THE LAST BOOKSHOP IN PRAGUE

HELEN PARUSEL

Boldwood

First published in Great Britain in 2024 by Boldwood Books Ltd.

Copyright © Helen Parusel, 2024

Cover Design by JD Design Ltd

Cover Photography: Shutterstock

The moral right of Helen Parusel to be identified as the author of this work has been asserted in accordance with the Copyright, Designs and Patents Act 1988.

All rights reserved. No part of this book may be reproduced in any form or by any electronic or mechanical means, including information storage and retrieval systems, without written permission from the author, except for the use of brief quotations in a book review.

This book is a work of fiction and, except in the case of historical fact, any resemblance to actual persons, living or dead, is purely coincidental.

Every effort has been made to obtain the necessary permissions with reference to copyright material, both illustrative and quoted. We apologise for any omissions in this respect and will be pleased to make the appropriate acknowledgements in any future edition.

A CIP catalogue record for this book is available from the British Library.

Paperback ISBN 978-1-83751-551-6

Large Print ISBN 978-1-83751-552-3

Hardback ISBN 978-1-83751-550-9

Ebook ISBN 978-1-83751-553-0

Kindle ISBN 978-1-83751-554-7

Audio CD ISBN 978-1-83751-545-5

MP3 CD ISBN 978-1-83751-546-2

Digital audio download ISBN 978-1-83751-548-6

Boldwood Books Ltd
23 Bowerdean Street
London SW6 3TN
www.boldwoodbooks.com

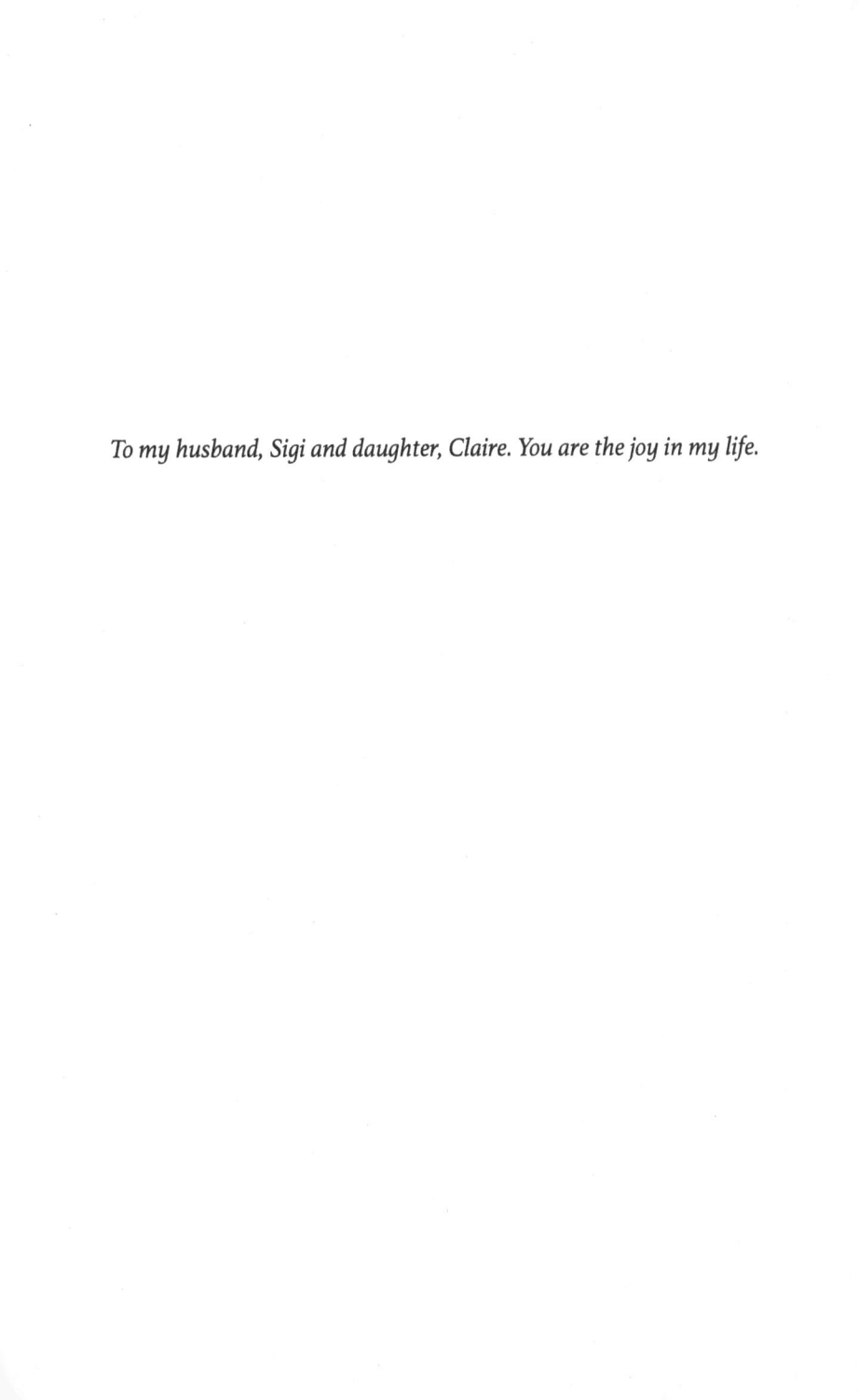

To my husband, Sigi and daughter, Claire. You are the joy in my life.

1

PRAGUE, FEBRUARY 1942

The bookshop was Jana's refuge. Here she could shut herself away from reality and choose to enter any world she chose. Adventure, travel or romance was just a book away.

She ran her fingertips along the spines, breathing in the scent of paper and the wood of the old bookcases that ran down one side of the wall. Opposite, shelves displayed the hand-carved puppets her father crafted, dressed in clothes Jana had sewn. She had taken over the dressmaking from Mama, who'd died whilst Jana had been studying at university. And now she ran Mama's beloved bookshop too; the ache from losing her mother two years ago was a constant companion.

She was alone in the bookshop, except for the small boy who sat on a stool in the children's section at the back. Five-year-old Michal came here after school most afternoons. Jana wasn't sure if his visits were due to his love of books or his desire to escape bullying on the streets; most probably a mixture of both. She watched his narrow, earnest face bowed over a book, deep in concentration.

She moved to the armchair beside him and patted the worn upholstery beside her.

'Come, Michal. Sit here and read to me.'

He jumped up eagerly and pressed his skinny body next to her, laying out the large book of Czech myths across his lap. He began to read – his favourite story about Bivoj, the hero who caught a boar by the ears. The change in Michal once he started to read never failed to fascinate Jana. His voice came to life, his tone assured. There was no sign of the shy, nervous boy who stared at the floor when spoken to. It had taken Jana months to win his confidence but now they were firm friends.

As Michal finished one story and turned the page to start the next, Jana glanced to the front of the shop. It was getting dark; she had lost track of time.

'It's time you got off home, Michal. It's late.'

He nodded, shut the book and handed it to her before shuffling from the chair. He picked up his coat, which he'd thrown over one of the small stools, and huddled into it before making for the door. Jana felt a pull at her heart; he was small for his age and darkness was sweeping in—

'Wait, Michal. I'll walk you home.'

She grabbed her hat and coat, locked up the shop and the two of them stepped out into the freezing February evening. Prague had been covered in snow since before Christmas and the low cloud promised a fresh fall that night.

She held his hand as they walked the short distance through icy alleyways towards Josefov, the Jewish Quarter.

A group of boys was hanging about on a corner and as they approached, she sensed Michal stiffen. The boys stared at him and then at Jana.

'Are they the ones?' she asked.

Michal gave a slight nod.

'Ignore them,' she said, gripping his hand tighter and marching towards them. She thought about confronting the boys about their bullying, but then was unsure. She wouldn't be with Michal next time he met them and worried she might make things worse for him. She needed to think before she acted; something her mother had told her many times when she was a child.

They passed by and a boy called out a jibe, but his words were lost in the wind that whistled down the narrow street. Michal showed her the way to where he lived: a row of worn houses that sat in the gloomy shadows of Gothic buildings on each side. Ahead, a small crowd had gathered. A police car was parked by the kerb. The crowd parted and two policemen and an officious-looking man in plain clothes exited a house. Cowering between them was a woman, her coat flapping unbuttoned in the wind. She wore no hat and her dark hair flew across her face.

'Mummy,' said Michal, pulling forwards.

Jana gasped and grasped his hand tighter.

In that moment, the dark-headed woman spotted her son and shot a terrified glance at Jana, giving a shake of her head, before she was bundled into the car.

Jana pulled Michal to her, and as the plain-clothed man paused beside the car and surveyed the street, Jana turned away, pulling the small boy back the way they'd come. As he was under the age of six, he was not yet required to wear the yellow star, and no one paid them any attention.

* * *

Back at the bookshop, Jana settled Michal in the armchair with a blanket and a mug of hot chocolate. She snuggled next to him.

'Where is your father, Michal?' she asked.

'I don't know,' he said in a small voice. 'He didn't come home from work yesterday. Why have the police taken my mama?'

'It must be a mistake. Try not to worry.' She stroked his head. He had every reason to worry. The round-ups had increased in the few weeks since a new German had been appointed in charge of Prague. His name was Reinhard Heydrich and it was rumoured that the high-ranking SS official intended to rule the city with an iron fist. Jana had no idea if and when Michal's parents would return. What should she do about him?

'Do you have any other family?'

'A baby brother or sister is coming soon.'

Oh, no. Michal's mother was pregnant.

'How wonderful,' she said, her voice gentle. 'How about a grandma or aunt?'

He told her he had an aunt and two cousins, but he wasn't exactly sure the way to their home.

'We can try and find them tomorrow in daylight. Meanwhile, you can stay with me tonight. We can tuck ourselves up in bed and read till really late. Would you like that?'

He gave a slight nod. 'Where do you live?'

'Upstairs, above the bookshop. With my father – you've met him a couple of times.'

A sudden hammering on the front door of the shop startled them both. The knocks were aggressive, not those of an enquiring customer.

Jana took Michal by the hand, putting a finger to her lips, and led him swiftly through a door at the back of the shop and into a small kitchen area. She glanced around, trying to quell her panic.

Under the sink hung a curtain which hid an array of cleaning materials. She pushed the things to one side with a sweep of her arm.

'Michal, you must be as brave as Bivoj when he caught that boar by his ears,' she said as she helped him crawl under the sink, 'but quieter than a mouse.'

After closing the curtain, she moved to the front of the shop where the door was still shaking from the pounding fists. She put on her most indignant expression and undid the bolt. Two grim-faced Czech policemen faced her.

'How can I help you, gentleman?'

'What took you so long?' said the one with the moustache.

'I'm here alone and a lady must use the cloakroom at times.'

'May we look around?' said the other – a young, cleanshaven one.

'Anything in particular?' said Jana, allowing them in and indicating the bookshelves. 'Fiction or non-fiction?'

Moustache was unamused. 'We're not interested in books. We're searching for a Jewish boy and a pedestrian reported seeing a young child enter your bookshop earlier.'

'That's not unusual. We stock a wide selection of children's books.'

'It's one particular child we're looking for,' said the cleanshaven one.

The men pushed past her and strode to the back of the shop. There were two doors: one led to the backyard, the other to the kitchen and toilet.

Jana held her breath. Moustache strode out into the yard, Clean-shaven towards the kitchen. What a terrible hiding place she'd chosen for Michal. But where else was there? How she hated these Czech police betraying their own people and working alongside their Nazi occupiers. Her heart raced as she waited for the young, arrogant policeman to haul Michal from hiding and march him away. Where would he be sent?

To the Terezin concentration camp on the outskirts of Prague most likely.

The men, grim-faced, returned to the shop.

'No sign of him in the yard, Captain Kovar,' barked Moustache.

'Nothing out back,' said Clean-shaven.

'We should check the apartment upstairs,' growled Moustache.

'Let's be quick,' said Clean-shaven, checking his watch. 'Our shift ends shortly.'

Jana guided the men out of the shop and through the entrance next door that led up to the apartment she shared with her father. She then had to endure the policemen stomping through her home. She bristled as Moustache opened her wardrobe and peered at her clothes. At least they were quick, losing interest, eager to get home.

Once they had left, she rushed down to the bookshop, into the kitchen and tore back the curtain. Michal stared at her, his wide, brown eyes filled with terror.

Pulling him into her arms, Jana made soothing noises, assuring him he'd be safe now.

* * *

A short time later, she was in the apartment, stirring soup on the stove whilst Michal read at the kitchen table. Her father would return soon from the puppet theatre performance he was giving at a nearby school. She'd have to explain the presence of Michal; harbouring the Jewish child could put them all in prison.

When the key turned in the lock, she moved straight to the door to greet her father with a kiss on the cheek.

'Papa, we have a visitor.'

She watched his expression as he looked across at Michal, recognising him from the bookshop, but surprised to see him in their home. He'd already told Jana of his concern about the recent legislation stating that Jews were not allowed in Aryan shops. How would he react? He shot a look of surprise at Jana, then assessing the situation, composed himself quickly. He put down his suitcase full of puppets, joined Michal at the table and began to chat about the book he was reading.

Later, in her bedroom, Jana dug out a pair of her childhood pyjamas from the back of a drawer and gave them to Michal. They were too big and he looked forlorn in the long sleeves and trouser legs that trailed on the floor. He was silent as she knelt down and rolled the pyjamas up and then tucked him up in her bed.

She sat beside him, stroking his head.

'Sleep now, Michal and I'll come and join you in a little while.'

His eyes were glassy with tears as he spoke. 'Will Mama and Papa be home soon?'

Her breath caught as she struggled to find the right words, but there were no right words.

'I'm not sure exactly, but we'll know more tomorrow when I find your aunt and cousins.'

He nodded solemnly and she gave him a light kiss on his forehead before returning to her father. They talked in hushed, urgent voices about the day's events: the dangers, the options.

* * *

The following morning, Jana's father took Michal to his puppet workshop in the attic at the top of the building, whilst Jana walked to the Jewish Quarter to make enquiries about Michal's family. The city was a grey-white spectre that morning; the skyline barely distinguishable from the snow-clad buildings in the early-morning mist. Jana tied her scarf closer to her neck in an attempt to keep out the cold, moist air. She hurried past shops yet to open, wincing at each red V sign she passed. How cruel of the Nazis to adopt the Czech's initial victory symbol used at the beginning of the occupation, now as their own. The sign was plastered around town with all the other Nazi paraphernalia: flags, banners and posters desecrating her land's beautiful culture. Everywhere, street signs had been changed to German with the Czech name written in smaller letters underneath. All part of the plan of Germanisation.

As she entered the area of Josefov, the Jewish Quarter, her heart raced. While there was no specific law that forbade her to be here, she would likely be questioned if a Wehrmacht soldier saw the absence of the yellow star on her coat.

When she saw two soldiers ahead on patrol, she darted down a parallel street to make her way to Michal's house. There she hoped to find a neighbour who might know the whereabouts of the boy's aunt.

This part of town fascinated her: the mix of architectural styles, a surprise on every corner. The Spanish synagogue that looked like a Mediterranean palace contrasting with the tall, narrow, worn houses that clung to winding, cobbled streets. Many shops were boarded up and closed and those that were open displayed a sad choice of wares. She passed two bearded men clad in long, black coats, their heads bowed together in contemplative conversation. Two red-cheeked girls ran in front of her playing catch, looking like any other children in Prague except for the stars stitched to the sleeves of their coats.

She neared the area where Michal's family lived and as she checked for traffic to cross a side street, she froze. A long row of people lined the kerb, each with a solitary suitcase. It took a moment for Jana to realise why their figures were bulky and misshapen; each person was wearing layers of clothes, coats over jackets, women with several head scarves covering their head, children clad in woollen hats, multiple scarves wound around their necks. The group was quiet and sombre; their eyes darted up and down the street, their feet shuffled. Some glanced at the apartment block behind them, faces creased in sadness. These were not people being arrested like Michal's mother. They had been summoned by the Nazis to evacuate their homes and hand them over to the Reich, leaving their belongings behind.

The sound of motor engines broke the silence, and a series of military trucks rumbled up the street. Jana retreated and stood back against the wall of a building. Wehrmacht soldiers sprung from the vehicles and shouted instructions, ushering the people into the back of the trucks. Jana's stomach roiled as she watched the people scramble aboard clutching their precious suitcases close to their bodies; an elderly man stumbled, his case flying from his hand. A teenage girl went to his aid, but as she reached for his case, she was shoved aside by a soldier and ordered to climb aboard. Another soldier hauled the elderly man to his feet and flung him in the back of the truck, before kicking the suitcase further down the street and into the gutter. A couple of soldiers laughed.

Unable to watch any more, Jana hurried on. Where were the people being taken? Did they even know themselves? Cold doubts seeped through her veins.

As she approached Michal's house, she saw a woman with a broom clearing snow from the pavement. The Germans were very particular about citizens clearing the pathways outside their homes. If a German slipped and sustained injuries, the penalty was severe, especially for Jewish citizens.

When Jana greeted her, the woman looked up, pushing a stray lock of hair beneath her headscarf. Her eyes flittered to Jana's left arm and noticing the absence of a star, her expression turned wary.

'Can I help you?' The skin on her thin lips was cracked and raw.

Jana paused, collecting her thoughts. She had to be careful not to put Michal in further danger, so best to keep details brief.

'My name is Jana Hajek. I'm concerned about a small boy, Michal. I expected to see him at my bookshop yesterday but he didn't show up.'

Her face flushed at the half truth.

The woman's expression saddened and shaking her head, she leaned on her broom.

'His mother was arrested yesterday, and there is no sign of him or his father.'

Her expression was so desolate that Jana's heart ached to tell her that at least Michal was safe for the moment. But what if the woman in innocence passed this information on to someone who was a collaborator? Or maybe she was a collaborator herself; the risk was too great.

'He told me once he had an aunt. Maybe he's with her. If you know where she lives, I could go and check if he's all right.'

'You don't need to waste your time. I heard she and her family are being taken in the round-up this morning,' she said, choking back a sob. 'It won't be long before it's my turn.'

Jana swallowed hard, not knowing what to say.

'Why are you here, exactly?' asked the woman, frowning.

'Like I said, I'm concerned for Michal.'

'Really? Isn't concern for Jews "*verboten*"?' Bitterness tinged her words.

Jana bit her lip.

The woman sighed. 'I must get on now.' Then she continued to sweep, signalling the conversation was over.

Jana made her way back home, her heart heavy. Michal had no family he could turn to now. His future lay in Jana's hands and this responsibility scared her. She pushed back on her fear. Fate or God or something had placed Michal in her care, and she would do everything possible to protect him. She would need help and she had faith that there were still good people in this world. Like her father.

* * *

Three hours later, she was climbing the stairs to the attic, her legs heavy with despondency. How could she tell Michal that when she'd finally found his aunt's house, no one was home? And that she'd learnt Michal's aunt and cousins had also been driven away in that morning's round-up?

As she pushed open the attic door, a dusty beam of pale sunlight greeted her. Michal sat on a high stool peering at her father at his workbench, chiselling features and life into a wooden puppet.

They looked up at her with eager expressions. Jana gave a slight shake of her head and before she could formulate her words, Michal, his face solemn, turned from her and studied the half-carved puppet in front of him.

Her father gave her a knowing look. 'We'll work something

out; I have a plan. Now, sweetheart, you need to get ready for your appointment.'

Amidst the morning's events, she'd nearly forgotten about her interview. She had applied for a job at Prague Castle; once the ancient domain of Bohemian kings and emperors, it now housed the Nazi central command.

2

The Wehrmacht soldier studied Jana's papers, including the official letter inviting her to an interview at Prague Castle, and satisfied, let her pass through the imposing Matthias Gate, flanked on each side by monumental statues: fierce, titanic warriors slaying their prey.

Snowflakes fell from a bleak sky as she entered the first courtyard surrounded by various buildings constructed in differing architectural styles: baroque, Gothic and Renaissance. Prague Castle was not one building but a vast complex of palaces, churches and monuments that had grown over one thousand years, hosting emperors, kings and presidents. And now the Nazi occupiers.

Jana's best friend from school, Lenka, had recommended her to take over her job at the Castle now that Lenka was pregnant. The thought that her friend was to become a mother gave a Jana a warm glow in her chest, despite the freezing wind that whipped around the courtyard. She made her way past the Saint Vitus Cathedral, the Gothic edifice that dominated the castle grounds, and found the nearby building indicated on her letter.

The interview with Miss Jezek, a petite woman with deep furrows between her eyebrows, was brief. Jana's background and references had already been thoroughly checked. After twenty minutes, Jana left the castle with a new position on the early-morning cleaning team; she was grateful at the chance to earn more money. The bookshop was her passion, but since the German occupation, business had depleted, and they were struggling to pay the rent. She could work the two hours before she opened the shop. Of course, she could have applied for a cleaning job somewhere other than at the Nazi HQ, but that was the point of it all.

Thin, icy snowflakes fell on her cheeks as she wound down the steep Nerudova Street that ran from Prague Castle to the Charles Bridge below, once the royal way where the coronation parades had passed. She glanced at the elegant, baroque houses with their intricate house signs that told a story of the families who had lived there; her favourite was the placard decorated with three violins representing generations of musicians. Shops too clung to the hillside, and she sighed as she noticed a second-hand bookshop had closed. It was no wonder; the list of banned books grew daily.

As she approached her own bookshop, she saw a bundled-up figure peering through the shop window. Lenka.

'What are you doing out here in the freezing cold?' called Jana as she neared.

'I wanted to know how you got on at the castle. No one is answering the door of your apartment,' Lenka said through chattering teeth.

Jana thought of Michal hiding up in the attic amongst the puppets. Her father would be ignoring callers.

'Let's get you inside and warmed up,' Jana said, retrieving the keys from her handbag and opening the shop door.

Once inside, Jana settled Lenka in the armchair where she had sat yesterday with Michal and went out to the small kitchen to make Lenka a hot cup of chicory coffee; there had been no real coffee for years. When she returned, Lenka was leaning back against the chair, her coat unbuttoned and her hands resting on her swollen stomach; she looked so vulnerable, Jana thought, as she pulled up a stool.

'I'm pleased you're stopping work next month,' Jana said. 'And the good news is I'm taking over.' She grinned; excitement tinged with fear sparking inside her at the opportunities ahead.

Lenka sat up and clapped her hands. 'I knew our plan would work and you'd get the job.'

'You must think of yourself and your baby now,' Jana said. 'Let me take over. And don't you worry; I'll keep an eye on Reinhard Heydrich, "*Reichsprotektor* of Bohemia and Moravia".' Her voice was tinged with derision when she said his title.

Lenka's eyes clouded. 'I miss the time when we were Czechoslovakia.'

'Me too.' Jana's voice tightened. 'And when we weren't under the tyranny of a man who's nicknamed "The Butcher of Prague".'

'You must be extremely cautious,' Lenka said, taking Jana's hand. 'Heydrich is a cruel, dangerous man, determined to stamp out any resistance to the occupation.'

Jana nodded. They were silent for a moment, then waving her hand around the shop, she said, 'What do you see?'

'Books?' Lenka leaned her head to one side.

'Only remnants of what my mother stocked on these shelves. Most of the international literature you and I studied at university has been banned and handed over to the Nazis.' Jana's voice caught. 'And now I'm forced to sell German authors that tell of the glory and honour of fighting for the *Vaterland*.'

She cringed as she looked towards the windowfront where she had been ordered to hang a swastika.

'Mama would be devastated if she knew what was happening to her beloved bookshop. To books. To words.' Jana fought back her wistfulness and squared her shoulders. 'You've been so brave, Lenka, but now it's my turn to fight back. I've been so wrapped up in my grief over Mama, I've become a passive bystander. Taking over from you will give me a new purpose: one Mama would approve of. Tell me what I need to know.'

* * *

After Lenka had left, Jana took some time to gather her thoughts before going upstairs to see Michal and her father. She moved around the bookshop, touching and straightening things: the depleted selection of second-hand books, the display of writing paper fanned out on a table, and the bookmarks lying next to the cash register. She'd crafted the bookmarks herself out of cardboard and remnants of fabric left from the puppet clothes. Sadness washed over her as she recalled her six-year-old self, sitting at the kitchen table making bookmarks with her mother as Christmas presents. Had her relationship with her mother been so close because she was an only child?

Still reminiscing, she moved to the front of the shop. Her jaw clenched as her eyes swept over the German books lining the shelves and decorating the front window.

'Oh, Mama,' she whispered to herself. 'It's better you're not here to witness this all. You put so much of yourself into your choice of books to sell. You'd be horrified…'

She shook her head to halt the downward spiral of her thoughts. It was better to be angry, and channel that anger to good use. She put a *back soon* sign on the door and went outside, glancing up at the sign above; at least they'd been allowed to keep the family name of the shop: Hajek. She locked the front door before letting herself into the apartment entrance a few steps away.

* * *

Michal was gazing in awe as her father expertly worked the strings of the marionette. The puppet was Hurvinek, the playful young boy with a shock of red hair. Her father recited lines from a recent comedy he'd performed at the children's theatre, speaking in a high-pitched voice. Michal almost smiled, but Jana's entrance broke the spell and his eyes turned dull as he returned to reality.

'I got the job, Papa,' she said, kissing her father's cheek.

He didn't know there was another reason she'd applied other than the need for extra income. She ruffled Michal's hair.

'Has my father been behaving himself?' She smiled.

Michal gave an earnest nod.

'And the puppets?'

Another nod.

'They can be an unruly bunch.' She pointed to a wooden chest in the corner. 'In the box over there are some half-finished ones I attempted as a child. They are quite bad, I'm afraid. Shall we sort through and choose which are the best and which are the worst?'

Papa chuckled, a warm sound full of memories. Then his expression saddened and Jana knew he was thinking of her mother.

'Go and have a peep,' she said, encouraging Michal. 'I'll be right there.'

He trotted over to the chest and kneeling, started to pull out the old puppets.

Jana lowered her voice. 'What are we going to do, Papa? You mentioned a plan.'

He smoothed his salt and pepper moustache with his fingers. His voice was gravelly when he spoke.

'Leave the shop closed and stay up here while I see a friend about a car. We'll drive Michal to your grandma. It's Friday and there will be more traffic, so hopefully the patrols won't check every vehicle.'

'We need a diversion,' Jana said, adrenaline kicking in. 'And I know just the friends who can help.'

3

Jana watched out the attic window till she saw her father arrive, then led Michal down the stairs. She opened the front door and peered out, keeping Michal behind her. Papa had the back door of the car open and was arranging the back seat; it was one of those cars where the seat clapped forward, leaving an opening to the boot. Perfect. He turned to her and looked up and down the street. Then gave a quick shake of the head. She waited. Two men in long coats and fedoras passed by. She waited some more. An old woman with a bent back shuffled by. A few more moments passed and then Papa nodded; the coast was clear.

Jana rushed Michal to the back door of the car and he scrambled inside, climbed over the folded seat and crouched down in the boot. She looked down into his wide, trusting eyes.

'I'll close the seat, but will open it as soon as we're out of town. Don't be scared. We can speak to each other the whole time; you'll still be able to hear me.'

'I'm not scared,' he said, his voice determined.

'I know,' she replied and then pulled up the back of the seat before clapping it shut.

Papa started the engine, but instead of getting in the passenger seat, she moved to the driver's side and spoke to him though the open window.

'I think I should drive alone,' she said. 'The guards are less suspicious of young girls. They'll see a middle-aged Czech male as more of a threat.'

'Who are you calling middle aged?' Her father protested with fake indignation. Then he gazed at her, his face troubled.

'I'll be fine, don't worry,' she said. 'We have a better chance that way.'

He sighed and climbed out.

Once seated, Jana pushed the gear stick into first and after giving her father a reassuring wave, drove off down the cobbled street.

'Can you hear me, Michal. Are you all right?' she called.

A small, muffled affirmative came from the back.

The light was fading and Jana flicked the switch on the dashboard for the headlights. As she approached the local Czech restaurant, her three friends from university were already there. They stood outside, Pavel leaning on his father's car, the other boys smoking. Pavel grinned at her and motioned his friends to climb inside. She slowed, allowing them to drive in front of her, before they travelled through the maze of cobbled streets that weaved through the centre of Prague.

Throughout the journey, she shouted encouraging words to Michal, who remained hidden behind the back seat.

Finally, they came to the checkpoint on the outskirts of the city. There were four or five vehicles ahead of her including Pavel. She bit her lip.

'Not a sound now, Michal. I'll tell you when we're through.'

The army truck and official government car in front were waved through. As she halted behind Pavel, she heard his loud radio music and saw the back of three heads bobbing from side to side. The music was Czech. She gave an inward smile. She had known Pavel would help after she'd paid him a visit that afternoon.

So far, everything was going to plan. Pavel pulled up alongside the patrol hut and Jana inched up behind, raising a hand to shield her eyes from the spotlight. The Wehrmacht soldier frowned and gestured to Pavel to wind down the car window. He did so and leaned out casually. As they exchanged words, the second soldier marched to the boot of Pavel's car and pulled down the door.

Inside the boot was a large cardboard box. The soldier shouted something to the other guard, who motioned Pavel to get out of the car.

Another car drew up behind Jana. Her stomach clenched. She waited. This must work. The car moved slightly as Michal adjusted his position. She wanted to say something reassuring to him but she couldn't risk being seen talking to herself.

Pavel joined the soldier at the boot of his father's car, who then started gesticulating one hand, the other on his pistol. Jana held her breath as Pavel reached into the boot. As the soldier waited for Pavel to heave out the box, he turned to her, peering through the windscreen.

Her breath caught.

He glanced at her empty passenger seat and then with an irritated look, waved her on. Relief swept through her as she pushed her foot on the accelerator.

Moments later, she was heading out into the countryside, leaving the majestic City of a Hundred Spires behind her.

* * *

Fat snowflakes danced in a frenzy in the beams of the car headlights. The windscreen wipers could barely keep up as the snow flew at the glass, and Jana had to peer into the darkness through a snow-fringed rectangle of glass. She glanced at Michal beside her; his head lolling to one side as he slept, jolting from time to time as they drove over potholes in the road. After they had left town and reached a quiet spot on the road, she'd called out to him, and he'd pushed the seat down and scrambled to the front of the car. She hadn't even needed to halt.

She checked the petrol gauge; the tank was half full. How had Papa managed to find fuel and the money to pay for it? His friend obviously had contacts on the black market.

When they arrived, it was only just past seven o'clock in the evening but in the thick blackness, it seemed like the middle of the night. Jana gave Michal a gentle shake.

'We're here,' she said.

The small, wooden house appeared to be in darkness from the outside; heavy drapes closed to keep the cold out.

Jana rapped the round iron knocker. Grandma would have a shock. There wasn't a telephone in her home, so there had been no way of warning her. But even if there was, conversations were routinely monitored by the Nazis, and announcing the arrival of a Jewish refugee would have been far too risky.

Hearing the creak of floorboards on the other side of the door, Jana called out, 'Babi, It's Jana.'

The door opened and in the dim light of an oil lamp stood her dear Babi, grey, tousled hair in whisps around her face. She wore her favourite full-length, crimson, wool housecoat and old, fur-lined slippers.

She looked at Jana and her young companion with an expression of shock mixed with pleasure, and ushered them in.

'Jana, I wish I'd known. I would have baked or cooked—'

'Don't worry, Babi. Everything happened so fast.'

They sat in front of the small open fire. The few pieces of coal that lay there would not burn for long. Babi usually went to bed early to conserve fuel and buried herself under layers of blankets.

'And who is this handsome young man you've brought to visit me?' Jana's grandmother said, looking at Michal with kind eyes.

'This is Michal. Papa thought you would be happy to look after him for a little while till his parents return,' said Jana, choosing her words carefully and giving her grandma a meaningful look.

'How wonderful,' she said, clapping her hands. 'I love company.'

Then, she busied herself in the kitchen, rustling up some supper with her meagre provisions. Jana added the day-old bread that she'd brought from home. It never ceased to amaze her how young and fit her grandma was. When Jana thought of the typical grandma as portrayed in most stories she'd read, she always thought how her Babi was nothing like them. She had been only nineteen when she had given birth to her first child and at sixty-seven was not really old.

They put Michal to bed in the room where her father had slept as a boy, a room he'd shared with his elder brother, who sadly had died in the Great War. Once Michal was asleep, Jana told her grandmother the full story of their escape from Prague. When she came to the part about the guard ordering Pavel to pull the box out of the car, she paused, biting her lip.

'What was in the box?' asked Babi.

'Just old clothes. The box was meant purely as a distraction,' Jana replied. 'I hope Pavel won't get into trouble.'

'Had the boys been drinking?'

'No, they were just singing along to the radio, that's all.'

'Well, it's hardly against the law to drive old clothes around and have a bit of a singsong.'

Jana gave a wry smile. 'So long as you're not singing the Czech national anthem.'

Babi nodded and gazed into the dying embers of the fire. 'Michal will be safe here with me,' she said. 'The Nazis won't bother with an old woman, living out in the country.'

'You're not old.' Jana smiled.

'I can pretend to be,' she said with a twinkle in her eyes.

'You must be careful. If anyone comes knocking, send Michal straight up to the attic. I don't like putting you in danger—'

'Don't you worry about me.' She gave a mischievous grin. 'I like a bit of adventure.' She tapped the side of her head with her forefinger. 'And I'm sharp.'

Once the fire was out, they turned in for the night, Jana climbing into the spare bed beside Michal where her uncle had slept as a small boy. Hearing Michal's gentle breathing, Jana's mind drifted back to her happy childhood, filled with the magic of her mother's books, and their stories performed by her father. Her parents had built a small puppet theatre at home and Jana had been proud to bring her excited friends to watch plays. Papa had been taught by his father; the heritage of puppetry stretched back generations. Tomorrow, she would show Michal her grandpa's workshop at the back of the house. Although Grandpa had died eight years ago, Babi had not touched the workshop since; a half-finished puppet and his tools were still spread around as if he would return at any moment.

She thought of Michal. What would his childhood look like now if his parents weren't released? What would happen to his unborn sibling? Tears pricked against her closed eyelids. No, she must stay positive, she told herself, stilling the wave of sadness.

She would make further enquiries about his parents' whereabouts when she returned to Prague.

At some point in the night, the mattress dipped as Michal climbed in beside her. She pulled him close and stroked his back till his body stilled and she could hear his steady breathing.

4

Seven tiny stools stood in a circle. Jana pulled up a taller one for herself and placed the Czech book of fairy tales on top. She was ready to receive her little guests who came every Saturday morning to listen to her read aloud. The older children escorted their younger siblings, or mothers brought their small children, browsing around the bookshop whilst Jana entertained their children. The women were particularly interested in the second-hand books; they had little money to spare.

Last week, one of the mothers, Karolina, had been turning over an old copy of *Pride and Prejudice* in her hands.

'I've read it before,' said the woman in a wistful voice. 'But that was a long time ago. It would be nice to read it again.' She had placed the book back on the display table.

'Why don't you take it?' said Jana.

The woman shook her head. 'I don't have the money for such luxuries.'

Jana picked the book back up and placed it in the woman's thin hand.

'It doesn't cost anything.'

'How can you make any money if you give books away?' the woman asked.

'I take money from the Germans.' Jana smiled.

And it was true Jana, thought now. She was forced by the Nazi regime to stock German authors and German translations of approved books. The only way to pay the rent on the bookshop was to sell to the Wehrmacht and other German officials who'd become her customers. She burned with resentment every time she served them, but she had to be practical. Losing the bookshop her mother had so lovingly built up was not an option. Her hand went to the locket at her neck, a gold book that opened up to reveal a wedding photograph of her parents. It had been an anniversary gift to her mother from her father, and it was the most precious thing she owned.

The door of the shop opened, and a flurry of snowflakes tumbled in with the first of the children. They darted excitedly through the narrow shop to the back, where the room opened out, and sped around the stools playing catch. The noise level raised several decibels. Jana would allow them a few minutes to expend some energy before she called for them to sit down.

The door opened again and Karolina appeared with her three-year-old daughter. She ushered her to join the other children, then turned to Jana and opened her handbag.

She held out the *Pride and Prejudice* book. 'I enjoyed this so much, thank you. I'm returning it so someone else can read it.'

The spark of an idea formed in Jana's mind. Why didn't she lend all the mothers her second-hand books and ask them to return them when finished? A book exchange.

She told Karolina about her idea.

'I think that would be wonderful. Of course there is the library, but it's stacked with German books now they've made

German the official language in Prague. And the place is always full of Germans. Anyway, it's cosier here.'

'I could hold a regular exchange day, just for our little community,' said Jana, enthusiasm swelling. 'We don't have extra copies of a title to hold a book club, but everyone can give an introduction to the book they've just read before passing it on.'

'I could spread the word amongst the other mothers,' said Karolina, enthusiastically. 'I'm sure they'd be interested.'

Jana went to join the children, her mind full of ideas. She would form a club. A book exchange club.

* * *

Jana was tidying up after the children had left when she felt a gust of cold wind. She looked towards the door.

She recognised the man. It was the young, clean-shaven police officer who had searched the shop and apartment whilst Michal was hiding behind the curtain in the kitchen. His colleague had called him Captain Kovar.

She bristled, deliberately continuing to shelve the books. She was much calmer than the last time he was here and didn't jump to attention. He greeted her.

In German!

Her head shot up.

'I believe we are both Czechs, are we not?' she said, pointedly. Her German was good, but she refused to speak it with another Czech, even if he was from the fascist police.

He gave a curt nod. She looked at his face more closely than the last time he was here. He had wide, prominent cheekbones, sharp like the chiselled features of one of her father's marionettes. And that's what he was. A marionette whose strings were pulled by the Nazis, a being as wooden and hard as—

'I waited till the children had left. I didn't wish to alarm them,' he said, mimicking that stiff way the Germans spoke. But at least he had continued the conversation in Czech.

'Most kind of you,' she replied in a clipped voice.

Annoyance flickered across his face.

'I have come with a warning.'

That got her attention. She squashed the fear that sprung up, angry at herself for becoming afraid so easily. She swallowed the lump in her throat. Did this involve Michal in some way? Or was it something to do with her new job at the castle, which she was starting next month? Or Lenka? Did they suspect her friend in any way? Lenka was extra vulnerable now that a baby was on the way.

'There will be an updated list of banned books issued tomorrow and I wish to remind you to be extra vigilant when checking your stock.'

What stock? The regulations had already left little behind. She would have laughed out loud if the censorship had not been so terrifying.

'As you see, Officer, there is not that much stock to check.'

'Nevertheless. And, of course, your second-hand books too.' He looked across at the pile on the round table. Her new book exchange table. Hopefully she wouldn't have to hand any more of those over to the authorities. 'You should be aware,' he continued, 'there will be random checks by the authorities.'

She'd got the message. Why couldn't he just leave? Was he trying to scare her?

'I have nothing to hide,' she said.

He gave her a strange look, then nodded and turned to leave. As he walked past the shelves of German books at the front of the shop, he paused to study the titles on the spines. Seemingly satisfied, he opened the door and left.

'Arrogant traitor,' Jana muttered under her breath as she went to the cash register to count the cash. It didn't take her long.

* * *

Later that afternoon, Lenka arrived at the bookshop, pale and unsteady on her feet. Jana immediately settled her in the armchair at the back and went to make her a mug of chicory coffee. She wished she could offer her friend a biscuit, but there had been no flour available for baking for months.

As she pressed the warm drink into Lenka's hands, she said, 'Is everything all right?'

Lenka looked across at the couple of people browsing the books and murmured, 'Wait a moment.'

Jana understood. The customers were Czech, but still one had to be cautious. Collaborators were everywhere, willing to betray friends as well as strangers for Nazi favours. It was terrible not knowing who you could trust, living under the spectre of treachery. Jana sat on a stool beside Lenka, talking about inconsequential things, till the shop emptied.

'What's the matter, Lenka? You look strained.'

'I have to stop work now instead of next month. I was bleeding slightly yesterday—'

'Oh, no.' Jana reached out her hand.

'The baby is fine,' said Lenka. 'But the doctor said I should rest as much as possible. Can you take over at the castle?'

'Of course. I can start later this week.'

That would give her time to visit her grandma and see how Michal was getting on.

'There are things you need to know. How the transfer of information will work.' Lenka's tone was solemn.

Jana sat up straight and held her breath in expectation.

'There are several of us who work at the castle and collect information for the resistance. I don't know who the others are exactly, but I have my suspicions. Anyway, a contact will approach you soon and advise you which Nazis they want you to keep an eye on. All the SS top brass who run Prague have a desk at the castle.'

'I'm ready to play my part,' said Jana, her voice earnest, her fingers playing with her gold locket. When Hitler had invaded Prague in March 1939, she'd been outraged, and she and her university friends had been resolute in their opposition to the Nazis, even more so when they closed down Charles University. She and her fellow students had taken to the streets but the Wehrmacht were merciless in their response, forcing the resistance to go underground. Jana and Lenka had joined a group along with Pavel and his friends, but the death of Jana's mother changed everything; after that, there was room for only one thing in her life. Grief. But since Lenka had become pregnant and had persuaded Jana to take over from her, something had shifted; Jana wanted to be active again. And now she was even more resolute since she'd personally witnessed Michal's mother being wrenched from her home.

Now she listened to her friend intently as she spoke about contacts and passwords, eager to step up to the challenge.

Lenka sipped her coffee and, placing a hand on her rounded belly, said, 'You must be alert at all times, Jana. Don't trust anyone and don't underestimate the enemy. And I don't just mean the Germans. There are plenty of fascist Czechs too.'

'I know.'

Jana thought of the Czech policeman in her shop that morning, Captain Kovar. She had a feeling he would be back. The skin at the back of her neck prickled.

5

Pavel was waiting for her outside the Café Slava, his hands deep in his pockets and his scarf wrapped around the lower part of his face. She'd told him countless times to meet her inside if he arrived first, but that wasn't his style; he preferred to accompany her when she entered.

His eyes lit up as she approached and they hurried inside out of the biting wind.

The interior was art deco style with huge mirrors on one wall reflecting the view through the large windows opposite: the ancient Prague Castle and Saint Vitus Cathedral towering above the icy, grey Vltava River. They sat themselves down at a round, marble top table and peeled off their outer garments, which they draped over the back of their chairs.

Pavel grinned at her, revealing the familiar dimple in his left cheek and chipped front tooth. Jana felt a rush of affection for her friend; he was one of the crowd from university. They had only been able to study for one year before the Nazis marched into Prague and closed down Charles University. One day, a large group of students protested in Wenceslas Square, including

Pavel's elder sister. The Nazi's machine gun fire tore through the crowd, young lives brutally extinguished within mere heartbeats. Jana had cradled Pavel through the night as he mourned the loss of his sister.

'I can't thank you enough for diverting the guards as I drove past with Michal,' she said in a low voice, shaking herself from her reverie.

'Did you get him to safety?'

'Yes. But what happened to you?'

'Nothing.' Pavel laughed. 'Transporting old clothes isn't illegal. Yet. Where is the boy?'

A breath of hesitation. But if she couldn't trust Pavel, then she couldn't trust a soul.

'He's with my grandma, but it's been two days now and I must see him. The buses aren't running. Either because of the snow or lack of fuel, or both.'

'I'd borrow my father's car again and drive you out there, but we're out of fuel now too.' He gave her one of his earnest looks that lasted a fraction too long. Jana knew he liked her. A lot. But although tempted a couple of times at parties, she hadn't crossed that line between friendship and romance.

The waitress arrived and took their order.

'How's Lenka?' he asked, after the waitress left.

'She's fine but must take things easy till the birth. I'm taking over her job at the castle.'

His eyes flickering with concern, Pavel leaned across the table and whispered, 'She never said what she was up to there but it was obvious she was working for the resistance. Things have got really savage now that Reinhard Heydrich is the new *Reichsprotektor*. As well as heading the Gestapo, he's one of Hitler's top men and is out to prove himself. No one messes with Heydrich.'

'I won't either.'

The waitress brought their coffees and moved on to the next table.

Jana glanced around her. People were either talking animatedly or reading books and newspapers. It was the usual crowd of actors, writers and artists. Or was it? Some were missing, like Kafka and his friend Brod. Writers who were Jewish, communist, socialist, or who even hinted against the Nazi ideals were persecuted, their work banned or even burned.

'It's better we don't talk here any more,' said Jana. 'You can always find me at the bookshop.'

He nodded and placed light fingers on her wrist.

'Be careful, Jana. Heydrich has his office at the castle.' Then he withdrew his hand quickly and they drank their coffee in silence.

* * *

That evening, Jana sat on her bed in her long, flannel nightdress and slipped on her warmest woollen bed socks. She pulled open the drawer of her bedside table, lifted out two books with gentle hands and lay them on her lap.

Mama's books.

She caressed the top book with soft fingertips, feeling the worn, burgundy fabric and the embossed, gold lettering. The book, *Little Women*, had transported her and Mama many times to Massachusetts in the 1840s, and into the life of headstrong Jo and her sisters. She placed the book on the bed beside her and gazed at the other that lay on her lap. Now her throat ached with unshed tears. She held the book covered in dark-green cloth to her chest. *Jane Eyre*: the emotional, personal story had become a talking point between her and

Mama for years. It had been her mother's favourite book. And Jana's too.

Her eyes moistened as memories of Mama swallowed her up and swirled in her brain till she was dizzy with love and sadness. Tears fell, which she quickly wiped away with the sleeve of her nightdress, not wanting to dampen the books.

She popped *Little Women* back in the drawer, and opening *Jane Eyre,* she removed the photograph she used as a bookmark. She gazed at the image: Mama posed in front of the majestic, domed Frauenkirche in Dresden, wearing an ankle-length skirt and a high-necked blouse. Her mother peered up at the camera from beneath a straw boater, a shy smile playing on her full lips. She looked so young and beautiful, barely seventeen. Papa had taken the photograph on an outing to the city. The young couple had been so in love and Papa had drawn a row of hearts on the back of the photograph he had taken.

Jana sighed, crawled under the covers and began to read, the familiar words bringing her comfort.

As far as she knew, these two books had not yet been banned. But others from Mama's collection were. Not able to bear handing them to the Nazis to be destroyed, she had hidden them away somewhere safe.

* * *

The following morning, a sour-faced official entered the shop and presented Jana with a list of newly banned books. She was to search through her stock and bring any of the offending works to the town hall within two days. He left, his boots leaving clumps of dirty snow across the wooden floor.

She fetched a cloth and was on her hands and knees mopping up the dirt when the door opened again and two men entered: one wearing a wide-brimmed hat and full-length, black, leather coat, the other the uniform of a police officer.

She sat back on her haunches, momentarily paralysed. The leather-coated man was Gestapo and the policeman was the young one with the high cheekbones, Kovar. He'd only been here two days ago with his warning of a new banned book list and here he was again. And he'd brought the Gestapo with him.

Bitter dislike tainted her tongue.

She got to her feet, fighting her instinct to frown, instead pinning a polite wooden smile to her face, like one of Papa's marionettes.

'How can I help, gentlemen?' she said, averting her gaze from the increasingly annoying policeman.

The Gestapo man spoke, his voice a quiet rasp. 'Just a routine check on banned books.'

'But I've only just received the list and haven't even started to sort through.'

'Nevertheless...' His leather coat flicked her hip as he passed by. She cringed at the touch, her mouth dry as she watched him approach the bookshelves.

The young policeman, Kovar, turned his attention similarly to the books.

Don't panic, she told herself. She had been meticulous in her last check, handing most of the banned books to the authorities, except for the couple she'd hidden away. Surely, there couldn't be any more forbidden editions on her sparse shelves. On the other hand, the list she'd glanced at briefly this morning had been a long one.

The Gestapo man moved to the second-hand book table whilst the policeman studied the classics section, pausing at the Shakespeare shelf. Jana waited, her feelings of uneasiness mixing with resentment.

Checking his watch, the leather-coated man let out an exasperated sigh. 'I have to leave. I'm to assist with an interview. You carry on here, Captain Kovar.'

'Yes, sir!' He stood ramrod straight, his back to the bookshelf.

After the Gestapo had left, Jana and Captain Kovar stared at each other in silence.

Finally, he asked, 'Are you Miss Hajek?'

Jana was relieved he spoke in Czech not German this time.

'Yes. The family name is on the shop front. Unlike other shop names, it has not been Germanised. Yet.' Her voice was flat.

He reached for a book behind him and flicked through the pages.

'*Hamlet*,' he said.

'Do you know the play?' she asked, her tone implying she clearly didn't expect him to.

'Yes, but I admit to reading it in translation. This edition, however, is an English original: a valuable book.'

'As far as I'm aware, Shakespeare is not forbidden.'

'Well, yes and no. The rules are complicated.'

This Captain Kovar was really beginning to annoy her.

'What do you mean?'

'The Reich has published a new version of the play, where Hamlet plays a pro-German warrior.'

A laugh of astonishment burst from Jana. 'You must be joking.'

Kovar's lips twitched and she saw his eyes light for a brief moment. They were a deep blue, almost navy.

'It's no joke, I'm afraid. This book might be taken from you next time, unless…'

Unless what? Was he suggesting she hid it? Surely not. He was a fascist, pro-Nazi, collaborator and traitor, turning his own people over to the SS. She just wanted him to leave.

'The list of banned books that you received this morning was a long one. Maybe you need some help. I'm off duty in an hour if you require assistance.'

Her mouth dropped open.

He removed his police cap to reveal a tuft of short, black hair, which he smoothed back with one hand. His expression softened. 'We could talk about the books on the list.'

Jana finally found her voice. 'That won't be necessary. Absolutely not.'

He nodded, looking embarrassed, asked her to excuse him and promptly left.

She stared after him, not having the faintest idea what that had been all about.

As the day wore on, each time the small brass bell clang above the door, she caught herself looking up with a hint of expectation. But Captain Kovar did not return.

6

The snow continued to fall, enveloping the city in a silent, white cloak; a fairy tale of sparkling towers, glistening roofs and mysterious statues, their faces hidden by masks of white crystals. But the fairy tale was a façade that hid the brutal oppression under the new Governor, Reinhard Heydrich, and Jana's anger burned.

It was another three days before the skies cleared and the buses out of Prague were running again. Jana and her father took the first bus available to see Michal. Jana was anxious for the boy. She could hardly imagine how he must be feeling, torn from his family and forced to live with a stranger; where he must remain hidden, unable to meet with other children. And worst of all, the news of his parents was bad. Jana had found out that Michal's father and pregnant mother had been sent to Terezin, a former fortress that was now some sort of relocation camp. There were conflicting reports about the place; everything from it being a spa town for recuperation to an overfilled, filthy prison. Jana chewed her lip as she stared out the bus window, her father dozing by her side. The idea that Heydrich would send Jews on holiday was ludicrous propaganda.

She and Papa were still stamping the snow from their boots on the front step when the door flew open and they were greeted by Babi's warm smile. 'I saw you through the window, Gustav,' she said, embracing Papa, and then Jana.

As they entered, Michal appeared in the small hallway. Bending down on one knee, Jana held out her arms. 'Hello, Michal. I'm so happy to see you.'

He bounded towards her and buried his head in her coat. He said nothing as she and Papa shed their coats and boots, just watched her with round, brown eyes. She took his hand and they all moved to the living room where they were welcomed by the warmth of the coal fire and the inviting smell of something cooking on the stove.

'When I saw the clear weather this morning, I knew you would come, so I've made us a hearty lentil soup.' Babi went to the large pot and lifted the lid, checking the contents.

'We've brought you some provisions too,' said Jana, placing her basket on the kitchen counter and unpacking tins of food. Then everyone drew chairs up to the fire and Michal sat on a cushion at Jana's feet.

'Have you found Mummy and Daddy?' he asked in a tiny voice.

Jana exchanged looks with Papa and drew a deep breath.

'We have indeed, and they are well,' she said with a forced brightness.

'Are they coming home?'

'Not yet. They are staying at a settlement just outside Prague.'

'Then I can go to them.' Michal's voice was stronger now.

Her chest tightened. 'It's better for you not to. Your parents would want you to stay with us.' She remembered the fear on Michal's mother's face as she was tumbled into the car and the shake of her head as her eyes swept from her son and settled on Jana. The look had been a plea to protect him, and Jana would do everything in her power to do so.

Michal bowed his head and started pulling at the tassels on the cushion.

'It's because we're Jewish, isn't it? People don't like us.'

A heavy silence filled the room, each adult struggling to find a reply. Jana was overwhelmed with the responsibility of finding the right words. An explanation. For a five-year-old child. But none came to her.

'I like you,' said Jana, simply. 'Very much. And so does my Papa and Babi.'

She leaned forward and stroked his fringe back from his forehead. She sought to find the right words.

'But yes, there are some unkind people, but there are also good people in the world, and they will win over the badness and until then we will keep you safe.' Jana wanted to add that he would see his parents again, but she faltered at giving him a promise she could not keep.

They ate their lunch and afterwards, Babi brought a crate into the living room that was filled with Papa's old toys. The adults watched as Michal unpacked the hand-carved farm animals crafted by Jana's grandfather and lined them up on the floor.

'How has he been?' Papa asked Babi in a quiet voice.

She sighed. 'What can we expect? He hardly says a word, mostly communicating with a nod or shake of the head. Or when he has no answer, he stares at the floor. It will take time but I'm sure I can win his confidence eventually.'

'It was traumatic for him. First, he saw his mother arrested and then he had to hide like a hunted animal under the sink,' said Jana.

'He mentioned the policeman who drew back the curtain,' Babi said.

Jana's stomach flipped. 'What do you mean?'

'That a police officer pulled open the curtain, looked at him and put a finger to his lips. Then he closed the curtain and went away.'

Jana jolted. 'He saw Michal?'

'Apparently, yes.'

Jana watched Michal gallop a wooden horse across the floorboards, making the accompanying neighing sounds. Why hadn't he mentioned the incident to her? But thinking about it, he'd been so traumatised by events, he'd hardly spoken at all, only asking after his parents. It had been Captain Kovar who'd searched the kitchen and then announced the all-clear. And a few days later, he'd returned to the shop with the Gestapo. What was this fascist Czech up to? Was he setting a trap? She would be starting work at Prague Castle next week, right in the heart of the Nazi government, and this sudden appearance of Captain Kovar in her life made her uneasy.

7

Jana had been assigned to work on the first floor of Salm Palace, situated in one of the numerous courtyards of Prague Castle. Here were the administrative offices of the SS command. She had slipped into fill Lenka's role perfectly.

She was just finishing her shift, flicking dust from a large oil painting of a general with a bushy moustache astride a magnificent black horse when firm footsteps made her look up.

She recognised him immediately; he was young, tall, athletic looking with a long, narrow face. As he marched towards her, he removed his cap with the skull insignia and smoothed back his blond hair. His long coat was unbuttoned, revealing his black SS uniform underneath. He swished past her without a glance, leaving a charged energy in the air that buzzed around her. She shuddered.

Reinhard Heydrich: the Butcher of Prague.

He unlocked the door of his office further down the corridor and slammed it behind him. Jana glanced at her watch; her shift finished ten minutes ago. She would put away the cleaning articles and then hurry down the hill to open the bookshop. As she collected her feather duster, bucket and bottle of disinfectant, she saw a secretary approach. She was balancing a tray with a pot of coffee and a glass of water and managed to free a hand to open the door to Heydrich's office. Jana watched as the secretary flipped her foot back at the door to close it, but the door didn't quite shut. Hearing Heydrich shouting into a telephone, Jana edged towards the gap in the door.

'...I don't give a damn how full the dump is. Put them six to a bed for all I care. Anyway, transportation will begin imminently—'

Footsteps. The secretary was retreating from the room. Jana scuttled away down the long, elegant hallway, past the portraits of fierce faces and impassive expressions of past generations.

She collected her coat and walked across the courtyards, taking a moment to stop in front of the majestic Saint Vitus Cathedral, which could be seen from all over Prague. She craned her neck up at the spikey, snow-tipped towers that pierced the insipid February sky. Here beat the Czech heart of Prague, where coronations had taken place and where saints were entombed. Yet the Nazis were trying to squeeze that heart out of existence, Germanise the people. Engulf and swallow up the small Czech nation until it dissipated within the black soul of the Third Reich. The thought sickened her to her stomach. She was eager to receive her first instructions from the resistance.

* * *

Later that morning, Jana prepared for the first book exchange meeting. She didn't have enough chairs for everyone so she improvised by covering upturned crates with blankets. As she positioned them in a circle, Heydrich's words spun in her mind.

What was the 'dump' he mentioned. Terezin? A chill went through her as she thought about Michal's parents.

She turned her attention back to the task in hand and arranged an array of children's books on a low table. Should she bring out the toy box too? No. The focus today was books and the joy of reading.

Five mothers arrived with their children including Karolina, the woman who'd returned the Jane Austen book and given Jana the idea for the book exchange club. Lenka also joined the group and Jana insisted she take the armchair.

Once the children were settled with books on their laps, the older ones reading to the younger ones, the woman pulled the books they'd brought for the exchange from their handbags.

They took it in turns to give a brief introduction of their book. These stories were of course all approved by the Third Reich, many portraying wholesome romances where women waited at home with a brood of children whilst their beloved went to war as a hero. Or light, frivolous tales set in the *Heimat*, the homeland.

Once all the books had been discussed and everyone had agreed which books they wanted to borrow, Karolina leaned forward and lowered her voice. 'You know what I would find interesting? To hear if anyone has read one of the banned books, and what it was about.' She smiled. 'I've read *The Great Gatsby*.'

Jana looked towards the children. 'Wait, one moment, Karolina.'

It was time for the children to make more noise so they didn't hear this change in conversation.

'Time to close books now children and play.' She pulled out the toy box and animated the children into liveliness. Jana put the *closed* sign on the shop door.

Now with the increased noise level from the children,

Karolina continued. 'It is set in America in the twenties when everyone was partying, and dancing to jazz and having affairs. All very decadent!'

The women edged forward on their stools, their eyes shining. Jana smiled; it was good to see everyone enjoying themselves. The mood turned more serious as they discussed the Czech author, Franz Kafka, who, as a Jewish author, had been banned years ago in Germany. Then Jana talked about another banned author, Helen Keller. The women held their breath as Jana told how this courageous woman, despite her blindness and deafness, became an author and activist. 'A truly inspirational woman,' she finished.

'They've been burning books in Germany,' said Lenka, shaking her head.

'I don't know if you've read anything by Heinrich Heine,' said Jana, looking around her group of friends, 'but he wrote in a play, this...' She paused, taking a deep breath, then quoted, '"There where they burn books, they will ultimately burn people."'

Her words plucked the air from the room; no one moved or spoke as each of them tried to process what they had just heard. Jana hadn't intended to end the meeting on such a terrifying note; the words she had read at Charles University had come to her unbidden. But the noise of the playing children brought them quickly back to their immediate surroundings.

As everyone prepared to leave, bundling children into hats and coats, Jana said to Lenka, 'How ironic it is that by banning books, people want to know even more about them.'

'Absolutely,' said Lenka, struggling to do up her coat buttons over her baby belly. 'It was a very good meeting today. I think we all got a lot from it.'

'Like I told the others, we can meet here every two weeks and put the world to rights.'

Lenka put an arm on Jana's shoulder. 'We must be careful no one discovers what we're talking about.'

Jana nodded, and mimicking a severe German accent, said, 'Free speech is *verboten*.'

'What isn't forbidden these days?' Lenka said in a wry tone, pulling her hat firmly over her ears. Then she kissed Jana on her cheek and left with the other women ushering their children out of the bookshop.

When quiet descended, loneliness fell upon Jana. It occurred to her she had been the only woman at the book exchange without a family. The only one without a partner. She was already twenty-two, but she had never met a young man that had captured her heart. She was very fond of Pavel, of course, and his recent help with getting little Michal out of Prague had made her warm to him even more. She knew he had feelings for her; maybe she should give their relationship a chance to grow.

That night, as she lay on the edge of sleep, a memory came to her: Mama's horrified face as she looked at the newspaper, a gasp escaping from her lips. Jana saw her twelve-year-old self, a glass of lemonade in her hand, look over her mother's shoulder. On the front page was a grainy photograph of a bonfire surrounded by people tossing something into the flames. When Jana had peered closer, she saw what was being destroyed. Books.

She fell asleep and dreamt of those bonfires; she could smell the burning paper, felt the flutter of ash on her cheeks. The quote from Heine swept into her sub-consciousness.

There where they burn books, they will ultimately burn people.

She was so hot; the heat from the flames scorched her skin.

Her heart was racing, sweat pouring from her. In a silent scream, she wrenched herself from sleep, forcing herself up through the waves into reality. Panting, she sat up in bed, the images fading. But the quote remained emblazoned in her mind.

It was nonsense, she told herself. Burning books was one thing, but people? That was something from the Middle Ages, not something that happened in civilised society.

* * *

The following afternoon, as Jana sat at the counter next to the register, crafting bookmarks, Lenka hurried in, her coat covered in snow, her teeth chattering. Jana pulled the armchair close to the small, iron stove, settled her friend down and brought a blanket which she draped around her shoulders. She then approached a Wehrmacht soldier who was browsing through the German section and asked if she could be of any assistance.

He had pockmark scars on his cheeks and eyes set close together.

'Have you got a copy of our Führer's master work, *Mein Kampf*?' he asked.

Jana balked at his request, momentarily speechless.

'I can't seem to find it,' the soldier continued.

'I don't have it in stock,' she said, her voice tight.

'Really? Why ever not? I think our SS General Heydrich should make it compulsory.'

This was her bookshop. Her mother had opened it with the freedom to sell what she chose. And now the Nazis were turning the shop into an outlet for their propaganda. Indignation boiled within her, but she strained to keep her voice even.

'Thank you, sir, for pointing out the omission of a – sorry, what did you call it? A master work,' she said, her voice thick with sarcasm. 'I seem to have overlooked it and of course shall rectify the situation.'

He stepped closer and Jana could smell a sickly-sweet odour emanating from him which she couldn't quite place.

With a sneer, he said, 'Good, then I shall return next week for a copy.'

Jana clenched her jaw as he stamped out the shop, his army boots leaving filth all over the floor.

The shop now empty, she went and sat with Lenka at the back of the shop and sighed.

'I'll have to get the wretched book now. I can't wait to get back at the hateful Nazis. But the resistance hasn't contacted me yet.' She had been waiting expectantly since Lenka had told her the password.

'Be patient,' Lenka said. 'You've only been at the castle three days.'

Not long, but she'd already heard disturbing things; Heydrich's words about transportation worried her. She was tempted to tell Lenka about it, but looking at Lenka's baby belly, she decided not to involve her. Instead, she asked, 'How's the little one?'

'Quick, put your hand on my tummy.'

As Jana reached out, she saw the whole of Lenka's stomach shift sideways, and as she placed her hand on her stomach, Jana felt the strong kick of baby feet, or maybe the punch of little fists. It was incredible: a little being beneath her fingertips, hidden by a few centimetres of her friend's skin. Jana's eyes welled up and she looked into Lenka's grinning face.

'How amazing. You and Ivan have made a little miracle. I'm so pleased you're out of danger now. Ivan never knew about your activities, did he?'

'No, he didn't.' Lenka paused and fidgeted with her wedding ring.

Unease flickered in Jana's stomach.

'You have finished with it all, haven't you?'

Lenka gazed into the distance.

'Lenka?'

Her friend shrugged. 'It's just one last thing. Then I'm finished. Promise.'

'No, that's crazy. Your baby is due in a few weeks. I don't know how the resistance can expect a highly pregnant woman to take risks.'

'That's the whole point. A highly pregnant woman is less suspicious.'

Jana let out an exasperated sigh. 'What are you going to do?'

Lenka looked towards the front of the shop. There was no one around.

'Transport some radio parts. That's all.'

'That's all?' shouted Jana. 'Forget it. I'll do it.'

'I don't want you involved in another resistance group. You've just started at the castle.'

Jana stood up and started to pace. 'Wouldn't it be better if all these separate groups co-ordinated with each other?'

'I'm not sure.' Lenka shifted herself in the chair, trying to find a more comfortable position and the blanket fell from her shoulders. Jana picked it up and wrapped it back around her.

'Thank you.' Lenka gave a weak smile. 'I suppose small separate groups are safer if anyone gets caught by the Gestapo. Fewer people to betray under interrogation.'

Nausea crept up into Jana's throat at the thought of Lenka and her unborn child in the hands of the secret police. 'Say no.'

'I can't let them down.'

'Let me do it. Please, for your baby.'

'All right. I'll think about it. The job won't be for another week or so.'

Jana was about to say something more but the conversation ended when the bell over the door rang and an elderly couple entered the shop.

8

He was here again. That policeman, Captain Kovar. Only this time, in civilian clothes. Jana was kneeling in the front shop window rearranging the book display when she glanced up to see his face, cheeks reddened from the cold, peering in at her from the other side of the glass. One corner of his mouth lifted slightly, as if in an embarrassed smile for being caught out watching her, but it disappeared instantly when she glared back at him. He stepped back from the window and shuffled around on the pavement. Annoyed at being interrupted, she crawled out backwards and stood up, pulling down her dress that had become hitched up on her woollen stockings.

What did he want now? She waited impatiently for him to enter the shop. When he still hung around outside in the grey, frozen air, she moved to the cash register and stabbed a stray cash slip onto the long spike that held the record slips of book sales. There weren't many. Maybe he hadn't intended to come into the shop but had just stopped to look through the window. No doubt found it amusing to find her scrabbling around on her hands and knees. She huffed to herself and looked at the door.

Finally, it opened and he stepped inside, his stride less assured out of uniform. He approached her, removing his brown fedora and held it against the breast pocket of his coat.

Running a hand over his hair – it looked freshly washed, a glossy black – he greeted her.

'Good afternoon, Captain Kovar,' she replied. 'What can I do for you?'

'My mother's birthday is coming up and I'm looking for a book for her.'

'Czech or German?'

'Czech.'

'New or second hand?'

He looked around the empty shop as if assessing the lack of business.

'New,' he said.

'Well, since most new Czech books are banned or discouraged, the choice is limited.'

She moved out from behind the cash desk, saying, 'I'll show you what we have,' and led him to a section of bookshelves towards the back of the shop. New instructions dictated the front of the shop be kept for German titles. 'What type of books does your mother like to read?'

He paused for a moment, his forehead wrinkling.

'Hmm, maybe you can recommend something? What does your mother enjoy?'

'Nothing. She's dead, Captain Kovar.' Even Jana was shocked at her hard burst of bitterness, and she regretted her harsh tone instantly.

His eyes widened in surprise.

'I'm sorry to hear that.' He looked at her with a dismayed expression.

Pressure built in her chest and she fought back the tears.

Why had she said that? She fingered the small, gold book that hung just below her neck, visible at the opening of her blouse. Kovar's eyes lingered a moment on the locket.

A long awkward, silence followed.

Then, her voice softer now, she said, 'It was a couple of years ago.'

He waited.

'She'd been a nurse in the Great War and contracted TB. She suffered from ill health after that, one chest infection after another. Then one winter, she caught flu which turned to pneumonia and she passed away within two days.'

He gave a slow, thoughtful nod. Again, he said, 'I'm sorry.'

Why had she just told him all this? She didn't owe him an explanation. She gave herself a mental shake and pressed back her shoulders.

'How about a family saga?' she said, lifting her voice.

Captain Kovar seemed grateful for the change of subject and looked at the books she suggested. The tension between them eased as they discussed the titles; he knew more about literature than she had expected and they fell into easy conversation. His expression had lost its arrogance and as she observed his high cheek bones and strong chin, she acknowledged his good looks.

He caught her studying him and gave her a warm smile. Annoyingly, her stomach fluttered.

She swallowed. This seemed like a good time to bring up what had been bothering her for days.

'You saw him, didn't you? Why didn't you denounce him?'

He stiffened. 'I'm not sure that I quite understand you.'

'You opened the curtain under the sink, saw him and closed it again. Why?'

'I'm afraid you're mistaken. I have no idea what you're talking about.' His expression had turned hard, their companiable conversation from a few moments ago shattered. 'I'll take this one,' he said, pulling a random book from the shelf and strode towards the cash desk.

He paid in silence, gave a curt goodbye and put on his hat. Jana stared after him as he walked out into the street. She was disappointed. She'd wanted to hear that he was one of them, a good Czech, a humane policeman who would not betray a young boy because of his religion. Because of what the Nazis demanded. But now she was confused.

Had Michal made a mistake that Kovar had seen him? Was Captain Kovar, in reality, an enemy? A collaborator? If so, she had just made herself look very suspicious, as well as putting Michal in possible danger.

* * *

As she approached the bookshop on her return from working at the castle, Jana saw a slightly built man wearing a worn coat and a cloth cap standing outside. It was unusual to have a customer so early. She smiled at him and asked if he was waiting for her to open up. He answered that he was and, after she had unlocked the door, followed her inside. Whilst she bustled around, removing her coat, turning on lights and lighting the stove, the man browsed the shelves.

Jana moved to the cash register and inserted a small key into the side of the machine and pulled down the handle. There was a ping and the cash drawer opened. She counted the small amount of change. All was correct.

When she looked up, she found the man standing before her; he was young with pale skin and intense, black eyes.

'How can I help you?'

For some reason, he made her feel uneasy as he checked

over his shoulder before speaking. "'Our true nationality is mankind.'"

Jana froze. The words he'd just uttered were a quote from H. G. Wells. But it wasn't the fact that the man had quoted a banned author that startled her; it was the fact that it was the code Lenka had told her to expect from her contact.

Jana's heart thudded as she gave the required reply, a quote from the Jewish, Czech author, Franz Kafka. "'God gives us the nuts but he does not crack them.'"

He gave a brief, thin smile and took a step closer to the cash desk.

'I presume you have a copy of *The Gardener's Year* by Capek.' She gave a nod and he continued. 'Messages will be a series of numbers coded to align with words and letters in the book. The first two numbers are the page number...'

Jana hardly breathed as she took in his words; this couldn't be happening. It was like something she would read in a book; not a real event in which she was involved. Concentrating hard, she memorised the code and repeated it back to him.

Nodding his approval, he handed her a slip of paper. 'It's your first assignment. Destroy when you have decoded the message.'

Her hand trembled as she took the note from him.

'How do I reply?'

'In the same code. It's best that you hide the note in something when you hand it to your contact.' He looked down at her handmade bookmarks displayed on the counter.

She nodded her understanding.

'How will I know the contact?'

He recited a quote and turned to leave just as the door opened and the first customer of the day entered.

* * *

Before locking up the shop that evening, Jana took the book *The Gardener's Year* and a handful of her handmade bookmarks. Then she climbed the stairs and let herself into the apartment. Luckily, her father was still working in the attic so she could start to decode the message without being disturbed.

Sitting cross-legged on her bed, she flipped through the pages, noting down the appropriate letters until the message appeared: she was to note the exact arrival times of Heydrich at Salm Palace each day. An easy enough job, she thought as she went to the kitchen sink, struck a match and set light to both her translation of the code and the coded message of numbers.

She returned to her room and cut a piece of notepaper to slightly less than the width of her bookmarks. Then she started painstakingly to compose her message, keeping it as concise as possible, writing her list of numbers with precision. Her coded note read:

HH talks of imminent deportation.

She then chose a bookmark she had made recently – floral fabric stitched over a piece of card, a golden tassel hanging from the top. She reached under her bed for her sewing basket and took out a tiny pair of scissors which she used to carefully slit open the stitches at the bottom of the bookmark. Once the fabric was free, she eased her note inside and then restitched the fabric. She sat back to admire her handiwork and smiled, pleased with herself.

An innocent bookmark. Mama would've been proud of her venture.

We'll show them Mama. They can burn and ban our books, but we won't be silenced.

9

The following evening, Jana met Pavel in a small Czech restaurant in the Hradčany district not far from Prague Castle. They chose here because it was a small, run-down place – one of the few spots not frequented by Germans. The shabby appearance belied the quality of the inexpensive food and the two friends dug into their hearty onion soup hungrily.

'Delicious,' said Jana, sipping melted cheese and baked croutons from her spoon.

'It's the local beer that gives it that rich flavour,' Pavel said in between gulping down large spoonfuls. His brown hair was tousled and his cheeks flushed. He glanced at her, pausing to eat and gave her one of his boyish smiles that instantly produced the dimple in his left cheek. Jana's chest expanded with appreciation of their friendship.

Whilst they ate, he asked about Michal.

'Well, considering the situation, he's doing very well. Papa took some time off to visit him today while I was working at the bookshop. He'd just returned as I was getting ready to meet you.'

'How's your grandma coping?'

'I think coping is the wrong word.' Jana laughed. 'She's thriving! Papa said that Babi and Michal put on a full puppet performance with my grandfather's old marionettes, with a script they'd written themselves and even sang Czech folk songs.'

Once they'd finished the soup, their conversation turned to Lenka and Ivan.

'Soon to be a family.' Jana beamed.

'It was love at first sight when those two set eyes on each other.' Pavel's expression turned wistful. 'They became inseparable after that.'

'Not everyone falls in love straight away,' said Jana. 'I think sometimes, love can grow.'

She grew warm and looked away. Why had she said that?

They sat in silence for a while, Pavel studying her, then he checked his watch.

'Time for me to walk you home since that damn Heydrich has ordered an early curfew again.'

Jana flinched at Heydrich's name and wondered what Pavel would think if he knew she was now spying on the tyrant herself.

They crossed the Vltava on the Charles Bridge, passing the brooding statues that loomed in the dark. Jana knew everything there was to know about the thirty statues that lined the bridge. Some days, she would touch the sandstone of the monuments, absorbing the vibrations of history: of priests, saviours, saints and kings. Her mother had told her as a child the myths and legends surrounding the bridge, some of them quite terrifying.

She linked her arm in Pavel's. It was an innocent action. The two friends often walked like this. The night air was freezing and she yearned for summer when the city was bathed in golden sunshine and the Gothic buildings appeared more enchanting than sinister.

They arrived outside the front door that led up to her apartment.

'I hope you're keeping out of trouble, Pavel.' She smiled.

'Just annoying the odd German here and there. A few slashed tyres, a bit of graffiti, and helping smuggle the occasional child out the city.'

'Thanks again. I appreciate it.'

'I'm always here for you, Jana. Always. You know that, don't you?' His voice had turned husky.

'I know,' she said, stepping towards him.

She hesitated. She was filled with the warmth of gratitude, but could there be more? She felt lonely, yearning for something. For Pavel?

It was time to find out.

On tiptoes, she lifted her face and pressed a kiss on his closed lips. She could sense his shock. Putting her arms around his neck, she kissed him again, prising his lips apart with her tongue. His chest heaved with a sigh and he retuned her kiss.

Their embrace was brief; the chatter of passersby and a low wolf whistle broke them apart.

'You better go,' said Jana. 'It must be nearly curfew.'

'What just happened, here?' asked Pavel, breathlessly.

'Let's think about it.'

'I definitely will.' He adjusted his hat and walked away with a bounce in his step.

* * *

As Jana turned out the light later, she thought about that kiss. She had yearned for it to ignite some passion within her, reveal her true feelings for Pavel, fulfil something missing in her life. But as they kissed, she'd felt very little. It wasn't unpleasant, just a bit awkward. A little cumbersome. Nothing like the earth-moving, overwhelming flood of emotion she'd read about in books such as *Wuthering Heights* or *Anna Karenina*. Now, she felt disappointed, but most of all guilty. She had given Pavel the wrong signals. No, worse than that: false hope.

10

Michal grabbed Jana's hand excitedly and pulled her into her grandfather's old workshop. Papa and Babi followed. It was Sunday and she and her father had taken the bus out of Prague early that morning. Now, Michal eagerly showed off the puppeteering skills he had been learning.

'Wonderful!' exclaimed Papa, clapping his hands. 'My father would have been proud of you. Did you know that he was a renowned puppeteer?'

'Yes, Babi told me. And he travelled the countryside with his theatre and made everyone laugh, even the adults because he made secret jokes that the children didn't understand.' He beamed as he spoke and it warmed Jana's heart to see his uplifted mood, and to hear him refer to her grandma as Babi.

They passed a happy couple of hours in the workshop lost in the historical, Czech world of puppets, fairy tales and legends. Papa didn't, of course, introduce Michal to the satirical skills of the foregone puppet masters: the scathing jokes about government and royalty or the lurid sexual references. The shows had been an open, all-round entertainment. Until the Nazis arrived and strictly censored the content.

It had started to snow again and Michal looked out the window longingly. 'Can I play outside?'

He had been at Babi's three weeks now and had not been allowed out for fear of him being seen. The sudden appearance of a strange child in the area could arouse suspicion. But Babi now looked at her son and Jana.

'He won't be seen at the back of the house,' she said. 'The nearest neighbour is two kilometres away and no one will be out and about on a Sunday in this weather.'

Papa frowned as he considered, then nodded at Michal. 'Only if I can build a snowman with you.'

Babi smiled. 'I'll pull out some old boots and a jacket of yours for Michal.' She bustled away with her usual energy.

Ten minutes later, Jana and Babi stood at the window watching man and boy rolling balls of snow around the garden.

'How are the two of you getting on?' Jana asked.

'He's a treasure.' Babi's eyes were alight. 'He's a sensitive, intelligent boy who responds to gestures of love. And he gives me so much pleasure.' She put an arm around Jana's shoulders. 'I'd take a whole troop of children hiding from the Nazi's.'

Jana laughed. 'I believe you would.'

It continued to snow into the late afternoon. Jana and her father stamped their way to the bus stop and looked up and down the thick mantle of undisturbed snow that covered the road. The darkening sky was a whorl of thick snowflakes. There would be no more buses back into Prague that day; they would have to spend the night here.

The weather worsened and Jana and her father had no choice but to stay a further two days with Babi. The bookshop would have to remain closed but what worried her most was being absent from work at the castle; she didn't want to lose the job she had just started, and she was eager to keep her eye on Heydrich.

Jana had brought some more books for Michal and the two of them passed happy hours snuggled up on the settee reading together. Her father found some blocks of linden wood in grandpa's workshop and showed the attentive Michal elementary skills in carving the fine-grained wood. Jana stood in the doorway watching them work. Papa was smiling and laughing more than she had seen since the death of her mother. Michal was good for him; they looked like father and son.

I wish you could see them, Mama. The thought sparked a burst of pain so fierce, she gasped. As tears welled up, she turned away, rubbing her eyes with the back of a hand.

Babi looked up from sweeping the floor. She stood the broom against the wall and moved towards her, spreading her arms.

'You miss her,' she said in a knowing voice. 'Of course you do. We all do.'

Jana leaned into her comforting embrace and cried softly into her shoulder.

* * *

It was mid-morning Wednesday before the buses were running again and they were able to return to Prague. Jana went directly to open the bookshop and her father to the attic to prepare for a children's performance the following evening. She worried about her job at the castle and wondered if she would be fired for not showing up for three days. Now that she had started real resistance work, it would be awful to lose the advantage she had of being so close to Heydrich.

The shop was quiet, so she closed up for five minutes to fetch a newspaper from the stand on the corner. The vendor was stamping his feet and rubbing his arms in an effort to keep warm.

'Read all about it, Miss,' he said as she approached. He tipped his cap at her. 'Heydrich has had another bunch of Czechs executed for so-called crimes against the state. Fifty men and three women.'

Jana put a mittened hand to her mouth. 'So many?' she said, aghast.

'Seems our new governor is really getting into the swing of things. And is more than happy to have it in the press as a warning.'

She shivered but not from the cold. She paid for the newspaper and took it back to the shop where she read about the latest incident with mounting horror. It was terrifying that the accused had not only been resistors, but also petty criminals accused of theft or black-market trading. Heydrich's fist was squeezing Prague's heart.

The latest news made her even more eager for her contact to appear so she could pass on her bookmark with her message: Heydrich's conversation that she'd overheard. Had the contact come to the bookshop in the last couple of days whilst she'd been snowed in with Babi?

It was six o'clock when, feeling weary, she was about to turn off the lights and reach for her coat to leave. The door opened and Captain Kovar stepped in, wearing civilian clothes with snow piled on the shoulders of his coat.

Goodness! Not again.

'I'm just locking up,' she said tersely.

'Oh, I don't mean to be a nuisance. I was a bit worried about you.'

A gust of freezing wind blew a flurry of snow through the open door, causing wet flakes to settle on her stockinged legs. Agitated, she beckoned him further into the shop and shut the door.

'Worried about what?' Her voice came out a little too high, her forehead wrinkling.

Had he come to confront her about Michal?

'The shop has been closed a couple of days and I feared you were unwell.'

She stifled a sigh of relief. 'No, I'm fine. I became snowed in whilst visiting my—a friend.'

Careful. She needed to steer the conversation in a different direction.

'Was your mother pleased with the book?' she asked.

His expression relaxed and he started to talk about his mother's birthday. He related a joke his mother had made about the shortage of candles actually being an advantage for the top of a cake of an older woman. For the first time, she saw him laugh, and was surprised at his wide smile, his large mouth. She thought of her kiss with Pavel; he had a small mouth, not much larger than her own.

'You look freezing. Would you like a hot coffee?' She was shocked at the words that had come from her mouth. But there was something else. A sliver of a thrill.

He looked surprised but pleased, and she led him to the back of the shop where she indicated the armchair.

'I'll put the kettle on the stove.'

He sat instead on a stool and removed his hat. This was bizarre; only a few weeks ago, he had been here in very different circumstances, marching through the shop, scaring her and Michal to death. She had thought his high cheekbones made him look arrogant, but now as she studied him, she found his face attractive.

He met her gaze and she turned away.

In the small kitchen, she put the kettle on and took out the jar of acorn coffee – only Germans had access to real coffee these days. She placed cups and saucers on the countertop, and watched the spout of the kettle, waiting for the first droplets of steam to appear.

She heard his tread behind her and turned. He'd removed his coat and she could now see he wore a shirt and tie with a navy pullover. His chest was broad and he had strong arms. *Policemen's arms*, she reminded herself, awaking from some strange stupor she'd fallen into.

He glanced down to where she was standing – in front of the curtain that ran beneath the sink. Where Michal had hidden.

Her heartrate quickened. 'You did see him,' she whispered.

Uncertainty flickered across his navy eyes. Such an unusual colour.

He didn't reply. Why didn't he just admit he'd seen Michal?

He took a step towards her. So close. Nearly touching. She stood backed up against the sink, her hands clutching the countertop behind.

She looked up at him, her breath catching in her throat.

His face was soft, questioning.

Her lips parted.

He bowed his head.

The shrill whistle of the kettle pierced the energy-laden air and he stepped back, allowing her to remove the kettle from the stove and pour the boiling water into the two cups.

Her voice shaky, she said, 'Let's take our drinks back into the shop, Captain Kovar.'

'I think it's time you called me Andrej,' he said, a glint in his eyes.

* * *

After he left, half an hour later, Jana sat in the armchair, mulling over what had just happened. Had he intended to kiss her or had she imagined it? After that moment, conversation over their coffee had been stilted. There had been a tension between them, but not an unpleasant one. More like a charge of expectancy. When he said goodbye, she felt a pang of disappointment that there was no kiss. But actually, that was a good thing. She certainly didn't want to get involved with a fascist policeman when she was taking part in anti-Nazi activities. Tomorrow, she would be back at the castle spying on Heydrich, who with Himmler, was one of Hitler's top men.

Was she incredibly brave or incredibly stupid? Neither. Just a bookshop girl doing what she could against her country's oppressors.

11

Dressed in her black maid's uniform and carrying a basket with cleaning materials, Jana waited outside Heydrich's locked door. A few moments later, her manager, Miss Jezek, who had interviewed her, bustled along, keys in hand. She had accepted Jana's excuses of being absent with a pinched expression earlier that morning, and had warned Jana to in future refrain from travelling in bad weather conditions on a Sunday.

Miss Jezek always opened the office doors for the cleaners and locked it again when they finished. Security was tight on the first floor of Salm Palace. It was strict protocol that the office doors were left wide open when cleaners were inside, and Miss Jezek patrolled the landing, keeping an eye on the staff. There was also an armed guard on duty at the end of the hall.

Jana set to work. Heydrich's office was what one would expect in the baroque palace: large with an imposing desk, grand chair, and oil paintings on the wall. Looking somewhat incredulous alongside the artwork was the obligatory portrait of Hitler. Jana gave his face a good slapping with her long feather duster before moving over to the sideboard.

On a silver platter stood a cut-glass crystal, brandy decanter and two glasses made from the finest Czech crystal. She took a small cloth and with delicate hands wiped the precious crystal before turning to Heydrich's desk. Everything was immaculately tidy, the surface of the desk empty except for an ink pot and a picture of his wife and four children. His wife was apparently an ardent Nazi and fully supported her husband's career within the Nazi party.

Jana's eye was caught by something she'd not seen in the office before: a violin case propped up against the wall. Heydrich played violin? The thought of this barbarian handling such a beautiful instrument jarred her; it must belong to one of the children.

Next, she dusted the antique bookcase, pausing to read the spines of the books. Many were beautiful, old, leatherbound copies and she guessed special editions. The authors were mostly German, such as Goethe and Schiller.

'Do you enjoy German literature?'

She spun round to see Reinhard Heydrich appraising her. He had fine features and an aquiline nose which gave him an almost regal quality. His blond hair, blue eyes and athletic physique made him fit the Aryan ideal far more than any other top Nazi.

Her mouth went dry and she took a moment to answer.

'I do, sir. I studied the subject.'

'Indeed?' He placed his briefcase on the desk, strode to a coat stand, hung up his coat and smoothed down the jacket of his pristine uniform. His boots gleamed and the silver SS pin on his collar shone.

'Good to hear a Czech speak articulate German. Most of you lot can't string a sentence together.' He seated himself and waved his hand dismissively. 'You may leave.'

He didn't look at her as he reached for the phone.

'Yes, sir.'

She hurried from the room, relieved to get away from him. The man was arrogance personified. She checked the watch on her trembling wrist and made a mental note of the time: twenty past eight. From now on, she would note his arrival times as requested and pass the information on to her next contact. She finished her shift and wound her way down Nerudova Street and on to the bookshop.

* * *

Later that afternoon, as the light was fading from a bleak sky and Jana was switching on the table lamps, Pavel arrived. He stamped the snow from his boots on the doormat and looked at her shyly. Normally, she would have given him a warm hug as greeting, but now she just managed an awkward smile.

He looked around the shop as he approached. He too didn't hug her. She asked how things were at the warehouse where he worked near the shore of the Vltava River.

'It's pretty hectic. The Reich has stepped up production at the steel works, and hundreds of boxes of ammunition are passing through our warehouse now the war is raging.' They were both silent for a moment as they considered the implication of his words.

'I have to work double shifts starting from next week,' he said, then added in a soft voice, 'I was wondering if you would like to have dinner with me this evening at our favourite little restaurant.'

Jana looked into his hopeful eyes. Everything within their friendship had changed since their kiss: the way they spoke to each other, their body language and the atmosphere that emanated between them. Having dinner with him would, in his eyes, be a date. She had made a mistake and she owed it to him to be honest.

He reached out, touching her hand briefly, his eyes shining.

'I haven't stopped thinking about you since the last time we met. I've wanted this for so long, and when you kissed me, it was the most wonderful moment of my life.'

'Pavel, I'm not sure—'

'Don't worry. I won't get heavy on you,' he said quickly, as if realising the weight of his declaration. 'We can take things slowly. Just dinner.'

Jana gazed at his boyish face, his expression full of longing. She stalled at crushing him completely.

'I'm sorry, I can't this evening. Another time, maybe?'

His face dropped. 'That's a shame. I'll be working long hours in future, but I'll let you know when I have some time.'

'Yes, do that,' she said, smiling in an effort to lift his spirits.

As there seemed nothing more to say, he left, leaving her with the feeling she had just lost her closest friend.

* * *

The book exchange group was lively the next morning. Seated next to Jana was Dasha, an old school friend with whom she'd lost contact until recently. It was good to have her join the book club. Dasha had just passed on a worn copy of an eighteenth-century romance and was now chatting about her brother's new job.

'...you would think, living in Pilsen, he would have found work in the beer factory, but actually he's been recruited to work at Skoda.'

'Don't they make weapons there for the Wehrmacht?' asked another.

'Yes. My brother would've preferred to brew beer, but he has to work where the Germans send him.' Dasha sighed.

'Free will died back in 1939,' piped in a prematurely grey woman. 'The Germans try to placate us with better employment, but they use our skilled work force to drive their war machine.'

Dasha nodded. 'At least our men don't have to join the Wehrmacht.'

'True,' Lenka said, 'but that's because we're not considered good enough to be German citizens, although our country is being Germanised. The Reich just wants our workers because all their men are away fighting.'

There were murmurs of agreement from around the circle. Jana glanced across at Karolina, who had inspired the book club in the first place. Today, she was unusually silent, her face pallid and drawn.

When the group came to a close and the mothers were getting their children into their coats, Jana approached her and gave a sympathetic smile.

'I just wondered if you were all right. You were a bit quiet today.'

'Just tired, that's all,' said Karolina as she struggled to get her little girl's arms through her coat sleeves. 'I'm not sleeping well.'

Jana reached out and helped with the child's coat. 'If you ever want to have a chat—'

'Thanks,' said Karolina, 'but really, I'm fine.' She didn't look at Jana as she spoke, concentrating on her squirming daughter, and then gave a vague wave to everyone as she left.

* * *

Lenka groaned as she lowered herself onto the settee next to Jana.

'Thank goodness Ivan likes to cook,' she said as she arranged cushions in an attempt to get comfortable. Homely sounds and smells emanated from the kitchen: the clink of pans, the aroma of onions frying. Jana looked around the apartment where Lenka and Ivan had lived since their wedding just over a year ago. It was small and cosy and would soon be filled with baby chatter and cries and the cooing of parents over the little wonder they had created.

Jana gave a small, wistful sigh. 'How are you feeling?' she asked.

'Exhausted, clumsy and ugly.'

'You could never be ugly.' Jana took her friend's hand and squeezed it. 'Only three weeks to go.'

'I want you to be godmother to the little one,' said Lenka, her face pale and earnest.

As Jana hugged Lenka awkwardly around her baby mound, she said, 'It would be an honour. And I fully intend to be the best godmother ever.'

What sort of world was it that the baby would be born into? If only their small nation hadn't been deserted by the rest of Europe.

'I wonder how different things would have been if we had resisted the German invasion,' Jana said.

'We would have been slaughtered and Prague razed to the ground.' Lenka sighed. 'Hitler threatened to bomb our historical city mercilessly if we didn't comply.'

'I know. I mean, if countries like England and France had supported us instead of literally putting us in Hitler's hands in order to pacify him... It was only when he invaded Poland that the rest of Europe reacted.' Jana couldn't keep the bitterness from her voice.

'We just weren't important enough.' Lenka sighed again. 'A tiny landlocked country, far away from London...'

'We were the sacrifice,' Jana said. 'But the beast wasn't satisfied.'

Ivan popped his head around the kitchen door. 'Not long, ladies. Hope you're hungry.'

Lenka patted her swollen stomach. 'We are starving.' She smiled. 'Our child has a huge appetite. Must be a boy.'

Ivan's brown eyes, soft with love, gazed at his wife, his chest heaving with emotion before he returned to preparing the meal. Jana was moved to see the deep love between her friends but her stomach flickered with concern. She lowered her voice.

'Have you been contacted about the radio parts? Surely they wouldn't expect you to take that risk in your condition.'

'I haven't heard anything. I expect someone else has been assigned the job.'

'Good. Promise me you won't do anything stupid.'

'Promise. Now let me bore you with baby stuff.' Lenka leaned to the side of the settee and pulled a basket onto her lap that contained balls of wool, knitting needles and tiny pieces of clothing already completed. 'I've been busy,' she said, holding up a delicate, cream bodysuit.

'How adorable,' Jana exclaimed. 'I have something for my new godchild too. It'll be finished in time for the birth.' Jana lay a hand on her friend's stomach, choking back a well of emotion. She leaned forwards. 'Can you hear me, little one? I can't wait to meet you and hold you in my arms.'

12

It was ten days after the first contact had appeared in the bookshop. During this time, Jana had noted the times of Heydrich's arrival each morning and added it to the slip of paper that she kept hidden in the bookmark. Although she had kept her writing small, the paper was full on both sides, and she was beginning to wonder whether she should start a new bookmark.

A stout, middle-aged woman in a bulky coat had been limping around the bookshelves for half an hour ignoring the Wehrmacht soldier who stood near the front surveying the selection of new German editions. After he'd left – without buying anything – the woman approached Jana at the cash register.

'"You cannot find peace by avoiding life",' she said, after Jana asked whether she could be of any assistance.

Jana's breath caught at the quote. It was from Virginia Woolf and was the password she'd been waiting for. She replied with a quote from the same author.

'"Why are women so much more interesting to men than men are to women?"'

The stout woman burst out laughing. 'Never a truer word spoken.'

Jana laughed too, and after a quick glance at the door, she retrieved a book of Czech poetry from beneath the counter. The all-important bookmark lay within the pages.

As she slipped it across to the woman, she whispered, 'There's an important message; I've added a conversation I over—'

She stopped short as the woman put a warning finger to her lips.

'If you tell me nothing, I know nothing.'

Jana nodded, angry with herself for breaking one of the basic rules of the resistance: the least known, the better. Then she looked at the woman questioningly. Did she have any further instructions?

'Next time,' said the woman, interpreting Jana's gaze. She pulled her own book from her shopping bag and slid Jana's bookmark inside. She moved to the door, surprisingly sure footed and then, Jana saw through the window, she adopted her shuffling gait once more. Jana smiled to herself; resistors came in all guises.

At lunch time, she put the *closed* sign on the door and strolled towards Josefov, the Jewish Quarter. She had the urge to see Michal's home; maybe speak to a neighbour, find out something more about the boy's family. Soldiers were patrolling the area so she took a detour but lost her way and found herself in a dark alleyway lined with rubbish. A putrid smell punctuated the air.

She heard a cat wailing and slowed her stride. The alleyway came to an abrupt end, a high stone wall blocking the way. The cat's wail came from what appeared to be a heap of abandoned clothes on the ground. Maybe the animal was injured, she thought as she approached, noticing the wall splattered with paint.

The bundle of clothes moved and Jana yelped. Before her was a tiny woman in a man's overcoat, kneeling, her hands folded in prayer, letting out cries of anguish.

Jana rushed to her side, 'Are you hurt? What's wrong?'

'My beautiful boy, my grandson. Why dear, God, why?'

In a horrifying moment of clarity, the scene became crystal clear. There was no injured cat hiding in a pile of clothes. There was a devastated grandmother, shrunken from hunger and grief, huddled on the cold ground. And instead of a wall covered in graffiti, she bowed before a wall peppered with bullet holes and scarred with black-crimson blood.

An execution wall.

One of many, where under Heydrich's orders, Jewish men and women were rounded up and promptly shot.

Their crime? None other than their religion.

* * *

In bed that night, Jana stared into the darkness, her eyes wide, aching with tiredness, her mind whirring. She turned and thumped her pillow. Images of the woman crumpled before the execution wall fought with pictures of Lenka holding up the baby clothes. She went over every word of her last conversation with her, worried. Had Lenka been evasive about the assignment to carry radio parts?

Sleep eluding her, she climbed out of bed and went to her bedroom window, which overlooked the narrow, cobbled street below. The street lamp was out and not a soul was around – such a contrast to a few years ago, when the noise of footsteps and voices of passersby always accompanied her to sleep. Curfew and electricity shortages had changed the way of life.

Leaning her forehead against the cold glass, she let out a deep sigh. In the short time Heydrich had been in charge, the brutal persecution of Nazi opposers and Jews had dramatically increased; opposition to the Reich was dealt with by interrogation by the Gestapo, torture and execution. People murmured about Heydrich's reign of terror, their eyes full of fear. Citizens walked the frozen streets of Prague with their shoulders slumped. Oppressed. That's what they were. An oppressed people. And Jana was afraid that Heydrich's unrelenting policy of stamping out the resistance was beginning to take effect.

No, that mustn't happen. They couldn't let Heydrich defeat them.

Shivering, she climbed back into bed, and her thoughts returned to Lenka. Tomorrow, she decided, she would ask Papa to mind the bookshop whilst she went to check on her.

Eventually, she fell into a troubled sleep.

* * *

Ivan was surprised when he opened the front door and saw Jana. 'Oh, you just missed Lenka. She's on her way to meet you at the coffee shop. To be honest, I would've preferred her to stay at home. She looked very pale, and she's so heavy on her feet—'

'I'll catch her up,' said Jana, already dashing down the apartment stairwell, a sick feeling in the pit of her stomach. Lenka had arranged no meeting with her, in a coffee shop or anywhere else. Jana fought down the panic, forcing herself to think clearly. As she stood on the pavement, she looked left and right, trying to decide which way Lenka might have gone. If she were meeting a contact to pass over radio parts, would she have headed towards the busy Old Town centre and attempted a handover in full view of so many people? Or to the quieter streets where she was less likely to be seen?

Precious moments ticked by, indecision paralysing her. Either scenario was possible. She imagined the scene. Lenka jostling through the crowds, maybe around the Astronomical Clock where people pressed shoulder to shoulder looking upwards, waiting for the figures to parade at the top of the hour; Lenka touching arms with a stranger, possibly a woman who'd surreptitiously take a shopping bag from Lenka's hand...

Jana bolted off down the street, heading towards the town centre. As she ran, she chided herself for not having suspected that Lenka would do the drop herself. Jana should have been more alert, taken better care of her friend.

Today was market day in Wenceslas Square: the perfect place to be carrying shopping baskets and bags filled with produce that concealed small electrical parts.

Ivan had said that Lenka had not long departed, and Jana was sprinting at a fast pace. Why hadn't Jana caught up with her? Lenka, heavy with child, would be moving slowly. Cold doubt seeped into her chest; she had got this all wrong. Made the wrong decision. Gone the wrong way.

Ahead, a maze of alleyways wound away from Wenceslas Square; there would be no chance to find Lenka if she turned down one of these.

Despair set in and she slowed her stride, trying to figure out what to do next. A short distance ahead, an old man stood under a lamp post playing a violin. It was a familiar classical tune, beautifully played. A few people had gathered to listen. One passerby threw a coin into the violin case that lay open on the ground. The old man nodded his thanks and as the passerby withdrew from the small group, a figure behind came in to sight.

Jana sighed with relief.

Lenka.

Jana called out, but Lenka didn't turn. Suddenly, two policemen stopped her friend pointing to her shopping bag. Jana's heart plummeted. Why had they stopped her? Was this one of the increasing routine stop and searches that Heydrich had ordered? Or had Lenka been betrayed by a collaborator?

Jana couldn't just stand by and watch; she had to do something.

She ran up to the policemen, shouting, 'Help, officers. A pickpocket has just snatched my purse. That way.' She waved her hand behind her. 'Back there.'

They looked up at her. Dull, disinterested eyes.

'You need to go to the police station and file a formal complaint,' one said as the other reached for Lenka's bag.

Jana dared a glance at Lenka's face; it was frozen in terror.

She jabbered on, 'The thief knocked a woman to the ground and... he punched someone too...'

The first policeman gave her his attention now, but the one with his hand in Lenka's bag continued his search, grim-faced. He pulled out a scarf, newspaper, knitting wool, patterns for baby clothes and tossed them to one side. His partner, looking in the direction Jana was pointing, said, 'Shall I take a look at what's going on up there?'

Yes, please, prayed Jana. 'Come, quick, lest the thief gets away.'

'He'll be long gone,' said the policeman rummaging in Lenka's bag. He frowned as he pulled out a small package wrapped in newspaper. Jana stopped breathing and watched as everything slowed; he peeled open the paper and the small metal parts were revealed. He stared at Lenka with a triumphant expression. Lenka's eyes fluttered as she clutched her stomach and her knees gave way, and she sank towards the ground. But the police grabbed her and hauled her upright, iron fists gripped around her upper arms, any interest in Jana's fictional thief forgotten...

Jana let out a moan.

The crowd swam before her eyes.

Helpless, lame in mind and body, she witnessed her beloved friend being dragged along in the direction of the police station. She saw how she stumbled and was yanked up, how people stared at the pregnant woman being marched away.

* * *

Curled up in the armchair, Jana sought to find solace in the silence of the bookshop. She had moved the chair to face the shop front where she sat in darkness, watching moonshine rays dim and glow as clouds scurried across the full moon. Her eyes were hot and swollen from tears, and her throat raw from her sobs. Now, drained, she sat still and motionless, waiting.

After witnessing Lenka's arrest that morning, she had run back to Ivan who was just about to leave for his work shift. Barely able to get the words out, she'd told Ivan what had happened. His face froze with shock and confusion.

'What on earth was she doing with radio parts?' he stammered.

Jana's whole body trembled. She was unable to speak.

Ivan held her by the shoulders.

'What's going on here?' he demanded.

Jana had then told him then about Lenka's work for the resistance, but how Jana wanted her to stop, how she'd pleaded with her to stop. Ivan listened to her words, his face a mask of disbelief, before grabbing his coat and racing out the door. Jana chased after him.

When they arrived at the police station, Ivan marched up to the officer behind the counter, and visibly trying to control his emotion, asked to see his wife. He was told to take a seat. Jana sat with him. They waited two hours before they were told that yes, Lenka was being held for questioning; no, she was not allowed visitors. Furthermore, Ivan and Jana were instructed to leave the police station immediately.

Ivan's chest had heaved with rage and his hands curled into fists.

'I'm not going anywhere till I see my wife!'

The officer, his face impassive, said, 'Any moment, you will be going somewhere. And that's directly into a cell.'

Jana had tugged at Ivan's arm. She'd managed to persuade him to avoid further confrontation and they left. As they descended the steps outside the police station, she promised Ivan she would find out more information.

She'd wandered around the city in the rain, up and down the alleyways, back and forth over Charles Bridge, past the statues where rivulets of raindrops ran down their anguished stone faces. Once she'd thought things through, she returned to the police station, hoping that the same officer was not there. He was.

'You again,' he said.

'I would like to talk to Captain Kovar.'

The officer raised his eyebrows.

Jana pushed back her shoulders and kept her gaze firm.

The officer eventually shrugged and picked up the phone.

A few minutes later, Andrej appeared and with a jolt of surprise beckoned her into an office. She told him what had happened and he assured her he would find out about Lenka and come to the bookshop that evening.

Now she waited for him, desperate for any news.

'Oh, Mama,' she whispered on a sigh. 'How can this be happening?'

It had been a nightmare ever since Hitler arrived in his motorcade in March, nearly four years ago, and strode triumphantly into Prague Castle. In order to stamp out any resistance, there had been ongoing mass executions.

Ice fingers closed around Jana's heart. Surely not Lenka and her baby.

As the bookshop door opened, Jana flicked on the switch of the standing light beside her and sprung across to meet Andrej. In the dim light at the front of the shop, she saw the strain on his face and her heart hammered inside her chest. He removed his hat and placed it on the counter.

'Tell me,' she said.

'Lenka was questioned this afternoon—'

'Not – not the Gestapo.' Nausea sprung up her throat.

'No. I managed to talk the chief out of handing a highly pregnant woman, whose arrest was witnessed in a full market square, over to the secret police. I highlighted the unrest it would cause amongst the citizens.'

'Thank goodness,' she murmured. 'Will there be a trial?'

Andrej looked at her with pained eyes.

Of course not. What a stupid thing to say.

'She was sent away about half an hour ago.'

'Where?'

'Terezin concentration camp,' he said, softly.

Jana's head swam and her legs went limp. As her body slumped, Andrej steadied her. She fell on his chest, her throat so tight, she could hardly breathe. He held her and stroked the back of her head as she cried.

'What about the baby?' she asked, her voice muffled against his coat.

He drew back and lifted her chin, his face solemn. He wiped away a tear, his thumb stroking her cheek. A gesture so gentle, it made her stomach twist.

'I have a contact in Terezin and will try to get news. There are doctors there: good Jewish doctors who will take care of her.'

'But to be born in a concentration camp? What a start in life. And poor Lenka without Ivan by her side. I must see her, I must...'

She knew she was babbling nonsense, but at that moment, it was better than facing the harsh reality.

'You know that's not possible. But I might be able to get a letter to her.'

'You could do that?'

'Luckily, I've just been promoted and I have connections...' His voice trailed off.

'I'm confused. Are you a fascist?' she whispered.

'You are beautiful.' He drew his face closer. His eyes were nearly black in the shadows, but she saw a glimmer before his lips hovered over hers, his warm breath caressing her skin. He brushed a kiss so light over her mouth that it was barely tangible. Then he straightened himself.

'I'd better go.' His voice was low and tender.

He parted himself from her and picked up his hat. At the doorway, he paused, looking up and down the street before stepping out into the darkness. He hadn't answered her question.

13

Jana moved through her daily routine like an automaton: washing and dressing, making breakfast for her and her father, trudging up Nerudova Street to Prague Castle with leaden legs. Grief made her body heavy and slow, but had left her mind in unrelenting activity. With every breath, she thought of Lenka. How terrified she must have been as she was arrested. The fear she must have felt for her unborn child. And what would she be doing now? Lying in a narrow bed, in an overfilled, filthy room with desperate people. Was she in the 'dump' that Heydrich had talked about? And what about the transportation he'd mentioned? What did it mean?

As she tidied the bookshop before opening up, she worried about Lenka's baby. Andrej had said there would be doctors in the camp, but what access did they have to medical supplies and equipment? And Lenka had already been bleeding during her pregnancy and could be in danger during the birth. Desperate for news, she was tempted to visit Andrej at the police station, but realised that might look suspicious and put them both in a difficult situation.

Still, at lunch time, she hung around the area nearby, hoping to see him, but it appeared that since his promotion, his duties were less on the streets.

That bothered her too. He'd been promoted. Obviously, his Nazi boss was pleased with his work of keeping the citizens under Heydrich's thumb.

It was four days since Lenka's arrest, and Jana walked the streets, shivering in the March wind. She looked at the people who passed her by, going about their daily lives. How the citizens of Prague had changed. The cheerful, bustling crowd punctuated with laughter that epitomised the Czech sense of humour had vanished. Now, weary expressions with dull eyes were all she saw. Despair clawed at her as she recognised what those faces held. Defeat. After over three years of occupation under the might of the Reich, people needed a sign of hope. But Heydrich was systematically crushing the resistance and Lenka had just become another of his victims.

She walked past the newspaper man, shaking her head as he proffered her the daily paper. The propaganda sickened her. She fumbled in her handbag for her shop keys and glanced up to see Andrej walking towards her, wearing civilian clothes. Thank goodness. He must have news. Her heart began to thump as she tried to read his expression, gauge the news he had to impart.

He greeted her with a small smile but his eyes were earnest. Hands shaking, she unlocked the door and as soon as he'd followed behind her, she swirled to face him.

'Have you heard anything? Is Lenka all right?'

'She went into labour shortly after arriving at Terezin. Another prisoner, a doctor, oversaw the birth. Although she lost a lot of blood, and is weak, she's expected to recover.'

'And the baby?' she whispered.

'A healthy girl.' This time, the smile reached his eyes and he placed a hand on her arm, before looking over his shoulder through the window and removing it again. 'Could we move away from the window?'

'Of course,' said Jana, her head light with the news. Warmth spread through her chest; Lenka had a baby girl.

They moved to the back of the shop out of view from the street.

'Has her husband, Ivan been informed?' Jana asked.

Andrej nodded. 'This afternoon. I've organised to get a letter to Lenka. But keep what you write neutral in case it is intercepted by the Nazis. I've told Ivan he can write one too.'

She nodded eagerly. 'Thank you.'

He looked slightly embarrassed, or uncomfortable. She couldn't quite make it out. He hadn't removed his hat like the last time he'd come. She felt a twinge of disappointment as she realised he didn't intend to stay.

'What are the conditions like at Terezin? Will Lenka and the baby have enough food?' If Lenka had lost blood during the birth, she would need iron. Meat would be ideal, but there would be little chance of that. 'Can I get food to her somehow?'

He shook his head. 'Sorry. But write your letter, and I'll collect it in a couple of days. Now, I must leave.'

His voice had turned matter-of-fact and he turned to go. She thanked him again but he was already walking away from her. It was hard to believe that this was the same man who had wiped the tears from her cheek and had brushed her lips with the most tender of kisses just days ago.

* * *

Throughout the day, she thought of Lenka: sometimes with an inner smile at her becoming a mother, other times with fear for her and the baby's future. Andrej had avoided her question about conditions in the camp. Jana tried to picture her friend cradling her newborn but the image dissolved before it could fully form.

That evening, she visited Ivan. He reached for the basket with the baby clothes Lenka had knitted and held up a tiny, pale-yellow cardigan.

'I don't even know my daughter's name,' said Ivan.

Jana swallowed hard. 'Will you tell Lenka's parents the news?'

'I'll post a letter first thing in the morning.' He folded the cardigan carefully and lay it back in the basket.

Crossing Wenceslas Square on her way home from Ivan, Jana stopped at the point where Lenka had been arrested and tipped her head to the night sky. The night was a black, frozen mirror awash with glittering stars; the creamy half-moon suspended over the hundred spires. She imagined how Lenka's parents must feel at that moment. The pain. Continuing her journey home, she made up her mind to visit them in the spring. They'd moved out of Prague and now lived in a small, picturesque village about twenty kilometres outside the city. It was called Lidice. They felt safer there, Lenka had said.

* * *

Jana stared at the blank sheet of pale-lilac writing paper before her, her fountain pen limp between her fingers. No words came to her. She'd selected her prettiest paper and reached for her finest pen, but now her actions seemed inane. They would be of no consequence to Lenka.

Sitting next to the cash register in the bookshop, Jana heaved a sigh and put down her pen. The shop, now closed, was in partial darkness; only the small reading lamp beside her threw a circle of light. She had been desperate to write to Lenka, but now she had no idea what to say.

She gazed into the shadows, as if searching the books for answers: a treasure of heroines and heroes overcoming adversity. But had any one of them been in the situation that Lenka now found herself in? What words of comfort or hope could she write to her friend? Lenka had been there for her when Mama had died: quietly by her side, her mere presence a comfort. Jana couldn't even do that for her friend. Tears of frustration clouded her vision. She stood up and moved to the shelves where she ran her fingers along the spines of the books; it was an automatic reaction when she needed comfort. Where there any books in Terezin that Lenka could turn to?

Books were often her solace. And books were made of words: words that could contain a world of emotions. She couldn't be with Lenka, but she could write down her feelings, simply and honestly. Nodding to herself, she returned to her paper and pen and began to write.

My dearest friend, Lenka.

As I sit here struggling to decide what to write, it has occurred to me that you don't need false platitudes or trite expressions of sympathy. What you need is my love, and I hope these words can covey how much you and your baby girl are in my heart. I think of you constantly and try to imagine your daily life, but of course I can't. But please know, I will never give up on you. I will pray for you every night and think of you each morning when I wake. I love you like a sister and will be waiting for you when this terrible ordeal ends. Stay strong, my darling. We will see each other again.

I love you,

Always in my heart,
Jana.

She wiped the tears from her cheeks on the sleeve of her cardigan and as she re-read her letter, she worried that it was insufficient in both length and content. Her chest ached with sorrow as she folded the letter and slipped it into the matching envelope. She would write again soon.

14

He swung open the door and halted, legs astride, filling the doorway as he surveyed the shop, his face impassive. A cold draught blew in. The three customers looked up, and Jana, sorting books in the children's area, followed their gaze. She froze.

Heydrich.

Heydrich, here in her bookshop. Heydrich, dressed in a black, leather trench coat, a pistol holster clipped to the belt at his waist. Taller and even more imperious on the threshold of her small bookshop. Incongruous outside the castle and stepping into her realm. Her heart raced and she fought to get her thoughts in order. Why was he here? Was she under arrest? She should greet him, move towards him, pay respect. But her legs would not move.

His cool eyes found hers. He waited.

Jana blinked and awoke from her daze. She walked towards him as he took a large stride into the shop, closing the door firmly behind him.

'Good day, *Herr Reichsprotektor*,' she said, with all the politeness she could muster. Did he hear the tremble in her voice?

He stared down at her, his face closely shaven. A waft of his sharp cologne mingled with a slight smell of cigarette smoke drifting around her. His presence filled the shop, sucked the oxygen from the air, replacing it instead with choking, dangerous power.

'Good afternoon, *Fräulein* Hajek. As you must know, I'm a cultural man, and decided to pay your bookshop a visit.'

She hadn't mentioned a bookshop, but he'd obviously read her file and decided to check her out. But, in God's name, why? She was a lowly member of the cleaning staff. Of absolutely no importance. Unless...

He drew off his black gloves in exaggerated slowness, one finger after the other, and slapped the gloves in his right hand. He had unusually long hands; his nails were clipped and clean.

'You may show me around.'

She looked through the shop window. Heydrich's black Mercedes-Benz convertible was parked outside; the chauffer, an enormous man, had climbed out and was surveying the street. He too had a pistol strapped to his waist. She saw no other security, which was typical of Heydrich. The man was so arrogant and self-assured that he often moved around Prague freely; the man from the castle, surveying his subjects that had bent to his will. He had tamed the Czechs and was king of his domain. She could taste the acid coating her tongue.

Jana turned. 'Shall we start with our classics section?' She gestured to that part of the shop, her arm outstretched.

The customers now dared to move and within moments, they had scurried out the door.

This was the first time she had been so close to the Butcher of

Prague. His affected, refined air so at odds with the barbarian acts he ordained. He too was more than capable of committing cold-blooded murder himself. She'd heard the story from Pavel of how, earlier in the war as Heydrich was on the eastern front, a soldier had hesitated in harming a young Jewish girl – of around eight years old. Heydrich had drawn his pistol and shot her in the face. At point-blank range. When the officer had vomited on the ground at Heydrich's feet, he'd looked at the man with disgust.

Her skin turned to ice at the thought.

'I enjoy autobiographies of the great composers. Beethoven or Handel, for example.'

'I have both. I'd be happy to show—'

'I'm sure you are aware my father was a composer. Bruno Heydrich.' He lifted his chin and gave a self-satisfied sniff.

She wasn't aware. As she struggled to find a suitable response, he continued to talk, running narrow eyes around the bookshop. 'There will be a concert in May, at the Wallenstein Palace. My father's piano concerto will be featured.'

'How wonderful.'

'Indeed.' Heydrich fixed his gaze back on Jana, his steel-blue eyes boring into her. She had the dreadful sensation that he could see exactly who she was; that he was testing her, baiting her. Any moment, the Gestapo would burst into her little bookshop, pumping her body with bullets, spraying her blood over the books. Or worse, drag her to their headquarters where unspeakable things would happen in the basement.

Heydrich turned his attention to the opposite wall where Papa's marionettes were displayed.

'Ah, the quaint tradition of Czech puppetry. Selling books and puppets is an interesting combination.' He raised an eyebrow at her, compelling her to explain.

'My father is a puppeteer. He crafts the figures himself.'

Heydrich made no comment as he stepped closer to peer at the figure. This one was of a peasant girl in traditional dress. Jana swallowed.

'How curious the Czech people are,' he said, thoughtfully. Then he shot her a look, his eyes steel-hard. 'Remove the doll,' he shouted, flinging his arm out. Jana jumped at the sudden outburst.

'Yes, sir.'

'And tell your father to craft some German puppets. I want a Hansel and Gretel in *Lederhosen* and a *Dirndl* for my children.'

Jana nodded. 'I'll tell him, sir.'

'Now, I must get to my next meeting,' he said, checking his wristwatch. 'I'll return maybe another time.' He nodded towards the bookshelves.

Then in a few strides of his black, polished boots, he was back out the door. Jana watched him wave an arm at his chauffer and climb into the driving seat himself. The chauffer jogged round to the passenger seat and had hardly closed the door when Heydrich revved up the engine and accelerated down the street.

Jana's heart pulsed in her throat. Feeling faint, she collapsed in the armchair. What had that been all about? He hadn't stayed to look at any books. Why on earth would he show interest in her modest bookshop? There were far grander ones in Prague more suitable for the custom of the *Protektor* of Bohemia. The answer was obvious: either he was curious and checking her out, or he suspected her already. Both scenarios were terrifying.

* * *

Jana was still mopping the shop floor when a figure appeared at the locked front door. As she always opened at ten o'clock, half an hour after she got back from the castle, she was surprised at the early customer.

Squinting against the early-morning sun, she realised it was Pavel, whom she hadn't seen for a couple of weeks. Her heart sank and her reaction saddened her. In the past, her spirits had always lifted at seeing her friend, and now her impulsive behaviour had completely altered their relationship. She must now be honest with Pavel and put things straight.

Standing the mop in the bucket, she took the keys from her apron pocket and unlocked the door.

Pavel's smile made her feel uneasy; there was more than friendship in his expression. She invited him in and he sidestepped the wet floor.

'Sorry I'm early, but I wanted to see you before my shift starts.' He studied her face. 'I miss you.'

'Pavel, I must tell you something.'

He tipped his head to one side.

'I'm so very sorry that I misled you about my feelings for you. Our kiss was a mistake. My mistake. I love you very much, but like the brother I never had. I wondered if our friendship could bloom into romance, but I realise now that's not the right way for us.'

He stared at her, not saying anything, the light in his eyes gone.

'I'm sorry,' she repeated.

'Is there someone else?' he murmured.

Andrej's tender lips filled her thoughts, his gentle fingers on her face. She tingled at the memory of him.

'There's no one else.'

Relief flickered across his face.

'You just need time to adjust to the change in our feelings. We can take things slowly—'

'But my feelings haven't changed. I thought that maybe—'

Pavel reached for her shoulders, his face urgent.

'There is something special between us, more than friendship. You can't deny it.'

'Don't. Pavel, please let's not spoil our friendship. Let's go back to how we were.'

His arms dropped and he shook his head. 'It's too late for that. All or nothing, Jana.' His voice had turned hard, not like Pavel at all. 'You think you can play with my feelings: want me one moment than reject me the next.'

She was astounded at his reaction. What to her had been an exploratory kiss had obviously meant much more to him. Guilt flushed her cheeks.

'Pavel, I didn't mean to hurt you. Please let us stay the good friends we were.'

'Like I said: all or nothing. You better think about it carefully.'

He turned and left, his bitter tone ringing in her ears.

* * *

Jana locked the shop for the day and breathed in the fresh, evening air. Her father was having dinner with a friend so she would take the opportunity to get some exercise – a walk around the city, maybe treat herself to something to eat from a street vendor.

The street lamps were dimmer than usual; shortages in electricity had increased as the war lingered on. In the gloom, the city took on a bleak beauty, its statues and intricate carvings on the building's façades whispering the horrors and triumphs of history.

She crossed Old Town Square just as the astronomical clock

in the town hall tower began to strike. There were always people who stopped, often parents with children, and looked upwards; two doors above the colourful clockface would open and the mechanical figures, twelve apostles and a skeleton, would begin their parade. Jana thought of the hundreds of times her mother had pointed out each figure and told a story until she had learnt them off by heart. And she would one day recount the same stories to her children.

But as she watched the figure of the skeleton tip the hourglass, she had a strange sensation of being watched.

She turned to look around her but only saw faces tipped up to the clock, or people scurrying past without giving her a second glance. She was fantasising, ancient tales creeping under her skin. Giving herself a shake, she carried on and passed through the Gothic stone arch that led to Charles Bridge. She paused a moment to take in the view of the Vltava River and Prague Castle opposite. Again, she had an uneasy feeling, the skin prickling at the back of her neck. Frowning, she walked onto the bridge.

People bustled past, eager to get errands done before curfew, or stood in conversation whilst looking out on the river. Jana walked down the avenue of statues lit by lanterns and halted at the statue of St Wenceslas. Leaning against the low, stone wall, she gazed out at the inky-black water splashed with patches of lamplight. She let out a sigh at the sight of the Vltava River. The Nazis had renamed it the Moldau; well, they could call it what they liked. In her heart, it would always be the Vltava, and no one, not even the Nazis, could take that from her.

There was movement beside her.

Breaths in the cold air.

'Don't turn.' The voice was taut. Familiar.

Despite the command, she flicked her eyes to the side and back to the water.

Andrej Kovar. Her stomach did a small flip.

'Have you been following me?' she said under her breath.

'Sorry. Yes. It's not safe to come to the bookshop any more.'

Not safe? For her or for him?

She wrinkled her brows as he continued to speak.

'Bring the letter for Lenka to Tyn Church at midday tomorrow. The left aisle, row seven.'

'Will you be there?' she whispered.

There was no reply. She repeated her question and unable to resist, she glanced to the side.

He was gone.

She swirled around, looking up and down the bridge. Sudden darkness dropped. All around her, the lamps were out. There were cries of surprise and annoyance: another power cut.

She saw the shadows of people shuffling around her. A few stars overhead gave a minimal glow. People had no torches with them; what was the point when no batteries were available? She moved slowly back along the bridge amongst the grumbling crowd, through the arch and across the square. Massive, dark buildings loomed around every corner but she was not afraid of the city she knew so well.

However, when she turned alone down a narrow alley, tall, unlit buildings pressing in on her, cold sweat dampened under her arms. Her brief encounter with Andrej and his warning that it wasn't safe to meet at the bookshop had her unnerved. It wasn't buildings and ghosts that scared her. It was the Nazis. The Gestapo.

She hastened her step and the toe of her boot caught on the kerb. She flew forwards and hit the ground hard, her forehead bouncing on the narrow pavement.

Dazed, she remained motionless for a few moments. Her right wrist hurt, but her gloves had protected her hands from severe grazing. She eased herself to sitting. Something warm trickled down her face and, removing her glove, she dabbed at the blood. The cold of the ground was seeping rapidly through her long coat; she must get up. The sky had clouded over and she was in complete darkness. The noise of the city had faded as people sought their homes.

Her heartbeat thrummed in her ears.

A scraping sound. She stiffened. Then chided herself; it was probably a mouse. But mice didn't scrape, they scuttled. She jumped to her feet, winced at a stab of pain in her knee, and sped off blindly in the direction of home. She visualised the execution wall, the sound of bullets ripping through the air. She was sure she was being followed; any second, her back would explode and her life would flip off like the lanterns along Charles Bridge.

Another of Heydrich's victims.

Her hand shook so violently that it took several attempts to get the key in the lock, before she fell through the front door of her home.

Papa greeted her, a candle in hand. He narrowed his eyes as she removed her hat, noticing the smear of blood on her face. She was fine, she assured him as she hung her coat on the coat stand; she had merely stumbled in the blackout.

But as they ate their cold supper in the semi-darkness, she felt badly shaken; not from the fall, but from the fear that had overcome her: the feeling of being followed by the police or Gestapo.

As the lights were still out when she went to change for bed, she lit a candle and placed it on her night table. She removed her high-necked pullover and threw it on the bed. From habit, her fingers reached for her locket. She froze. It wasn't there. Her hands tapped wildly at her chest, searching for the feel of cool metal. She spun to the mirror on the wood-panelled wardrobe and was horrified. In the flicker of the candlelight, she saw the naked place where it normally hung.

Her stomach clenched as she tried to remember if she had worn the locket under or over her clothes. Frantic, she searched her pullover inside and out. Nothing. Had the chain on Mama's locket become undone and fallen to the street as she'd stumbled? She must fetch a torch and search outside. Papa would ask what she was up to. *My God*, she couldn't tell him she had lost the most precious thing in their world. Wearing the locket meant Mama was always with her, but now she was gone.

She heard the water begin to run in the bathroom and the sounds of her father preparing for bed. It was already curfew but she would be quick. There was a pocket torch under the sink in the kitchen; they seldom used it to save the battery, which was the last one they had. She yanked her pullover back on, fetched the torch and her coat, and crept out the door.

Outside, she swept the small circle of light along the ground, back to the spot where she had fallen. She knelt down on the trodden snow and ran her bare hands over the ground, trying to swallow down her despair. Dirty footprints and small scattered stones were all she saw. And a few drops of her own blood. Mama's locket wasn't there. She'd lost her most cherished possession. Papa's too. He had entrusted her with Mama's locket, something that encapsulated his love for her, that held so many poignant memories.

She didn't know how long she'd spent scrabbling on the ground, but eventually the torch dimmed, the battery fading, and she was forced to return home.

Her father, dressed in pyjamas, was waiting for her, his face anxious in the flame of the candle he held.

'Thank goodness! I was out of my mind with worry! Why were you out past curfew?'

'Sorry, Papa.' Now she would have to tell him.

As she sought the right words, her heart breaking, the hall light blinked on and a blast of music came from the radio in the living room. The electricity was back. Averting her father's gaze, she bowed her head to compose herself. It was then she saw something glinting on the floor next to her father's neatly positioned shoes under the coat stand.

She let out a cry of relief and scooped up the beloved locket, gazing at it as if it were a butterfly resting on the palm on her hand.

Tears filled her eyes as she embraced her father, clutching the locket tight. They sat together at the kitchen table. She recognised that glazed look in Papa's eyes: the one when her likeness to Mama overcame him, when her auburn hair and green eyes swept him away in memories. She reached across the table and squeezed his hand, feeling the rough skin on his craftsman's fingers. His voice cracked as he began the story of how he'd met her mother in spring on the banks of the Vltava River... She'd heard the story a thousand times, but it still brought a lump to her throat.

His eyes fixed on the gold locket that hung again around her neck.

'She loved reading of course, always had a book nearby. She read even while she cooked, stirring the pot with a wooden spoon in one hand, her book in the other,' he said, his face soft with reminiscence. 'I bought her the locket for our tenth anniversary. I went to goldsmith, Herr Katz, just off Wenceslas

Square. He was a kind, family man with a good reputation. "Tell me about your wife," he said, before designing the book locket.'

She listened patiently as he recounted the memories yet again, as he told of her mother's delight at the gift, and how she'd lifted her long, auburn hair to allow him to fasten the necklace around her pale neck.

'I know, Papa,' she said softly and lay her hand on the locket, so much more than just a piece of jewellery at her neck.

They fell silent then, both thinking the same, she knew. The Nazis had taken Herr Katz's shop and his home, and in return, Herr Katz had taken his life.

15

The following morning, Jana entered Old Town Square at a quarter to twelve, walked past the astronomical clock and paused to take in the view. The Gothic Tyn church dominated the old town, its spiked turrets, spires and twin towers shooting towards the sky. Jana had always thought the building looked more like a castle from a fairy tale than a church – sometimes macabre, sometimes enchanted, but always magnificent. Emotion welled up inside her. The church was an ancient symbol of Prague and it saddened her to see the grey-green uniforms of the Wehrmacht in evidence around it.

The entrance of the church lay behind a line of elegant mansion houses. She passed through the archway that led to the church courtyard and the main door. Once inside, her eyes ran over the beautiful and ornate interior. There was a scattering of people amongst the pews, some with heads bowed in prayer, others still and contemplative in the silence. Each one of them, thought Jana, had had their lives upturned by the occupation.

Treading softly, she made her way to the far left and walked along the rows. She limped slightly from her fall yesterday, her knee grazed and swollen. That morning, she'd woken up to a purple bruise on her forehead and had tried to conceal it with face powder. Now, she tipped forwards the brim of her brown, felt hat, hiding her face.

Stopping at the seventh row, she shot a glance along the long, wooden bench. She didn't recognise anyone and sat on the seat by the aisle. Was this the right place to sit? Maybe she should move one place along, leaving the end seat free. She did so.

Her heart fluttering with expectation, she clasped her bag close to her, the letter for Lenka tucked inside.

As the church bells announced midday, Jana held her breath.

Nothing happened.

People walked to the altar. Some turned away. A priest appeared with a candle.

It was freezing in the church, and the chill seeped through the soles of her shoes and up her legs. She pressed her knees together to stop them shaking.

Footsteps on the stone floor.

The creak of the wooden pew beside her. The swish of a coat against hers.

From under the brim of her hat, she cast a sideways look and saw Andrej's handsome profile: his high cheekbone and firm jaw, a muscle pulsing. She turned her gaze to her lap, and bowed her head, her heart beating too loud in the silence of the church.

He slid a bible along the pew rack in front of her, tapping the book pointedly with his forefinger. She nodded to herself, removed her gloves and pressed the catch on her bag. It made a loud click. Her hands froze. *Nobody is watching*, she told herself, and prised the bag open. With a quick, deft motion, she slipped Lenka's letter from her bag to inside the bible which she gave a casual shove back in Andrej's direction. Then she rested her hands on the pew.

Andrej reached for the bible, shuffled briefly with his coat, and was still again. He put his hand on the pew beside him, his little finger grazing hers. It was a murmur of a touch but it sent a shiver through her body. She thought of the feel of his lips when he'd kissed her in the bookshop. A kiss that was hardly a kiss. More a promise of a kiss.

His finger curled around hers. He squeezed softly. It was the tiniest action but it made her gasp. The gesture held so much; he was on her side, here to help, he cared. He sat close, their bodies not touching, just their little fingers entwined. And then he withdrew his hand and he was standing up. She wanted to pull on his elbow, make him stay a moment longer, tell him about her fear last night in the blackout, but she merely stared at the altar. The pew creaked and shifted and then he was gone, leaving just chilled air behind him.

She tipped her head up to the cavernous ceiling. The sun had come out and shafts of light shone through the stained-glass windows, making the array of golden artefacts glow. Was God here and listening? She prayed for Lenka. Then for Michal. Then for the broken woman at the execution wall. There were so many to pray for that the task overwhelmed her and tears blurred her vision.

Steeling herself against a feeling of helplessness, she rose from the pew. She must stay resolute; despair would not help anyone. She must believe that every action of humanity, no matter how small, would make a difference to the world.

* * *

Early next morning as she hurried to the castle, a figure emerged from a doorway and stepped into her path. Jana started. The woman in front of her wore a fringed shawl draped over her head and shoulders, her hands clutching the ends tightly. A pale, strained face peered out at her.

'Sorry to startle you,' said the woman.

Jana recognized her; it was the woman with cracked lips who'd been sweeping snow outside Michal's house: the woman who'd told her Michal's aunt and cousins had been taken too. Jana had explained she was a friend of Michal and that she ran a bookshop, but the woman hadn't been interested in conversation and had turned back to her broom.

The woman looked around nervously. 'My name is Lillian. We met briefly when you were searching for Michal.'

'I remember,' said Jana.

'Please, I need your help.' Lillian clasped Jana's arm. As she did so, the shawl slipped aside, revealing the yellow star on her coat sleeve. She was taking a risk being outside the Jewish Quarter whilst concealing the star; the Nazis considered that a serious offence.

Jana cast a cautious glance up and down the street. Two older men were approaching.

Jana guided Lillian to the side of the pavement and in a loud, chatty voice complained about the long winter and food shortages. Lillian drew her shawl tightly around her and nodded her agreement at Jana's protests.

When the men had passed, Lillian continued. 'We'll be next. I know it. My children... please help them, like you helped Michal.'

Jana jolted. Lillian knew? No, she might suspect.

'I don't know if I can help. I...' Her voice trailed off.

'I'm a widow with two daughters, aged ten and four years old. If you know of someone, some way to help them escape. My eldest, Yveta, nearly made it out of Prague four years ago. There was a British man, a Mr. Winton, organising transport to get the children to England and Yveta was on the list. But on the morning the train was due to leave, the German tanks arrived and took over the city...' Her voice broke and her shoulders sank.

Jana's heart squeezed. What could she do? Borrow a car again? Pull the same trick? But that would involve Pavel once more and putting him in danger a second time. She didn't want to use his affection for her; it wasn't fair. But who else could she ask for help?

As she looked into Lillian's desperate eyes, she found herself saying, 'I'll do what I can. I'll make enquiries.'

Lillian's face softened with gratitude and Jana became scared of the enormity of the task. Not of the risk to her own safety, but at the risk of failing this mother.

Both of them looked around as the door of the alchemist shop opposite opened. A thin man in a white coat appeared with a shovel in hand. He nodded his head in greeting before he dug into the overnight snow that had landed on his doorstep.

'I'd better head back,' said Lillian. 'You'll contact me?'

'Yes, yes, I will,' Jana replied, with all the reassurance she could muster, eager to ease the woman's pain.

Jana watched Lillian hurry away, head tucked to her chest. She turned the corner and was gone. Jana had to wait a few moments to compose her thoughts before carrying on up the street.

* * *

At the castle, Jana regarded the staff with intrigue, wondering who else might be working for the resistance. Obviously, her small contribution was only part of a bigger scheme to keep a watch on the Nazi headquarters: the movements of the SS chiefs, their visitors, anything at all. There was the broad-shouldered groundsman who Jana passed each day as he shovelled snow from the drive that swept up to Salm Palace, the electrician who knelt beside his tool box unscrewing plug sockets and repairing wires, and the carpenter who was repairing wood panelling on the ground floor. Not to mention anyone from the team of maids, cooks and delivery boys. They all had one thing in common; they were Czech.

Lillian's plea was on Jana's mind as, on her hands and knees, she scrubbed at a non-existent carpet stain a few feet from Heydrich's office.

Her manageress, Miss Jezek, strode up to her and frowned. 'What's the problem here?' she asked.

'A nasty stain, probably coffee.'

As Miss Jezek squinted down at the carpet, Jana sploshed more soapy suds onto the offending area and leaned over, obscuring the woman's view.

'Don't worry, Miss Jezek. I'll get it clean.'

'Very well,' she said tartly, 'I shall check back shortly.' Her thin hand scribbled on her clipboard and she bustled away.

Raised voices emanated from behind Heydrich's closed door. Jana had seen him enter his office with three SS aids for an early-morning meeting. She'd made a mental note of his arrival: twenty to eight. Now Heydrich was clearly upset about something.

'...am I surrounded by a bunch of incompetent fools?' he yelled.

There was a murmur of voices as a response but Jana could

not make out what was being said. Heydrich's retort was furious, his high-pitched voice screaming, '...I don't give a damn if these vermin fought with us in the Great War; they're all traitors. And don't whine to me about popular public figures, writers, artists...'

He was ranting now, his angry diatribe disturbingly similar to Hitler's speeches. Jana sat back on her haunches, listening.

'...damn public opinion!' She could hear the pound of his fist on the desk. 'Then tell them what they want to hear: that the rats are going to a holiday camp. We'll put on a show of our humanity and in the meantime, I want a least a thousand per train load...'

A soldier appeared at the end of the corridor for a routine check. Jana avoided eye contact and leaned forward, diligently scrubbing the carpet.

Heydrich's rage continued behind the door. '...it's results I want to see, numbers. Now, get out of here!'

Muted voices were followed by footsteps. Heydrich's office door opened and three pale-faced SS men exited. One had to step around her as he walked.

'Get out the way, woman,' he barked, venting his anger.

The soldier on guard frowned at her.

'Finish up there, now.' Narrowing his eyes, he studied her face beneath the headscarf that hid her hair. She stiffened. It was the soldier with pockmarked cheeks that had come to the bookshop and ordered a copy of Hitler's book, *Mein Kampf*. His name, Private Brandt, came back to her now; for some reason, he'd not returned to collect the book.

Her own flippant tone from that conversation also returned to her mind.

'I know you.' He took a stride closer.

An SS officer appeared and Brandt snapped to attention. As

they exchanged a few words, Jana quickly gathered her cleaning materials and bucket.

As she scuttled away, she could hear the strains of a violin drift out from Heydrich's office. Tendrils of ice pierced through her; how perverse that such a beautiful melody should be played by such an evil man: the Butcher of Prague.

16

At lunch time, Jana closed the bookshop and sat at the back, tucked out of sight in the armchair, *The Gardener's Year* on her lap. She carefully counted lines and words, jotting down the emerging code in a small, spiral notebook. Several times, she started a new attempt; it was a challenge to convey the message as concisely as possible. Finally, the message read:

Request help in aiding transport of children to safety.

She prayed that help for Lillian's children would come. She turned the paper over and started the urgent task of conveying Heydrich's tantrum of words: the ominous mention of thousands on a train, and what did he mean about putting on a show? Again, it was a painstaking job, but finally, she was satisfied.

On the table beside her lay a bookmark covered in navy fabric, the end open. It was safer to use dark colours as they concealed the secret within. She cut the note to size and slipped it inside before stitching the end closed. For extra safety, she stitched a narrow pink ribbon along both of the short edges. Then she took the book holding the bookmark to behind the cash desk.

As she was bending down, there was a rap on the window.

She looked up to see a woman's large, round face pressed up against the window, frowning, her hand cupping her eyes. Although Jana acknowledged her, the woman's knuckles struck the glass again.

Jana went to unlock the door for the impatient customer, unable to get Heydrich out of her mind.

* * *

Days passed and Jana waited for a contact to show. She hadn't been able to sleep, Lillian's pleading eyes dominating her thoughts. Maybe Lillian and her family had already been taken and any help would be too late. And the other information was urgent. At times, Jana despaired that resistance against Heydrich was futile, and other times, she was driven with determination to stand up and act; the rollercoaster of emotions was exhausting.

* * *

It was the fifth day after her conversation with Lillian when the bell above the shop door jangled and Jana turned. Heat rushed to her cheeks. It was Andrej. Her joy at seeing him was mixed with confusion; he'd said he couldn't come to the shop any more, yet here he was at nearly six in the evening, the collar of his coat turned up and his hat pulled down low. He wore clothes she hadn't seen before and a pair of spectacles. He must have been watching the shop because a customer had just left.

'Did Lenka get my letter?' She lowered her voice, although the shop was empty.

'I passed it on so I'm sure she did. Hopefully, you'll hear from her soon.'

She sighed with relief, then waited. Why was he here?

He took a step closer and she caught the scent of his cologne: a warm, woody smell that was inviting, sensual. She hadn't noticed him wear cologne before.

'I have something to say to you.' His gaze was so deep, her breath halted.

'Yes?' she whispered.

'"Words are like X-rays; if you use them properly, they'll go through anything."'

She stared at him, confusion fuddling her brain. Had she heard correctly? Was Andrej speaking the words from Aldous Huxley? Was he speaking the words the last contact had given her as a code? Was he...?

Andrej gave a small smile and nodded.

'I'm as surprised as you are that we've been put in contact with each other,' he said. 'I knew, of course, you'd helped Michal. But learning that you passed on secret messages, here in the bookshop, was a shock; it puts you in terrible danger. Just me coming here puts you at risk.'

'Are you with the resistance?' she asked, trying to sort her jumble of thoughts.

'Are you?' His dark, eyes shone with intensity. He was following protocol, avoiding direct answers. He had given her the correct code, the book quote, so surely she could trust him. She had to.

'Can you help me? Help some children in terrible danger?'

'I'll do everything I possibly can.'

'How will you help?' she asked, hope for Lillian and her children igniting inside her.

'First, I need some details. How many and how old are they?'

'Two sisters, aged ten and four.'

'They'll need a safe house.' He gave her a meaningful look. 'I presume the small boy found one.'

Babi had been more than willing to have Michal but should she turn up on her grandmother's doorstep with two more children? 'I'd take a whole troop of children hiding from the Nazis,' she'd said. Jana was in no doubt she meant it, but still...

'I can arrange it.' The words flew from her mouth before she could stop them. 'How can we get the children out of Prague?'

'I've already got things in motion.' He threw a glance at the door, then said, 'We need to move quickly. There will be more round-ups in the next few days. Heydrich is putting pressure on the police.'

Heydrich's furious words sprung to mind. Jana bit her lip to stop herself from bursting out what she'd overheard. Just in time, she remembered the rules: information was to be coded inside a bookmark and passed on. But if Andrej was a contact, then she could give him the message. Or simply tell him. But then he would know she was spying at the castle. On the other hand, he probably knew about her cleaning job...

'Jana...?'

'Yes, we must act quickly. What should I do?'

'Meet me on the Charles Bridge in an hour. At the statue of Saint Christoper. I'll have it all arranged by then.'

His eyes fell on the yellow bruise above her eyebrow. 'What happened?'

Her hat had hidden it from view in Tyn Church when she'd handed him Lenka's letter.

'It's nothing. I stumbled in the dark.' She didn't want to talk about that now; there were more important things.

'Take care, Jana. Till later.'

She opened her mouth to speak but he was already retreating out of the shop.

* * *

Twenty minutes later, she was climbing the stairs to the attic, her mind racing. What would Papa say when she told him what she'd agreed to do? There was no way to contact Babi and ask if she were prepared to commit further treasonable acts against the Reich. Acid rose in her throat, as the image of Babi being manhandled into a police car sprung in her mind.

In the attic, Papa was bent over his workbench.

'Are you working on something new, Papa?' She peered over his shoulder at the wooden figure he was crafting to life.

'It's for Michal,' he said, pausing, and smiling up at her. There was a light in his eyes she hadn't seen for a long time. 'He told me he's always wanted a dog of his own, and that's what I'm making him. He's a quick learner and will soon have his new four-legged friend scampering across your grandma's floor.' It seemed that having Michal in his life had lifted his spirits despite the background of the circumstances. What would he think about Michal having some friends to play with?

'I need to speak to you about Babi,' she started.

He raised his eyebrows and she took a deep breath. His face turned grave as she told him she'd met a woman called Lillian who'd suspected she was behind Michal's escape and had asked for help. Jana was careful to make no reference to messages passed via the bookshop, or Andrej stepping forward as a resistance member. She told him simply that Lillian had a contact and Jana would find out more later.

'I don't want Babi to be more at risk than she already is, but...' Her words drifted away.

Papa was silent. He bent his head and massaged the bridge of his nose before he sighed. 'Babi would say that it's no more illegal to hide three children than one. We both know she would want to help these children...'

She planted a kiss on his cheek. 'Thanks, Papa.'

'I haven't done anything yet. Tell me how I can help.'

'I'm meeting Lillian this evening to get details of the plan.' She felt a pang at the half truth.

'I'm scared for you, my darling daughter. If anything should happen to you...'

She turned, avoiding the sorrow in his expression; it reminded her of when he talked about the loss of Mama.

'I'll be fine, Papa. I know what I'm doing.'

Even to her ears, her platitude sounded lame.

17

Shortly before seven o'clock, Jana stepped onto the Charles Bridge wearing a cloche hat and a belted coat that had belonged to her mother. She doubted anyone would recognise her in the clothes. As always, the bridge was busy, people making their way home for the evening.

He wasn't alone at the statue. Two men in railway uniforms were chatting and smoking. She hesitated. Andrej caught her eye and shifted along the bridge. She approached, then halted. A young couple, arm in arm, stopped next to Andrej to gaze out over the river. Jana's heart thudded. The bridge was a good place to go unnoticed in a crowd, but they must be careful not to be overheard.

Taking a breath to calm herself, she rummaged around in her handbag for nothing in particular.

When she glanced back up, she saw that Andrej had distanced himself from the couple and was now a little way further down the bridge. He lit a cigarette and studied the smoke as it spiralled away in the wind. She stood a stride away from him, her eyes fixed ahead.

As he spoke in a low, urgent voice, her stomach knotted with nerves. The plan must work, she thought; the children's lives depended on it.

She left Andrej a few moments later and walked off the bridge, through the stone arch and back across Old Town Square. Avoiding streets where Germans patrolled, she entered Josefov and arrived at the house where Lillian lived.

She rapped on the door. Hope sprung to Lillian's face when she saw Jana, and beckoned her in. The heads of two girls peeped from a doorway off the hallway, one above the other, long plaits dangling to their shoulders. Lillian waved the children away. The young faces disappeared.

'Have you news? About the girls?' she asked in a hushed voice.

Jana nodded and quietly told Lillian the plans for the following day.

* * *

The next morning after she finished work at the castle, instead of opening up the bookshop, Jana hurried to the local community centre. She hadn't seen Dasha since the last book club exchange, when Dasha had spoken about her brother's new job at the Skoda munitions factory.

Inside, women rummaged through the second-hand clothes spread out on trestle tables. Dasha, behind one of the tables, was helping a woman find the correct children's size from an array of donated clothes. Her face lit up when she saw Jana.

'This is a nice surprise,' she said.

'I wasn't sure if you were working today,' Jana said.

The ruddy-faced woman who Dasha was helping tutted loudly.

'I'm being served at the moment.'

Jana raised a conciliatory hand. 'Please continue, I'm just browsing.'

She shot Dasha a wry smile and started to examine the clothes while the woman continued to fuss around.

Jana looked through a small pile of children's hats and scarves at the end of the table. She stopped to consider a small, navy beret. Would it be the right size for a four-year-old? Holding on to it, she searched further till she found a green, felt hat trimmed with a black ribbon. The hat was worn and had a muddy stain on the brim; it was perfect. She then chose two hand-knitted scarves and waited till the ruddy-faced women was satisfied with her haul and left.

'Can I take these for a friend?'

'Of course,' said Dasha. Then with a smile, she asked, 'How's Lenka? Any news on the baby?'

A lump came to Jana's throat. None of the book club girls knew yet about Lenka's arrest.

'She's had a baby girl,' she said quietly.

'How wonderful! What's her— Is everything all right? Jana, what's wrong?'

She choked back her tears. 'Lenka's been arrested; she's in prison.'

'In prison?' Dasha's cry turned a few heads. She composed herself before speaking again in a quiet voice. 'What on earth has she done wrong?'

'Nothing. It must all be some terrible mistake.' Jana didn't want to have this conversation now; she needed to stay focused on getting Lillian's children to safety. 'I'm sure I'll know more at the next book club meeting: Thursday morning in two weeks.'

Dasha nodded, her face pale with shock.

As Jana turned to go, Dasha said, 'I hope your friend likes the clothes.'

* * *

The city was every shade of grey as the March wind whipped through the narrow streets and stone arches. The only colour Jana could see was the blood red of swastika flags that cracked back and forth in a frenzied dance. Church bells rang the hour: one o'clock.

Exactly on time, Jana arrived at the meeting point, on the corner next to the bicycle shop. She waited opposite the path that wound away into the Josefov district.

Lillian appeared, ushering the girls along. Andrej had insisted they travel with no possessions, and the trio carried no suitcases or bags that could invite a stop and search. Not even a doll in the hands of the smallest girl had been allowed; a toy might imply a longer trip was planned. Their only belongings were the clothes they stood in.

Staying on the opposite side of the street, Jana looked around her. Although they had chosen a quiet spot, there were nevertheless a few pedestrians. A cyclist passed. Lillian wore a tightly bound headscarf, her hair tucked out of sight, her face as grey as her surroundings. She spoke to the eldest girl, who Jana had learned was called Yveta. The girl nodded solemnly at her mother's words. Yveta clearly knew the truth: that she was about to be wrenched from her parents and sent to an unknown destination. Her young sister, Maddie, however, bore an expression of anticipation, jumping from foot to foot, pulling on Yveta's hand, as if she'd been told she was going on holiday.

Anger spiked in Jana's chest; she hated the Germans, hated

their flags, soldiers, and marching music that blasted from radios. But most of all she hated that tyrant, Heydrich.

Taking a breath to steady her nerves, she scoured up and down the street. The coast was clear. She locked eyes with Lillian. The mother heaved her chest in realisation that this was the moment, and it had to be quick. She took Yveta's arm and peeled the yellow star from her coat sleeve, having loosened the stitches as planned. Some hasty kisses on the girl's cheeks and she gave her daughters a shove in the backs. Yveta grasped Maddie's hand tightly and the sisters crossed the street towards Jana.

'We're playing dressing up,' she said, pulling the hats and scarves from her shopping bag. As agreed, the girls wore no accessories, and within in moments, Yveta was sporting a felt hat and Maddie, a navy beret. Jana tucked their plaited hair beneath their hats and draped the knitted scarves around their necks.

'You're the lady who came to see Mama yesterday,' said Maddie.

'That's right, and I'm going take you both on an adventure.'

'Can Mama come too?'

'No, she can't,' said Yveta, fiercely, yanking Maddie's arm.

Across the street, Lillian was hovering, her yellow star clearly visible, whilst her inconspicuous, gentile children were to be accompanied by a close friend for a day out. That was the story Jana would tell if anyone asked. Jana said it was time to go, and Maddie gave her mother a bright wave. Yveta's face was like stone as she swallowed hard. She lifted her hand, but let it fall again.

Jana ached with sadness as she gave Lillian one last look before forcing herself to walk away, taking the woman's children with her. She'd agreed to meet Lillian the following evening at the same spot. If Jana carried a book under her arm, all was well and the children were in safety. No book meant something had gone wrong.

Jana led the children around the back of Old Town Square and passed under the Powder Tower, leaving the ancient town behind. They went to the tram stop and waited a few minutes until the red and white tram arrived clanging its bell. Once they had settled in their seats, Jana breathed a sigh of relief: so far, so good. She rehearsed the story in her head: she was looking after a friend's children for the day. Yes, she had her identification papers with her. No, she hadn't thought to bring papers for the children. A coy smile would follow; she'd applied lipstick that morning, pouting into the mirror. She would flutter her eyelashes if she had to.

'I love trams,' said Maddie, twisting herself on the wooden bench to look out the window. An older woman who sat opposite, wearing a traditional embroidered shawl across her shoulders, smiled indulgently in Maddie's direction. Jana gave a brief smile, not wanting to draw attention by being unfriendly. People remembered unfriendliness.

Jana wondered if the girls ever rode the trams. There were only certain times Jewish citizens were allowed to travel. She mentally corrected herself; they were no longer citizens according to German law.

She looked across at Yveta, her heart going out to the stone-faced girl. She longed to say something but what could she say in public? Even in private, she wouldn't know what words of comfort she could offer. After all, she was a stranger to the children.

The tram filled up as it crossed town. At every stop, Jana held her breath, terrified that an official would get on, asking for papers. A Wehrmacht soldier boarded, but he paid them no attention. Two men, smartly dressed, speaking with German accents, rode two stops with the tram; they too showed no interest in Jana and her charges.

They alighted at the tram terminal, crossed the street and boarded the bus that would take them out of Prague. If all went well – Andrej had said crossing the checkpoint out of town would be the most dangerous.

The three of them squeezed together into a double seat, with Maddie pressed up against the window and Yveta in the middle. From her aisle seat, Jana had a good view of the driver and through the bus windscreen.

She glanced around at the passengers, their heads jolting from side to side as the bus bumped over tram lines and cobblestones. They were normal citizens, not police, soldiers or officials. But a normal citizen looked no different to a collaborator, a traitor, who, for favours, or out of desperation to aid a loved one, would betray a fellow Czech.

The traffic slowed until the bus came to a stop. They had reached the queue to pass through the checkpoint. Sweat trickled down the back of Jana's neck as she leaned into the aisle to peer through the windscreen. In front of the bus was a white delivery van and ahead of that, a military truck, its flap open, revealing seated soldiers clutching rifles.

The bus driver cut the engine and leaned back in his seat as if anticipating a long wait. The vibrations of the bus stilled and an ominous quiet hung in the air. The passengers shuffled; a man tutted and snapped open his newspaper; a woman sighed and pulled out her knitting, her expression one of resignation.

'What's happening?' asked Maddie, her loud, childish voice causing some heads to turn.

'Nothing, sweetheart,' said Jana, reaching across Yveta to pat Maddie's knee. 'We'll be off in a moment.' Yveta gave Maddie a sharp nudge with her elbow which Maddie reacted to with an exaggerated, 'Ouch!'

More heads looked up. Panic gripped Jana; passengers were looking at them, wondering who they were, if Jana was the children's mother and where were they going – *no, stop Jana. Keep calm. Breathe.* A smile at the woman with the knitting. A nod at the man who glanced over his newspaper.

Ahead, a policeman waved the military truck through and held up his hand at the delivery van. Jana watched as the driver was asked to get out and open the back doors. She checked her watch; something was wrong. Andrej should have been here by now but there was no sign of him.

The delivery man had begun hauling out tins of paint from the back of his van. Then a second policeman appeared at the side of the bus and spoke to the driver through the open window.

Where was Andrej? Her right knee began to jitter uncontrollably; he wasn't coming. The whole plan was a mean and terrible trick to catch her and the children red-handed.

The driver activated the doors, which swished open as the policeman approached the steps. Or maybe Andrej had been discovered, betrayed and arrested. And now the police would demand to see passes, and the children... Her heart twisted; the children...

The policeman had his boot on the first step when a shout made his head jerk round. A police captain was yelling instructions and waving his arms, motioning to get the traffic moving.

Andrej.

Jana slumped with relief. The policeman snapped to attention and retreated. The doors hissed shut, the engine started up, and after a few moments waiting for the delivery man in front to reload his wares, they were on their way. Jana saw Andrej scanning the bus as they passed and as she leaned into his line of vision for the briefest of moments, his expression registered with her – a trace of a smile.

* * *

When the bus stopped at the small village of Lidice, Jana was reminded of Lenka's parents who lived there and again determined to visit them soon. Her thoughts about Lenka were distracted from a downward spiral by a group of noisy children climbing aboard. A boy shoved a girl and she shoved him back. Twice as hard. The others laughed and bounded through the bus. Yveta gave the children a hard look as they passed. They were about the same age as she was, and would no doubt be finishing school that summer when their formal education would end; the Nazi regime had closed secondary schools deciding the Reich needed workers, not intellectuals.

The bus left Lidice behind and bumped along through the countryside, the children getting off one by one as they reached their homes.

Jana decided to alight at the next stop. It was a still a distance to Babi's house but they would walk the rest of the way. She'd deliberately chosen an indirect bus route so as not to leave a trail.

As she led the children off the bus, a thin-faced man glanced up from his book. He gave her a blank stare and returned to his reading. The title of the book was German.

Maddie's initial enthusiasm for their adventure after they left the bus waned as her little legs grew tired.

'When are we there?' she whined. Jana had told Maddie they would be visiting a kind woman who had lots of toys, in particular puppets, and they would all have tremendous fun putting on a show. But now, the young girl's lip wobbled. 'I'm hungry,' she said.

'Be quiet,' snapped Yveta.

'No, I won't.'

'I'll give you a piggyback,' said Jana, stepping in to avoid a fight, and she hoisted Maddie onto her back, making neighing noises. Yveta rolled her eyes.

'That's a horse, not a pig,' laughed Maddie.

When Jana set her down again a short while later, the child remained silent, eyeing up her older sister warily.

They followed a path that ran alongside a field. The months' old snow was shrinking, revealing muddy patches of earth beneath. It was now late afternoon but the sky cleared and a soft sun appeared.

'Look,' said Jana, pointing at a cluster of snowdrops, the pretty flowers whiter than the tired snow around them. 'It will be spring soon.'

A few moments later, Babi's house came into view and Jana's heart lifted.

'We're here,' she said.

* * *

In the darkening twilight, Jana hurried towards the Josefov district, a book under her arm, eager to let Lillian know her daughters had reached the safe house. She could picture the anxious mother waiting on that windy corner, praying for the sight of Jana with that all-important book. What Jana couldn't imagine was the courage and pain Lillian must have endured to reach the decision: to put her beloved children in the hands of strangers and send them away, not knowing if she would ever see them again. She had no husband with whom she could share the responsibility of her actions.

With tear-filled eyes, Jana picked up her stride and arrived a few minutes before the allotted time, six thirty in the evening.

Lillian wasn't there yet. Jana stood opposite the corner where Lillian had said goodbye to her children the previous day. Moments passed. She clutched the book firmly, anticipating the moment Lillian arrived. They had agreed it was better not to be seen talking together, hence the plan of using the book as a signal. However, Jana was toying with the idea of exchanging a few words if no one was in sight; it seemed too cruel not to offer Lillian some words of comfort.

A nearby church struck the half hour. A mother with three children in tow walked past without giving her a second glance. A light rain began to fall. The snow in the city had nearly disappeared and the transition into spring had begun.

Jana shuffled from one foot to another, her eyes fixed on the alleyway, lit by a dim lantern, where Lillian would emerge. A figure appeared, bundled up in winter clothes, the face hard to distinguish. But from the height and figure, she knew it to be Lillian.

Heart thudding, Jana held the book firmly across her chest, looking around her as she considered crossing the road to give the poor mother some reassurance.

Only it wasn't Lillian.

It was a much older woman who bustled away without looking in Jana's direction. Jana's stomach dipped with disappointment, and she checked her watch, which she continued to do every couple of minutes. Something was wrong. Lillian would've been bursting to hear news of her daughters.

When the church chimed seven o'clock, with a surge of fear-fuelled adrenaline, Jana strode across the street and took the alleyway into the heart of the Jewish quarter. She received some inquisitive looks as she hurried along, but she kept her head down, her face half hidden by a large-brimmed hat that had been her mother's.

There was a morbid silence in the street where Lillian lived. Jana walked softly past the narrow, terraced houses, their windows dark. There were no cooking smells drifting into the street, no voices or children's laughter to be heard. One of the houses had its front window smashed, and Jana, peering in to the dark room, could just make out belongings strewn around.

Filled with dread, she came to Lillian's house. A 'V' in red paint defaced the front window, and a clumsy Jewish star had been splattered across the front door. In desperation, she rang the bell and thumped on the door. Then she called Lillian's name through the letterbox but heard only her own frantic voice echoing beyond.

Breathless, she stood back from the house and combed the street for any sign of life. But all she found were a few personal items lying amongst shards of glass: a child's hat, a wallet ripped open and a baby's empty feeding bottle.

The air was heavy with malice and Jana visualised the scene of Lillian being wrenched from her home and shoved into a car, just as Michal's mother had been.

Immobilised by sorrow, she stood a moment gazing into the sky, watching the first of the evening stars flicker to life. She wondered if Mama was looking down on the dreadful scene.

I don't understand it, Mama. Any of it.

A gust of wind blew a newspaper down the street, the rustling sound bringing Jana out of her reverie. She sped away, desperate to leave the melancholy scene behind her.

18

The three children bowed, puppets dangling from their hands. Their audience, Jana, her father and Babi clapped, enthusiastically. Michal and Maddie grinned, looking very pleased with themselves, while Yveta's expression remained earnest, but Jana noticed she threw a shy look at Babi, as if seeking approval. She got it.

'Bravo! A wonderful performance!' Babi beamed and gave Yveta a wink. A ghost of a smile traced the young girl's lips. Jana was glad to see how Babi was winning Yveta's confidence and hoped one day that she could do the same; till now, the girl had viewed her with suspicion.

Whilst the children took the puppets back to the workshop, the three adults stretched their legs and moved over to the garden window.

'How have the girls been?' asked Jana.

'Yveta is older,' said Babi in a quiet voice. 'She understands a lot of what's going on. Of course she is scared and angry, but I think I'm slowly winning her trust. Maddie, on the other hand, seems to have adapted fairly well.'

'Children sometimes amaze me by their resilience,' said Papa. 'I've seen it at some of the puppet shows I've given in the poorest of areas.'

'And Michal?' said Jana, glancing in the direction of the workshop, where the children's chatter could be heard.

'Oh, he's enchanted by Maddie. Even though she's younger, she bosses him around and he happily complies, following her around the house with wide eyes. He's perked up since the girls arrived. Children need other children.'

Jana was relieved to hear about Michal. Temporarily, with Babi's care, he was managing. But what about the long term? When would he see his parents again? She had to find out how they were.

She gazed through the window and up at the sky. It was a sunny day, small whisps of cloud skating along in a stiff breeze.

'The children have been stuck at home for weeks,' Babi said. 'I can't keep them indoors the whole summer.'

Papa squinted into the garden and ran his fingers over his moustache. 'The fence I put up to protect the chickens is still intact and high enough to conceal the children from view. Plus, there are your bushes and trees. But children can be heard, and that's too risky.'

'Who's going to hear them?' said Babi. 'There isn't a neighbour for miles, and the woods start not far from the back of the garden.'

'True, but the woods are not very deep, and behind that is farmland. Labourers might wander in this direction.'

'Only when the wheat is being harvested. I'll keep the children inside in the autumn.'

'You'll have the children till the war ends, Babi. There is nowhere for them to go,' Jana said.

'I'm delighted to have them; they enrich my days, give me a

sense of purpose. Anyway, the war can't possibly last much longer. Now, this is what I propose: the children can play outside for an hour with instructions of no shrieking.' She gave a wry smile at the implausibility. 'I will keep watch from the attic window, looking out for anyone who might stumble out of the woods. One of my impressive bird whistles would alert the children to come inside immediately.'

Jana looked at her Babi with admiration; she was a remarkable woman.

* * *

Jana had been expecting him ever since he'd recognised her scrubbing the carpet outside Heydrich's office.

Private Brandt made an impressive entrance into the bookshop, throwing the door wide open, an exaggerated sneer across his face. He was going to make a show of this, thought Jana, wincing.

The timing of his arrival was unfortunate; the book club had just broken up, and both women and children were there to witness any unpleasantries. She would have to be humble.

She pinned a smile on her face as she greeted him. 'You have come for your book, Private Brandt.'

'Indeed, I have. It appears I've come at a busy time, which surprises me as I thought business for bookshops was quieter these days.' His tone was accusatory, as if waiting for an explanation. He frowned towards the children who now, released from their book-reading session, were exercising their lungs as well as their legs. Jana had no choice but to offer an explanation.

'I offer the occasional read aloud hour for children.' It sounded more harmless than an adult book exchange meeting, and Jana was certain Brandt was now on the lookout for anything untoward.

As she moved to the cash desk, she caught Karolina and Dasha glancing at her with concern in their eyes. Brandt oozed hostility and even some of the children had quietened down as the mothers hurried their children from the shop. Jana retrieved his order from behind the counter and waited. But Brandt was in no rush as he perused the German books. After she'd encountered Brandt at the castle, she'd stocked the shelves with several copies of Hitler's odious book in anticipation of a visit from Brandt.

He almost looked disappointed when he found his Führer's books stacked neatly on the shelf. He then moved onto the Czech section, hoping no doubt to find some forbidden work. Meanwhile, Karolina and Dasha hung around, uncertain if Jana needed their support, or whether it would be best to leave. She gave her friends a subtle nod of reassurance, eager for them not to be involved if there were to be a confrontation with Brandt.

Once everyone had left, an uncomfortable silence filled the bookshop. Just the noise of Brandt's army boots clomping on the wooden floor remained as he moved from shelf to shelf, inspecting the titles. Jana's heart quickened. Although she had been thorough in removing undesirable works, there was always the chance she'd missed something from the ever-growing list. Brandt was prowling for trouble.

'Can I assist in some way?' she asked, approaching him.

With a harsh laugh, he swung his large frame to face her.

'You may assist me,' he said, mimicking her tone, 'by telling me what you are doing at the castle.'

'I have a cleaning job there.'

'And why, may I ask?'

'To earn money,' she said, and then, afraid that she sounded flippant, added, 'as you rightly remarked, business is quiet and I need to earn extra to pay the rent.'

He stepped up close, his hands clasped behind his back. The sheer bulk of him was intimidating but she forced herself to stand firm and lift her chin. Not too much to appear insolent, but enough to show she was unafraid. That strange odour, sweet and nauseous, wafted on his breath, turning her stomach.

'And why of all the places you could clean, have you ended up at the command HQ?' His cheeks flushed, highlighting the angry scars of his pockmarks.

Jana's tongue went dry as she sought a suitable answer: one that didn't mention a pregnant friend who had previously worked there.

'I heard about the vacancy.'

'From whom?'

'I can't remember exactly. Word of mouth.'

'Do not mess with me, *Fräulein*!' He bellowed at her, so loud that this time, she did step back. 'I don't trust you, bookshop girl. Not for one moment. I'll be watching.'

She remained rooted to the spot as he marched out the shop, leaving without his book, which meant he would be back. And now, as it seemed he'd been assigned to duty at the castle, she would be confronted with him daily.

19

The atmosphere at the market in Wenceslas Square had deteriorated over the last couple of years. Jana remembered the excited cries from the vendors exalting their fine produce, the citizens bustling around the stalls eager to fill their baskets with the best produce. Today, people looked at the meagre wares on display and shook their heads.

'They'll be issuing ration cards next month,' said one stall holder, whom Jana had known since she was a child, 'and not everyone will be receiving them. No ration cards, no food.'

Jana didn't need to ask who would be denied ration cards – anyone deemed undesirable by the Reich. As she left the stall holder, she thought about the weary shrug he'd given her; it seemed endemic amongst so many people these days: they saw things but looked away. A poisonous, complicit silence that smothered empathy for the suffering of others, born of fear and helplessness. *We must keep fighting*, she told herself. *We mustn't give up.*

An unexpected blow jolted her shoulder and as she stumbled slightly, a steadying hand gripped her arm.

'Please excuse me, are you hurt?' said a voice. It was Andrej.

'No, I'm fine,' she said, her stomach flipping.

'Follow me,' he whispered. 'At a good distance.' Then, in a raised voice: 'Apologies for my clumsiness.' He tipped his hat and moved on.

Adrenaline pumped through her. She had been longing to share the success of their mission with the girls and was eager to speak to him about the possibility of further attempts. And she realised, she ached to see him, even if for the briefest of moments. She had no idea what he wanted from her, but she was filled with sweet expectation as she watched his tall frame bob between the crowds.

He walked at a steady pace across the square and turned down one of the numerous side streets. Keeping her distance and allowing several people to walk between them, she followed him through a maze of streets into an area where jazz clubs and music bars had once thrived. The narrow buildings had become worn and boards were nailed across some windows. She glanced up at a sign written in German advertising a nightclub; through the window, she saw chairs stacked on tables, and...

She'd lost him. Seconds ago, he was there and now he was gone. The street was empty. She ran down the street searching left and right, her breaths shallow and fast. She yelped as something gabbed her arm and yanked her into a doorway. A hand clamped across her mouth.

'It's just me, Jana. Don't be afraid.' Andrej pulled her through the door into a dark room, still clutching her close. She could smell the wool of his coat, his woody cologne and something else: a warm musk of sweat and skin. A pang of desire stirred in her so deeply that she gasped.

He let go of her.

'Where are we?' she asked.

'A friend's music bar. It's been closed down at the moment because of the new curfew.'

The windows were shuttered, the only daylight coming from a small, milky window high on the wall, but it was enough for her to make out her surroundings: the wooden bar, round tables and a small, raised stage at one corner of the room.

'We did it, Andrej! We got the girls out,' she burst out.

'You got them to safety? After I saw the bus disappear, I kept praying that everything would go well.'

'Yes, we arrived—'

'Don't tell me where they are.'

Jana bit her lip, understanding the need for discretion. She thought of what she'd overheard from Heydrich, and although she'd passed the information hidden in the bookmark, there had been no response. If only she could share what she knew with Andrej. Her knowledge was a burden that sat heavy in her stomach.

'I brought you here because I have a response from Lenka,' he said, slipping a hand inside his breast coat pocket.

Her heart raced as she took the letter. 'I'd like to read it now, but it's so dark in here.'

'Come, sit down. The electricity is off but there are candles behind the bar.'

Jana sat at a round, wooden table, and Andrej brought two empty wine bottles with candles inserted in the top which he lit with his lighter. She pulled off her gloves and her hand trembled as she slit open the crumpled envelope and slipped out a sheet of paper.

As she held the letter to the candlelight, her eyes welled up at the sight of Lenka's handwriting.

My dearest Jana,

I cannot tell you how much it meant to me receiving your letter. To read your words and know you are thinking of me has lightened my heart. On days when my spirits are low, I re-read your letter and feel comforted.

You need not worry about me. Conditions here are quite adequate and both my beautiful daughter, Alena, and myself are well. When I first arrived here, I was imprisoned in the barracks, but was allowed out for the birth to a hospital, of sorts. Once Alena was born, I had the good fortune to be permitted to stay in the town area of Terezin and now have relative freedom.

I was surprised to find that we are allowed some recreational facilities like a choir group and there is even a small library, although we need more books. People here find great solace in reading, losing themselves in other worlds, leaving their worries temporarily behind. I'm even thinking of starting a book club!

I've received letters from my parents and Ivan. Please can I ask you to keep an eye on Ivan and reassure him I am well; he sounded so lost in his last letter. My parents of course are desolate. I pray that I will somehow see them at least once more in life.

Please take care of yourself, dear friend. Stay well and find happy moments even on darker days. You are always in my thoughts.

Yours always,

Lenka

Jana remained silent as she digested Lenka's words. Then she reread the letter, her chest tight with emotion. Andrej, sitting opposite her, said nothing, smoking a cigarette, giving her the time she needed; she welcomed his reassuring presence.

She exhaled a deep breath and held the letter out to him.

'Please, read it, Andrej.'

'Are you sure you want me to?'

'I need to know what you think. I need to be able to talk to you.' There was urgency in her voice.

Taking off his gloves and putting them on the table, he took the thin piece of paper from her.

She watched his face in the candlelight as he read, his brow furrowed, as he leaned in towards the candle. Jana shivered in the cold room and rubbed her arms.

He set the letter down on the table and rubbed his forehead.

'Well?' she said, impatient to hear his reaction.

'Of course, Lenka has written aware of censorship and has chosen her words carefully. But I think we can believe she and the baby are as well as can be expected.'

'Thank goodness she was released from the prison barracks and is living in the so-called town area.'

A satisfied expression flitted over Andrej's face.

'You arranged that, didn't you?' she said. 'With your contact.'

He nodded but without elaborating, continued, 'What's interesting is Lenka's reference to shops, theatres and the library.'

'It sounds much better in Terezin than I had expected.'

'Exactly.'

'You don't believe it?'

'It's something I'm going to look into.'

'Lenka sounds different,' Jana continued. 'Stifled somehow.' She shivered again and pulled her coat tighter around her body.

'You're cold. Let's get you out of this cave.'

She shook her head. Not knowing when she would have this opportunity again to be alone with him, she fixed her gaze on him and took a deep breath.

'There are some important things I want to share with you,' she said.

Andrej stood up and removing his coat, draped it over her shoulders before pulling up a chair next to her. Then he took off his hat and placed it on the table with his gloves. He touched her cold hand.

'You're like ice. Give me your hands.'

She held them out in front of her, wrists together as if offering herself up for arrest. He cupped her hands in his and began to rub them warm. She composed her thoughts and then spoke.

'I know the rules of silence in the resistance and I understand they're for our protection. But if there is vital information to pass on, surely we must sometimes break those rules.'

'You will have been given channels to convey anything you've discovered.' His tone was cautious.

'But I don't know if my messages have been received. I haven't had any response.' Her frustration rose. 'I don't know that the system is working. Precious days go by and more and more people are disappearing, being locked up, shot. Do you know I stumbled upon an execution wall, and met a grandmother on her knees...?' She choked on a sob, unable to continue.

Andrej squeezed her hands. 'Oh, Jana, I know it's—'

'I work at Prague Castle,' she blurted. 'As a spy.' Defiance welled up in her. 'I eavesdrop on Heydrich,' she said before Andrej could break her flow.

'I know,' he said.

'You know?'

'I am in the police force.' He gave a half smile. 'But if you have information...'

She yanked her hands from his, heat rising to her cheeks.

Unable to contain herself any longer, the words tumbled from her mouth, telling him everything she'd heard about transportation of thousands of people, how she noted the times of Heydrich's arrival, how he'd talked about putting on a show for the public. She ploughed on, not caring care if she was being reckless; the relief at being able to connect and share with Andrej was so sweet, and when she finished, she slumped forward, hanging her head in exhaustion.

Andrej's hands lifted her face, his eyes wide and grave. 'You can trust me, Jana. Yes, theoretically you should only share information with your chosen contact, but what you've heard is a terrifying development. I know Heydrich is sending people from Terezin on work details like the railway in Dresden...' His voice tailed off as he stood up and paced the room, his face deep in contemplation.

'What about your contact in Terezin who passed on Lenka's letter? Will he know anything?'

'He's a low-level policeman who does me favours for a small reward. I doubt he would know the details of such a high-level operation and if he does, I'd need to tread carefully with my enquiries.' Andrej ran his hand through his hair. 'But it's a starting point. I wish I could get inside Terezin and see what's really going on.'

As Andrej continued to pace in silence, a flicker of an idea came to Jana. And as the idea took form, the desperation she'd felt a few moments ago began to fade as new energy revived her. She jumped up and halted Andrej mid stride.

'Lenka said in her letter that they are allowed books and have received some clothes. I have a friend, Dasha, from my book club, who works for a church charity. I believe they are affiliated with the Red Cross. Maybe the Terezin authorities would permit a charitable delivery.'

'They may allow it – to enhance their propaganda campaign of humanity,' said Andrej, studying her as he tried to figure out where she was going with this.

'Maybe I could get into Terezin, under the guise of a volunteer bringing books.'

'You?' he said, startled.

'Why not?' she said, disappointed at his lack of enthusiasm at the idea.

'Because you're already in deep danger with one of the most feared men in the Reich.'

There was a pause before she said quietly, 'How many times can they execute me?'

'Oh, darling Jana. They can do so much more than kill you.'

He'd called her darling.

She gazed up at him, her lips parting, as wrapping his arms around her, he kissed her cheeks, the side of her mouth, his lips travelling down her neck, sending a shudder through her. She sought his mouth; their kisses at first tentative, then demanding, passionate. He pulled the hat from her head and drove his hands into her hair, twisting it around his fingers. Frantic with desire, she kissed him with unrestrained force. Hearing him moan filled her with longing and she pressed herself hard against him, heat throbbing through her. Her hands roamed over the contours of his lean, muscular back.

'This is the worst possible scenario,' he panted, withdrawing from her lips.

'Why?' she said, breathless and hot, her legs weak. She gazed into his handsome face and traced her fingers along those incredible cheekbones.

He took her hands gently from his face. 'Because I have feelings for you that I shouldn't have. They could cloud my judgement, weaken my resolve in the moment of a crucial decision. And that applies to you too. We must stay focused.'

As he stepped back from her, a pang of pain spiked her chest. She wanted to throw herself back at him, kiss and touch him till he could no longer help himself, draw him into her body and soul, but instead, she just nodded. Of course he was right. And she would show him that she could be as strong and disciplined as he was; that she was up to the tasks that lay ahead. Their own desires must be pushed aside; other people mattered now: Lenka, Michal, Yveta, Maddie – as well as so many others that needed help.

Taking deep breaths, she picked up her hat from the floor where moments before, he had flung it, and pulled it on, tucking her hair beneath it. She was aware of him watching her every movement.

'You should go now,' he said. 'I'll lock up in a short while.'

'How can I contact you once I've spoken to the church charity organisation?'

He looked doubtful.

'I'm going to get myself inside Terezin somehow,' she said, determined not to let his reticence deter her.

'Not as a prisoner, I hope,' he said wryly.

She rolled her eyes.

'All right. Let's meet here for an update in five days' time at 7 p.m.,' he said. 'I don't need to tell you to check you are not being followed. And wear different clothes.'

'Especially another hat. You didn't seem to like this one.' She gave a cheeky smile.

20

'I've had a letter from Lenka,' whispered Jana, leaning over the trestle table.

Dasha dropped the clothes she was unpacking back in the crate and stared at her. 'Tell me everything! Is she all right? And the baby?'

The community hall was crowded today and as three women began to hunt through the clothes on Dasha's table, Jana and Dasha retreated to one side. In a lowered voice, Jana outlined the contents of Lenka's letter and then went on to her idea about a charity delivery of books and clothes to Terezin.

Dasha turned pale. 'You want to go into Terezin? We don't even know what the place is. A prison, a town, a work camp? There are all sorts of rumours flying around.'

'Exactly,' said Jana. 'That's why I want to see for myself. Maybe I could even get to see Lenka. You know someone from the Red Cross, don't you? I thought maybe you could put me in touch with her.'

Dasha's expression was dubious. 'Miss Novak from the Red

Cross will be here tomorrow morning to speak to the pastor. I could introduce you then, but I don't know if she can help.'

'Thanks, Dasha. It's a starting point.'

* * *

The following morning, Jana and Dasha spoke with the pastor and Miss Novak about the proposed idea; they were both enthusiastic about the plan but realistic about the hurdles to be overcome.

'Getting inside Terezin is something the Red Cross has been pursuing for some time,' said Miss Novak, 'but the German authorities are dragging their feet. And now with Heydrich…' Her voice tailed off and she shook her head.

They talked about the rigid bureaucratic channels to be negotiated and Miss Novak suggested they meet again in three weeks' time. By then, it would be the beginning of May; everything took so long and Jana dreaded to think what might be going on in the meantime. Heydrich's words of transporting thousands still haunted her and although she had no proof this was happening at Terezin, uneasiness kept her awake at night. She wondered what the resistance were doing with her information, if anything at all.

* * *

Jana rolled out the grass-green paper in the window front and scattered over the flowers she had crafted from scraps of material. She was determined to make the spring display as cheerful as possible despite the ugly swastika she was obliged to hang in the window. As she laid out the selected books, her thoughts kept returning to the contacts who came for her coded messages. It was frustrating; their visits were irregular and it seemed the resistance movement had become extremely fragmented since Heydrich arrived in Prague. She would like to be able to notify a contact if she had an important message; give some kind of sign.

Mulling this over, she laid out her handmade bookmarks as always amongst the book display; sometimes, she split them into two colourful fans, other times just one. Passersby often looked at her window even if they never entered the shop.

Leaning back on her haunches, she narrowed her eyes. That would be it; the bookmarks would act as her sign. Two fans of bookmarks would mean no news. One fan would mean an urgent message was waiting. She smiled to herself. It would be easy enough for the resistance to find inconspicuous passersby to note how she'd done her window display. She would notify the next contact of her idea.

She didn't have to wait long. A couple of days later, a tram driver, still in uniform, made contact with her and she passed on her proposal.

* * *

The early-morning breeze that drifted through the open office window was cool, but when Jana looked out at the blue, cloudless sky, her heart lifted. The April sunshine of the last days had melted any remnants of snow and all over the city, green shoots were emerging announcing the arrival of spring. Working in the office adjacent to Heydrich's, she was rolling the carpet sweeper over the ornate rug when the noise of an engine halted her.

The sound of the motor car was unmistakable: Heydrich's Mercedes-Benz convertible. She left the sweeper standing, snatched up a duster and began to polish the glass as she peered down from the first-floor window. Heydrich climbed out of the driver's seat and adjusted his SS cap. He had driven through the city alone, the roof of the convertible down, without even a security guard; the *Reichsprotektor* of Bohemia and Moravia, self-confident and arrogant.

Jana watched as he allowed himself a moment to admire his vehicle before striding into the palace as upright and proud as a king. She checked her watch: twelve minutes past eight. She would note down everything she'd just observed in her secret code.

Moments later, she heard him enter his office next door, followed by someone else. It wasn't long before Heydrich was engaging in his favourite pastime: thumping his desk. Jana collected up her cleaning things and walked into the hallway.

The door of Heydrich's office opened, and a member of the SS exited, beads of sweat on his forehead. Heydrich stood in front of his desk, legs astride, glaring at the back of the man, but on seeing Jana, he beckoned her to him. She looked at him questioningly, her stomach in knots. Did he really mean her? What could he possibly want? She was a mere cleaner, not worth his time. His sudden attention made her nervous.

'*Fräulein*,' he shouted, impatiently.

She bolted into his office.

'*Guten Morgen, Herr Protektor*,' she said in her best German accent.

His greeting was a curt nod of the head. As usual, he looked immaculate, lean in his pristine, black uniform with its gleaming insignia pins and buttons. His cool-blue eyes studied her a moment, before he waved a hand at his floor-to-ceiling bookcase.

'I inherited this office. It is like a library, which would be charming if the shelves were not so chaotic. You're interested in literature – sort it out for me. That's more useful than flicking a duster around.'

'Yes, sir,' she said, glancing down at the bucket in her hand. Did he mean now instead of finishing her duties? Her shift ended in half an hour. But of course, no one questioned Heydrich, least of all a cleaning maid.

Seeing her uncertainty, he frowned. 'Forget the damn bucket and start now.'

She put down the bucket and moved to the mahogany bookcase which she had dusted earlier that morning.

'How would you like the books sorted, sir? Alphabetically—'

'However you think best. Just get on with it,' he said, reaching for his Czech crystal whisky decanter. Heydrich was not in a good mood, and she wondered how often he had a drink before nine o'clock in the morning. He took a cigarette from the silver box on his desk and stood at the window, cigarette in one hand, whisky in the other, his expression hard, calculating. As she turned to the books, she wondered what terrible things he was scheming.

He had just spent a couple of days in Berlin and it was rumoured he'd had a high-level meeting with Hitler and Himmler. A shiver went down her spine just thinking about what might have been discussed: countries to attack, people to persecute and murder, nations to oppress and bend to the will of the Reich.

Heydrich's secretary entered the room, laden with a pile of files. The plain-faced German woman with hair tightly braided around her head placed the files on Heydrich's desk. She glanced, surprised, at Jana, who averted her gazed and busied herself with the books. Heydrich dismissed his secretary and then sat at his desk shuffling through the files in silence.

Jana's nerves were as taut as the strings of Heydrich's violin that lay in its open box. It was bizarre and terrifying to be in the same room with this man who could turn on her in an instant and order her execution. The more she tried to work quietly, the louder were her movements: one of her shoes squeaked, a book collapsed with a thud on the shelf, and then to her dismay, her stomach began to rumble.

Heydrich, however, did not seem to be disturbed, and continued to ignore her as he worked.

A shrill noise pierced the room and Jana jumped. Heydrich grabbed the telephone receiver and after a few moments of listening – to what Jana could make out as a man's urgent tones – Heydrich barked, 'I'm on my way.'

'Finish up in here,' he said to Jana before shuffling the files together and pushing them to the side of his desk. He strode out the room, leaving her frozen to the spot. She had only ever been in his office early in the morning when his desk top was empty. She had once tried the drawers but they were, of course, locked. But now files of information lay on his desk a couple of steps away.

The office door was wide open. It would be madness to start rifling around in the *Protektor's* paperwork. Anyone walking past would see her immediately. She bit the inside of her cheek, thinking hard, then heaved a pile of books from the shelf and put them on Heydrich's desk, shielding the files from view if someone appeared at the doorway. Keeping her eyes on the open door she flicked through the files, scanning the covers. A beige one with an official emblem of a spread-winged eagle, clutching a swastika between its claws, caught her attention. She opened it, concealed behind the pile of books, her heart pumping. There were a few carbon copies of recently dated letters signed by Heydrich.

Fear clouded her vision; the typed words, a smudged carbon

blue, jittered before her eyes. She forced herself to focus: a letter to his immediate superior, Himmler.

Snatches of words sprung out at her:

> Not only is the idea of extradition of undesirables to Madagascar ridiculous, it is logistically and financially inviable. Please rest assured that I take our Führer's concerns seriously and that I'm in the process of implementing a solution—

'Ah, the bookshop girl.'

Her head shot up. Brandt stood in the doorway, his eyes small and hard.

'And what might you be doing in our *Protektor*'s office?'

In a swift movement, she flicked the file shut and pulled the book pile on top of it.

'Herr Heydrich asked that I sort his bookcase. It's easier when I lay the books out.' She spoke with as much authority as her parched throat would allow.

'That's a very important job for a cleaning woman,' he said snidely.

Sweat ran down the back of her neck as he approached. She lay her hand on the pile of books that now covered the file underneath. Brandt's bulk neared, his scarred cheeks reddening.

'My goodness. It's like a party in here.' Heydrich's secretary entered with a small watering can. She stared at them both.

'The cleaning girl here has some story about tidying books,' said Brandt with a sneer.

'Well, Herr Heydrich has requested that she do so.'

Brandt's face dropped.

'But I've just heard Herr Heydrich has been called away for

the rest of the day,' continued the secretary, 'so I'm here to lock up.'

She gave Brandt a fixed look and he retreated from the room, but not before glowering at Jana. 'I'm watching. Always watching.'

The secretary sighed as if she wasn't particularly fond of Brandt and moved to the windowsill to water an impressive cactus.

'Please replace the books and leave now,' she said, paying attention to avoid the huge prickles as she watered.

Jana used the moment the woman was distracted to lift the books and slide the file back to the others and then stacked the books on the shelf.

The secretary stepped back, admiring the swollen plant. 'Even something so vicious needs a few drops of loving care,' she said.

Jana said goodbye and raced from the room, wondering what or who the secretary had been referring to.

* * *

Jana flew through the door of the bookshop and went straight to the window. First, she removed one display of the bookmarks and then fanned out the remaining ones prominently in the centre of the window: urgent news. She hadn't understood the reference to Madagascar, didn't even know where that was, but the words 'extradition' and particularly 'solution' were ominous; a word often bandied about by Hitler with reference to Jews.

She fetched *The Gardener's Diary* and began work on the coded message. Annoyingly, the shop was busy that day, and every time she sat behind the cash desk with the book on her lap, a customer came in and she had to snap it shut and shove it beneath the counter. It wasn't until four o'clock in the afternoon that she'd finished and her note was securely hidden in a daffodil-yellow bookmark. How long would it take for her sign in the window to be seen? She needed to tell Andrej the latest news; maybe he could speed things along.

* * *

Two days later, hearing the unmistakeable sound of the Mercedes-Benz convertible, Jana checked her watch – eight twenty-three. She had deliberately left cleaning Heydrich's office to last, and although she'd finished, she continued to sweep her duster over the already clean surfaces. As usual, the office door was open and Miss Jezek had already stopped by to check for signs of missed dust.

Jana continued to repeat the words in her head that she'd been practising most of the night. But now that Heydrich's arrival was imminent, nerves paralysed her brain and the words became a jumble of nonsense.

He wore no coat over his black uniform and removed his hat as he entered his office. His heavily creamed, blond hair was swept back, which made his face longer and more severe than usual, doing nothing to ease her nerves. He halted, tall and rigid when he saw her, his expression one of annoyance.

'Haven't you finished yet? I don't expect to find cleaning staff still here when I arrive.'

'My apologies, *Herr Protektor*. I am finished now but was just wondering if you would like me to continue with the bookshelves.'

'Not this morning. You may leave,' he said, folding his long frame into the chair and putting his briefcase on the desk.

She nodded. This wasn't going to work. What on earth had

she been thinking that she, a mere cleaner, could strike up a conversation with the *Reichsprotektor* of Bohemia and Moravia? It was a ludicrous idea.

He opened his briefcase and glanced up at her, frowning.

'Why are you still here?' he said.

Her legs trembled. Now was her chance. She tried to swallow over the rock in her throat.

'Spit it out, *Fräulein*, or get out of here.'

'Sir, I'm involved with a church charity that is affiliated with the Red Cross. We are trying to get approval to deliver donations to the people of Terezin.'

He fixed her with emotionless, cool eyes. 'The settlement now carries the German name, Theresienstadt.'

'Yes, sir, yes, of course,' she stumbled.

'Furthermore, I am aware of the requests of the Red Cross.' His voice was quiet, but his words cut the air with slivers of ice.

Careful, Jana, careful.

'Yes, of course,' she repeated, fighting to find the right words without enraging him. 'It seems to be taking a long time, and I think the Red Cross just want to allay any fears and tick it off their list,' she said, trying to sound casual, as if the visit was of no great importance.

'Allay fears?' Alertness flickered across his features.

Her stomach lurched: bad choice of words. She'd thought the idea might suit the German propaganda that Jews were being treated humanely.

Seeking to diffuse the situation, she shrugged her shoulders. 'You know how the Red Cross are. Sorry to have bothered you, sir.'

He studied her for a long moment, his pale face impassive, as immobile as a mask.

She clamped her jaw to stop her teeth chattering. He scared

her more like this than when he was thumping his desk and shouting. Behind his glacier eyes, he was calculating, assessing, planning. And then as if bored with her, he turned away and reached inside his briefcase.

'I have work to do,' he said, dismissing her.

With great relief, she retreated from the room, and stopped in the hallway, one hand on the wall to support herself, taking deep breaths to slow her racing heart.

21

On the way down Nerudova Street, Jana berated herself. How could she even think of taking on a man like Heydrich? If he hadn't been suspicious of her before, she had no doubt he was now. She'd jeopardised everything by her inexperience and naïvety. Fear twisted her stomach in knots, not just for herself but for Papa, Babi, the children, everyone who knew her. Heydrich was head of the Gestapo and once they got involved…

She shuffled home on weak, boneless legs and slumped into the armchair at the bookshop, her mind whirling with scenarios of horrific outcomes.

That evening over their meal, Papa remarked on her sombre mood. 'What's wrong, sweetheart? Something is weighing on your mind.'

She shook her head, saying she was merely tired; he would be sick with worry if she told him what had happened. But he persisted.

'Talk to me, Jana. We're already both involved in illegal activities and I've suspected for a long time you're up to something at the castle.'

But she wouldn't be drawn into conversation. She went to bed early, citing a headache.

When she woke the next morning, she was filled with dread at the thought of seeing Heydrich and considered staying at home, claiming to be sick, but that would achieve nothing. She dragged herself from bed and left home before her father woke.

When she arrived on the first floor of Salm Palace, Miss Jezek informed her she would not be required to clean Heydrich's office as he would be away for a couple of days and his room would remain locked. Jana sighed inwardly, grateful at this short reprieve.

Throughout her early shift as she pushed the carpet sweeper over elegant rugs and polished the crystal chandeliers with a long feather duster, thoughts of Andrej sprung into her mind: his hot lips sweeping the length of her neck, his hands plunging into her hair after flinging her hat from her head. The force of desire that pulsed through her was something she'd never experienced before. He had even said he had feelings for her; but he'd also made it clear that their relationship was to remain professional. She was eager to meet him again as arranged and share her discovery of Heydrich's letter referencing a 'solution,' even though she wasn't supposed to discuss information with anyone. But she and Andrej had already crossed that line and she no longer wanted to work in complete isolation.

* * *

Later that same morning, the book club was due to meet. As Jana was preparing the chairs, the bell above the door rang and she looked up to see Karolina with her daughter. She glanced at her watch; Karolina was twenty minutes early.

When Jana went to greet her, she was shocked; Karolina's eyes were red and swollen, her face drawn.

'I'm sorry I'm early, but I'm not staying for the book club today,' she said in a raw voice. Then, placing a hand on her daughter's back, she told the child, 'Run along and find a nice book.' The girl skipped away and Karolina turned to Jana. 'I don't want her to hear what's happened to her father.'

'My goodness, whatever is the matter?'

'Petr has been arrested. It's bad, I'm afraid.' Karolina swallowed a sob.

'But why?' Jana put a hand on Karolina's arm.

'It's been coming for a while. I knew this would happen but he wouldn't stop. I begged him but he wouldn't listen.'

Jana remembered how withdrawn Karolina had been at the last book club. She waited for her friend to continue, fearful of what she would say.

'He's been writing anti-Nazi articles and distributing them in an effort to activate more resistance. I don't know what they will do to him. If only I knew how to help him, if only...' She broke down in tears and Jana wrapped her arms around her, murmuring words of comfort.

'There must be something we can do. Don't despair.' She knew the situation was dire, but her thoughts turned immediately to Andrej, who she was due to meet that evening. He was Karolina's only hope. She suggested that Karolina leave her daughter at the bookshop to play with the other children who'd be arriving shortly. Then, later, either Jana or one of the other mothers could bring the little girl home.

'Thank goodness I have friends like you,' said Karolina, wiping the tears from her eyes.

'I'm here for you,' said Jana. 'We all are.'

* * *

Jana went through Mama's wardrobe, examining the clothes that she and Papa hadn't been able to bear to give away. After Mama's death, Papa had suggested Jana should wear the clothes, but Jana had thought that too sad. Now, however, she decided her mother would have approved of Jana's resistance activities and would've been delighted that her clothes were aiding Jana in her disguise. She picked out a smart, black, wool coat and a traditional embroidered headscarf that would keep her auburn hair out of sight.

After weaving her way through the back streets of Prague, she arrived at the nightclub, waiting till the street was empty before she rapped on the door.

Despite her resolution to keep her feelings in check, her cheeks flushed when Andrej's face appeared. He waved her inside.

Andrej had found a small oil lamp which he'd place on a round table, and the two of them sat opposite each other. There was a charged tension between them immediately and Jana knew they were both thinking of their passionate kisses last time they'd been together.

She swallowed and diverted her attention to recent events, starting with Heydrich's letter.

Andrej looked aghast. 'You read one of his letters?'

She wasn't sure whether to be proud or indignant at his surprise but continued to discuss the contents.

'What do you think Heydrich means by Madagascar?'

Andrej paused in thought, rubbing his chin before he spoke.

'Before the war broke out, Germany's aim was to expel Jews from the country, stripping them of their wealth and belongings before they left. The persecution, humiliation and violence were part of a plan to make life untenable for the Jewish citizens in order to drive them out, or arrest or murder them. But now the war's begun, all the borders are closed and they are trapped within the Reich.'

'So now they are forced into Ghettos around Europe,' said Jana.

'Exactly, but the Ghettos are at bursting point and problematic for the Nazis. There were rumours of a plan to send all the Jews away to some place, another location, an island or—'

'Madagascar,' finished Jana.

He nodded. 'I heard an SS officer talking about it after he'd downed half a bottle of Becherovka at Christmas. But the cost and logistics of such an operation make the idea infeasible, of course.'

'So the Nazis are looking for another solution, like Terezin.'

Andrej pushed back from the table and started to pace, something Jana now recognised he did when agitated.

'But Terezin is a small fortress. What happens when it's full?' he said, more to himself.

Jana told him about her talk with Miss Novak from the Red Cross, but stopped short of recounting how she'd approached Heydrich on the subject; Andrej would reproach her for being reckless and she didn't want him to worry about her even more.

'One last thing, Andrej. A friend of mine needs your help.' She sighed at the thought of poor Karolina.

'Go ahead,' he said, halting his pace and leaning on the bar to light a cigarette.

After she'd told him about the arrest of Karolina's husband, he hastily stubbed out his cigarette. 'I'd better get to the police station straight away. Once he's in the hands of the Gestapo, there is nothing I can do.'

As they made their way to the door, Jana said, 'I must be able to contact you if I need you.'

She thought she saw a flicker of amusement in his eyes and her neck grew warm. 'I mean, if I have some urgent information.'

They needed some type of code like the one she had with the bookmarks. The idea came in a flash.

'I always have a display of bookmarks in the shop window.'

'I know; very pretty ones you make yourself.' He smiled.

'That will be the sign. If I remove them all, it means we need to meet.'

He looked at her with admiration. 'You're getting good at this. I can walk by each day on my way to the police station. If the bookmarks are gone, I'll meet you at the club that evening at seven.'

She smiled, proud of herself.

'But every time we meet, there is a risk we'll be seen. So only in an emergency,' he added.

She touched his arm lightly. 'Shame, I thought we could meet here in the dark three times a week for illicit goings-on.'

Her words made him blush; something she hadn't seen him do before and she thought it made him look charming, slightly vulnerable. She would try it more often.

As the last time, she left the nightclub first, and Andrej shortly after.

As she hurried home to prepare dinner, she worried about Karolina and her husband, hoping that Andrej could help in some way.

* * *

There was nothing remarkable about the middle-aged woman who approached the cash register with the book she had chosen.

Her face and clothes were non-descript, and Jana, distracted by thoughts of Andrej, would never have remembered her had the woman not slid a bookmark across the counter; Jana's own bookmark that she'd previously given a contact with a concealed message. Startled, she shot the woman a look. Jana's display in the window had signalled she had urgent news, summoning this contact within three days.

Coded book quotes were exchanged, and Jana retrieved the bookmark she had waiting beneath the counter: hidden were her notes on Heydrich's letter to Himmler and his ominous words about a solution.

Her stomach flickered with nervous excitement. Would the message she received be a new assignment? Till now, she'd only been required to note Heydrich's arrival in the mornings.

As soon as the church bells outside sounded midday, she flipped the sign on the door to *closed*, grabbed *The Gardener's Diary*, and hid herself at the back of the bookshop.

Half an hour later, she'd deciphered the message and was leaning back in the armchair, pondering over the new instructions. She was to monitor when Heydrich drove himself, was driven by a chauffeur and when there was an escort car. Any of these variables, she'd noticed were possible on any given day. But was there a pattern, or did it all hang on the erratic whim of Heydrich?

It was obvious that the resistance was monitoring all Heydrich's and probably other top SS officers' movements too. She had long suspected there were several spies at the castle, who, like her, had filtered through the security checks when being hired. The enormity of being tasked to spy on the top man weighed on her. Her new instructions had sparked her adrenaline. But something else too: an uneasiness about the resistance's intentions.

The following morning, Jana found herself glancing out the window a hundred times on the off chance she spotted Andrej passing by. His shifts were irregular so she never knew when to expect him, but he'd promised to check her window display for a sign if she needed to speak to him urgently; all she had to do was remove all the bookmarks and go to the nightclub to meet him.

She'd slept badly, worries assaulting her from every angle: Lenka, the children with Babi, Heydrich and his so-called 'solution', and how she or the Red Cross would gain entry to Terezin to find out what was really going on. The only thought that had distracted her from her tumult of fears was the kiss she had shared with Andrej, but this too kept her from sleep, as yearning, hot and fluid, had coursed through her, covering her skin with a sheen of sweat.

The morning at the castle had passed by without incident as Heydrich was still out of the office which Jana was relieved about. Now back at the bookshop, she was unnerved and longed to talk to Andrej. Yes, it was breaking the rules, but her new assignment had thrown up a lot of disturbing questions.

She paced around the bookshop, moving books around, then placing them back again in the same place. A few customers came and went but no one bought anything. At lunchtime, she closed the shop door, went into the kitchen to fetch some bread and cheese and hurried back to the cash desk where she ate her lunch staring out the window. The food gave her indigestion and then in a spurt of determination, she rushed to the window and scooped up all the bookmarks. She simply had to see Andrej that evening.

The sun came out in the afternoon, highlighting the dirty window pane. Fetching a bucket of water from the kitchen and some old newspapers, she slipped on her coat and went outside to clean the glass. From there, she had a good view up and down the street and as she worked, her heart fluttered with anticipation that she would see him.

He didn't come.

Disappointed, she returned the bucket to the kitchen, rinsed it out, and took the dirty newspapers to the rubbish bin in the backyard. Maybe he was walking past right now whilst she was in the backyard; he would notice the absence of bookmarks and meet her that evening at the nightclub.

Later, a group of children occupied her at the back of the shop and she was unable to keep an eye on the window, but she felt sure he'd have passed the shop by the time she locked up. Before she left, she twisted her hair and tucked it under a plain, brown beret. She took a compact mirror from her hand bag and studied her pale skin and the black circles under her eyes. It was a shame she had no makeup with her. She pinched her cheeks and her lips till a pink tinge appeared and left the shop.

As she crossed Old Town Square, her head down, she tried to analyse her emotions. Did she want to see Andrej to discuss Heydrich, or did she have other reasons? Unbidden, an image of her and Andrej kissing and touching in the dark nightclub darted into her mind. She sighed inwardly; she was overthinking everything and it was exhausting.

Dusk was creeping into the alleyway where only one streetlamp emitted an insipid glow. Her heels clicked along the cobblestones as she passed the tall, shadowy buildings. A dog barked in the distance. Alone in the street, she hurried to the nightclub door and rapped the iron knocker softly. It was just past seven so he was bound to be here. Any moment, his face would appear; her pulse quickened. Would he smile at her? She liked his smile: wide, generous lips. He should smile more often; in another place and time, he would be smiling as he listened to her talk, as he looked at her, as she kissed his cheek and stroked the back of his neck.

There was no sound of footsteps or the clunk of a bolt. She knocked again, louder this time, glancing up and down the street, nervously. Her knocks echoed on the other side of the door. Surely, he'd seen her sign; he wouldn't let her down. Had he passed the shop before she took the bookmarks out of the window? Sometime in the morning? But she'd been staring into the street all morning, looking for him. Was it possible she had missed him?

The familiar sound of army boots on cobblestones startled her. Her mouth dry, she looked up to see two Wehrmacht soldiers approaching her.

The older soldier frowned at her. 'What are you doing here, *Fräulein*? If you are wanting a drink, you're out of luck. The bar is closed.'

When she didn't reply, the younger soldier looked her up and down. 'She's touting for business, sir.' He smirked.

'I'm doing no such thing,' Jana said indignantly. 'I've merely lost my way.'

'Let us escort you, then,' said the older man, surveying the building behind her. 'I thought I heard you knocking on the door,' he added, narrowing his eyes as his gaze slid over her.

'I–I wanted to ask for directions,' she stammered.

'Show me your papers.'

She fished her pass from her handbag and held it out. He shone a slim torch over her details, taking his time, making her tremble. She caught the younger soldier's smug expression and looked away. *Steady, breaths, Jana. Your papers are in order. Don't show your fear.*

'Very well. Follow us.' The soldier returned her pass and she was led away down the alleyway.

22

Sweat had pooled under her armpits by the time she stumbled into the bookshop. It had been a mistake to try and meet Andrej; he was right about the risks. If he had been there at the nightclub, the Wehrmacht would have caught them: a police captain in a clandestine meeting. Questions would have been asked. If she were merely a girlfriend, then why the secrecy? It would be easier if she and Andrej were a pair; after all, a policeman was entitled to a private life. But of course, Andrej was protecting her; in the terrible event of him being uncovered as a spy, people connected to him would be interrogated by the Gestapo. And she was putting him in jeopardy by summoning him to meet her.

Gathering the pile of bookmarks she'd removed, she knelt in the window and spread them back out in full view. She would deal with her assignments alone and not drag Andrej into her activities. It was clear to her now. She had her role and he had his.

But as she trudged up the stairs to the apartment, frustration gnawed at her. The resistance seemed so fragmented, different groups with their own agendas, one group not knowing what the other one was doing. And it had taken three days to respond to her signal of bookmarks in the window.

As she put her key in the lock, a smell of cooking greeted her and she smiled. Dear Papa. He had started preparing their meal without her.

* * *

Four days after the arrest of her husband, Karolina came into the bookshop. Jana threw her arms around her.

'What news have you?' she asked.

'It seems Petr was lucky enough to escape the Gestapo.'

Andrej had managed to help, thought Jana. Thank goodness.

'So that's something to be grateful, for.' Karolina sighed heavily. She peered at Jana. 'Did you have something to do with that?'

'Me? Why would you think that?' said Jana, startled.

Her friend shrugged. 'Just a feeling. The way you spoke about sorting something out.'

Jana shook her head vehemently and diverted the conversation. 'Where is Petr now?'

'He's still at the police station, but will be transported to Terezin later today.' Her last words choked on a sob and her head fell into her hands. 'He'll be in prison for years. I don't know if he'll ever come out.'

'Yes, he will. The Germans won't be here forever. The allies will come and we'll fight back.'

'What allies? We've been abandoned, and that's the truth,' Karolina said, her voice wrought with bitterness.

Jana had no answer, so she sat quietly with her friend, her own tears slipping down her cheeks.

* * *

'We have permission!' Dasha panted, her cheeks pink with excitement as she skipped into the bookshop.

Jana looked down from the ladder where she stood rearranging her father's marionettes. 'For what?' she said, stepping down and smiling at Dasha's own huge grin.

'Permission for the Red Cross to visit Terezin. Authorised by Heydrich himself.'

'My goodness, that's fantastic.' Jana was flabbergasted.

'We don't have a date yet, but I'll start sorting clothes to donate.' Dasha bobbed around like a school girl; she looked too young to be married with a child.

'I'll start collecting books, approved ones of course. Do you think that I'd be allowed to accompany the visit?' said Jana, bubbling with excitement.

'I don't know,' said Dasha, doubtfully. 'You know the Germans are sticklers for regulations. Probably only Red Cross members are allowed.'

'Then I'll join up.'

Dasha laughed. 'Speak to Miss Novak. She seems to like you.'

Jana liked the Red Cross supervisor too; she had a gentle persuasiveness about her and kind eyes. She prayed that somehow, Miss Novak could persuade the authorities that she needed Jana for the visit.

Over the next days, Jana started to collect books. Her first obvious port of call was to ask the book club ladies for donations. Then at lunch time and in the evenings, she went house to house, a large basket over her arm. One sour-faced woman announced she certainly would not donate a thing to criminals and Jews and slammed the door in Jana's face. But mostly people were happy to give what they could, even if it was one shabby, well-loved children's book.

Meanwhile, she carried out her new assignment at the castle, watching Heydrich's arrival each day. Mostly his chauffer, a huge boar of a man, drove; occasionally, Heydrich drove himself and sometimes, he was accompanied by an armed security car. And unless it was raining heavily, Heydrich travelled with the roof of his convertible down. Jana noted every detail.

She had little contact with Heydrich until, one morning, he marched in her direction as she was carrying towels to the cloakroom at the end of the corridor. There was no way to avoid eye contact so she greeted him politely, hoping he would pass her by.

He stopped close to her, his long frame looming over. '*Fräulein* Hajek. Have you heard that I've authorised a Red Cross visit to Terezin?'

There was a look of cold amusement in his eyes.

The only words that came to her were, 'Yes, thank you, *Herr Protektor.*'

A strange smile touched his thin lips. 'Why thank you?' He feigned puzzlement.

He was playing with her but she didn't know the rules of the game. She paused as she scrabbled her thoughts together.

He stared at her, no doubt enjoying her discomfort, then before she could speak, he waved his hand. 'Leave what you're doing and finish sorting my bookshelves.'

After she'd rushed to deposit the towels, she went straight to his office and stifled a groan. Brandt stood erect, legs apart directly next to the open door. He glowered at her as she passed.

Heydrich was not in there, his desk clear. As she moved to the bookshelves, she wondered if Heydrich had told Brandt to stand guard. Had Heydrich suspected her of snooping? Of course not. If he had, she would be lying in the basement of the Gestapo, her body smashed and broken, or crumpled against an execution wall, riddled with bullets.

23

Most of the garden had been turned into a vegetable patch, and the first green sprouts poked through the earth. Jana sat with Lenka's parents on the back porch of their modest house in the picturesque village of Lidice.

'I've planted carrots, turnips and potatoes and a few herbs.' Lenka's mother, Marie, waved her arm at the garden. 'That, with the eggs from our chickens, is more than enough to keep us going. Isn't it, dear?' She flicked something from her husband's trouser leg.

Lenka's father nodded amiably and sipped at his barley coffee.

'Do you miss Prague?' asked Jana.

'Of course life is very different from when we lived there, but we had no choice. When our business went bankrupt in the thirties, it made sense to join my sister and her family here in this small mining village. Actually, we're very settled here. I have a very nice job at the school; so lovely to be surrounded by children. Stanislav is too old to work in the mines but he has a job at the metal factory, don't you, dear?'

Stanislav smiled, knowing an answer wasn't required.

'We were so happy when Lenka studied in Prague and got married. And we became grandparents...'

Marie's nervous chatter faltered and her face crumpled. Her husband reached out and clasped her hand as she heaved a racking sob. She shook her head, indicating she was unable to continue.

'We've received one letter from Lenka,' Stanislav said in a low voice. 'She said little, just that her and the baby were doing well. Have you heard anything different?'

'The same as you,' Jana replied, 'but I do know she's not being kept in prison and is allowed to live freely within the Terezin fortress. I'm hoping to find out more and will keep you informed.'

Jana looked at Marie, who was crying openly now. She sniffed loudly and Stanislav pulled a handkerchief from his pocket and tenderly dabbed at her tears.

A hard lump formed in Jana's throat. How terrible it must be to have your daughter at the hands of the Nazis and be unable to do anything about it. She felt a swell of affection for this warm-hearted couple who had always made her so welcome at their home, and at their kindness when Jana had lost her mother. If only there was something she could do to ease their pain. The idea of getting donations of clothes and books into Terezin via the Red Cross wouldn't let her go. She'd spoken to Miss Novak about aiding the visit and now visualised getting inside the fortress town herself. Then somehow, she would find Lenka and her baby.

After a pleasant – and often emotional – few hours, Lenka's parents accompanied her back to the bus stop, showing her the village on the way. Marie pointed out the school where she worked, and they took a few minutes to stand outside the small church. Beside it was an orchard where apple blossom bobbed in the breeze. Two young girls lay on their stomachs in the grass, reading books.

'It's very peaceful, here,' remarked Jana as they crossed a small square.

'That's why I like it so much,' said Marie. 'And the people here are very friendly and community minded, always ready to lend a helping hand.'

A silver-haired woman on a bicycle gave a cheery wave as she rode past.

'That's the school mistress. Lovely lady,' whispered Marie.

It occurred to Jana in that moment that she'd never heard Lenka's mother speak ill of anyone.

They reached the bus stop where Marie and Stanislav waited with Jana until the bus trundled up the road. They all hugged each other fiercely, promising to keep in touch. Marie's parting words were, 'Pray for Lenka.'

'Of course,' said Jana and kissed her cheek before climbing aboard. She took a place by the window and waved as the bus juddered forward, twisting in her seat to take a final look at the couple before they disappeared from view. She would visit them again soon.

* * *

As days passed into May, contacts appeared more frequently at the bookshop. Occasionally, one that had been before: the tram driver, the woman who limped but had a healthy leg. She sensed a new urgency from the resistance: her increased observance orders, the regular contacts. And there was a charged energy in the air as Prague erupted into spring and the city glowed golden in the sunlight.

After lunch on the second Sunday in May, Jana had a whole afternoon at her disposal. She would walk down to the Vltava River and find a quiet spot to read. Feeling too warm in her long-sleeved blouse, she went to her wardrobe and pulled out her favourite summer dress – yellow and floaty with short sleeves and a print of tiny, white daisies. Her mother's gold locket sat perfectly above the sweetheart neckline.

Feeling romantic in the dress, she did a little twirl in the mirror, and then for no reason other than to please herself, she applied a dab of face powder and a pale-peach lipstick. She brushed out her hair and left it loose on her shoulders, and completed the outfit with a wide-brimmed sun hat. Picking up her copy of *Jane Eyre*, she set off.

As she walked through Prague Old Town, a light breeze ruffled the hem of her dress. Despite the occupation, nature continued to weave its magic and spring had brought out the lovers in Prague. And she was alone. A wave of self-pity rose but she quashed it. She would enjoy a few hours disappearing into her book and try, even for a short while, to retreat from reality.

She sauntered towards the river, which was fringed with trees heavy with blossom. Swans glided along the blue water, sending ripples across reflections of the grand buildings that lined the riverbank. Two white butterflies, the first she had seen this year, fluttered in front of her. She let out a deep sigh and breathed in the sweet scent of spring. And then she saw him.

Andrej.

A jaunty walk and a newspaper clutched under his arm as he mingled with the Sunday crowds. He wore light-grey trousers and a white shirt, the collar open, no tie. He'd exchanged his police cap for a cream boater with a black band, and looked as handsome and relaxed as movie star, Clark Gable. Her heart skipped as she fell in line behind him, keeping her distance.

She meandered after him, hiding amongst families bearing picnic baskets and blankets, and groups of teenagers horsing around. He stopped under a tree. She halted and watched him sit down, his back against the trunk, and shake out his newspaper. And now? What should she do now? In another life, she would run up to him, exclaiming what a coincidence it was to see him. And he would tell her to join him. They would chat and laugh, watching people walk by, and he'd take her hand and lean over to kiss her.

A shrill scream close to her shook her from her fantasies and she looked across at a small boy having a tantrum in his pushchair. People glanced up at the noise briefly. Including Andrej.

She froze as his face registered surprise at seeing her. He looked at her questioningly, but she just stared back at him. She should just walk away but as she started to play with her locket nervously, he stood, gestured with a nod to follow him, and walked further on down the river bank.

He strolled slowly, as if measuring his long-legged stride to her shorter one. She held her distance as they left the crowds behind them and the stone embankment dwindled to a low wall then to a gravel path on the edge of the water. Ducks splashed in the reeds alongside her. The river was quiet here, the current slower. To her right was a derelict building, the iron gates padlocked. They passed under linden trees, their yellow flowers beginning to bloom. She wondered where he was leading her.

Finally, he stopped by a spot where trees, shrubs and long grass hid the view of the water's edge. He checked the area around them, then motioned her to follow before darting through the bushes and disappearing. She gave a furtive glance over her shoulder and went after him.

Passing through bushes and bright-yellow forsythia shrubs,

she came to a secluded, stony beach. A small disused steam boat half out of the water was tethered to a rusty pole; the boat reminded her of the small passenger ferries of her childhood. Andrej appeared from the wood cabin and reached out an arm.

Heart fluttering, she let him haul her up over the side and they entered the cabin.

He sat on the floor, his back against the cabin wall, his head just below the window.

'If we stay down here, we won't be seen,' he said, patting the space next to him.

She slid down beside him, her legs straight in front of her, arranging the folds of her dress to cover her knees. She felt self-conscious as he watched her every movement.

'We'll be safe here for a while,' he said. 'Has something urgent happened?'

'Oh, no. Why do you ask?' She was confused why he'd brought her here.

'When I saw you on the embankment, I thought you were looking for me because something had happened. I led you here so you could tell me.'

This was embarrassing; she couldn't say she'd been following him simply because her heart had skipped when she'd spotted him, that feelings of romance and the promises of spring had drawn her to him.

'Everything is fine. It was just a coincidence I saw you.'

Even as the words left her mouth, she thought how stupid they were. Nothing was fine. She so badly wanted to tell him about Heydrich's letter to Himmler, but she had decided to keep to her orders and inform her contacts only. Now she was uncertain, so she moved to a safer topic.

'Thank you for saving Karolina's husband from the Gestapo.'

'It's not that simple.' He sighed. 'I managed to keep him out of their hands here, but Terezin prison is run by the Gestapo. I can't make promises for his future.'

They fell silent. Jana gave him a shy look. 'I'm glad I ran into you today.'

'Me too,' he said, a rare smile touching his lips. She looked at his mouth, her own instinctively parting.

He leaned over and they kissed. Deeply. He moved his lips to brush the base of her throat, a feather of kisses to her collarbone. She stretched back her neck with a small gasp as her skin tingled and heat spread through her. This was so decadent, romance on the floor of an old steamboat. This could be their illicit meeting place, where they could be together, talk, touch, love.

He ran his fingers along the neckline of her dress, and she ached to feel his touch on her breasts. But instead, he drew back and gently lifted her gold locket in his fingers.

'A book, so fitting for you.'

'It was my mother's,' she said, short of breath, 'an anniversary gift from my father.'

'It must have been very hard to lose your mother so young.' He sat back, visibly trying to compose himself, distracting his passion.

'I was twenty, technically an adult. But I felt like a child. I wasn't in any way prepared to face my life without her...' Her voice drifted away, emotion threatening to overcome her.

They were silent for a moment as he placed the locket softly back against her skin. She didn't want to talk about herself; she knew nothing about him and had so many questions she wanted to ask.

'Tell me more about your family. I know you have a mother who you bought a book for when it was her birthday.' She reached out and stroked the back of his neck.

'My mother is the only family I have. My father died in the Great War when I was just one year old. I have no memories of him, just a few blurry photographs. But I feel I know him through my mother's stories.'

'And your mother never married again?'

'She loved my father too much, she said, to want to another man in her life. Anyway, there were hardly any men left after the war. And then came the Spanish influenza. The country was full of widows. But nevertheless, there was a new wave of hope sweeping the land. We were a democratic nation, a new country, Czechoslovakia. Twenty years of freedom, something my father lost his life for.'

He paused.

Jana continued, 'And then came the Germans, chopping off pieces of our country before invading what was left of us.'

She watched his eyes cloud over and then dropped her head to his shoulder. His arm curled around her waist. She shifted and, tucking her legs beneath her dress, snuggled against him, breathing him in.

'Is that why you do what you do?' she asked, glancing at his profile, but knowing the answer to her own question.

He said nothing, but his chest heaved. Then she asked something she'd wanted to know for a long time.

'Has there ever been someone important in your life?'

She judged him to be about twenty-eight. Surely, he'd been in love at some time. In fact, most men his age were married.

'Yes,' he said, quietly. 'But that was a long time ago, now. In my line of work, it's for the best I'm no longer in a relationship.'

His words were shards in her heart. What was *she* then? Nothing. What were the kisses they'd just shared? Nothing. What on earth did he think they were doing right this moment?

The brief spell had shattered. She pulled away from him and sprung to her feet.

'I think I should go.' Her voice was tight.

He grabbed her hand. 'I'm sorry. That sounded harsh. It's not that I don't like you, it's just—'

'No, really, I understand.' She yanked her hand free and strode to the cabin door. 'Bye, then.' She threw the words over her shoulder and ran across the stony beach, half expecting him to call her back.

He didn't.

Fighting back the tears, she exited through the small clearing in the bushes and gave out a cry.

Pavel stood grim-faced, arms crossed in front of him, his eyes challenging.

'What are you doing here?' she stammered.

'Oh, Jana. You of all people. How could you?'

Her mouth fell open, but the confusion in her brain would not allow her to speak.

Pavel shook his head. 'You can't give your affections to me, a loyal, caring friend. But you throw them at a fascist policeman.'

'Have you been following me?'

'Watching, I'd say.'

'Why?' Her voice was shrill.

He shrugged. 'Looking after you, I suppose.'

'You've been spying on me?'

'You'd know all about spying.' He cocked his head.

Her chest tightened. Did he know about her work at Prague Castle? She tried to gather her thoughts. What was happening here? Pavel had, aside from Lenka, been her best friend. She'd confided so much in him; Pavel always there with a listening ear, a comforting word. He knew her well. Too well.

'Does your fascist pig of a boyfriend know about the little Jew boy we smuggled out together?'

The venom in his voice shocked her; this couldn't be Pavel talking.

'Don't use that tone with me. And Andrej is not my boyfriend.'

'Oh, Andrej, is it? On first name terms, are we?' A mocking smile played across his small mouth.

She cringed at herself for her stupid mistake. But what was more worrying was Pavel's reference to Michal. She fought the impulse to snap back that Andrej not only knew about Michal, but had helped smuggle out two further children.

'I think we should end this conversation,' she said, nervous that Andrej would appear any moment. She moved to bypass Pavel, but he sidestepped and stood in her way.

'Is this how you treat your friends?' His eyes had turned sad.

'I'm sorry,' she said over the lump in her throat.

'Sorry for what? Using me?'

'I never used you.'

'Stop lying to yourself.' He stepped aside, waving out his arm in a weary gesture. 'Go.'

Not knowing what more to say, she sped away, her head spinning with Andrej and Pavel, kisses and rejection, dangerous secrets, children in jeopardy. What had started out as the most beautiful day that had held so much promise, had ended up in only one thing. Disaster.

24

As Jana approached the back entrance to the castle, she saw the gardener raking over the earth in the flowerbeds, careful not to disturb the red tulips and bright daffodils. He was young, his strong forearms already tanned from the spring sunshine. With the change of the season, she saw him working around the castle grounds often. He had an easy smile that sported a gap between his front teeth.

As always, he greeted her, but today, he asked her name. She told him, and thought it only polite to ask in return. He told her it was Janek.

'Have a nice day, Jana,' he called out cheerfully as she made for the entrance. The surly guard checked her bag, and a female official with sharp fingers patted her down. She went to the cloakroom where her uniform hung on a peg and got changed.

Heydrich rolled up into the front courtyard, his convertible toady driven by his chauffer. An escort car followed. Jana made a mental note of the details and continued her duties.

Half an hour later, when she was polishing a silver table lamp in one of the back offices overlooking the neat lawn, she heard a commotion. Men's shouts. She moved to the window, turning rigid at what she saw. The young gardener, Janek, was held by two SS men and Heydrich was screaming at him. Jana couldn't make out the words but she heard the viciousness in his tone. What could the young gardener possibly have done to anger Heydrich to such an extent? Janek just tended the flower beds; smiled at the staff as they came to work in the morning.

But now his face was full of hate and defiance as he glared back at Heydrich, who then turned silent, his body still as stone. The *Protektor* and the gardener stared at each other. The seconds stretched; Jana held her breath. Then, Heydrich nodded at the SS officers who hitched Janek under his arms as if to march him away. Janek raised his head and spat out a few words at Heydrich.

Heydrich's arm flung to his side, whipping out his pistol; his legs stood firm, his right arm extended, his face a mask of fury.

'No,' gasped Jana.

A gunshot pierced the air. Janek's body jerked backwards, convulsing.

She just had time to take in the SS men's surprised faces covered in Janek's blood before she screamed and collapsed to the floor. Not even an hour ago, Janek had greeted her with a smile on his young, cheerful face, and now... Bile filled her mouth. What she had just witnessed was the most horrific thing she had ever seen. Her stomach spasmed and she crawled over to the cleaning bucket and vomited till she was hollowed out.

When she had finished being sick, she lay rolled up in the corner of the room, shivering. Poor Janek. What had he done to rile that monster? Revulsion and fear coiled in her stomach. He had been working for the resistance, no doubt. And so was she.

'Had a shock, have we?' Brandt's snide voice came from the doorway. She was too weak to raise her head from the floor. The thump of his footsteps came towards her and she soon saw his black, shiny boots in front of her face.

'No one messes with our Blond Beast.' He used the term with fondness and pride.

Hating to be at his feet, Jana lifted herself to sitting. Her voice thin, she said, 'He shot him in cold blood.'

Brandt let out a cruel laugh. 'That's nothing. When we were out east, I saw him shoot a small girl. At point-blank range.' He paused for effect before he said, 'But she was a Jewess.' He shrugged.

So the rumour she'd heard was true.

Images of Lillian's daughters sprung into her mind, goosebumps crawling over her skin.

'You'd better pull yourself together, *Fräulein*.' He shoved her knee with his boot. 'And get on with your work.'

With that, he stomped out the room.

Jana stayed where she was for a long time, her body and mind gripped with inertia as she tried to process what she had just seen. Eventually, she forced herself to her feet. How she detested Heydrich. That vile, evil monster. Anger and hate surged through her. The man wasn't human. He didn't deserve to walk on this earth. She wished with all her heart that he was dead.

* * *

In bed that night, Jana relived the invasion of Prague by the Germans.

It happened on the morning of 15 March 1939. She had woken in the middle of the night to low voices coming from the living room and had switched on her bedside light, squinting at her alarm clock. It was 4.35 a.m. Dread settling in her stomach, she climbed out of bed and padded in woollen socks from her bedroom. Mama and Papa were huddled around the radio, listening to their president addressing the nation in solemn tones.

'What's going on?' Jana had asked.

'The Germans are coming,' said Papa, his voice hollow. 'Hitler has declared that if we don't surrender, he will wreak devastation across the land.'

Mama, her face pallid, reached out an arm to Jana and draped it around her shoulders. 'The Wehrmacht will cross our border at six o'clock this morning.'

'There's a snow storm blowing in. Let's hope that stops them in their tracks,' Papa said, adjusting the dial as the radio crackled. Jana stared at the radio in shock. Although the Czechs had been living with this threat for some time now, everyone had hoped the government could come to some agreement with Hitler. But the disaster they'd all feared had become reality.

The sky had been hazy, the clouds grey and low, as a light snow drifted across the city. And Jana and her parents had joined the Czech citizens lining Wenceslas Square.

They stood next to an anxious-faced woman, a shawl draped over her head. Beside her, a workman in shabby clothes shouted defiantly to those surrounding him, his words met by cheers.

It was just past ten thirty when the ground vibrated beneath their feet and silence fell on the crowd.

A roar of motor cycles, a rumble of tanks. And the thump, thump of heavy boots.

The Wehrmacht arrived, soldiers in grey-green uniforms marching five abreast, their rifles high on their shoulders. Tanks rolled in, leaving their tracks in the snow. Some people hissed and jeered at the Germans; others looked on in horrified silence. A lone male voice began to sing the Czech national anthem and was quickly joined in an uprising of emotional singing. Then trucks arrived bearing loudspeakers warning that any resistance would be met by brutal repercussions. The crowds quietened as the Germans set up machine guns pointing at the gathered citizens and planes flew low over the city. The hopelessness and despair that Jana felt was reflected on her parents' faces.

They stood in the frigid air watching events unfold. Mama coughed into her scarf and Jana worried she was developing yet another chest cold. Ever since she had contracted tuberculosis in her nursing days during the Great War, she had been prone to illness.

'Come, Mama, let's go home and have some hot soup,' she said coaxingly.

But Mama shook her head, saying she needed to witness what was happening to believe it.

Within hours, the city was splashed in blood-red swastika flags, adorning buildings, statues and historic monuments.

And early evening, Hitler himself stood at the open window on the first floor of Prague Castle, looking down in triumph.

A few days later, Himmler paraded around the city with a tall, imposing figure, rumoured to be his new protégé; that was when Prague's citizens first laid eyes on Reinhard Heydrich.

At home, Mama developed a high fever. She was admitted to hospital and diagnosed with pneumonia. One week after the Nazis had entered Prague, Jana's mother passed away.

25

The Wehrmacht soldier waved the Red Cross truck past the check point and Jana caught her first glimpse of Terezin. Lenka had explained in her last letter some of the set up there:

The compound is made up of the small fortress which is the prison, surrounded by a moat, and the large fortress where I live, which is laid out like a small town. I've been moved from a maternity area and now live in a three-storey barrack named Dresden, which I share with other mothers and their children. There are a lot of us here, so no chance to get lonely. We take it in turns to look after each other's children when one of us has work duty, and have designed a rota. I've been assigned to the laundry which is hard work, but I'm rewarded with a meal at the end of the day.

The men live in Sudeten Barracks and are assigned the heavy physical work such as building a railway. There is a silly rumour going around that a group has been tasked with building a swimming pool for the SS families, using just spoons to dig out the earth. Ha! As if...

> *I'm one of the few here not wearing a yellow star and was worried at first that I'd be treated by the other woman as an outsider, but the contrary is true. I have encountered only kindness and companionship.*
>
> *I feel sorry for the elderly and sick amongst us who are unable to work. Their rations of food are smaller, but they don't complain as the Germans have explained they need more food for our children. It is war time after all and we all have to make sacrifices.*
>
> *There is a cellar in Dresden Barracks and we are allowed to use one of the rooms for community meetings. These are the best times of the day. We have many musicians amongst us and we have started a small choir. We also hold literary evenings, not only to discuss published works, but also to read aloud our own poetry and stories. Some of the readings are rather sad, but life is like that sometimes, isn't it?*
>
> *The last few weeks it got a bit crowded here, but some of the women have left to be rehoused in a fine new development (we don't know where). Trains have begun to leave regularly to take men, women and children to their new home. I wonder if I will be sent too. With my precious little one, of course.*

Jana was finally within the Terezin compound. She sat on the front seat of the Red Cross truck, between Miss Novak who was driving and Dasha who had also been allowed to assist with the delivery of the donations. Miss Novak had given both girls Red Cross caps to wear with their white, short-sleeved dresses.

The soldier had given Miss Novak instructions to follow the police cyclist to the Magdeburg Barracks, the building that housed the Jewish Council of Elders. This was where they were to deposit their donations and were told to return to the check point within half an hour.

They drove down a street lined with three-storey barrack-style buildings, the façades faded and peeling, the curtainless windows all flung open to catch the spring air. The housing very much fitted Lenka's description, but what surprised Jana were the lack of crowds; there were only a few pedestrians along the pavements, and although their clothes were shabby, and their faces thin, they looked not so different to the citizens who walked the streets of Prague.

The truck passed a grocery shop and a bakery, both displaying wares, although Jana noticed that none of the citizens were carrying bread or shopping bags. A group of smiling children waved as they passed; the girls with neatly plaited hair wore faded but pretty dresses. She was surprised when she saw a building with a sign: *Post Office*. The words on the wooden placard glistened as if freshly painted.

The police cyclist pulled up outside a small, stone building and Miss Novak parked the truck outside. They all climbed out and waited on the front doorstep as the policeman thumped on the door, shouting, 'Delivery!'

A man with a black beard and wire spectacles opened up and greeted the women with a bow of the head. 'Welcome. My name is Samuel.'

Samuel called behind him and two teenage boys appeared.

'My sons will help carry the things inside.'

Watched by the policeman, Jana, Miss Novak and Dasha were aided by the boys to unload the boxes from the truck. Samuel ushered them inside, directing the clothes cartons upstairs and the book cartons to a room on the ground floor. Miss Novak and Dasha went upstairs with the boys and Jana stayed with Samuel.

'I hope these will be of use,' she said as she opened a carton and pulled out a couple of books to show him.

Samuel smiled but his eyes were moist with tears. 'You don't know how much these books will mean to us. I'm very grateful—'

'How long will this take?' The policeman poked his head round the door. 'My cigarette break is overdue already.'

'I need to make a quick check that no banned books have inadvertently found their way in here,' said Samuel. 'Give me twenty minutes. Why not take your break and we'll be finished here by the time you're back?'

The policeman eyed Samuel, huffed and marched out.

Jana lowered her voice. 'Samuel, can you help me? I'm trying to find a friend of mine, Lenka. She's in the Dresden Barracks. Is that far from here? I'm desperate to see her.' The words tumbled out.

His eyes widened. 'They won't allow you in there.'

Jana gulped. 'I could sneak out now. I have twenty minutes. Please help me.'

Samuel shook his head.

'Please.' She grabbed his thin arm. 'I don't want to get you into trouble. If anyone asks for me, say I was unwell and went to the lavatory.'

'We do have one at the back of the building,' he said, slowly. 'The window opens onto the street—'

'Show me.' Jana's adrenaline was pumping now; she couldn't waste this opportunity. Who knew when she would be this close to Lenka again?

Samuel set his jaw, his expression resolute. 'Come,' he said. 'It would be good if an outsider saw this place. Many of us paid to come here.'

'Paid?' said Jana, bewildered.

'Many artists, from all over the country, were led to believe this was some kind of cultural haven. I'm a pianist... But enough of that, there isn't time.'

Samuel led Jana to the lavatory at the back of the house. As she clambered onto the toilet seat and pulled open the window, Samuel gave her hurried directions to Dresden Barracks. 'Be back in twenty minutes,' he urged.

'I will,' she said, checking her watch.

'You'll stand out in that,' He pointed at the white cap with the Red Cross insignia.

She whipped it off, stuffed it into her dress pocket and jumped into the street.

She was instantly enveloped in a scene very different to the one that had met her on arrival in Terezin. This street was packed with people – sitting on the kerb, pulling carts, shoving along children whose clothes were no more than rags. Tired, gaunt faces glanced at her pristine white dress and clean, neatly rolled hair as she pushed her way through the masses.

Hurrying across a junction, she glanced down a side street. There was a barrier at the end and an armed soldier was turning people away. She jolted with realisation. The side street led into the road they had used to enter Terezin. It had been cordoned off, keeping citizens out of the peaceful model street with its shops and post office, all staged to give visitors a positive impression. But she was now behind the stage, witnessing the reality. This place was not the fine town being touted by the Nazis. It was a concentration camp.

She lost her bearings and stopped to ask directions before she arrived at a long, low, stone building. In the courtyard in front, women were sitting on the ground; there were no benches. They were watching a group of toddlers playing, screaming or crying.

Jana approached an older woman with frizzy, grey hair who looked up her curiously.

'You certainly look new here,' the woman said.

'Please can you help me? I'm looking for my friend, Lenka. I don't have much time. She's just had a baby.'

The woman gave a sardonic laugh. 'Do you know how many there are of us here? Who are you anyway?'

'I know a Lenka,' came a thin voice. 'The storyteller.'

Jana looked at the young woman bouncing a baby on her knees.

'She's inside looking after a sick child.'

Aware of time ticking, Jana rushed through the barrack's open door and came to an abrupt halt. Entering from the bright sunshine into the darkness, she was blinded, black zig-zag lines dancing before her eyes. A fetid smell assaulted her, and her brain tried to identify the mixed odours: stale air, sweat, urine, vomit and strangely, disinfectant that made her eyes sting. Her vision came into focus, and she saw a young woman on her knees, scrubbing ferociously at the wooden floor. Strands of hair had come loose from her bun and hung damp across her shrunken cheeks.

The woman looked up at Jana and in an apologetic voice, muttered, 'He's been sick again. I'm sorry. I'll clean it up quickly. Sorry.'

She continued to scrub. Beside her on a bottom bunk bed, a scarlet-cheeked baby screamed.

Jana took in the scene around her, her throat closing. Rows of narrow bunk beds stretched to the ceiling. Items of clothing, both adults' and children's, and stained, threadbare towels lay strewn on each bed. Seeing the several make-shift pillows of rolled up clothes, Jana realised that people were sharing beds with more than one person.

Jana kneeled down to the woman and put a hand on her bony arm. The woman flinched at the touch and her eyelids flickered wildly.

'Don't be afraid,' said Jana, her voice hoarse with emotion. 'I'm just looking for my friend, Lenka.'

But the woman looked at her blankly and continued scrubbing and apologising. Jana's heart wrenched as she realised there was nothing she could do for the woman. And the clock was ticking. She hurried on down the narrow aisle that ran alongside the rows of beds, mostly empty. The women were most likely at work, and some of the children, the younger ones were outside. But where were the older children? Working too?

'Lenka,' she called, in a raised whisper.

A woman stirred on one of the bunks. A baby whimpered.

Jana called louder. 'Lenka! It's me, Jana. Are you here?'

'Jana? Is that you?'

Her heart stopped. She peered to her left and in the shadows, she saw a figure seated on a bottom bunk, cradling something.

'Lenka,' she cried, and squeezed herself between the beds to reach her friend. Lenka rose, a swaddled baby in her arms, staring at her, her mouth open in disbelief. Jana choked back a gasp. The last time she'd seen Lenka, she'd been pregnant and rosy cheeked; now she hardly recognised the sunken-faced woman with sallow skin, her limp hair tucked behind her ears.

Jana leaned across the baby and wrapped her arms around Lenka's shoulders.

'How? Why...' Lenka stammered.

Jana quickly explained about the Red Cross delivery and that she'd sneaked away to find her. She looked down at the fretful baby in Lenka's arms.

'Is that Alena?'

Lenka shook her head. 'It's a friend's baby. He's sick and I'm taking care of him till my shift at the laundry starts. That's Alena.' She nodded to the sleeping child on the bed. Alena lay on her back, her little head tilted towards them, her arms flung out, tiny fists on each side of her head. She wore a nappy and short-sleeved top. Jana noted the lack of baby rolls on her arms and legs. She ran a gentle finger along Alena's cheek. The feel of the baby's skin sent a quiver of love and longing through her.

'She's beautiful,' she whispered.

'She needs more milk.' Lenka sighed. 'Mine dried up after only a week. We get milk powder, but it's rationed. Some of the women here give favours to the policemen for extra rations. I haven't done that yet, but...'

Jana's eyes welled up. 'What can I do for you? There must be something.'

'Just seeing you is more than something. And I can't wait to look at the books you've brought. I've started a sort of book club here.'

The baby in her arms had stilled and Lenka placed him next to Alena on the bed. She took Jana's hands and fixed her with intense eyes.

'Please, make me a promise.'

'Anything.'

'If anything happens to me, please try and get her back to Ivan. And watch over her. Please.'

'Nothing will happen to you.' Jana fought to control the panic in her voice. 'Stay strong. You must stay strong.'

'I will. But just in case. Listen, I'm lucky to be here. I was destined to be imprisoned in the Small Fortress.' She shuddered. 'The Gestapo are doing terrible things to the inmates. We hear the screams. And rifle shots.'

Jana thought of Andrej's intervention, which had helped

Lenka to be moved out of the Small Fortress, and she swallowed hard.

'Alena is here because of my crime,' Lenka continued. 'But she's not Jewish like most of the people here; their future looks bleak. But if I died—'

'No!' gasped Jana.

'Listen. If I died, what reason would there be to keep her here? You and Ivan could persuade the authorities to release her. She would not have a mother, but she would have you, her godmother.'

Jana bit her lip and nodded solemnly.

Heartbeats passed as they held each other's hands, their faces wet with tears Jana's gaze fell on her watch and she jolted. Twenty minutes was up and she still had to get back to Samuel at the Magdeburg barracks. Even if she ran, it would take five minutes.

The wrench as she left Lenka behind was a physical pain in her chest. She fled from the woman's barracks, gulping the fresh air and swiping tears from her face.

Running past the women and children in the courtyard outside, she raced back in the direction she came. People looked at her, and when she saw two policemen up ahead, she was forced to slow her pace. She mingled with a group of women, and dropped to one knee to adjust the strap on her shoe, avoiding the glance of the police passing by. Then she bolted onwards.

Heart thudding and sweat pouring down the back of her neck, she came to the open window of the lavatory, and tried to clamber up inside. But here she had no toilet to stand on.

As she struggled, a young man, handsome with wavy, dark hair sidled up to her.

'I have no idea who you are or what you are doing, but you

look as if you need help.' He stretched out his arms and cupped his hands, his fingers tightly linked. 'Here, let me give you a leg up.'

Breathing hard, she pressed one foot into his hands and he heaved her up to the windowsill. She scrambled across and dropped down on the other side but when she turned to thank the man, he was gone.

She heard voices in the hall outside the closed lavatory door: Samuel's conciliatory tones, the policeman's gruff ones. She turned on the tap and let water run into the discoloured, cracked sink.

Thump. Thump. Thump. The door shook.

'Are you in there? Show yourself immediately!' bellowed the policeman.

She slipped her hands under the brown water and turned off the tap. There was no towel, so she shook her hands and opened the door. Wiping a damp hand across her forehead, and slumping her shoulders, she spoke in a weary voice.

'I don't know what's come over me. I feel quite poorly.'

The policeman eyed her up and down, whilst Samuel stood behind him and gave Jana a wink over his shoulder.

'Then you'd better get yourself back to the truck. You're overdue anyway,' he barked.

Miss Novak and Dasha stood outside with concerned expressions.

'Are you all right, dear?' asked Miss Novak. 'Samuel told us you were quite unwell.'

Jana assured her she was feeling better and the three of them climbed aboard the truck.

As they drove off, Samuel stood on the doorstep watching. Jana gave him a wave and hoped her small smile signalled her gratitude for his help. His reciprocal nod told her he did.

* * *

That evening, over a bowl of turnip soup, Jana told her father about her visit to Terezin.

'You saw Lenka?' Papa stopped eating, his spoon halfway between his bowl and his mouth. He put the spoon back in the bowl. 'My, goodness. How did you manage that?'

Papa looked horrified as she relayed the story. She had thought twice about telling him about her antics, but her need to share her experience in the camp was overwhelming. She and Papa were already involved in anti-Nazi activities together anyway.

When Papa had recovered from the shock, he asked, 'How was she?'

'She looked so different. She was...' Jana put down her spoon, her appetite gone, and told him about the few precious moments she had spent with her friend and her promise to look after Alena if anything happened to her.

'Papa, have you heard anything about the transport of Jews and other so-called enemies of the Reich?'

'You mean transport to new housing areas? Yes, I have.'

'No. I mean transport out of Terezin. Thousands at a time. The place is so crowded and filling up all the time. The Nazis are sending people on somewhere else.'

'How do you know all this?' He frowned, watching her closely.

'I overheard something at the castle.' She shrugged with one shoulder to make light of how she had gleaned the news.

Papa heaved a sigh. 'Oh, Jana, I'm not totally naïve. I've suspected for some time you're doing more than cleaning at the castle.'

Jana waited for the admonishments and the warnings, but

was surprised when her father's eyes softened and filled with tears.

'I'm so proud of you, darling. And your mother would be too, if she was still with us. You have a big, courageous heart, just like she did. I'm proud and terrified at the same time.'

Jana's fingers fluttered to her mother's locket and slid it gently from side to side along its chain; a habit that gave her comfort and connection to her mother. Papa's words made her heart swell. His approval and love for her gave her strength; how she loved him.

Both of them were choked with tears.

'If one of us goes down, we all go down. The whole family, and the children,' Papa murmured, his voice hoarse.

'I know,' she said. Then she squared her shoulders and took a deep breath. 'But we won't. We mustn't let fear stop us from fighting back, Papa. If we stay passive, then we give up on hope.'

26

Jana dragged herself out of bed and trudged to the bathroom, exhausted after another sleepless night. Her thoughts had not let her rest, as if poking her with a stick each time sleep began to lure her in. At first, it was the images of Lenka in the foul-smelling, airless barracks, rammed full with women and children, weak, hungry and desperate. Then just before dawn, it was Andrej that slipped into her mind, with his fingers on her cheeks and his feather-light kisses on her neck. The memory of the two of them tucked away on the derelict steamboat filled her with romantic longing and she ached to feel his touch again. But then his words came back to her: '...it's for the best I'm no longer in a relationship.'

Andrej obviously didn't acknowledge a romance between them. Then what was she to him? Why did he look at her the way he did, kiss her with a passion that left her weak and breathless? Yes, he'd spoken of danger and risk and all that stuff, but maybe that was all just an excuse. He'd kissed her a couple of times and had lost interest. And at that thought, she'd lost all hope of falling asleep and got out of bed.

Now she looked at her small, tired eyes and white skin in the mirror. Splashing her face with cold water several times, she decided to go to Prague Castle earlier than planned, visit the St Vitus church and try to find some peace of mind, get her thoughts in order.

But as she sat beneath the vast, vaulted church ceiling, there was no peace to be found, just an onslaught of images and questions triggered by her visit to Terezin. It was clear that the Nazis' portrayal of Terezin was a complete deception, another piece of propaganda to fool the Czech citizens, the Jewish community and even the outside world. Theresienstadt, as the Germans called it, was being proclaimed as a self-regulating town, with good living conditions, perfect for retirement with a relaxing environment. Samuel had said cultural members of society such as artists, writers and musicians had even paid to go there, believing they would be living in some budding, creative milieu.

The church bells rang, the sound reverberating around her and through her. It was time to start work.

As she made her way to Salm Palace, she wondered how she could let people know about the reality she'd seen without being accused of spreading anti-Nazi propaganda. Would anyone believe her? A heavy weight lay in the pit of her stomach. She was just a bookshop girl. How could she possibly climb the mountain of obstacles that stood in the way?

One step at a time, she told herself.

This morning, her job was to keep an eye on that murdering, tyrant, Heydrich.

As she walked from the shadow of the church into the May sunshine, a shiver went down the back of her neck.

* * *

A light mist drifted through the streets of Prague as, just before seven o'clock, one Wednesday morning in May, Jana climbed her way to the castle. The air was still cool, like the past few days, but she knew that by midday, the sun would burn through the haze and the city would glimmer under a cloudless sky.

When she passed the guards, showing her staff pass made her uneasy. The feeling reminded her of the moments before an examination at school. As she crossed in front of the mist-shrouded St Vitus Basilica, and a black cloud of crows took flight from the turrets, the feeling intensified; the craw and flap of the birds jangled her nerves and her stomach knotted.

It's no wonder, she reasoned with herself, that she was uneasy entering the offices of the Nazi high command. But there was something else she couldn't identify.

It was the usual routine: show her bag to the security guard, change into her black uniform in the downstairs cloakroom, report to Miss Jezek and collect her cleaning materials. She started work at the end of the corridor, working her way towards Heydrich's office. All the while, Miss Jezek flitted around, locking each room after Jana had finished.

It was nearly eight thirty when she reached Heydrich's office. She opened the window and looked out. The mist had cleared and the blue of the sky was deepening, the birds chirping loudly. Automatically, she glanced down at the courtyard below, but the Mercedes-Benz had not yet arrived. In this weather, Heydrich would arrive with the roof of the Mercedes down. Would he drive himself today or would the chauffer be at the steering wheel?

'Waiting for our Blond Beast?'

She winced at the voice and with an inward sigh, turned to face Brandt's smarmy expression.

'I'm here to clean,' she said, turning from him and wiping down the windowsill.

He continued to talk to the back of her head, undeterred. 'I doubt our *Protektor* will be on time after his late night. Yesterday evening was the grand concert at Wallenstein Palace, the opening of the Prague musical festival.'

The upcoming event had been widely heralded in the press and Jana recalled Heydrich telling her about it when he'd visited the bookshop; he'd been so proud that his deceased father's composition was to be a highlight. She imagined Heydrich's preening face as he soaked in the atmosphere of the imposing venue, the adulation of the audience, his cool, pristine wife at his side, glorifying in her husband's success and power. Then the image of the gardener, Janek, facing Heydrich's pistol rose up and her stomach clenched.

Thankfully, Brandt's footsteps retreated, and she was spared from further conversation. It was nearing the end of her shift, nine o'clock, and there was still no sign of Heydrich, which was actually a relief. Since she'd witnessed the terrible murder of the gardener, her fear of Heydrich had increased tenfold.

Rolling the carpet sweeper to the end of the hallway, she noticed a scuff mark on the skirting board, so she pulled a cloth from her apron pocket and kneeled down to wipe the mark.

A thud of feet and two polished boots appeared under her nose, the leather so shiny, she saw the reflection of her own face. She craned her neck.

Brandt. Again. Why wouldn't he just leave her alone?

He smirked as he looked down at her.

'What a lovely sight. You on your knees before me. I'm sure to think about that when I lie in bed tonight.'

Revulsion spiralled through her, sending bitter bile onto her tongue. She sprung up, her head whirring with retorts. How dare he speak to her like that, uttering disgusting inuendoes. She gave him a withering glance.

'And I am sure no thoughts of you will cross my mind. They never do.'

She lifted the carpet sweeper in one hand, and her cleaning things in the other, and with an exaggerated sniff, she marched away, her chin held high. His laugh followed her down the hall. Her hands trembled as she changed back into her summer dress and hung her uniform in the locker. Brandt had unnerved her further and her courage dipped. He was watching her, no doubt longing for an excuse to report her to Heydrich. But there was no proof of her doing anything wrong. All she did was observe. The notes she made were hidden inside a bookmark, and what was the chance of that being discovered?

Walking back to the bookshop, she took off her jacket and placed it over her arm, the sun warm on her face. Her thoughts turned to Andrej. She longed to talk to him about everything; it was so unfair that the man she had feelings for was posing as a fascist policeman and for both of their safety, they had to keep apart. What other resistance activities was he involved in? His actions were far more dangerous than hers. If he was discovered as a spy, the Gestapo would torture him to find out what he knew. They would break him utterly. Then they would execute him.

Jana halted, putting an arm against a shop window for support. Her head spun. *Andrej. Not Andrej. Breathe, breathe.* She saw him in her mind's eye strolling down to the river, his long legs taking easy strides, his shirt sleeves rolled up, and his straw boater on his head set at a jaunty angle. Shaking the thoughts from her head, she stumbled on to the bookshop where she rushed to the kitchen, desperate for a glass of water.

Once she had calmed, she went to the cash desk, retrieved

the bookmark and slipped out the piece of paper. Today, she simply drew a dash to indicate that Heydrich had not shown up during her shift, and slipped the bookmark back between the pages of *The Gardener's Diary*. Then she opened the shop door, ready for the day's business.

About an hour later, Karolina burst through the shop door with such fury that the three customers and Jana jumped and stared at her.

'Something is going on!' she panted, her hat clutched in her hand, her fair hair hanging lose from its roll.

'Whatever is the matter?' said Jana.

'All hell has broken loose in Wenceslas Square. A mass of police and soldiers are storming the streets. There's shooting and people are screaming!' She leaned over, hands on her thighs, gulping deep breaths.

'Oh, God. Papa is in town. Stay inside the shop, Karolina, and lock the door.' She nodded at the customers. 'You too if you wish. I'm going to find my father.'

Jana was halfway through the door as Karolina called, 'Be careful. It's crazy out there.'

The sound of gunshots echoed down nearby streets as Jana fought her way against the oncoming stream of people and was buffeted from side to side. She tried to ask a woman what was going on but the woman rushed past her, pulling a child behind her. A bulky man knocked against her shoulder and yelled, 'You're going the wrong way, girl. The Germans are on the war path and arresting everyone in sight.'

Jana bit her lip and pushed on. Papa had planned to visit his friend, a shoemaker who had a small shop just off Wenceslas Square. She hoped he hadn't already left the shop and was taking refuge instead. But as she stepped around the corner, she realised her mistake. Wenceslas Square was writhing in the grey-green uniforms of the Wehrmacht, rushing in all directions, waving their pistols. Czech police jumped and yelled, their faces nervous as the panic-stricken citizens fled, trampling down the side streets, shoving each other and screaming for loved ones.

The Wehrmacht soldiers appeared uncoordinated; citizens were being haphazardly rounded up and let go again. The police made some frantic arrests, grabbing anyone that passed by. There was no way she could cross the square; she could wind her way around the back of it to the shoe shop, but as she battled against the onslaught of people, barely able to breathe amongst the throng, she knew it was the wrong thing to do. Papa could be already back at the bookshop now and finding her not there, might even set out to search for her. The Old Town was in pandemonium and the most sensible thing she could so was return to the bookshop.

She turned back and was shoved along with the crowd. Words tossed in the air, hasty questions as to what was going on, but no one seemed to know. Elbows jarred at her; feet trod on hers. There was a sudden push from behind, and the people in front had come to a halt. But the pressure of the crowd behind her gathered momentum.

Jana's face was forced up against the back of a man in front. Screams filled the air. Jana's heart raced as she tried to suck in breath; fibres of the man's jacket filled her throat and nostrils.

She couldn't breathe. She couldn't breathe.

Nausea overwhelmed her. The weight against her back grew and grew, pain spiked in her ribs and her head spun. The noise around her was fading. No, she mustn't faint.

Abruptly, the man she was pressed against moved forward, and Jana teetered, her feet struggling to gain purchase. She was falling.

'I've got you,' said a firm voice, as she was yanked up by her elbow.

'Keep moving.' A strong arm hauled her along. As Jana's vision cleared, she looked at the middle aged, well-built woman by her side, her jaw set, her cheeks crimson.

The crowd dispersed slightly.

'Are you all right now?' asked the woman.

'Yes, I can't thank you enough. You may have saved my life.'

'I have a daughter your age. Now get off home.' The woman took off with firm strides.

Jana arrived at the shop, bathed in sweat, her yellow dress smeared with dirt. Karolina ran to unlock the door and let her in, relief flushing across her face.

'You were right, it's crazy out there,' said Jana, her throat parched.

The three customers looked startled as they took in Jana's appearance, one woman jumping out of the armchair and guiding her to sit down, whilst Karolina fetched a glass of water.

They all stayed huddled at the back of the shop, afraid to go out until the street quietened. Jana stared through the shop window, willing the arrival of her father.

After an agonising two hours, he appeared and she ran into his open arms, sobbing with relief.

* * *

Late afternoon, upstairs in their apartment, Papa tuned into the Prague radio station, eager to make sense of the day's chaotic events. The answer finally came in a news broadcast: there had been an assassination attempt on Reinhard Heydrich, *Reichsprotektor* of Bohemia and Moravia. He had been attacked in his open-top Mercedes on his way to work and was now in Bulovka hospital undergoing emergency surgery. An intensive search was underway for the two men responsible for this heinous crime.

A conflict of emotions tumulted through her: awe at the men who had attempted to put an end to The Butcher of Prague, satisfaction that revenge on this monster had been taken, and fear at what would happen next.

Jana and her father stared at each other, stunned.

'I wonder how serious his injuries are.' Jana's voice was a whisper. 'Will he die?'

'And what happens if he does?' Papa added.

The broadcaster went on, his tone grave: the city was now under curfew as house-to-house searches were being made for the culprits and their accomplices. Anyone found aiding the atrocious criminals would be punished in the most severest of terms. Citizens, however, who came forward with evidence as to the whereabouts to the perpetrators would be richly rewarded. A state of emergency had been declared for the whole country.

Papa's eyes searched her face. She could see his raw fear.

'Do you know anything about this?'

Her heart thumped loudly into the silence of the room. She shook her head slowly. 'No. No, I don't.'

Or did she?

They sat glued to the radio set till the light outside faded and a half-moon rose over Prague Castle.

Jana and Papa talked back and forth after each new announcement.

'This will give our resistance a surge, give the Czechs hope that we can fight back.' Jana was pumped with adrenaline now that the initial shock had subsided. 'It shows the Nazis that they can't do what they like to us.'

'It will certainly shake them up,' Papa said. 'And gives the world a sign we are still here, still fighting back. But an attack on one of the highest-ranking SS officers in the Reich will cause repercussions. The Nazis will come down hard on anyone with the slightest involvement.'

'I hope the two men, whoever they are, get away. How courageous they were.' She could hear the euphoria in her own voice.

Papa remained silent, his brows furrowed. A tendril of fear slipped into the back of her mind, but she pushed it away and continued to listen to the broadcast.

The details of the attack came out over the course of the evening, so by the time Jana went to bed, she had a clear idea of the sequence of events. She lay in the darkness, her eyes closed, but her mind was buzzing. She put the story of the day's events together and let the images play out in her mind.

Heydrich had breakfasted later that morning, no doubt chatting with his wife, Lina, about the previous evening's concert. He would have sipped his real coffee with a self-satisfied air, recalling how all eyes had been on him as the most celebrated musicians had played his father's composition. The magnificent Wallenstein Palace had been packed with the Nazi elite, all witnesses to Heydrich's power and success. He was the rising star in the German Reich. After breakfast, he'd have checked his appearance in the hall mirror, put on his SS cap, the silver skull emblem gleaming, and gone outside to where his chauffer was waiting for him. It was ten o'clock.

Jana didn't know what Heydrich's house looked like, but had heard it was a grand building that had been formerly the home of a Jewish merchant. She imagined the Mercedes roaring down a sweeping drive, Heydrich in the passenger seat, self-assured, his cruel brain scheming terrible things.

Heydrich took the same route each morning, passing through the suburb of Kobylisy. A hairpin bend in the road always forced the car to slow down, and that morning, two men had sprung out, ambushing the car. At that moment, a tram stopped on the opposite side of the road, witnessing and later reporting events. Jana pictured a man aiming his Sten submachine gun at Heydrich, but unbelievably, it jammed. Heydrich had stood up in outrage, and drawing his pistol, fired at his attacker, but the second man threw an anti-tank grenade and the Mercedes convertible exploded. The impact had shattered the windows of the nearby tram and screaming passengers fled the vehicle, whilst in the chaos, the two attackers escaped.

Jana sat up in bed and stared into the darkness, imagining Heydrich's broken and bleeding body. She then thought of the gardener he had shot and she was pleased. Pleased that Heydrich had got what he deserved. She thought of Michal and the sisters, Lenka and the woman sobbing at the execution wall. She thought of the deception of Terezin and Heydrich's talk of transports and solutions. And if Heydrich died? Something cold and hard formed in her chest. If he died? She would be pleased.

Finally, hours later, her adrenaline began to subside, and the fear that had been gnawing at her would not be silenced. Would she be implicated in any way? Had her spying and coded messages aided the attack? After all, she'd noted Heydrich's arrival at the office for months. At first, she'd assumed the resistance wanted to keep a general surveillance on the movements of the SS officers. But had another idea come to her as she'd watched the open-top convertible pull up each day? No, she'd never dreamed that anyone would actually dare an assassination attempt. It had been an unrealistic daydream that Prague could rid itself of the evil man.

She lay waiting for dawn, waiting for the first news broadcast. Was Heydrich still alive? His haughty face as he glanced around the bookshop and had set eyes on Papa's puppets sprung to mind. She hated the man; he didn't deserve to live.

It wasn't yet light when she heard a motor car rumble down the street. Car headlights swept her window. The motor stopped. Down below, heavy feet trampled the cobblestones. She held her breath. Moments later, there was shouting and banging on the front door.

And she knew.

They had come for her.

27

A shove in the back and Jana found herself in a small cell packed with women, some shouting through the open bars as the police guard locked up.

'Why are we here?'

'I've done nothing wrong!'

'I'm thirsty.'

'I need the toilet.'

It took her some moments to take in the scene: the dishevelled, hastily dressed women who'd had no time to brush their hair; pale, drawn faces; red, swollen eyes and each expression etched with fear. She was surrounded by about thirty women, some leaned against the wall, others sat on the cold, stone floor.

Jana pulled her coat tightly around her; she'd been allowed two minutes to get dressed and had grabbed the blouse and skirt draped over the back of her bedroom chair. There had been no time for stockings and her bare legs prickled with goosebumps.

Looking around her, she noticed a young girl that she recognised from the castle staff. There was a brief acknowledgement between them but then the girl looked away. Jana was considering approaching the girl when someone else caught her eye. She gasped. Huddled against the back wall, her long hair unpinned and wild around her narrow shoulders, was Miss Jezek. Jana's manager, usually immaculate and confident, hair swept back in a severe bun, a slash of red lipstick on her lips, was barely recognisable.

Jana edged her way past the other women to get to her.

'Miss Jezek. What are you doing here?' It was a stupid thing to say – what were any of them doing there? – but somehow, it was more surprising to see her superior looking so vulnerable and locked up.

'It's an outrage,' said Miss Jezek, pursing her lips. 'Me, of all people: a loyal employee of the castle.'

Jana had always thought her a Nazi sympathiser which added to her surprise to see her there. But obviously, no one at the castle was above suspicion.

'As if I would have anything to do with an attack on our *Protektor*.'

'Have you heard any news on his condition?' asked Jana.

Miss Jezek shook her head.

'I hope he's dead,' a voice hissed. Jana turned to see an elderly woman with several missing teeth. 'He's responsible for the death of my nephew.'

Another voice piped up. 'We're all in enough trouble as it is. God knows what will happen if he dies...'

The clank of steel silenced everyone for a brief moment. Two guards ushered three more women into the cell.

'We soon won't have enough room here,' said one guard to the other.

'They'll have to start sending them to Petschek Palace,' came the reply.

At this, women started shouting again. Jana shivered.

Despite its name, Petschek Palace was not a welcoming destination. The four-storey, grey, stone building was the headquarters of the Gestapo. If Jana was sent there and interrogated about her work at the castle, her bookshop...

Her legs giving way, she slid down against the back wall onto the floor. She caught Miss Jezek watching her.

The women in the cell had grown tired, and the noise of chatter had been replaced by the sounds of people: a shuffle, a sigh, a cough. Jana thought of Papa and his face, frozen in horror as she was arrested; he must be frantic with worry. She wondered where Andrej was. She'd looked for him when she'd been herded inside the police station but there had been no sign of him. Maybe he wasn't in the building but out with the force rounding up suspects. How did it feel to play the fascist and arrest his fellow Czechs when he was really on their side? How difficult it must be to try to help without arousing suspicion. And how frustrating to witness the fate of those he was unable to help.

Her thoughts spun further. What if Andrej himself was under suspicion? Being interrogated? She let out a cry. But no one looked at her; each woman was battling her own nightmare. Overwhelmed with exhaustion, she slumped forward, laying her throbbing head on her drawn-up knees.

Hours dragged by until heavy footsteps outside the cell made everyone look up, nervous with anticipation. This time, there were three armed policemen.

The tall, lean one stepped forward, clipboard in hand, and raised his voice.

'Step forward if you hear your name.'

As each name was called, a woman stumbled up to the bars. Jana's chest tightened. Were these the ones to be sent to Petschek Place? To be handed over to the dreaded Gestapo?

The sound of her name when it came was almost no surprise. Her life had taken on some dangerous journey of which she had no control and all she could do was watch herself teeter on the edge of catastrophe. Her name was repeated, louder this time. She staggered forwards.

Eight of them were led from the cell and escorted from the basement to the ground floor. The woman in front of Jana lurched sideways, and as Jana held up a steadying hand, a gruff voice said, 'No touching.'

Jana looked up to find a pistol pointing at her.

They gathered in a small group and waited for further instructions. Looking through the front doors, Jana saw black cars lined up, waiting to take them away to interrogation. Her mouth was too dry to swallow. She glanced wildly around for Andrej.

He wasn't there.

Names were called again. Five women were shunted outside to the waiting cars.

Every muscle in her body was taut, her chest so tight, she could hardly breathe. Her fingers jittered around her locket. She and the remaining two women glanced at each other's frightened faces. A voice bellowed her name. Her head jerked up and a policeman beckoned her to a closed office door. He knocked and opened it, announcing her, and signalled she should enter. Her legs shaking, she went into the room.

At a desk laden with files and documents sat a police officer.

It was Andrej.

28

Jana would have liked to throw herself against his chest and curl her arms around his neck. She dreamed how he would hold her tight, murmuring words of comfort and stroking her hair. But here, in the real world, a young, petite secretary stood by Andrej's side, notepad and pen in her hand. Jana stood rooted to the spot, waiting for Andrej to address her.

He nodded at the secretary who left, closing the door behind her.

'Ah, Miss Jana Hajek,' he said in a loud, formal voice. 'Please, take a seat.'

Despite his tone, his face was full of concern.

'Thank you, sir,' she said for the benefit of the secretary who might be lingering outside the door, or the man in the next room with his ear against the wall; she was surrounded by the enemy. The only raft afloat in this poisonous ocean was the man who now held her gaze.

His worried expression told her how awful she must look: her clothes crumpled, her hair unkempt, her eyes sore from lack of sleep. He too was clearly under stress. It was the first time she'd seen him unshaven, a shadow covering his chin and upper lip. An impulse surged to run a finger over the stubble above his mouth, but instead she merely ran a tongue over her dry lips.

Responding to her action, he poured a glass of water from a jug on his desk and placed it in front of her. She reached for the glass, her fingers brushing his. He let his hand linger for a heartbeat before picking up a pen and studying a form in front of him. As she gulped down the water, she glanced at the clock; she had been in the cell eight hours without a drink.

'I have some questions...' he began, again in an exaggerated loud voice.

She played along as he asked her about her duties at the castle, the length of time she'd been working there and the last time she'd seen Heydrich. She tensed when she heard the name. Was the man still alive? But Andrej gave nothing away and continued with the routine questions, making notes of her answers.

Finally, he put his pen down and looked at her with dark, intense eyes that flickered with emotion. She grew warm under his gaze, the pull of their connection making her heart yearn. His Adam's apple bobbed as he swallowed hard and got to his feet.

'Staff will not be required at Prague Castle until further notice. Thank you for your co-operation, Miss Hajek.'

The interview finished, she stood up. Andrej moved to her side of the desk and after a glance at the door, he leaned in to her. His breath was warm on her ear as he whispered, 'Destroy all messages at the shop.' She breathed in his earthy scent.

Then, after a tiny nod, she turned her head, so that her cheek brushed against his mouth. Her exhaustion had evaporated and every nerve ending in her body tingled. Her stomach quivered.

He stepped back. 'You are free to leave now.'

And that was it. He walked to the door, opened it and indicated for her to go.

For a moment, she was lost. She needed more: questions answered, advice, but most of all his closeness. The fatigue returned, enveloping her in a mantel so heavy, she could barely stand. She wrenched herself from him and stumbled outside into the midday sunshine.

* * *

Papa cried with relief when she entered the apartment, and although all she wanted to do was sleep, she told him what had happened at the police station and how after some routine questions, she'd been allowed to leave. She didn't of course give any indication that she knew the investigating officer.

Finally, she had one more thing to do before she could rest. Downstairs in the bookshop, she withdrew the bookmark from *The Gardener's Diary* and slipped out the coded message within. In the kitchen at the back, she took the box of matches and set the piece of paper alight above the sink. The smell of burning paper filled her nostrils and seconds later, she turned on the tap and washed away the charred remains.

She was safe now, she tried to tell herself as she trudged up the stairs. And if she was safe then so were the many people connected to her. But was that really true? What about the contacts who had come to the shop: the tram driver, the woman with the artificial limp and others? If they were questioned, might they be persuaded either by threats, violence or bribery to give names? She knew that such a scenario could not be ruled out.

* * *

When she awoke, she was lying on her back, her right palm on her locket, the dream from last night still sharp in her mind. Mama had been in the bookshop rearranging the shelves when the door flew open and German soldiers rushed in wielding guns. Mama had looked around, a pile of books in her arms, and screamed. A soldier waved his rifle at her and she raised her hands in surrender. The books tumbled to the floor, their covers splayed, their bindings broken. The soldiers laughed and kicked at the pages that had come loose, and one went to the kitchen and returned with the box of matches. In her sleep, Jana had known what was coming, and tried to redirect the dream, but it refused to be swayed. The books were torched. Mama's gold book locket flashed at her neck as the tornado of flames rose and Jana knew both her and the books were gone forever. 'It's a sin to burn books,' her mother's voice whispered in her brain.

Jana took deep breaths to calm her pounding heart and dragged herself from her dreamworld back to reality. It was hardly better. The drone of the news broadcaster pulled her from her bed. She slid into her slippers and padded into the sitting room, still in her nightdress. Her father was already dressed and sipping chicory coffee from his favourite mug. She kissed him on the cheek.

'Any news?' It was the third morning after the attack.

'Plenty. And none of it good.'

She sat next to him on the settee. 'Tell me.'

'The reward has gone up. It seems if you know the wanted men, you can get rich or get shot.'

The Nazi threats had started immediately; anyone found aiding Heydrich's attackers would be executed along with their families. Red bilingual posters were splashed all over town offering either rewards for information or warnings of death. The citizens of Prague were on high alert as the dramatic events unfolded. Jana heard the whispers in food queues – the attackers were heroes – comments from customers in the bookshop – the attackers were foolhardy. She heard stories from friends. Dasha had said the Wehrmacht had raided the apartment block where she lived; dozens were arrested and a neighbour, a quiet young man, had been shot dead. The Germans were openly declaring the number of executions each day, although it wasn't always clear if these were acts of revenge or punishment. And the question on everyone's lips: was Heydrich recovering?

An hour later, as Jana unlocked the bookshop door, she thought about the other women she had shared the packed police cell with. Had her manager, Miss Jezek, been released? Now that employment had been suspended at the castle, she had no way of knowing.

She opened the drawer of the till and started to count the cash, but her thoughts wandered to Andrej and the charade the two of them had played in his office. How many times had she been forced to restrain her feelings for him? Was it as hard for him as it was for her? To be honest, she didn't know if he had any feelings for her at all. In fact, she realised, she didn't know him at all. The thought made her sad.

Just before lunch, Dasha appeared in the shop. 'Have you got time for a break?'

Jana looked around the empty shop. 'Looks like I do,' she said.

As the two friends walked into the sunshine, Dasha explained that her mother-in-law was babysitting.

'Where shall we eat?' she asked. They both had taken their meagre lunch with them.

'Down by the river. I can't bear the town centre at the moment, swarming with troops and police.'

Things weren't much better on the banks of the Vltava. Soldiers lined the Charles Bridge and marched along the embankment. The girls sat down, spreading their dresses on the grass and tucking their legs beneath them. They munched on their dark, heavy bread. Jana's was five days old; she had been slicing the loaf as thinly as possible to make it last the week.

'Do you think you'll be questioned as you work in the castle?' said Dasha.

'I already have.'

Dasha stopped chewing and stared at her. Jana went on to explain.

'Goodness. How frightening,' Dasha said.

'It was.' Jana sighed.

Jana longed to share more; she had underestimated the burden of secrecy. The only person who knew she was involved in resistance activities was Andrej, and it was too dangerous, especially now, to see or speak to him.

Dasha shuffled up closer and lowered her voice.

'Do you ever wish you could do something to help? Sometimes, I feel guilty for just sitting back and watching events unfold around me.'

'You help at the church,' Jana said.

'Yes, but is that enough? There are brave citizens that are fighting back against the Germans, whereas people like us are just passive observers.'

Jana shifted, feeling uncomfortable. Was Dasha fishing for information? Did she know something?

'What do you think of Heydrich's attackers?' Dasha continued.

'You mean the question everyone is asking: heroes or fools?'

Dash nodded and popped the last morsel of bread inside her mouth.

Jana considered it for a few moments before answering.

'They are heroes. Their courage to stand up against the Nazis is a symbol of hope. It shows even one of the highest-ranking SS officers is vulnerable.'

'But the attack didn't succeed.'

'No. But the attempt has lifted our Czech spirit, given us a voice. The news will have gone round the world; we will be seen again. Visible so that the allies don't forget us.'

Nearby, a ferry docked, and the travellers from the far bank were met by soldiers, questioned and searched. A steam boat chugged past.

'Have you heard any news from Lenka?' asked Dasha.

Jana shook her head. 'I hope she's all right.' Her own words sounded stupid to her. Of course Lenka was not all right. Jana had seen the conditions her friend was living under. 'I'm not sure when I'll hear from her again now we have this uproar going on.'

How could she pass letters on to Andrej when she had to keep her distance from him?

'The war must end soon,' Jana said, trying to convince herself as much as Dasha. 'Germany has taken on Russia and America. It's just a matter of time.'

'Let's hope the allies remember our tiny country.'

'They will now.'

* * *

Over the next couple of days, the tension escalated. More troops poured into the city. The police were jittery, reaching for their pistols unprovoked, and the Gestapo slid in and out of apartment buildings. Jana decided to not go out at lunchtime any more but took a stool and a book into the backyard for her break. Each day, the Germans were becoming angrier that the culprits were still at large, and the reprisals were growing greater. Then, one week after the attack, when Jana and her father gathered in front of the radio for the latest broadcast, the news came:

Reinhard Heydrich was dead.

Jana gasped, her hand flying to her mouth. She stared wide-eyed at her father, shocked and yet excited. The assailants had been successful in their assassination. The Butcher of Prague was dead. He hadn't survived his wounds. No longer would he terrorise the Czech people whom he'd called vermin, whose spirit and culture he'd systematically set out to destroy.

'They did it. He's gone.' Jana exhaled a long breath.

'Yes.' Papa gave a slow nod.

A flash of annoyance at his lacklustre response heated her cheeks.

'I'm glad,' she said, defiance in her voice. 'He deserved it.'

'He definitely deserved it,' said Papa, 'but what comes next?'

'A resurgent of resistance against the Nazis. An uprising!' Adrenaline pumping, she rose from the chair and paced the sitting room. 'Don't you see, Papa, this is what we've been waiting for.'

* * *

In the days that followed, Jana was fraught with emotions that swung between elation and despair; the Czechs were fighting back, the Czechs were being imprisoned and shot. The city was holding its breath as day after day, the sounds of fists on doors and boots on stone reverberated around the city.

One late Thursday morning, two weeks after the death of Heydrich, Jana was on her way to the grocery shop wondering how long the food queue would be, when a boy darted in front of her. Hopping out of her way at the last moment, he spun round and aiming two fingers and a thumb at a second boy, shouted, 'Bang, bang.'

Jana halted a moment to watch the boys as they 'fired' at each other, one proclaiming the other 'dead.' So sad to witness how the occupation influenced their play. Or was it sad? Maybe their choice of game helped them to deal with the world around them, protected them.

A woman in a lilac dress, an apron tied at her waist, appeared at a nearby doorway. She thrust her hands on her hips. 'You two get right back in here at once.'

'But, you said we can play, Mama.'

'Well, I've changed my mind. Get inside. Now.' The woman caught Jana looking at her. 'I wouldn't go into town,' she said. 'All hell will've let loose down there.'

'Why? What's happened?'

The woman waited until the boys had slumped past her into the building before answering.

'I just heard news on the radio. They've found the attackers, poor souls, holed up in that church on Resslova Street; the SS have surrounded the building.'

Jana's heart plummeted. She mumbled a thank you to the woman and sped back the way she came, eager to get home and listen to the latest bulletin. She ran up to the apartment, alerted her father, and the two of them held their breath as the radio crackled to life. Papa adjusted the dial impatiently to reduce the static, and the announcer's voice boomed into the room. There was a trace of glee in his tone.

'...the two perpetrators of this heinous crime have been

hunted down and are now under siege at the Church of Saints Cyril and Methodius. It is believed that five other criminals have also taken refuge there. The church is now surrounded by hundreds of troops, the SS, and police...'

'Oh, no,' whispered Jana. 'They can't escape now.'

She'd prayed so hard that the men would somehow evade capture, hide in the mountains, slip out of the country. But it seemed they hadn't even made it out of Prague.

She sat with Papa in silence, transfixed, not wanting to hear the news, yet desperate to know the outcome. The siege went on for hours, seven men holding off the might of the German army. It became clear there would be no surrender, no arrests or trials.

Finally, the announcement came: the men had fought to the death.

'Heroes,' said Jana and heaved a sob.

'They were brave men.' Papa put an arm around Jana's shoulders.

'Well, I hope the Nazis are satisfied now,' she said, shedding angry tears. 'They have what they wanted and can stop terrifying everyone.' She wiped her hot face with the back of her hand. 'They can leave us all in peace now.'

29

A soft, summer rain pattered against the bedroom window; a musical sound, thought Jana, romantic. She squinted at the alarm clock beside her bed. It was still early, so she closed her eyes again and allowed her thoughts to linger on Andrej. Her favourite place to imagine him was on that deserted little steamboat, hidden behind the trees and bushes. Now, in mid-June, the green foliage would be dense; the light through the cabin window would shine dappled onto the wooden floor, shadows from the trees shifting as the leaves trembled in the breeze.

A huge sigh escaped her lips as she relived kisses they'd shared, looks they'd exchanged. There had been so few opportunities for them to be alone together that she could remember every precious encounter between them: from when he'd come to the bookshop searching for a gift for his mother's birthday, to his face at the checkpoint as the bus passed by with her and the sisters seated aboard. It amazed her how only a handful of occasions could ignite such intense feelings inside her. And all the fear and drama of the past few weeks made her want him more than ever: to talk to, to share her thoughts with, to make love to.

She rose and went to greet her father good morning. As always, he was up and dressed before her, and listening to the radio. He sat in the armchair with his back to her, a tuft of hair on the back of his head sticking out. An image flashed across her mind: how Mama would smooth down that exact same stubborn patch for him, a tender smile on her face. Jana moved to do the same but catching a familiar name from the broadcast, she froze to the spot.

'...We will not hide what happened last night in Lidice—'

Papa switched off the radio.

She stiffened. Lidice? That was the village where Lenka's parents lived, where she had visited them and sat in their garden.

A guttural noise came from Papa's throat and his head fell into his hands.

She rushed to him and touched his shoulder. 'Whatever's happened?'

He turned to look at her, eyes welling with tears. 'It's gone,' he mumbled.

'What's gone?'

'The village. Lidice. Burnt to the ground.'

'No!' She went to kneel in front of him and grabbed his hands. 'Tell me.'

'The Germans stormed the village last night. They executed every single man and took all the women and children. Then the village was torched. The Germans are openly broadcasting that the destruction of Lidice is a reprisal for the assassination.'

'But they are innocent people.'

How could even the Nazis act in such a brutal way?

Cold fear filled her. 'Where are the women and children? Lenka's parents live there.'

'They're not saying what will happen to them. Nobody seems to know where they are.'

'Oh, Papa. That's terrible, that's horrific...' Her words tailed away and she lay her head on her folded arms across his knees like when she was a child. All the while, her father stroked her hair.

* * *

Unable to bear more newscasts, Jana went down to the bookshop. She kept the shop closed and sat curled in the armchair, staring unseeing at the bookshelves. She had silently celebrated the death of Heydrich, the most feared and hated man oppressing their land; the assassins were heroes who had stood up against the Nazi terror. Isn't that what one should do? Stand up and say what is right, whatever the consequences? But then no one had anticipated retribution on this scale. Arrests, yes. But mass murder? She couldn't imagine the horror the people in Lidice had faced; she didn't want to imagine it. Lenka's parents – kind, gentle people who had nothing to do with any of it.

But you did, a grim voice in her head told her.

She let out a moan as guilt swept over her, crushing her breast, squeezing the breath from her lungs.

She was responsible; she had spied on Heydrich, noting his arrival times and supplied the resistance with information. It was no use telling herself that her messages had been merely required to build a picture of the *Protektor*'s movements. What had she thought the information was for? She had wished him dead on more than one occasion. And she'd got her wish. *But the cost, my God, the cost...*

Her hand went to her mouth and she sucked on the fleshy

part at the base of her thumb. Had she thought it noble and brave to leave coded messages in bookmarks, using the bookshop as some sort of secret post office? Her jaw trembled and she pressed her palm against her teeth. *Stupid, stupid, naïve woman, playing spies, reckless games* – she bit down into her soft, tender skin. *Irresponsible, selfish, stupid, stupid.* Grinding her teeth into her flesh, the pain ripped through her but still she didn't stop until she tasted blood, metallic on her tongue, then she pulled at her hair, caught in a whirlwind of torment. Eventually, her energy spent, she gazed down at the fistful of hair and let it drift to the floor. She would pull out a strand of hair for every life lost, she would – but exhaustion overcame her and all she could do was take deep, shuddering breaths and cry hot, desolate tears.

* * *

The next days passed in a blur. Jana kept the shop closed and spent her time huddled in the armchair seeking solace in books, but it didn't come, her mind throwing endless recriminations at her. In the mornings, she pulled out strands of her hair and draped them on top of her chest of drawers. One evening, she sat on her bed in her underwear gazing at the tender white skin of her thighs. She thought of Lenka in the stifling barracks and imagined her receiving news of her parents. Jana scooped up the pencil from her bedside table and plunged the point into her leg. The lead broke but she continued to stab herself, clenching her jaw to stop herself from crying out.

At night, she thought about all the questions she wanted to ask Andrej. She had so many questions to ask him. What did he know about Lidice? If Lenka's father was dead, what had happened to her mother? And there was the question that burned in her brain. Had he known about the plan to attack Heydrich?

She thought about ways to contact him. Simply walk into the police station and ask to see him? Or maybe she could hang around outside and wait for him to show up. But she had no idea what shifts he worked. A while ago, they'd agreed that if she removed all the bookmarks from the display, it meant she needed to talk to him.

The following morning, Jana scrambled into the window and removed all the bookmarks. Taking a deep breath, she unlocked the shop door. She knew she had to face people but a part of her hoped there would be no customers today.

Sitting behind the cash register, she stared out the window, willing Andrej to pass by.

The day dragged on. There were no customers and no sign of Andrej. She only left her lookout post for a few moments at a time, to fetch a drink, something to eat or use the bathroom. Mid-afternoon, an elderly woman came into the shop looking for a book for her grandson. Jana was forced to leave her watch and move to the children's section where she couldn't see the window.

'Terrible, isn't it?' said the woman. She had pale, watery eyes and deep lines between her brows. 'Those poor people in Lidice. Doesn't bear thinking about.'

'No, it doesn't,' said Jana, a pang in her chest. This was exactly why she didn't want to see people; everyone would be talking about the mass murder of the villagers.

The woman went on, talking of the news reports she'd heard. Jana finally managed to bring her attention back to children's books and the woman left half an hour later with her purchase. Hearing the details of the massacre from the woman was more information than she wanted to hear, and feeling drained, she locked the door once more. She perched herself back on the stool and stared out the window.

* * *

The front of the nightclub was boarded up; a padlock hung on the door. Jana had decided to come here even though she hadn't caught sight of Andrej, in the hope she'd missed him. It was seven o'clock, the exact time they'd met here in the past. But then the place hadn't been boarded up. Even with the key, Andrej wouldn't be able to get in.

A man and woman ambled by and threw her a curious glance. She hurried on.

In the vague hope that Andrej might turn up, she walked around the block and came back up the street. He wasn't there. Ever more desperate, she walked again and again around the block, but finally slumped home just ahead of curfew.

After several days of hiding at the back of the closed bookshop, she decided to no longer hide from her crimes, unlocked the door and turned the sign to *Open*. She blinked as the sunshine streamed inside, highlighting dust motes dancing in the breeze from the open door. She dragged her feet to the kitchen to fetch a duster.

Her head was under the sink when she heard the clang of the bell over the shop door. Goodness, she'd only just opened up and the first customer had arrived. Breathing deeply to compose herself, she walked back into the shop.

Her heart took a double beat. Andrej. He had come.

He wore a pale-blue shirt tucked into grey trousers, which hung loose around his waist. Like everyone else, he'd lost weight. His eyes were dark against his ashen skin. He was freshly shaven, a nick from his razor red on his chin.

'Hello, Jana. How are you?' His voice was gentle.

'I don't know, really. We need to talk.'

'Yes, I thought so.' He gestured behind him to the window. 'Our code. I need to talk too. Do you remember the way to the disused steamboat?'

She nodded.

'Can you meet me there at seven this evening?'

'I'll be there.'

Silence stretched between them as their eyes met. Then he gave a ghost of a smile and left.

30

Winding her way alongside the embankment, Jana thought about all the things she would say to him, her pulse racing. It was a long list and she struggled to know where to start.

As she neared the spot where she thought the steamboat was hidden, she slowed her pace. The riverside was now lined with thick, green foliage and everything looked different; she was unsure. She had just passed the locked-up, derelict building on her right, so the opening through the trees should be on her left. Only there was no opening; the bushes and trees entwined with each other. The low sun broke from the clouds and she shielded her eyes with her hand. Where was the entrance?

Her eyes ran over the ground, dense yellow with dandelions. There was a spot where a few were crushed. Footprints leading into the bushes. This was the place.

She pushed her way through, releasing her clothes as they caught on branches. She wore the same clothes as this morning: a short-sleeved, white blouse and a green skirt that fell just below her knees. Before she'd left home, she'd brushed her hair, leaving it loose. A memory sprung up of Andrej ripping the hat from her head as they'd embraced in the nightclub, and her face grew hot. Then she scolded herself for allowing such thoughts in these terrible times.

It was a relief when she emerged onto the narrow, stony beach and caught sight of the boat. She approached, pebbles crunching under her feet. The boat was half hidden by a broad-trunked weeping willow, its elegant, yellow-green fingers dipping into the river; two swans drifted in its shade. The trill of a bird's evening song filled the air and a red squirrel darted back into the bushes at the sound of her tread.

Andrej appeared on deck and reached out an arm to help her on board. He led her quickly inside the cabin, which was dark in the shade of the willow. She took a moment to catch her breath and started when his hand went to her head as if to stroke her. But he merely pulled a leaf from her hair and tossed it on the floor. He wore the same blue shirt as that morning, the top buttons undone, revealing a dark curl of hair.

'I'm sorry you spent so long in the cell. As soon as I saw your name, I did what I could to get you out of there as quickly as possible,' he said.

'I'm grateful. But please tell me about Lidice. It's horrendous what happened to those poor people.'

He ran a hand through his ink-black hair. 'Come, let's sit down.'

She sat down on the floor, her whole body wound tight with nerves. He joined her and gave a heavy sigh before he started to speak.

'I'm shocked at the brutal reprisal from the Germans. It was to be expected they would take some action, but this is beyond comprehension. Normally, the Germans like to cover up their crimes. But this time, they want the Czechs to know what they are capable of. The massacre at the village is not just retribution but an act to spread terror, a warning.'

'I was glad when Heydrich was shot. I was sick with loathing for him and thought that the shooting showed the Nazis couldn't crush us. But the price was too high.' Her throat ached with emotion. 'Do you know who the assassins were?'

'Word has now got out. They were two young soldiers who were trained in Britain as paratroopers. We suspect they were sent by our exiled government in London with specific instructions to target Heydrich. They were flown here and parachuted in.'

'And the other men who died in the shootout in the church?'

'Also paratroopers working on other resistance jobs. All brave men.' Andrej shook his head and rested his elbows on his knees.

'Did you know the resistance were planning the attack?' she asked, her voice, tense.

'No. It was top secret, probably planned in London. But I had an inclination that Heydrich might be a target—'

'Why didn't you tell me? You knew I was involved in the resistance and working at the castle. You should have told me I was aiding an assassination!' Her voice rose.

'I didn't really believe the resistance would do anything so dramatic. No one did, least of all Heydrich, who felt secure enough to drive around in an open-top car. I assumed you were part of a general surveillance team.'

'No, Andrej, it seems I was more than that. And my involvement makes me guilty for the villagers' lives lost. The lives of Lenka's parents.' Misery welled up inside her.

'It's not your fault. If anything, it's mine. I should have suspected something. But even if I had, would I have tried to intervene if could? We are resistance fighters, after all.' But his last words lacked conviction and she saw the torment on his face.

'Surely, no assignment can justify the loss of so many innocent lives?'

'I don't know any more. It's easy to say with hindsight. What should we do, Jana? Not fight back?'

His words echoed what she'd thought when she first got involved at Prague Castle. She'd been determined to resist the German occupation, proud to be doing her part. It had felt the right thing to do. But it had in fact been irresponsible and reckless.

'The paratroopers knew the time Heydrich came to work because of me,' she said.

'There were many more people involved than you: people who knew the route he took in the morning, people who were watching when you weren't there.'

Jana thought of Janek, the young gardener. She shuddered.

'You're not to blame, Jana.' He reached for her hand.

In a burst of anger and frustration, she shoved him away.

'I am to blame. All of us are to blame. You too. I don't even know what you do. Who you are. All these secrets, all these schemes. I'm sick of it. Sick of it all.'

She broke down sobbing, her face in her hands, tears squeezing through her fingers. Her thoughts were in turmoil. Resistance or submission, that was the choice. But who was she to decide the risks to take, to put the lives of others in danger?

'I'm just a bookshop girl,' she whimpered, more to herself than Andrej. 'I'm no one.'

'That's not true. You're a very special person.' His voice broke as he tentatively took her hand.

Her heart throbbed with pain. She was too weary to push

him away, to fight her feelings for him. She turned to him and lay her head on his chest. He stroked her hair, made comforting sounds. She smelled the faint scent of his woody cologne and was reminded of the last time they were here together, their passionate kisses. Desire, warm and fluid stirred through her and she tipped her face to him, looking deep into his tear-filled eyes.

'Kiss me,' she said.

He hesitated only for an instant, then his mouth was on hers. Hot emotion coursed through her as their kisses intensified. She ran her hands across his chest and down his stomach before she yanked his shirt from the waist of his trousers. Her fingers slipped beneath his shirt, exploring every muscle, every hair. She opened the top buttons of his shirt with trembling fingers and ran her tongue across his skin, loving the saltiness of him. He moaned, a wonderful sound. He stroked her hip, her thigh, slowly hitching up her skirt. Her nerve endings were on fire her at the anticipation of his touch on her bare skin.

Her pleasure shocked her and guilt sprang up. She didn't deserve this joy; people had died because of her, and here she was desperate to fulfil her own needs. Panting, she pulled back, her cheeks burning and still wet from her tears.

'This is wrong,' she murmured.

He leaned his forehead on hers and heaved a sigh.

'I love you, Jana.' His words were choked and she realised he was crying. 'I don't know what's right or wrong any more. I only know that I fell in love with you that day in the bookshop; I was looking for a book for my mother's birthday and you were so angry and proud. So beautiful.'

She put a hand on his cheek and he lifted his head. His handsome, pale face with those beautiful cheekbones bore a look of such sadness and love that her heart wrenched and she wiped a tear from the corner of his eye. She loved him too but choked back the words.

'Let's have this moment,' she said.

It would be only the one moment, she knew.

They pulled at each other's clothes in the dim light of the cabin, their lips caressing each other's bodies, and when they made love, it was bitter and sweet, racked with pain and sadness, and heightened with desire that left then both depleted, quiet, together.

* * *

People queued in the hushed silence of Tyn church to light a candle. It seemed that the whole city had turned out to pay their respects for the victims of the Lidice massacre. Jana took her place amongst the distraught faces, shuffling forwards a couple of steps at a time. When it was her turn, she took a candle from the nearly empty box – candle wax had become scarce and she doubted the box would be replenished; the churchgoers at the back of the queue would be disappointed. She lit her candle, bowed her head and moved to the pews to find a place before the altar.

After she finished her prayers, her unbidden thoughts went to Andrej. She chided herself but she had no control of the images tossing in her brain: their desperate lovemaking in the steamboat, the way they had clung to each other, crying, before Andrej had to leave for his night shift. Before he'd left, she'd told him it was over between them.

'But it's only just begun,' he'd said, his expression bewildered. 'I know I said we mustn't be seen together, and that still applies. But now and then, we could snatch a moment together, like today. And when the war is over—'

'No.' She strained not to cry again. 'Don't you see, Andrej? I have no right to happiness or love. *We* have no right.'

'But what about what just happened between us?'

'We were searching for solace.'

'Is that what it was to you? A bit of comfort?'

Now, head bowed in front of the altar, she winced as she remembered the pain on his face, the disappointment in his voice. More than once, she'd bitten back the words that wanted to burst from her mouth: that she loved him. She didn't deserve to feel that precious emotion: something the murdered villagers would never feel again. She would sacrifice that love as penance for what she'd done. She would deny herself the pleasure of holding Andrej in her arms. And she would endure the emotional pain, which was nothing against what the women and children survivors of Lidice would be suffering – if there were any survivors.

She rose from the pew, her limbs heavy, and made her way out of the church into the incongruous sunshine. It was a hot, June day; the proud buildings shimmered in the midday sun, the spires glinted.

Dazzled by the bright light, she swayed for a moment, feeling light-headed. It occurred to her she hadn't eaten breakfast nor dinner yesterday; she had no appetite. But she needed to drink.

At a nearby water fountain, she cupped her hands, splashed her face and drank some water. She stared at her reflection, oblivious of the people around her. Two words spun in her mind: resistance or submission? She had tried resistance and what had it achieved? The slaughter of innocents. Maybe submission was easier; she was so tired of fighting. And the faces of the people in the church told the same story. They were crushed by the savage retribution dealt out to them.

As she approached the bookshop, Andrej's words came to her.

'I love you, Jana,' he'd said: the most beautiful words she'd ever heard. But she would not allow herself to hear them again. She wouldn't be able to stop thoughts of him pushing their way into her mind, but that would serve as part of her punishment: to taste love just once and never again.

31

The tram was packed that hot Saturday morning. Jana stood, gripping the bar as she was jostled by other people boarding from the market with their sad baskets of provisions. She herself had only managed to buy three small potatoes, some carrots and an onion. It seemed people went to market more to see friends and acquaintances than to actually shop; the market stalls had few wares and people had little money to spend. The doors swished closed and as the tram lurched forward, those standing swayed in one motion before steadying themselves again.

The young, flush-cheeked woman standing beside her giggled at something her boyfriend said and he curled an arm around her waist. With a contented smile, she leaned her head on his shoulder. The sight brought Jana a pang of misery; it was six weeks and two days since she and Andrej had made love on the old steamboat. The exquisite memory of his hands on her skin fought with the memory of the pain on his face when she'd told him it was over. And she had meant it too. Still, a small part of her was disappointed he hadn't contacted her since then and tried to persuade her to change her mind. Perhaps he hadn't

The Last Bookshop in Prague

loved her after all or perhaps he felt as guilty as her about the terrible events.

The tram screeched to a stop and Jana peered out the window to see where they were. Near the police station. It wasn't her stop, but in a rush of emotion, she pushed her way to the doors and jumped out.

This wasn't the first time she'd hung around the police station, gazing in shop windows or standing at a nearby bus stop, hoping for a glimpse of him. She'd never seen him here though and always went home disappointed. It was stupid of her, she knew, but she couldn't help herself. Although she remained determined their love affair was over, she needed to know that he was still there; a brief glimpse of him would be comfort enough.

Today, she dawdled in front of the ironmongers where, with her back to the police station, she watched the entrance in the reflection of the window.

She squinted at the black car parked out front, where a driver sat waiting. Her eyes moved to a woman hauling a screaming child up the steps. An old man in a shabby coat limped out the entrance. She pretended to study the tools displayed in the window, her eyes flitting up every few moments to the reflection of the police station.

After a while, she became aware that the shop owner was eyeing her from the other side of the glass, a puzzled expression on his face. She gave a weak smile and sighed; she'd have to move on.

At that moment, she started. In the reflection, she saw two men in the familiar long, leather coats and black hats descend the steps, and tucked firmly between them was Andrej in his police uniform. Startled, she spun round. Andrej had his head lowered, the men either side of him pressed close, their expressions unreadable. All three of them climbed into the back of the car which sped away from the kerb.

Jana's knees went weak and she placed a hand on the shop window for support. The shop owner's face appeared close up, frowning at her. She moved away and stumbled back to the tram stop in a daze. What had she just witnessed? An arrest? She'd seen no handcuffs but the way the men in black had been escorting him had looked threatening. She tried to reason that this was nothing sinister but any way she looked at it, one thing was for sure.

The Gestapo had Andrej.

32

Two sleepless nights followed with Jana's mind filled with horror scenarios. The worse part was the not knowing. She tried to reason with herself not to expect the worst from the situation; after all, Andrej was a police officer and could have been accompanying the Gestapo for all manner of reasons. Only the hostile body language of the two men escorting Andrej had indicated something else.

During the day, she was light headed and nauseous with worry. She had to know if Andrej was all right. It was impossible for her to carry on life as normal. Desperation made her act.

On the third day, she left the bookshop at six o'clock and headed straight for the police station. She knew it was risky to ask questions about Andrej but she was in such turmoil, she was past caring.

There was a long queue at the counter and as she waited her turn, she rehearsed what she was going to say, becoming more nervous each moment. She looked time and again towards the same office in which Andrej had staged an interview with her, willing him to stride out. But the door remained firmly closed.

When it was finally her turn, she stepped up to the counter where a flustered policeman in wire spectacles was scrawling across a form. After what seemed an age, he looked up at her.

'How can I help?' he asked in a monotone voice.

'I would like to see Captain Kovar,' she said. Her voice was too quiet to hear above the hubbub around her, and the policeman put a hand to his ear.

'I didn't catch that.'

Dismayed at having to repeat herself, she raised her voice and tried again.

This time, at the mention of Andrej's name, something passed over the policeman's face.

'May I ask why?'

'He's interviewed me in the past so I'd like to discuss something with him again.'

The policeman didn't look convinced and as she was grappling to add further explanation, he said, 'Captain Kovar doesn't work here any more.'

'I don't understand,' she stuttered.

He drummed his fingers on the desk. 'He's left us.'

'Where's he gone?' The words were out before she could stop them.

'I have no idea.' He gave her a suspicious look. 'Why do you want to know?'

Jana shrugged at the question, her face burning.

'Is this going to take all day?' A tall, elegant woman behind tutted. 'I have an appointment, Officer.'

The policeman ignored her and said to Jana, 'If you wish to see another officer, take a seat in the waiting area.' He motioned to where a group of people stood around the half a dozen occupied chairs. She nodded and stepped aside, the woman sidling up to take her place, mumbling, 'Finally.'

In the waiting area, Jana paused a moment as she watched the policeman at the counter, and as soon as he was distracted, she slipped out the front door and down the steps. Dread gripped her as she staggered along the pavement, her shoulders bumping with passersby.

'Watch where you're going,' an angry voice called.

She didn't remember the journey back, but somehow she reached the bookshop and, with trembling fingers, unlocked the door. Once inside, she leaned with her back against the door, and gulped deep breaths.

Andrej was gone.

* * *

Jana shuffled from foot to foot, chewing her lip as she watched the elderly man in the phone box shove another coin in the slot. How long would his call take? She searched her mind for alternative public phone boxes in the area. But there was no guarantee that they would be unoccupied. Her heart raced as she prayed for him to hang up. But still he shouted into the receiver. She was just about to give up and move on when he ended the call. She sighed with relief, only to become agitated again when he took the time to light up a cigarette.

Finally, he shambled away and Jana dived in to take his place. The phone directories were piled on a shelf beneath the telephone and she bent down to read the spines. For some reason, there were two copies for the beginning of the alphabet, then one for the end. It would be just her luck that the one she wanted was missing. It was four days since Andrej had disappeared with the Gestapo and she needed to act quickly. Her heart jumped when she saw the tatty volume she needed. She hauled it out and began to flick through the pages, spirits sinking at the number of torn-out pages. Why did people do that? It was so selfish.

But it was there: the page with the surname Kovar. Andrej had talked about his mother but had never mentioned her first name or where she lived. If she had a telephone, she would be listed. Jana ran her finger down the page, dismayed to see there were a number of people with the surname Kovar. However, looking more closely, she noticed that most of the forenames were male; there were two listed as Mrs. These women would likely be widows. Choosing one at random, she inserted her forefinger in the dial. It felt sticky. The ringing on the other end of the phone was faint but Jana didn't have to wait long till someone answered.

'Hello, Mrs Kovar speaking.' The pips sounded and Jana slipped the coin into the slot.

'Hello, Mrs Kovar. I'm sorry to disturb you. My name is Jana and I'm looking for a friend of mine, Andrej Kovar. Is there any chance you have a son named Andrej?'

There was a pause, and Jana could hear the woman's breaths.

'Are you from the police?' The woman's tone was suspicious.

'No, no. Like I said, I'm a friend and I have an important message for him.' She didn't want to cause alarm with stories of arrest and disappearance at this stage.

'Well, I don't know anyone called Andrej. Sorry and goodbye.'

The click sounded loud in Jana's ear. Now she was unsure if the woman was lying to protect Andrej, or if she was telling the truth. This was proving more difficult than she'd anticipated. But contacting Andrej's mother to see if she knew his whereabouts had seemed her obvious first move.

Jana, perspiration beading on her forehead, dialled the number of the other Mrs Kovar, trying to decide how to frame her enquiries more delicately. The phone rang and rang. She held on, imagining an elderly woman struggling out of her chair, stumbling down a hallway to where a telephone hung on the wall. *Give her time*, Jana told herself. But no answer came and she replaced the receiver despondently. She made a note of the address next to Mrs Kovar's name, deciding to visit in person that evening.

* * *

Climbing the narrow stairwell to the third floor of the apartment building, Jana wondered how an elderly person managed the stairs. Maybe Andrej's mother was fit, or maybe Andrej regularly brought her provisions. Or maybe the woman living at the top of the building wasn't Andrej's mother at all. Her heart plummeted at the thought but then she forced herself to remain positive: Andrej's mother would open the door and tell her Andrej had a new job and now had a new address; he would be safe and well. Or better still, he would open the door of the apartment, give a surprised, delighted smile at the sight of her. They would embrace. Not kiss, of course. That was over now. But she would be close to him and they would spend the afternoon chatting with his mother and laughing about Jana's worries over Andrej being arrested.

On the top landing, Jana took a moment to catch her breath and compose herself. Two apartment doors faced her. The left door with the number sixteen was the address she had from the telephone directory. She pressed the doorbell and listened. She heard no sound of a bell. After trying a couple times more, it was clear the bell was out of order so she knocked with her knuckles and waited. Nothing. She knocked again, louder. Already sick with nerves, panic gripped her. Finding Andrej's mother in the hope she would have information about her son had been Jana's main plan. Her only plan so far. What if her search ended here? She banged on the door again with her whole fist.

The door of the neighbouring apartment opened and a blonde-haired woman with a small, sleepy child on her hip looked out. The child, a boy, looked ready for bed, dressed in pyjamas and clutching a teddy.

'I'm so sorry if I disturbed you,' said Jana. 'I was hoping to catch Mrs Kovar at home.'

The woman gave her a puzzled look. 'She doesn't live here any more.'

'Oh!' Jana gasped with surprise.

'Yes, her son helped her clear out her possessions.'

'Was her son called Andrej?'

'Yes. Nice-looking man, always very polite when we passed on the stairs.'

Jana's heart beat faster at the possibility that this was good news.

'Was that in the last couple of days?' she asked.

'Oh, no. This was at least three weeks ago.' The child began to whimper and rub its eyes.

The brief moment of hope was dashed. Andrej went missing after he'd moved his mother out of her home.

'Did Mrs Kovar or her son say where they were going? Sorry to pester you but I need to find them urgently.'

The woman shook her head, adjusting the position of the little boy who had started to cry.

'I'm afraid I must get this little one in bed. Sorry I couldn't help.'

With heavy legs and dread in her heart, she descended the stairs and made her way back to the bookshop. Her enquiries had come to a dead end and she wrestled to make sense of what she knew: if Andrej had moved his mother from her home, it must have been for her safety. And that meant he'd suspected imminent danger. And a short time later, he was picked up by the Gestapo and not heard of again. Despite her attempts to imagine positive outcomes, her thoughts always ended in darkness.

* * *

In the weeks that followed, she found herself walking past Petschek Palace, the Gestapo headquarters, affecting a nonchalant air as her eyes drifted over the windows and front door. It was ridiculous to expect Andrej's face might appear at a window or he would trot out the entrance, but she couldn't extinguish the tiny hope in her heart that refused to die.

One night, two months after his disappearance, Jana was crying into her pillow as she often did; she missed him and was terrified for him in equal measure. She wondered if anything had been different if she hadn't rejected him and that as lovers, he'd confided in her; she would've been able to help him in some way. She had owed him that after he'd released her from arrest after the attack on Heydrich. She wouldn't give up on him.

The following morning, she strode back into the police station, pleased to see a different officer to last time at the front desk; she hoped he would be more knowledgeable and repeated her enquiries about Captain Kovar. This policeman had a friendly manner but unfortunately knew nothing.

'Is there a way I can find out about his whereabouts?'

'Oh, yes, you can request information from the Police Commissioner's department or the Gestapo. If you are a relative, I can help you complete a form.' He smiled and began rifling through papers on his desk.

Startled, Jana retreated, mumbling something about being short of time and returning later. Once outside the building, she breathed in the fresh air in huge gulps, her heart hammering. She was helpless, no closer to finding Andrej than she had been nearly three months ago.

The air had cooled in the last few days and the first leaves were fading to pale yellow. She buttoned up her jacket and set off for the bookshop, her mind desperately searching for another idea to find Andrej. But as summer gave way to autumn, she discovered nothing new. The man she loved and yearned more for at each passing day had simply vanished.

33

One evening in late September, Jana took a walk in the cool, autumn air. The colour of the leaves matched the city as it turned golden in the setting sun.

Lost in her thoughts, she wandered across Wenceslas Square where Lenka had been arrested. Without Andrej's help, she could no longer get letters to her friend; Ivan had been trying the official route to keep contact with his wife but without success. The absence of information on Lenka and baby Alena's well-being was torment.

She crossed Charles Bridge, weaving through the crowds, and found herself climbing the narrow, shop-lined street in the direction of Prague Castle. An inexplicable urge to see the castle drew her on. She hadn't been near its walls for months and her heart quickened as she approached.

Too late, she realised her mistake. A Wehrmacht soldier was marching towards her.

She stopped in her tracks, her breath catching at the sight of the wide, pockmarked face.

Brandt. His eyes lit when he saw her, a smirk crossing his lips.

The pavement was narrow, allowing only one person to pass. She stepped aside, glancing around for her nearest place of refuge, but he was faster and blocked her way.

'Ah, what a lovely surprise – the bookshop girl,' he sneered.

The last time she had seen the vile man was when she'd witnessed the shooting of Janek the gardener. An image of the terrible moment sprung up and she glowered at him as he continued.

'It was very fortunate that you were released from prison after the assassination of our beloved Blond Beast.'

'I had merely been helping with enquiries. It was standard procedure.' She kept her tone even.

'I was never convinced by your innocent, dust-cleaning charade.' He stepped closer, his beady eyes glinting with danger. 'One wrong step, my little cleaning woman, and I'll be on you like a ton of bricks.' She could smell it on his stale breath, sweet and sickly – that odour of his; it reminded her of something she didn't like. Then she noticed the black smear on his lower lip and the memory finally popped: liquorice. She had always hated liquorice.

'I really don't know what you're talking about, so if you would please let me pass?'

He remained still, leering at her. He was deliberating trying to intimidate her and she wasn't going to let him.

She stuck out her chin, turned on her heel and strode swiftly back down the way she'd come. It wasn't a surprise to hear his army boots clomping behind her, following her. She picked up her pace and so did he. Her mind raced. How could she be rid of him? Where could she go? She wasn't far from the little restaurant she used to frequent years ago. The last time she had been there was with Pavel. The memory of how she had given him an experimental kiss popped up. She brushed the thought away; she must focus.

Jana remembered the owners of the restaurant – a kind, hardworking couple. She would take a table there and hoped he wouldn't make a scene in front of them and the customers. Relieved, she turned down the narrow street. It was remarkably quiet, with only a couple of pedestrians. The familiar shops were now boarded up and when she came to the restaurant entrance, her heart sank; it was closed. Daylight was fading as dusk drew in.

She glanced up to see Brandt marching towards her, his expression intent.

She ran.

As she swerved to avoid a middle-aged couple who stood in her path arguing – the stout woman searching for something in her bag – Jana lost her footing on the cobblestones. Her left shoe flew off and she was about to slip it back on when Brandt was on her, his large hand clasping her free wrist. She yelped and tugged against his grasp, but she was no match against his steel grip. He yanked her arm so hard she thought her shoulder would be pulled out of her socket.

The startled coupled stared, mouths open. Jana caught the woman's eye.

'Excuse me, sir,' the woman said, addressing Brandt. 'Has this woman done something wrong?'

'Mind your own business,' he growled.

'It's just that you're being rather heavy handed with the young girl.'

A moment of gratitude towards the woman. But then hope faded.

'Get out of here before I put you all under arrest,' he bellowed, his free hand gripping his pistol.

Fear flickered across the woman's face. Her husband took her elbow.

'Come on, dear. Let's not meddle.'

Jana's heart sunk as the couple scuttled off. Glancing up the street, she saw a young man sloping away; she was alone with Brandt. With a strong tug of her arm, he threw her with her back against the wall, his boot clipping the edge of her bare foot. She winced from the pain.

She clutched her errant shoe in her hand as he held her by her shoulders, his face up close, his liquorice breath causing her stomach to turn.

'Let go of me,' she said. 'I've done nothing wrong.'

'Oh, I'll find something. Unless you can be more accommodating.'

His hand travelled from her shoulder, his fingers snaking towards her breast, but then paused, hovering over her locket.

'Nice,' he said and yanked the chain from her neck, breaking the clasp and stuffing it into his trouser pocket. Jana gasped and in the brief moment he weakened his hold on her, she flung out her hand that still held the shoe and smashed the heel against the side of his head. He howled, the sound echoing down the empty street. She struck again with all her might. His hands flew to his wounded head and she slipped from his grasp, bolting down the street, one shoe on, one shoe off. She threw back a glance before she turned the corner. He stood glowering at her, blood trickling down the side of his face.

'Next time, bookshop girl,' he called after her, 'next time.'

34

Several weeks had passed since the incident with Brandt, the golden autumn ending abruptly, and the beginning of November blowing in with an icy wind. Jana closed the shop for the day and decided to stay there a while before going up to the apartment. She went to the kitchen and made herself an acorn coffee, and then huddled up in the armchair taking small sips.

She lay a hand on her neck, the empty space where Mama's locket had hung, a gaping wound in her soul. For weeks, she had anguished over ways to retrieve the locket from Brandt; reporting the theft to the fascist police would only put her and her family in the spotlight and would get her nowhere. The police were unlikely to accuse a member of the Wehrmacht and Brandt would deny it anyway. Did he even still have her locket in his possession or had he sold it? Thinking the latter was most probable, she had begun to scour the second-hand jewellery shops but without success. She clenched her jaw; she would not give up till she found it and one day, somehow, she would wreak her revenge on Brandt.

It had been terrible telling Papa she'd lost the locket. She'd restrained from telling him that a German soldier had ripped it from her neck, afraid that he would be furious and cause a scene at the police station. Right now, it was important that they kept under the radar: the best way to protect the hidden children.

Jana shivered and took a gulp of her coffee. The shop was cold and there was no coal for the pot-bellied stove. How were her and Papa going to keep warm through the winter? There was no coal, no food and increasingly, no electricity. The Nazis were cutting power to homes in order to keep the factories producing armaments. And sturdy boots just for the Wehrmacht. Prague and the rest of the country had been occupied for over three years, and although there were rumours of Germany losing their grip in Russia, there was no sign of it in Prague. If anything, the Nazi hold was stronger than ever.

She heard a tapping sound and frowned as she listened. But all she heard was the patter of rain. Then the noise came again, louder: a knocking from the front of the shop. She put down her coffee and went to investigate.

A figure hovered outside the window. The street was in darkness, the lamps no longer lit. Goosebumps ran up her arms. Was it Brandt all these weeks later? Had he come for her? She could still smell the liquorice. Her stomach roiled.

But as she peered through the glass, she saw that the person was slighter and shorter than Brandt. She stepped closer.

'Oh,' she murmured in surprise. It was Pavel.

'Hello,' he said awkwardly as she opened the door.

She invited him in.

'Come and sit down.' She gestured to the back of the shop.

He shook his head. 'I was just passing and wondered how you were?'

The last time she'd spoken with Pavel, he'd accused her of betraying her country with a fascist policeman.

'I'm well, thank you,' she said cautiously.

Pavel sighed. 'Look, Jana, I'm sorry about what I said that time down by the river. It's not for me to judge your choice of boyfriend.'

'He wasn't my boyfriend then and isn't my boyfriend now.' She stopped short of saying Andrej had vanished without a trace.

He raised his hands in apology. 'I hate it when we see each other around town and look the other way as if we were strangers. Please, I'd like us to be friends again.'

At this, she softened, remembering how he'd always been there for her, before she had rejected him.

'I'd like that too.'

They exchanged a few words about their everyday lives. Pavel still worked at the warehouse packing supplies for the German army.

They fell silent for a few moments before Pavel spoke again.

'How is Michal? Still at your grandma's?'

A warning signal flashed in her mind; it had been a mistake to risk sharing that confidence with him all that time ago. She could say Michal was no longer with Babi but that would only lead to more questions; best to divert the conversation.

'He's fine. How about your activities? Still annoying the Germans?' She kept her tone light.

'Maybe.' His expression turned wary. He didn't trust her despite his claims of friendship. Why was he really here?

They spoke for a few minutes longer, their conversation stilted before Pavel said he needed to go. He didn't say why.

Jana's relief that he'd left soon turned to concern. It was

strange that he'd suddenly turned up at her door after all this time. She wanted to believe it was out of desire to renew their friendship, but their conversation had been far removed from the easy banter they'd once shared. She went back to her armchair and finished the coffee that had gone cold.

35

Only Dasha and Karolina had turned up for the book club that cold November morning. Jana was actually relieved as they were her closest friends and she had important news to share.

'I'm afraid I will be closing the bookshop in the new year,' she said and exhaled, her chest sinking.

'Oh, no,' gasped Dasha.

'Why?' Karolina asked with a shocked expression.

'It's not earning any money, and in addition, I lost my income when all the staff were fired from Prague Castle. The Germans need full-time factory workers.' She grimaced. 'I'll apply at the employment agency.'

'But your mother's shop!' Dasha looked around at the bookshelves.

'That's the good news. The landlord said he'll let me keep the shop, even if it's closed. Apparently, finding new tenants is impossible at the moment, and being a literature fan himself, he'll let me keep the premises. He's not a fan of the Nazi regime, it seems and is ever hopeful the war will end soon.'

Although the three girls were alone in the bookshop, Jana

still lowered her voice. 'The Nazis aren't doing too well in Russia, he told me.'

'That's not what we hear on the radio,' said Karolina.

'German radio,' Jana pointed out. 'I think my landlord has inside information.'

'If only it were true, and the war ended. My Petr would be free.'

Jana and Dasha looked at her with sympathy in their eyes.

'There's been another round up of resistance fighters, I read this morning.' Dasha shook her head.

'I'm surprised there are any left after the purge following the assassination,' said Jana. Since her dismissal from Prague Castle in June, not a single contact of the resistance had entered her shop; something that suited her, as she'd vowed to have nothing more to do with the resistance since the tragedy of Lidice. But she did hope the contacts she'd met were safe.

'I suppose that's the end of our book club too,' said Karolina, sadly.

'Not necessarily.' Jana gave a bright smile. 'Our gatherings are too important to lose. Let's arrange to meet here at the shop in the evenings or weekends even when it's closed. The landlord said I can leave everything here as it is, only the *closed* sign will be up.'

Karolina's expression lifted. 'That would be wonderful. We'll need to find a time that suits everyone as most of us are working or have children to look after.'

'It might be tricky, but leave it to me. I'll sort out a time that suits all of us. More than ever, we must stick together.' Jana spoke with all her heart. She as much as anyone needed her support group. Her life was so uncertain now; closing the bookshop and Andrej gone from her life were shattering blows and she relied on the steady support of her friends from the book club.

* * *

A few weeks later, she was making plans for how to make their Christmas book club meeting special. As she hung some paper stars in the window, she wished she could provide her friends with Christmas biscuits or sugared almonds, real coffee or hot chocolate topped with whipped cream. Her hollow stomach groaned at the idea and she shifted her thoughts onto other possibilities to promote some festive cheer. She would design some book-themed games and quizzes, but would focus on stories with happy or hopeful endings. Everyone's spirits had been so low the last months, the occupation taking its toll, and Andrej's absence had carved a chasm in her life. But at Christmas, she would pull herself together for the sake of Papa, Babi and the children. And she would make the last book club of the year as joyful as possible.

As she scrambled around the window display, positioning hand-carved, wooden angels, a memory popped up: Andrej peering at her through the shop window as she'd crawled around on her hands and knees positioning books. How annoyed she'd been with him then, thinking he was spying on her, that he was a danger. She glanced up, visualising he was there now, her heart wistful. But it was another man's face that glanced in and then made for the shop door. A familiar face.

She retreated from the window and turned to greet the man. He wore a flat wool cap and a brown coat, and even though he wasn't in his uniform, she recognised him: the tram driver who, on several occasions, had delivered messages from the resistance. This was the first time that any contact had entered her shop since the assassination of Heydrich. Her mouth went dry. What did he want? That part of her life was over now.

'Can we talk?' he asked, looking around the empty shop.

She nodded and led him to the cash desk where she stood watching the front door.

'How are you, Miss Hajek?' His soft voice belied his burly appearance. The sleeves of his coat were taut around the muscles of his upper arms and his hands were large and strong. He looked to be in his forties, and very fit considering he sat in a tram all day.

'Who are you, exactly? I doubt you're a tram driver.'

He laughed, his eyes bright. He raised his hands in mock surrender.

'I'm Egon, and you're right, I'm not a tram driver. I have another function now.'

'Why are you here? As you know, I'm no longer at Prague Castle and have no information that may be of interest.' Her tone was terser than she'd intended but his sudden appearance had unnerved her.

'I was wondering if you'd be willing to help our activities once more. Heydrich may be gone but there is so much still to do.'

Swallowing hard, she said, 'I'm still struggling with the repercussions of my last actions. Nothing can justify that loss of life.' She shook her head, pursing her lips. 'I'm finished with all of that.'

He sighed, his expression turning grave. 'Such a tragic loss of life, and I believe not one that was anticipated by anyone. Not to that extent... But it puts us in a terrible dilemma. Do we lie down and die, or stand up and die?'

'At least we're not dead if we do nothing.' She didn't want to have this conversation; it was making her flustered, uncertain. 'I'm sorry, but I can't be of any use to you.'

They fell silent. He held her gaze, his amber eyes intense, as if appraising her.

She shifted and looked away.

'Very well,' he said, disappointment in his voice. 'But we need clever, brave women like you. If you change your mind, I'm at the Masna coffee shop on the first Monday of every month around seven in the morning. In any case, I wish you a peaceful Christmas and all the best for the New Year.'

He left leaving Jana's thoughts in turmoil; the thrill of slipping coded messages into bookmarks fought against the terror of Heydrich catching her looking at his bookcase, the tremor of delight as Andrej whispered to her on the Charles Bridge in contrast to the despair of being thrown into a police cell. She had been balanced on a spinning top, rotating too fast for her to spring from, but now she had her feet back on solid ground, steady and safe.

Sitting at the counter, she lay out the bookmarks she was making for Christmas. As she cut out tiny, silver, paper stars to stick on the fabric, she realised she'd missed an important opportunity; She should have asked Egon if he'd heard anything about Andrej Kovar. Afterall, Egon and Andrej had both been involved in resistance activities and possibly knew each other.

At lunch time, she walked along the freshly fallen snow to the telephone box and after finding the Masna coffee shop in the directory, she made a mental note of the address. She returned to the bookshop, a quiver in the pit of her stomach.

36

On a bleak, January morning, Jana trudged up the hill to the Employment Office. She and Papa had discussed the closure of the bookshop on New Year's Eve as they'd sat together, the gramophone playing quietly in the background.

'I see no alternative,' she'd said.

'I'll seek full-time work too. There's no money to be made as a puppeteer any more.' His eyes clouded. A short time later, he went to bed, and Jana stretched out on the sofa with a book she'd borrowed from Dasha at their last meeting. She read until midnight and, placing the book on her stomach, she greeted the new year listening to the silence; the curfew meant no one was out celebrating. And what was there to celebrate anyway? Another year under the occupation of the Reich? So 1943 had slid in unheralded with a fresh sweep of snow.

There was a queue outside the Employment Office building, but Jana had become used to queues since the start of the war. She was actually grateful for the wait, each second delaying the moment that she would give up the bookshop and commit to a new job; although, the bookshop hadn't been a job to her, but a passionate way of life, a purpose and connection to Mama. Misery welled up inside her as she edged forward and stepped inside the building.

The thin, balding man frowned down at the questionnaire Jana had completed in the waiting room. Then he stubbed out his cigarette in an overflowing ashtray and immediately lit up a new one.

'Hmm, Literature student and bookseller.' Unimpressed, he looked back up at her. 'Any craft skills?'

'I can sew.'

His face brightened. 'Then you could stitch leather.'

'I suppose so.' She would rather stitch fabric.

'Good news. Positions are available at a factory that produces boots for the Wehrmacht.'

'Oh, I was thinking more in line of work as a seamstress. I'm experienced at making clothes for puppets and—'

He laughed out loud, exposing small, nicotine-stained teeth.

'Puppets? Books? Oh, come now. We need useful skills. Anyway, it makes no difference. My orders are that all applicants today are to be assigned to either boot or armament production.' He raised his eyebrows in a question.

'Boots,' said Jana, angry at his humiliation of her.

He shoved some papers across his desk which she signed and moments later, she left the building with a letter of employment to start at the factory the following week.

* * *

Jana spent the evening before her first day at the factory cleaning and tidying the bookshop. She removed the books from the bookcases and wiped the shelves, then carefully dusted each book with a short feather duster before slotting it back in place.

The pressure of unshed tears built behind her eyes as she cleared her window display and taped her hand-written sign on the inside of the glass:

CLOSED

So many bookshops had closed since the Germans had issued their banned book lists. The ones that remained open mostly sold books by German authors or German translations with altered texts deemed appropriate to Nazi ideals. Her shop, with its selection of Czech and international authors, was one of the last real ones: to her mind, the last bookshop in Prague. The tears burst through then, and as she took one last look around her, she whispered into the room, 'We'll be back, Mama. The day will come, I promise.'

* * *

Each dark morning, she dragged herself out of bed, dreading the day ahead of her: the noise of the factory, the cloying smell of the leather, the endless rows of soles to be stitched into the German Jack boots. Her fingers and hands were sore and she suffered daily from headaches. But at least she was earning money and was able to pay her landlord some of the rent for the closed bookshop. He waivered the rest.

As the first Monday of each month approached, she toyed with the idea of meeting Egon at the Masna coffee shop. She had no intention of joining the resistance again, but burned to ask him if he knew anything about Andrej. But then she worried Egon might manage to persuade her into some resistance activity, and she became afraid, letting the Monday slip past. *Maybe next month*, she told herself.

When April came and the snow melted, restlessness gripped her and nothing she did could appease her. Andrej dominated her thoughts day and night; she chided herself for her inaction to discover what had happened to him, and as the first buds unfurled their pink blossoms on an early Monday morning, Jana walked into the Masna coffee shop.

Egon sat near the back, his bulky frame hunched over a mug of coffee. Jana was surprised to see him talking to a pretty, dark-haired girl sitting opposite him. Jana hesitated but Egon spotted her and waved her over.

'Come, join us and I'll order you a cup of this awful coffee.'

'No, thank you. I'm on my way to work and can only stay a few minutes,' said Jana, taking the free chair.

'I'm delighted to see you. Are you no longer at the bookshop?'

'No, unfortunately. I work at a shoe factory.'

Egon dipped his head towards her. 'Are you here to join up with us?'

Jana glanced at the young girl whose face remained impassive.

'This is Nela; she's part of the group, so you can talk freely,' said Egon. Then he nodded at the elderly man behind the counter. 'The owner's all right too.' Egon looked back at her, waiting for her to speak.

'I actually wanted to ask a favour; if you know or can find out anything about a police captain called Andrej Kovar. He was working for the resistance and has gone missing.'

'People go missing every day. That's nothing new.' Nela's tone was clipped.

'I've heard of him,' said Egon, 'but I have no information other than he no longer works at the police station in Prague. Why do you want to find him?'

Heat crept up Jana's throat. *Because I love him. Because I'm terrified for him.* 'I witnessed him being driven away by the Gestapo and he's not been seen since.'

'So?' Nela's mouth formed a hard line.

Egon raised a hand to silence her.

'He was working against the Nazis. He's one of us. Please help me find out what happened to him.' Jana's voice wobbled on her last words and Nela gave her a knowing look.

'I'll do what I can. In the meantime, maybe you would consider working as a courier.'

This was exactly what she had feared: being drawn into operations again. As if reading her expression, Egon added, 'Nothing as involved or dangerous as your last assignments. I know what was asked of you then. You would just need to transport small packages. Radio parts, to be precise.'

Jana's stomach churned. That was exactly what Lenka had been doing when she'd been arrested. The memory of her pregnant friend dropping to her knees and being hauled away from the market spiked her chest and made her gasp. She reached for her locket before remembering it was no longer there.

'At least think about it. If you change your mind, I'll be here next month on the first Monday.'

Jana nodded, wondering where Egon was and what he was doing the rest of the time.

She rose to leave and said goodbye, knowing that Nela was staring at her as she walked away.

37

A month later, Jana returned to the Masna coffee shop, both excited and afraid about news Egon might have on Andrej. She'd also given careful thought about the courier work Egon had proposed. Cracks in her resolve to distance herself from the resistance had appeared since Egon had mentioned carrying radio parts; memories of Lenka's bravery as she'd carried out this same mission spun a loop in Jana's mind. Lenka had been highly pregnant, but that had not diminished her determination. And she'd paid a high price for the cause.

Jana had begun to wonder about her motives for her own inaction. Yes, the Lidice massacre had shaken her to her core and made her question the value of resisting the regime. She'd tried to assuage her guilt by denying herself the pleasure of love. But now all she did was wallow around in self-pity, even more so since Andrej was missing. She had become stagnant, with no purpose in her life. She really didn't like herself any more.

Her heart sank slightly as she walked in and saw that Nela was with Egon again. Although Nela was probably younger than Jana, she still felt intimidated by her. A coffee was already waiting for her and she slid into the chair beside Egon. After a brief exchange of greetings, he got straight to the point.

'I have no news of your friend Kovar, I'm afraid. The resistance has become fractured and extremely cautious since the brutal Nazi crackdown. Even if someone knew something, they would be reluctant to say.'

'He's dead.' Nela's tone was matter-of-fact.

'Why do you say that?' Jana snapped.

'Because you said the Gestapo had him.'

'That's true. But I don't know he's dead. He's missing.' Jana's voice shook with fear, mixed with anger at Nela.

Egon interjected, looking at Nela. 'This isn't helpful right now.' Then turning to Jana, he said, 'Have you thought any more about the courier work I suggested last time we met?'

Jana took a few breaths to calm herself and focus on the quick change of topic. It was time to stop dithering, pick herself up and let Lenka be her inspiration.

'I'll do it,' she said.

38

Over the summer, Jana's main contact was Nela. Egon had retreated to the hills outside Prague where he was rounding up and training new members of the resistance. Nela would give Jana details of the pick-up and drop-off points. At first, Nela remained curt and unsmiling, but as Jana continued to turn up for each assignment, a restrained camaraderie developed between them.

Jana's new role gave her a sense of purpose once more and helped offset the drudgery of producing those dreadful Jack boots for the enemy. And without Andrej in her life, her missions helped to give her a different focus, during the daytime at least. At night, he still dominated her dreams and she refused to believe Nela's view that he was dead.

Jana's long hours at the shoe factory meant her assignments were scheduled for either early mornings or evenings. On a hot, August morning, Jana strode towards the market in Wenceslas square. Each week, there were fewer stall holders – they had nothing to sell – but still the citizens turned out with their ration cards in the vain hope of finding a scrap of food to feed their families. Mostly people liked to meet up and talk.

Jana carried a nondescript, brown, nylon shopping bag stuffed with newspapers, which she would exchange for a similar bag stuffed with radio parts. Her left wrist was bandaged: a signal she was the courier. Leaning against the base of the Wenceslas statue was a petite woman holding a yellow notebook in one hand and a brown nylon bag in the other. Jana sidled up to her and they both placed their bags on the ground. Ignoring each other, they surveyed the square and watched the passersby. After a few moments, Jana checked her watch and as if realising she was late, snatched up the petite woman's bag and headed off across the square. Feeling the weight of the radio parts made her heart race.

She passed a violinist playing under a lantern, his case open on the ground before him. Two policemen appeared through the crowd, marching in her direction, the older, heavier one staring straight at her. Uneasiness rippled in her stomach; a feeling of déjà vu overcoming her. The same violinist under the same lantern, and the same spot where Lenka was arrested was where Jana stood now; two policemen about to stop and search her. It was kismet that she too would be captured doing exactly what Lenka had been doing in the same place. Inevitable really.

Beads of sweat broke out on her forehead as she halted and waited for the moment, her hand that held the shopping bag trembling. The police were in front of her now, both giving her strange looks. She would go quietly, not make a scene. Perhaps she would end up in Terezin with Lenka; that was if the Gestapo didn't get her first. Didn't do what they did—

'Are you all right, Miss?'

The older, heavier policeman was talking to her, frowning. 'You're looking very pale.'

'Just feeling a bit faint,' Jana murmured.

'It's the damn heat. Going to be another scorcher today. Take a drink from the fountain and get yourself in the shade.'

'Yes, thank you, I'll do that.'

He nodded and the two policemen walked on.

Jana pulled herself together and took her delivery to the Masna coffee shop where she handed it over the owner behind the counter, relief flooding through her at the successful completion of her task.

39

After the book club ladies had dispersed on a blustery November evening, Dasha hung back, a pensive expression on her face. Jana had noticed she hadn't engaged as much as she usually did in the meetings; it was obvious she had something on her mind.

'How are you and the family?' asked Jana, sitting back down on a stool, indicating she had time for her friend although she was exhausted after a day stitching boots.

Dasha shrugged and sat too. 'You know, fed up, like all of us. I hate handing over my daughter to my mother-in-law so that I can go to work in a factory canteen.'

'How are you getting on with your mother-in-law these days? Any better?'

'Worse, actually. And it would be nice if I had a husband that supported his wife rather than his mother.' Her tone was edged with bitterness. 'Actually, Valtr and I are having problems; our marriage wasn't what it was...'

Jana put a hand on Dasha's knee. 'Times are so hard at the moment that everyone is under terrible strain.'

Dasha shook her head. 'It's not that. There's a distance between us...' She broke off and with a false laugh, added, 'All these romantic books we're reading are not helping. Anyway, I better get off home now.'

As Jana locked up the bookshop and climbed the steps to the apartment, she considered Dasha's words. The recent exchanging of lighter romance novels was intended as escapism from the drudgery of the occupation, but maybe for some it ignited yearning, in Dasha's case, possible dissatisfaction. For Jana, reading love stories just highlighted everything she had lost. Her few brief encounters with Andrej would forever be embedded in her soul. And yet just after the one time they had made love, she'd pushed him away. Although she had told herself it was over, deep down, she'd believed she would always have the chance to relent if she chose.

She entered the apartment, eyes brimming with tears. He had been so courageous and selfless in his double role in the police force and yet she had never told him how brave she thought he was. He had told her he loved her and she'd not returned the words. If only she could tell him now the painful depth of her love for him. But for the first time, she faced the reality. Pain pierced through her, pinning her to the spot.

Nela was right.

Andrej would not be returning. Ever.

40

Babi's house echoed with the sound of children's voices. A joyous sound, thought Jana as she watched Michal, Yveta and Maddie rummage through Papa's old toy trunk, deciding what to play next.

Michal pulled out a wooden box. 'Ludo!' he exclaimed.

'Ah, my favourite when I was a child,' said Papa, as he settled himself down on the floor beside them. Michal slid open the lid, which served as the playing field and retrieved the four wooden tokens, each brightly coloured.

'I want red,' said Maddie, snatching up the figure and holding it behind her back.

'Well, that's decided, then,' laughed Papa.

Jana sat with Babi on the sofa, their weight causing the old springs to dip in the middle.

'It gladdens my heart to hear your father laugh again,' said Babi. 'The children are a balm for his soul.'

'And for yours too.' Jana smiled.

'Indeed, they are a blessing. Even though tragic circumstances brought them here, I am grateful for the purpose they've given me.'

Yveta rattled the dice in the cup and sent them skittering across the board.

'Your father and his brother used to play with that very set for hours, right up till they were teenagers,' Babi said fondly, her eyes with a faraway look.

'You must miss him,' said Jana, wishing she had known her uncle.

'The Great War took so many.' Babi sighed. 'Just young boys, they were. And now this madness is happening all over again.' She shook herself free of her thoughts and turned to Jana. 'And how are you, my dear?'

'Fine,' she answered automatically. But how was she really? It was now April, 1944, nearly two years since the assassination of Heydrich and the terrible reprisals.

Since then, she'd watched the people of Prague continue their lives as best they could, faces grim with resignation. The suppressed hatred against the Germans was poison in the veins that turned one bitter and hard and angry. People were starving, tired and overworked. The Germans demanded they work long hours in factories and transport services to keep their war machine rolling.

Her courier work had been temporarily paused because of a possible leak in their activities, but Egon would contact her again when the coast was clear.

It was also nearly two years since she and Andrej had made love in the little, old steam boat on a warm summer's evening, but she could feel his touch and taste his lips as if it was yesterday. And as each day passed, the pain of losing him scoured deeper into her heart.

'You are not fine, my angel.' Babi laid a hand over hers. 'Shall we go into the kitchen to talk?'

But although Jana would've loved to unburden herself, she didn't know where she would begin. Not a soul knew about her love affair with Andrej.

'Really, Babi, I'm fine,' she repeated.

There was a loud shriek from Michal; the faces of the dice showed a double six and he triumphantly moved his token around the board, counting loudly. Jana caught Yveta giving her a surreptitious glance from beneath her long, straight fringe. The girl, now a teenager, was still wary of her but was deeply fond of Babi. She had grown tall with long limbs, and beneath her dress, a small bosom was evident. The green, floral dress she wore had belonged to Mama once; Babi had altered it on her sewing machine, taking it in at the seams. Babi had used every piece of available fabric to sew clothes for the growing girls.

Jana gave Yveta a small smile but she looked away.

After the game, they ate lunch: a potato and leek casserole. It was a wonder, Jana thought, how Babi had kept the children fed for the last two years, but somehow with her chickens and vegetable patch, she managed. Jana and Papa brought what they could from their rations when they visited.

Babi had taken it upon herself to continue the children's education, and Jana helped with reading and writing on Sundays, keeping up a supply of books. After lunch, Jana unpacked the books she had brought and spread them out on the floor. The children gathered round to look through the books and claim their next read. After some quiet time reading, the children were allowed to play with a skipping rope in the garden while Babi kept lookout from the attic window. The children had learned to keep their voices low, and Jana was amazed how they had adapted to their confinement.

The afternoon passed quickly and soon it was time for Jana and her father to catch the bus back to Prague. They said their goodbyes with promises to see each other the following Sunday. Maddie gave Jana an extra fierce hug and whispered, 'Have you heard anything about Mama?'

Jana's heart twisted. 'No, my sweetheart. But that doesn't have to mean bad news.' In reality, she didn't even know if Lillian was still being held in Terezin. Perhaps she had been transported elsewhere. The not knowing was terrible, but Jana held on to the belief that no news was good news.

It was early evening when the bus dropped Jana and Papa back in the centre of Prague. It was warmer here in the city so Jana shrugged off her cardigan and slipped it over her arm. As they strolled down the busy, tree-lined avenue, the boy at the newspaper stand called out the headlines, his adolescent voice breaking on his words.

'International Red Cross approve Theresienstadt,' he shouted at the passersby, waving a newspaper in the air.

Jana and Papa exchanged sceptical looks. Papa bought a newspaper.

'Papa, would you mind if I sat here on a bench to read the newspaper a while before going home?'

He was happy to do so and handed it to her. She couldn't wait to read the article.

'See you later,' he said and strolled in the direction of home.

She sat down on one of the benches along the avenue and snapped open the newspaper, her eyes racing over the report: a delegation from the International Red Cross had visited the town of Theresienstadt at the invitation of Germany; the three inspectors praised the town developed for the largely Jewish community; the streets were clean and an array of shops provided groceries, including fresh daily bread. There was a school, post office and even a theatre. Culture of all types was encouraged, especially music and literature. The delegates had spoken with happy, well-dressed children and had even witnessed a well-attended football match. As proof of their findings, there were two photographs: one of smiling children in smart clothes, and one of a crowd cheering the football teams.

Jana's stomach churned. She was sick of the lies, the propaganda, the staged photographs. How could the Red Cross delegates be so easily fooled? Did they not look behind the scenes like she had done? She hadn't wandered very far to see the true conditions.

She slapped the newspaper down on the bench beside her in disgust. It was puzzling how the Germans had been open about Lidice, but were making such a big effort to promote assurance over humane conditions in Terezin; it made her uneasy, as if they were hiding something. Something big.

She thought of Lenka, who'd feared she might be transported. Jana hadn't heard anything from her friend since Andrej had disappeared. All communications with Terezin had been cut off. She didn't know if Lenka was still there or even alive. And what about Michal's parents and Yveta and Maddie's mother, Lillian? There had been no news from them either.

She heaved a deep sigh and closed her eyes a few moments.

A bus rumbled to a halt at a nearby bus stop. A dog barked behind her.

'Hello, Jana.'

Her eyes flicked open at the familiar voice. It was Nela.

'I saw you from across the street. What are you doing here?'

'I'm just reading the newspaper. I can hardly believe what they are saying...'

The words tumbled out of her as she told Nela what'd she'd

read about the Red Cross visit and the façade put on by the Nazis, her voice full of passion and indignation.

'It's propaganda, of course,' Nela said quietly. 'The international press will pick it up and show the world what the Nazis want them to see. Their humane solution to the so-called Jewish problem.'

'Oh, I know that. I saw it for myself at Terezin and told Miss Novak. She's the Red Cross lady who was with us at the time. Actually, I haven't seen her for a while...' She tailed off and cast a wary glance around her, wondering if it was all right for her and Nela to talk in public. She lowered her voice. 'Any news from Egon?'

Nela nodded. 'He's out in the countryside, gathering support. We have to be patient and wait for the right moment. Don't give up on the resistance, Jana; things are happening.' Nela gave the merest hint of a smile, then got up and sauntered away.

41

Jana let herself into the bookshop and immediately, her chest eased. It had become her ritual to come here every evening after she finished work at the shoe factory. The shelves of books were a welcoming embrace. The shop was a place of solace where she sensed a quiet power from the books and the connection to her mother. This was her purpose: to keep the shop alive behind the locked door, to preserve it until the day the city would be free again and she could welcome back book lovers. The day when she would be allowed to stock all books without fear of punishment, the day people could choose what they wanted to read. This dream kept her going.

She moved through the shop and out into the backyard where she picked up a watering can. She had transformed the yard into a little oasis; an array of mismatched pots were arranged around the pebble stone yard. In between the pots were some old garden ornaments Babi had given her. Jana had laid out a seated area consisting of a circular table with sun umbrella, two folding chairs and upturned crates covered in bright cushions.

As she watered the red geraniums, Nela's words from a few days ago spun a loop in her head. *Don't give up on the resistance. Things are happening.*

She fetched glasses from the kitchen, placed them outside on the table and then filled a jug with tap water. How nice it would be to offer her friends homemade lemonade. Her mouth watered at the thought of bright-yellow lemons, something she hadn't seen for years. Standing by the sink, she drank a large glass of water to fill her stomach; she would not eat this evening, saving her meagre rations for Babi and the children. The food situation was dire and the gnaw of hunger was her constant companion.

Just before seven o'clock, Jana went back into the shop and waited for the women to arrive. She was pleased she had kept the book club going; the group met once a month not just to discuss books but anything that helped their daily lives, exchanging tips for mending shoes and clothes, stretching rations and giving each other emotional support.

Dasha arrived first, followed by Karolina. When everyone was gathered in the shop, Jana led them into the yard where they made themselves comfortable in the evening sunshine. Jana was reflective as she looked around the group. Dasha, despite the lack of nutrition, had bright eyes and pink cheeks. Jana pondered how she'd seen Dasha a couple of times recently talking to the same German soldier, but she quashed her uncharitable thought quickly; despite Dasha's comments about troubles in her marriage, Dasha wouldn't be unfaithful to her husband, and certainly not with a German. Opposite Jana sat Karolina, her appearance the polar opposite of Dasha. Karolina's husband, Petr, was still incarcerated in the prison block at Terezin. It pained Jana to see her suffering. There had been little news about him and Karolina's face was etched with worry, her skin translucent.

The group chatted as the sun slid golden behind the buildings, throwing the yard into shadow. The women drifted off until only Dasha remained sitting outside.

'You saw the Red Cross article?' said Jana.

'Sickening, isn't it? But you saw the truth behind the façade.'

'But that doesn't help anyone. I wish I could tell my version to the newspapers; get a message out somehow.'

Dasha gave her a sideways look. 'I sometimes wonder if you and Lenka were involved somehow in resistance activities. If you still are.'

Jana was taken back at the direct question. For a moment. Jana imagined what a relief it would be to tell Dasha everything: from hiding Michal, to spying in Prague Castle and falling in love with a fascist policeman who wasn't a fascist at all. She could no longer talk to her best friend Lenka, and now Dasha was her closest friend. Still...

'You mean when Lenka and I were students,' laughed Jana. 'Sure, we wrote some slogans on walls and pulled down a few German flags. But that was a long time ago.' Jana rose and picked up the empty water jug from the table. 'Back in a moment.'

She went to the kitchen and refilled the jug, giving herself time to gather her thoughts. When she returned to Dasha, she said, 'How are things at home?' If Dasha noticed the deliberate change in conversation, she didn't show it. Again Jana thought about Dasha talking to that German soldier. Or had she been flirting? She had stopped herself from confiding in Dasha just in time.

42

Jana continued to go to the Masna coffee shop the first Monday of each month. Nela was always waiting for her, alone. Egon was involved in something big, she told Jana, but did not expand further. For several months, Jana was not required to act as a courier, but then one freezing December Monday, Nela's pale, pretty face was graver than usual.

'We need your help. The place we use for storage has been raided. We got a tip off and managed to move the goods to somewhere temporary, but we're looking for an alternative location.'

Jana's mouth went dry in anticipation of what was coming next. She took a sip of the coffee and glanced around her. There were no customers, just the owner behind the counter washing glasses. Outside was pitch black; dawn was at least two hours away.

'What do you want me to do?'

'You have a bookshop that is closed. A perfect hiding place.'

Jana's chest tightened. 'You want me to hide radio parts?'

Nela paused, chewing her cheek, then leaned across the small table. 'Ammunition.'

Jana jolted and she stared at Nela, speechless.

'Not weapons,' Nela continued 'Only bullets that are small and easy to hide. We need them here in the centre of Prague, ready for when the day comes...' She tailed off, waiting for Jana to speak.

'I don't know, Nela. It endangers so many people I have connections with: my father, the women who come to my book club...' Jana leaned her elbows on the table and put her head in her hands.

'Then cancel your book club. Tell your father nothing. Now is the time to show your courage for our country.'

As Jana looked up at Nela's flaming eyes and fierce expression, something inside her shifted. A surge of patriotism and defiance gripped her. 'All right. Tell me how it will work.'

* * *

Jana's first action was to cancel the book club until further notice, citing her longer work hours and feeling exhausted as a reason. Next, she rummaged around the bookshop searching for the ideal hiding place for ammunition. She had several cartons full of books: perhaps too obvious. Maybe under a floorboard. She tapped her foot along the firmly nailed boards, but found no suitable spot. Behind a bookcase? There were only stone walls. Under the kitchen sink where Michal had hidden, perhaps. Again, too obvious. Sinking into her armchair, her mind weary, she curled her legs beneath her. The seat was beginning to sag and needed new springs. She jumped up and removed the upholstered cushion before tipping the chair on its side and examining underneath. The base of the chair was stitched closed with coarse fabric.

Returning from the kitchen with a toolkit, she used a pen

knife to cut open the stitches and peeled back the fabric to reveal a row of coiled springs fixed to a wooden frame. She pulled at the frame; it would be a struggle to get it out, but she was determined that her idea was a good one. The base of the heavy chair was deep and could certainly hide a stack of bullets. Using a pair of pliers, she released the nails of the frame holding the springs and slid the whole thing out. Then peering into the cavity, she smiled, satisfied with herself.

* * *

Nela had told her to expect the delivery on the following Friday evening at eight o'clock. It was arranged the courier would come through the back entrance. Jana opened the back door of the bookshop and walked across the yard. The wooden door fitted into the fence was closed with a small, single bolt which she slid open. She peered into the narrow alleyway that ran behind but could barely see anything in the frozen night.

She rubbed her hands together, nervous and cold. Light footsteps on frosted cobbles, and a slight figure appeared before her. Nela, a bulky bag under her arm. She had brought the delivery herself.

The girls hurried inside and Jana tipped over the chair and pointed to the space beneath. 'Once we've packed everything inside, I'll loosely stitch the base back in place.'

Nela nodded her approval and knelt down, shoving the bag into the base of the chair.

'Perfect,' said Nela, standing back up and holding out her hand. 'I just need your spare key to the back door.'

This part of the plan made Jana uneasy. Nela was to have access to the bookshop so that the ammunition could be collected at short notice, for example if Jana was at the shoe factory and not contactable.

'I'll take care of the shop,' Nela said, reading her mind. 'I know how precious it is to you. The ammunition won't be here long; we need to get it to our fighters.'

Jana took the key from her dress pocket and dropped it into Nela's palm.

Nela walked out the back door and across the yard. As she walked through the door in the fence, she turned. 'Keep this door unbolted.'

'Yes. And Merry Christmas,' Jana whispered.

But Nela was already gone.

43

As the dreary winter months crawled into 1945, Jana's highlight was visiting Babi and the children on Sundays. Today, Papa was at home with a heavy cold, so on this crisp, March morning, she headed out alone to the bus stop. She had packed a bag full with young children's books for Maddie and Michal. For Yveta, now thirteen years old, she'd brought *Jane Eyre*.

As she approached the bus stop, she caught sight of Dasha on the other side of the road and stepped forward to wave. Something thumped against her elbow with such force that her bag flew to the ground, the books spilling out. The cyclist that had hit her did not stop but hurled abuse at her as he pedalled on.

Dasha hurried over and knelt to help Jana. 'Are you hurt? What an oaf that cyclist is. What are you doing with your old children's books?'

'Oh, donating them,' Jana said, flustered, rubbing her elbow.

'Why don't you bring them to the church where I help out. We need children's books and toys.' She retrieved the last book and handed it to Jana with a smile.

'Next time. I promised these to someone else.'

'No doubt you're taking the bus to your grandma as it's Sunday? Where does she live exactly?'

'In the middle of nowhere,' Jana forced a laugh and changed the subject. 'How's the family?'

The two friends chattered till Jana's bus arrived and Dasha waved her off.

* * *

A week later, Papa still had a bad cough, so Jana caught the bus on her own. She looked out the window and thought about her friendship with Dasha; they had drifted apart the last few months, since Jana had stopped the book club.

She pictured Dasha's enquiring look as she'd picked up the fallen books. Had she suspected something? Unlikely. And anyway, Dasha was a close friend and would never betray her. Surely?

No, Jana was more worried about Pavel; he had been actively involved in Michal's escape and knew that he was with Babi. But he had been involved in other anti-Nazi activities and hated the regime. Would he turn against her and collaborate with his sworn enemy? Did he still bear a grudge that she'd rejected him? Oh, for goodness' sake, she was being paranoid. Treachery was a spectre that loomed over everyone, each person suspicious and afraid of friends and neighbours. And as people became poorer and more desperate, the Germans were waiting to lure them into acts of betrayal.

Jana shook her head to clear her thoughts of traitors and spies and settled back for the half-hour journey, closing her eyes. Within moments, she was thinking about Andrej; it was nearly three years since he'd disappeared and there hadn't been one iota of news. He had simply vanished. But, of course, that's what the Gestapo did: made people vanish. She had to somehow come to terms that he was no longer alive. Her heart wrenched. Terrible images floated into her mind of how Andrej might have met his death and she sprung open her eyes to avert them.

The bus stopped and more passengers boarded. A young girl about Yveta's age approached the seat beside her, asking if it was free. Jana nodded her consent and the girl sat down, drew a book from her handbag and began to read.

If only Yveta could be free to do something as simple as ride a bus and read a book in public. She was going through puberty and if that wasn't hard enough, she was separated from her mother and in hiding from the Nazis. Jana would make an extra effort with her today, try to reach behind the wall the young girl had built and hope that she would eventually accept Jana's friendship.

As the bus neared her stop, she redid the top buttons of her coat and slipped her hands into her gloves. Jana checked her watch; the bus was on time and Babi would be expecting them. Her mood lifted at the prospect of spending the rest of the day playing and reading with the children, all in the warm company of her sprightly grandmother.

Jana walked the short distance from the bus stop but before she had a chance to raise the knocker, the door opened. Babi, her expression nervous and urgent, beckoned her in. The three children stood fully dressed in the narrow hallway, their faces barely visible beneath their thick scarves and woolly hats. Both girls were wearing boys' trousers, not the usual dresses they wore on a Sunday. Three pairs of solemn eyes met her gaze.

'What's the matter?' asked Jana, noticing the rucksack at Yveta's feet.

'Police are in the village asking questions. About Jewish children,' said Babi.

'No! Are you sure?' Jana said, fear closing her throat.

'The postmistress told me less than an hour ago. I walked into the village to collect my post.'

Jana's thoughts stumbled over each other, panic paralysing her.

'Now, listen. I've packed food and drink,' Babi said, pointing at the rucksack. 'You must leave immediately with the children.'

'But where should we go?' Jana said, overwhelmed.

'I have an old school friend in the village of Zbraslav. You've heard me talk of her: Milada Jesenska. She lives in the first house after the village sign at the side of the road.'

'But she doesn't know me. I can't just turn up with three children.'

'She's a good woman; we went through a lot together during the last war.' Babi held Jana's arm and looked at her with steady eyes. 'She will help you.'

'But how do we get there and how far is it?' Jana's voice rose in panic. This was all happening too fast. She glanced at the children, terrified at the responsibility. When she'd smuggled them out of Prague, she'd had time to plan. Looking wildly at Babi, she shook her head. 'It's too dangerous...'

Babi spoke in a calm, assured voice. 'You can do this, Jana. Breathe. Come on, Jana, Breathe.'

Jana did as Babi told her and after a few moments, her mind cleared.

'Tell me,' she said, her voice now resolute.

'You'll leave from the back of the house, over the fence and across the field till you come to the train track. Follow the track to your left, keeping yourself hidden between the trees until you get to Zbraslav station. It's about thirty kilometres which will take a few hours, but you'll arrive before nightfall.'

'And from the station?'

'Then follow the road for another kilometre which leads to the village. Now, let's go.'

Babi sped them through the house and into the garden.

'But what happens once we're there?' said Jana as she adjusted the rucksack on her back.

'We'll work it out once the coast is clear. I'll get word to you. But first, we need to get the children out of here.' Her words were vague but Jana knew Babi was thinking on her feet.

Babi lifted an old garden chair and carried it to the fence.

'But what will happen to you, Babi? The police will come here. Or worse, the Gestapo.'

'They have no proof of anything. The children and I packed away all the toys and books. If I'm questioned, I'll say the things are from my sons' childhood. You go over first, Jana, and I'll pass the children over to you.'

Jana looked at the chair and back at Babi, terrified for her. What did the police know? How did they find out about the children? Did someone betray them? But there was no time to dwell. She threw her arms around her beloved grandma, tears filling her eyes.

'Please, stay safe, Babi.'

'You too, my precious girl.'

Jana longed to linger in her embrace but Babi pushed her away gently, and held on to the chair. 'Hop up.'

At that moment, Yveta rushed at Babi and buried her head against her shoulder.

'I'm not leaving you,' she said.

'Now, now.' Babi patted Yveta's back. 'I need you to be strong. You must look after your sister and Michal. I'm relying on you.'

Yveta let out a muffled sob, shaking her head.

'Please, come,' said Maddie in a tiny voice, tugging on Yveta's coat.

Jana watched the scene, sorrow tugging at her heart.

'We'll come back again,' she said, not sure if she believed her own words.

Reluctantly, Yveta drew away from Babi and took Maddie's hand. 'I'm ready now,' she said with a sniff.

Jana climbed onto the chair. She gave Babi one last look, swung up her arms and grabbed the top of the fence. Then she scrambled over the top, grateful she was wearing a flared dress that allowed her legs movement. She dropped down to the other side with a thud. The earth was still hard, but the snow had nearly gone.

A shuffle, a grunt from Babi and Maddie's face appeared over the top of the fence. Jana held up her arms and Maddie jumped into them. Next came Michal, his eyes wide with fear and excitement. Jana caught him and swung him to the ground. Then she looked up waiting for Yveta. Seconds ticked past. Babi was saying something, her tone urgent. Still there was no sign of the girl.

A rumble of car engines broke the quietness.

'Yveta,' hissed Jana. If Yveta didn't come, she would have to flee without her. But she couldn't leave her to the mercy of the Germans.

Again, she called her name.

The noise of the car motors neared.

Then stopped... Car doors slammed.

Jana grabbed Michal and Maddie's hands and looked over her shoulder; they would have to be swift to reach the shelter of the conifers.

'Babi,' she called. 'What's—'

The fence shook, and Yveta scrambled over. Jana held out an arm to steady her, but she ignored the help and jumped down easily on her long legs. They raced away, Jana trying not to think of Babi opening the door to face the police. Her immediate task was to get the children to safety.

44

It was cold as they made their way through the gloom of the forest. Traces of snow lay beneath the trees, the last vestiges of winter interspersed with patches of snowdrops, heralding spring. Jana guessed they'd been walking about two hours, following alongside the train track as Babi had instructed. At first, Maddie and Michal had been animated, exchanging snatched words with each other, but now they walked in silence. It warmed Jana's heart to see how they had become close since they had been in hiding together, like brother and sister.

Yveta continued to stray a couple of paces behind, her face tight, waves of hostility radiating off her. Jana understood the girl; in Yveta's eyes, it was Jana who had led her away from her mother and now her substitute mother, Babi. The teenager was channelling her anger about the situation at Jana. But still, Jana struggled not to be hurt by it.

The shoes she was wearing were not ideal for walking. She had dressed that morning intending to spend a day indoors and not trampling through forests, and now, blisters had formed on both her heels. The children, however, wore sturdy boots. Babi had made sure they were suitably dressed for the journey.

They paused to eat the bread and tiny piece of cheese from the rucksack, sitting in a row on a fallen branch. It felt good to rest their feet but they soon began to shiver in the damp air.

They continued on their way, weaving through the fir trees, stepping over tree roots and broken branches Their pace slowed, and Jana heard the children panting; it occurred to Jana they had not taken a walk outside for such a long time. Although they had played and jumped around, they were not as physically fit as they should have been.

The sun was lowering in the winter afternoon and the shadows of the trees grew longer. She was just about to suggest a short rest when the ground began to tremble and the sound of an oncoming train alerted her. She moved her little group further from the tracks, and they crouched beneath a towering fir, waiting until the train had passed before marching on.

Hours had passed, and seeing the children's weary faces, Jana said, 'Not far now.' When a short time later, she peered through the trees to see a train platform, she said with relief, 'We're here.' But when she saw the station sign, her heart sank. It wasn't Zbraslav.

They retreated to the thickening forest and trudged on, daylight fading. Jana began to wonder if they had taken the right route; she didn't know the area at all. They were all so tired. Her own legs were weary, her heels rubbed raw. How long could they go on?

She kept her eyes peeled at the train track to her right, following its path through the countryside. The incline was steeper now, the landscape more hilly. Her rapid breaths swirled visibly in front of her as the temperature dipped. Finally, the grass verge gave way to a concrete platform, and a post with the sign *Zbraslav* came into view. They'd arrived.

Jana could see that the exit of the station was on the opposite side of the tracks, accessible by a wooden bridge. The bridge however was in full view of the stationmaster's hut, and although she couldn't see if it was occupied, she couldn't risk being seen. She led the worn-out children back the way they came till they reached a bend in the railway, and could cross the track unseen. They then made their way back to the station, crouching in single file behind her.

On one side of them lay the railway, and on the other, through a row of bare bushes, a road came into view. Jana halted and gathered the children.

'Wait here a moment. We've come to the village road, so the house must be nearby. I'll check the coast is clear.'

She pushed her way through the bushes to the side of the road and looked towards the station entrance. Her heart stopped. Two military trucks were parked outside. Several soldiers stood beside their vehicles, smoking. This was bad news. What were the Wehrmacht doing in this tiny village? She didn't know if they were searching for her and the children, but whatever the reason, she couldn't enter a village full of German soldiers. Retreating back, she began to panic. She and Babi had not discussed an alternative plan and she had no idea where they could go now.

The children were waiting with expectant faces.

She shook her head. 'I'm sorry, the Wehrmacht is in the village. We have to hide a while and hope that they leave.'

Maddie let out an exasperated moan and Michal's eyes filled with tears. Yveta looked crestfallen, her face white. She swayed slightly.

'Are you all right?' asked Jana. The girl looked ready to drop.

'I'm fine,' she said.

'As soon as we are back in the forest, we'll take a break and have a drink.'

Jana offered Yveta her arm but she pulled away.

They snuck back over the railway and headed for the trees, Jana's mind racing about her next move. The children were trailing behind her when she heard a soft thud. Maggie squealed. Jana sped round to see Yveta crumpled on the ground. She rushed to kneel by her.

'What happened?' she said to Maddie.

'Nothing. She just fell.'

'Yveta, can you hear me?'

The girl lay motionless on her side, her face translucent. Jana shook her shoulder and called her name again and again. Maddie and Michal joined in the chorus. Heartbeats passed. Jana sat cross-legged on the icy ground, lifting Yveta's head onto her lap and patted her stone-cold cheeks.

Yveta's long, dark eyelashes fluttered.

'She's conscious.' Jana sighed with relief. 'Maddie, fetch the flask of water.'

Maddie opened the flap of the rucksack on Jana's back and pulled out the flask.

'Help her to drink, while I hold her head,' Jana said.

Maddie held the flask to her sister's lips, murmuring encouragement for her to drink.

After taking a few sips, Yveta mumbled, 'What happened? Everything went black.'

'I think you fainted; not enough to eat or drink, exhaustion. It's not surprising. Let's lean you forward and get some blood to your head.' Jana heaved her to a sitting position and Yveta dropped her head to her knees.

'She'll be fine,' Jana said to Michal, who was watching with wide eyes, though she sounded more confident than she actually was. The chill from the ground seeped through her coat and she worried about Yveta; she had to get her up and moving. With Maddie's and Michal's help, they lifted Yveta to her feet.

She took a step, winced, and gave a small cry.

'I think I've twisted my ankle.'

Jana's heart plummeted. 'Can you walk?'

'I'll try,' she said, bravely.

Grimacing, Yveta tried a couple of steps. It was clear she was in pain and wouldn't be able to walk far.

Think, Jana, think, she told herself. Daylight was fading fast and the temperature was dropping by the moment. She had to find them somewhere to spend the night; she could keep watch, hoping that the Wehrmacht would move on and they could approach Babi's friend's house, or she could search for a nearby barn. Only, she hadn't seen a farm nearby. And Yveta couldn't traipse around looking for shelter. That meant she would have to leave the children here whilst she went looking. But how could she leave the children all alone in the forest? Perhaps the stationmaster's hut—

The crunch of breaking twigs.

The squeak of leather shoes, no heavier: boots.

Behind them, a grunt. Startled, Jana swung round and stared into the butt of a rifle.

45

'What do we have here?' The gruff voice belonged to a large, bearded man in ragged clothes, his broad hands clasped around the rifle. 'Who are you?' he said, frowning at Jana.

'Who are you?' she retorted, edging herself in front of the children, her arms stretched wide protectively.

He laughed. 'Perhaps a friend, if you're less cheeky. Are you thinking of staying out here all night?' He shrugged. 'Come with me if you want a roof over your head tonight, or not. As you wish.'

He turned away.

'Wait. Please,' said Jana. Dusk was turning to night as each second passed. They would soon be plunged into darkness. 'We need help. One of the children has an injured ankle and we have nowhere to go.'

She had no idea if she could trust him, but right at that moment, she saw no alternative.

He walked back towards them. 'Who's injured?'

Jana indicated Yveta, keeping a protective arm in front of her.

He grunted. 'She's just a slip of a girl. I'll throw her over my shoulder.'

'No.' Yveta recoiled. 'I'll walk.'

He laughed again, a deep, throaty laugh.

'Then follow me.'

They followed him through the trees, Yveta hobbling along, supported by Jana on one side and Maddie on the other. Michal hung on to Jana's coat sleeve. A short while later, they came to a small clearing. A soft glow lay ahead: an oil lamp in the window of a ramshackle building. Jana felt relief mixed with trepidation. She was taking a huge risk with this stranger but here was light and a roof, and the children were about to collapse with exhaustion. She took a deep breath as they all followed him through the front door and night closed in behind them.

A small woman with grey hair pulled up in an untidy bun looked at them with a startled expression. She stood at a stove in the sparsely furnished room, stirring a pot, the steam billowing around her lined face.

'Who are they?' she said sharply, putting her free hand on her hip.

'Fugitives, I'd say.' He threw Jana a glance. 'Running from the Germans, no doubt?'

She gave a tiny nod of the head.

'Well, they can't stay here,' the woman said.

'Just for the night. They'll move on tomorrow.'

He waved his hand to a sagging settee. 'You can rest there, all of you.'

Jana removed her rucksack and the four of them collapsed onto the worn, musty settee. Exhaling with relief to rest her aching muscles, she gathered the children close to her, where they remained huddled in their coats, teeth chattering.

The woman slammed two bowls and two spoons on the wooden table, then brought the pot over from the stove.

'There's not enough for them,' she said, ladling thin liquid into the bowls. 'There is barely enough for us.'

The man threw his coat over the back of one of the two chairs and sat down. The woman sat opposite and began to eat. The sight of them eating made Jana's stomach growl. The food that Babi had given them was all gone.

'I'm hungry,' whispered Michal.

The man looked across at them with an impenetrable expression, putting his spoon down. He picked up the bowl and carried it over to Michal.

'Drink,' he said.

Michal slurped at the soup and after a few greedy gulps, passed the bowl to Jana. She smiled at him and looked down at the broth; tiny cubes of carrot and potatoes floated in insipid liquid. It looked and smelt like heaven. She breathed it in and handed the bowl to Maddie. Jana didn't dare take even one sip, afraid she would drain the bowl completely once she got the taste in her mouth. Maddie drank and gave the bowl to her older sister, Yveta, who barely had the strength to drink, Jana thought, as she watched the girl with concern. 'Finish it,' said Jana, when Yveta held out the remains to her, and after a moment of hesitation, the girl sipped the last drops.

A little while later, when Jana had warmed up, she removed her hat and coat and helped the children do the same. She then knelt down and gently removed Yveta's boot and sock to inspect her injury. The ankle was swollen and already turning black.

'We need to bind that,' she said. She glanced over her shoulder. The man watched them dispassionately. Then with an irritated grunt, he pushed himself up from the table and rummaged around in the corner of the room where he produced a scrap of cloth and shoved it in Jana's hand. He returned to the table and poured himself a drink from an unmarked bottle. The woman said nothing as she continued to darn clothes, shooting Jana the occasional suspicious look.

Yveta winced and bit her lip as Jana bound her ankle.

'It looks like you sprained it when you fell, but I don't think it's broken,' Jana said.

Even so, Jana didn't know how they could continue their journey tomorrow if Yveta couldn't walk. And furthermore, a journey to where? Too tired to think about it, she clambered back onto the settee and shifted around with the children, trying to get comfortable, using their coats to cover themselves.

'Get some sleep,' she said as Michal and Maddie snuggled against her. Yveta propped herself up at the end of the settee.

Jana forced herself to keep awake, wary of the woman and man who sat in silence, he drinking and she sewing. Finally, they retired to their bedroom, leaving Jana and the children alone in the dark. She thought about slipping off her shoes, but her heels were rubbed raw and she was afraid she would never get them back on again. As she listened to the steady breathing of the children, her own eyelids fell and she drifted into a fitful sleep.

* * *

The creak of floorboards awoke her. Her heart jumped as her eyes snapped opened and she saw the man in rumpled clothes, bowed over her. She glanced with relief at the children still asleep by her side.

'Time to wake up, Sleeping Beauty,' he said and moved to the sink where he filled a kettle.

Jana eased her stiff neck from side to side and shook the children awake whilst the man put the kettle on the stove to boil. He made each of them a cup of fake coffee which Jana thankfully accepted; she had a dreadful taste in her dry mouth.

'Thank you for letting us spend the night here,' she said, sipping the bitter, brown liquid. 'I'm not sure what to do next, to be honest. Perhaps I'll check if the Wehrmacht are still occupying the village.'

Legs astride, he stood in front of her, slurping from a chipped mug.

'I have a better idea,' he said.

'You do?' she asked, desperate to hear any suggestion.

'I can tell you where some members of the resistance are hiding out. They'll give you shelter.'

Her heart leaped. 'Are you with the resistance?'

'I'm not with anyone but myself. But I'm no Nazi sympathiser, that's for sure.'

She stood up, shaking out her dress.

'I'd be very grateful if you could tell me where to find these people.'

'And I'd be grateful if you showed your appreciation. With payment,' a thin, hard voice said. The woman spoke as she entered the room, her dressing gown flapping, her grey, unbrushed hair loose around her shoulders. She looked old in the morning light.

'I'm afraid I've only a few coins in my purse,' said Jana.

'No payment, no information,' said the woman, exchanging a glance with the man, and stepping up close. Her eyes swept over Jana and settled on her wrist. 'Your watch.'

It was an inexpensive piece from a second-hand shop and Jana was willing to hand it over to buy their safety. She unfastened the strap and caught the man's eye. Could she trust him?

'You definitely know where the resistance are?' she asked.

'I know everything that goes on in this forest.' His expression was surly.

'Come on.' The woman folded her arms, tapping her fingers.

She handed the woman her watch.

'And the coins in your purse.'

Jana retrieved her purse from her rucksack and shook out the last of her money in the woman's outstretched hand. She thought about how Brandt had taken her locket and was sure if she'd been wearing it now, the woman would have demanded it from her too.

'What else do you have?' said the woman.

'Nothing,' said Jana, trying to keep the dismay out of her voice.

'Leave her be now,' sighed the man. 'I want to get going.'

Everything sped up after that. The man broke off a piece of hard bread for each of them, which the children ate hungrily, but Jana put hers in the rucksack before filling up her flask with water at the sink. When it was obvious that Yveta couldn't walk, the man fetched a rusty wheelbarrow and lifted the surprised girl into it before pushing it off down the track. Jana and the children followed him into a damp, grey morning, the woman slamming the front door behind them.

The group walked in silence through the forest, the man ahead pushing Yveta in the wheelbarrow, its wheel squeaking loudly. It had rained in the night and cold droplets fell from the needles of the pine trees. The promise of spring from a few days ago had disappeared. Jana was chilled to her bones and her leg muscles ached from the walk of the previous day. Hollowed out from hunger and lightheaded, she thought she'd keel over when a sharp gust of wind blew. Maybe she should have eaten that bread, but she'd saved it, not knowing where the next meal would come from.

Eventually, the man halted, set down the wheelbarrow and pointed to the ground. 'Follow this track. It leads to the home of a woodcutter. They call him The Bear. He'll help you.'

Jana's eyes followed the trail that weaved away between the trees.

'Aren't you coming with us?'

'I've work to do. It's not far: an hour or two. Keep to the track. You can keep the wheelbarrow.' He gave one of his now familiar grunts and headed off back the way they'd come before she could protest. She watched his receding back, hardly able to believe he'd led them into the middle of nowhere and then deserted them. Anger and frustration swelled inside her; she had given them her watch and the only money she had and he'd left them to their fate. She very much doubted there was a woodcutter's hut, let alone a man called The Bear. Perhaps the pair they had just spent the night with were collaborators with the Germans and for a reward were delivering her and the children into the hands of the Nazis; they would be greeted at the woodcutter's hut by cruel-faced men wearing long, leather coats.

Forcing back the despair that threatened to envelope her, she grasped the handles of the wheelbarrow and said, 'Let's get going.'

Despite Yveta's light weight for a thirteen-year-old, it was hard work pushing the old wheelbarrow with its wobbly wheel down the rutted path, and Jana's shoulders and arms soon burned. Yveta clutched the metal sides, grimacing at every bump, her face etched with pain. Maddie and Michal trudged by Jana's side, their faces miserable. As time passed, Jana wondered if they were going in the right direction: if there even was a right direction.

'Are we nearly there?' Michal whined.

'Not far now,' said Jana, frowning as the trail seemed to peter out.

'There is no woodcutter's house,' said Yveta, her voice full of bitterness.

'Don't say that!' shouted Maddie.

'It's true,' retorted Yveta. 'We've been left in the woods to die. Like Hansel and Gretel.'

Maddie burst into tears and Michal shouted at Yveta, 'Why are you always so mean?'

'That's enough.' Jana's voice rose above them. She set down the wheelbarrow and took a deep breath. 'Arguing will not help. I need you three to be brave and grown-up. We must support and encourage each other.' She turned to Yveta. 'I know you're in pain, but nevertheless, you are the oldest and I expect you to behave like it.'

Jana's tone came out more severe than she'd intended but the girl's face registered the rebuke and she quietened. Michal took Maddie's hand as she fiercely wiped at her tears.

They continued their journey in silence.

The trail ended abruptly, but ahead, the trees opened up and an imprint of cart wheels appeared on the ground. And horse's hoofprints.

Jana whirled her head at the children. 'There we have our woodcutter and his horse!'

With a surge of renewed energy, the small group ploughed on. Icy sleet began to fall, whipping their faces as they followed the tracks of the cart wheels. They seemed to go on forever and Jana was sure they'd been walking for far longer than an hour or two as the man had told her. Her wool coat grew wet and heavy and after a while, she saw that Yveta was sitting in a pool of water. Jana stopped, hauled the bedraggled girl from the wheelbarrow, tipped out the water and helped her back in again. Jana's knees threatened to buckle, but she gritted her teeth and pushed on. There was no other alternative.

She noticed the smoke first, billowing into the slate sky. A large cabin with a chimney emerged through the driving sleet. The cart tracks stopped outside a barn attached to the side of the cabin.

'We're here,' she said with a huge sigh. But her relief was tinged with wariness when she thought of the frigid reception at last night's accommodation.

They stumbled to the door. Doubt crossed Jana's mind as she knocked, her mind blank at what to say. She didn't even know the name of the man who'd sent them here.

A middle-aged woman with a large bosom opened the door and stared at them. Where was the woodcutter? Was this the right house?

'Does someone called The Bear live here?' asked Jana.

'My goodness, look at the state of you poor lambs. Come in,' said the woman, then called over her shoulder. 'Bear, you have visitors.'

Heavy footsteps approached behind the woman. She stepped to one side and Jana gasped at the burly man.

It was Egon.

46

The woman who had greeted them, Ramona, was Egon's wife. She was broadly built with a loud laugh and bright eyes; Jana liked her immediately. Egon beckoned them to the warmth of the woodburning stove whilst Ramona went to fetch food for the little troupe.

Egon explained that this was his home, from where he was organising his resistance group.

'But how on earth did you find me and what happened to you, Jana?'

She told her story and when Jana told of her experience at the couple's house the previous night, Egon laughed. 'They're a miserable pair, those two. But they hate the Germans and keep an eye out for us.'

Jana continued. 'But I had no idea that the woodcutter named The Bear would turn out to be you.' Her eyes welled with tears of thankfulness.

Ramona brought them all bowls of broth. 'Rabbit,' she said, proudly, nodding towards her husband. The soup was rich and meaty, and Jana sighed with pleasure at the taste.

After they'd eaten, Ramona fussed over Yveta, examining her ankle and rebinding it in strips of clean linen. Jana, seated on a lopsided, rickety chair, finally dared to remove her shoes and gave a small moan. Her stockings, smeared in dried blood, stuck to large open wounds on each of her heels.

'My, goodness, young lady, that needs seeing to straight away,' said Ramona, turning her attention from Yveta to Jana. Within moments, she'd brought over warm water and some type of tincture and helped to remove Jana's stockings.

'...and you pushed that young girl in a wonky, old wheelbarrow all that way, with feet like that...' Ramona was saying as she tended to the raw wounds. Jana caught Yveta watching, her face thoughtful. There was concern in her eyes, and something else: recognition and perhaps gratitude. Jana gave her a reassuring smile, which Yveta returned: the first smile she had ever given her.

Maddie and Michal revived quickly after their soup and jumped at Egon's invitation to visit his cart horse in the barn. Michal was now seven years old and looked so much older than the shy child that used come to her bookshop for refuge and escape. Jana thought of the day she'd witnessed his mother's arrest, her pleading expression to protect her son. Michal had said his mother had been expecting a baby. And what had happened to Michal's father who had simply not returned from work one day? She prayed the family would one day be united.

Her thoughts turned to Maddie as she watched her skip out the door in the direction of the barn. Three years had passed since she and her sister had seen their mother, Lillian. It was heartbreaking how many families had become separated during the war.

Ramona insisted that Jana rest in her rocking chair and made her comfortable with pillows and a blanket. Yveta was laid out on the settee with her ankle supported and raised, and the weary child closed her eyes and dozed. Jana would have liked to sleep too, but her mind continued to whirl; Papa would be frantic with worry not knowing what had happened to her. And what about Babi? Had the police suspected that she had been hiding children? Had she been arrested? Eventually, she allowed her eyelids to fall and drifted into a light sleep to the comforting sound of Ramona bustling around the house.

Sometime later, Egon returned with the children, their arms full of straw which Ramona used for four makeshift beds by the stove. Jana stirred from her rocking chair and padded over the floorboards in a pair of Ramona's socks, relieved not to be wearing shoes; it would take a few days for her feet to heal. Ramona had already said that she and the children could stay as long as they wanted. She was disorientated by the unexpected turn of events. Just yesterday she had been on her way to visit her grandmother for an afternoon, and now she was on the run with three children in tow. They were lucky to have found sanctuary with Egon and his kind wife.

* * *

Over the following days, visitors came and went. The men arrived on foot, on bicycle or horse. Egon talked with them in hushed voices as they smoked outside or they hid themselves in the barn till late in the night. She heard the muted sounds of radio broadcasts through the wall.

One evening, once the children were sleeping and Ramona had retired to the bedroom, Jana went to the bathroom to prepare for bed. She slipped on a worn, flannel nightdress of Ramona's and rubbed her teeth clean with a linen cloth. When she returned to the sitting room, Egon was gone. She guessed he was in the barn listening to the radio. After debating with herself a few moments, she followed.

Egon looked up in surprise at her footsteps, turning the volume down of the distinct tones of a BBC broadcast.

'Please tell me what's going on,' she said simply. 'I want to take part.'

He motioned to his stool, moving to sit on a bale of hay. 'Thank you for storing the ammunition at your shop. It's been collected without any problems.'

Jana sighed with relief.

Egon continued. 'The allies are advancing towards the German border...' His eyes shone with hope. 'The time is close when we will rise up and free ourselves from the Germans.'

'How can I help?' She sat down and pulled her nightdress over her knees.

'It will be dangerous,' he warned, 'but we'll need non-combatants who help with movement of supplies, building of barricades and tending to our wounded.' He looked at her with concern.

'I'm used to the risks. I've worked with you before.' She raised her chin. 'I'm ready to do so again.'

* * *

April brought swathes of bluebells to the forest floor and sunshine filtered through the branches. Egon's visitors became more frequent and Jana was invited to their meetings, often in the barn where they listened to the latest news. She was filled with nervous excitement as plans were made and the day that she would accompany Egon back into Prague neared. She dreaded the thought of leaving the children behind, but she knew they were in good hands with Ramona.

On the evening before the planned departure, Jana returned from the bathroom and passed the couple's bedroom door; it was ajar and she caught a glimpse of Egon and Ramona standing in a tight embrace. He stroked back her hair and murmured to her in a soothing voice. Ramona's shoulders shook with stifled sobs. Jana was moved by their love and when Jana lay down on her bed of hay, her thoughts turned to Andrej. If only he could have been with her when she returned to Prague, side by side, united in their fight.

That night, she had the most perfect dream: she and Andrej ran along the Charles Bridge, draping one Czech flag after another over the balustrades. Then hand in hand, they sped down the riverbank of the Vltava River to their steamboat where they slid off their clothes and made passionate love.

She awoke, her heart racing, her body tingling with desire. But reality crushed down on her; Andrej was gone, murdered by the Gestapo. She was sure of that now; it was the horrific but obvious conclusion. If only she had told him just once that she loved him. He had uttered those sweetest of words, kissing her tear-stained face that evening on the steamboat following the massacre, but consumed with guilt and misery, she'd bitten them back. Now she wished she'd returned his words and that before he'd died, he'd known how deeply she loved them. Now it was too late.

The children stirred as she prepared to leave. She hugged each of them to her breast.

'Be good to Ramona,' she said to Maddie. 'I'll come back for you,' she assured Michal. His lower lip wobbled and two pink spots appeared on his cheeks.

She turned to Yveta, who had watched the farewell with a stiff, white face, but it was Yveta who spoke first.

'I wish you weren't going.'

Jana wrapped her arms around her bony back and the girl's rigid body softened and grew limp against her. Yveta exhaled a shuddering sigh.

'Thank you,' she said in a small voice.

Jana swallowed the hard lump in her throat, knowing how difficult it had been for her to utter those words.

'It's time to leave.' Egon pattered her on the shoulder and she turned finally to Ramona and took both her hands.

'Take care of the children.'

'Rest assured I will. And you two take care of each other,' Ramona said, her eyes flitting to her husband and back to Jana again.

The air was so charged with emotion that Jana was relieved to leave the house and gulp in the crisp, early-morning air. The horse and cart were waiting, and Egon helped her up onto the front bench before settling beside her. As they trotted off, Jana looked over her shoulder and waved goodbye to the little group, their anxious faces imprinted on her mind.

Birdsong filled the spring air and at the sound of horse hooves, red squirrels scuttled through the undergrowth and darted up the trees. Egon, deep in thought, was silent as they rode, and Jana grew afraid of what lay ahead.

An hour later, they halted at a small farmhouse where three men, a teenage boy and a woman awaited them. Jana's spirits lifted to see that the woman was Nela. They smiled at each other. As they all boarded, Egon leaned towards Jana.

'Nela has been learning first aid. One of your tasks will be to assist her if necessary.'

She nodded. 'But what about the boy? He's so young.'

'Don't worry. He's just here to drive the horse and cart back home. Once we reach the outskirts of Prague, we will continue on foot.'

***

At noon, Jana, Egon, Nela and the three men mingled with the crowds in central Prague, lowering their eyes when they passed the soldiers on patrol. Egon slowed to a stroll and indicated a building across the street.

'That's our target,' he said. Jana looked up at the plain, four-storey building. It was the headquarters of the Prague radio station.

47

Jana climbed the staircase to her home, trepidation slowing her pace. How she hoped to find Papa at the breakfast table reading the newspaper, scowling at the latest German propaganda. She had told Egon that she must check on her father but she would meet up with him afterwards. Egon had warned her of the risk of being seen, but understood her concern.

Now, turning the key in the lock, she realised he might be at work, but if she found today's newspaper half-read on the table, she would know he hadn't been arrested.

She pushed open the door and her mouth fell open. Papa's coat lay flung on the floor, the pockets pulled inside out. The drawers of the hall table hung on their hinges, letters and bills strewn around the hallway. Dazed, she stumbled to the kitchen. Every cupboard door was open, the meagre contents tipped onto the countertop. Jana stepped over smashed crockery and knelt to pick up a piece of porcelain depicting a purple-blue blackberry; it was a shard from Mama's favourite vase.

As if in a dream, she moved to her bedroom. Her clothes lay scattered on the bed and floor. She cringed to see her brassiere dangling from the chest of drawers that housed her underwear. The intrusion made her nauseous. Bending to pick up a pile of writing paper and old birthday cards, she tried to make sense of what had happened, but she was too stunned to focus.

The book from her mother, *Little Women*, that she kept in her bedside table lay spread open on the floor. She gathered it to her and smoothing a crumpled page, placed it back in its drawer. But what about her mother's other books? Those that were banned? Hidden. Heart pounding, she turned to her heavy based wardrobe. The doors were wide-open, her clothes ripped from their hangers. Kneeling on the floor where the wardrobe met the back wall, she slipped her slim fingers along the narrow gap; they touched a metal clasp which she opened with a practised flip. There was a creak as the compartment hidden in the wooden base popped open. She crawled to the front of the wardrobe and looked inside the cavity, then heaved a sigh.

The books were there; titles from Kafka, Hemingway, Thomas Mann and others. Jana snapped the compartment shut, the joins disappearing into the ornamental carvings. Papa had done a good job crafting this secret place to conceal his wife's beloved books.

Jana was met by a similar chaos in her parents' bedroom. It was painful to see Mama's clothes treated with such disrespect. The sight of a dirty footprint on an old, cream petticoat sickened her. She picked her way across the room, careful not to trample on anything, and stood in front of the open cupboards; every shelf had been emptied. Old family photographs had been tossed about and she knelt to gather the precious pictures. Her head began to thrum. What did this chaos mean? A burglary? But the truth was likely more sinister: Babi had been arrested for harbouring so-called undesirables and her son was the subject of a wider investigation. Cold dread clutched at her heart. The Gestapo had been here and taken Papa with them.

No, not her dear, kind, gentle father. Mama was gone, but please God, not Papa too. She must do something, but what?

Glancing at the shambles around her, Jana scooped up a couple of items from the floor, but it was hopeless. There was no time to tidy up; she had to return to Egon and the others.

Her throat aching from unshed tears, she ran from the apartment and down the stairs. Had they been in the bookshop as well? The Gestapo, the police or whoever they were? Best not to look. There was no time now.

But she opened the bookshop door, unable to help herself. As soon she entered, she wished she hadn't; books thrown from the shelves lay splayed on the floor, their spines broken. Odd pages lay desolate, ripped from their stories. Papa's puppets, their limbs disjointed in a grotesque pile amongst the carnage. Her breath came in short gasps as she took in the sight.

Sacrilege: that's what it was.

These people were barbarians. White-hot fury flamed within her, driving out the fear that had paralysed her a few moments before.

'Enough!' she screamed into the empty shop. 'It's enough.' She balled her hands into fists.

As she fled the shop, anger and resolve fuelled a new surge of energy. *Enough is enough*, her mind screamed at her. The people had been oppressed too long. She too had wavered in her resolve after the massacre, allowing guilt to paralyse her. Where was the brave girl who had worked in the heart of the Nazi regime, gathering information? Where was the girl who'd hidden coded messages in her own handmade bookmarks? She'd been desperate to fight back against the occupiers of her country.

Where was that girl?

As she passed her fellow citizens on the street, she glanced at their gaunt, exhausted faces. People were starving on their feet whilst what little food there was went to the Wehrmacht. The Lidice villagers had been murdered. But had they died in vain? She thought of Lenka's parents and rage pumped through her veins. It was enough, and the girl that had refused to passively stand by, where was she now?

She was here and ready to do battle.

48

Jana spent the next few days camping out in the cellar of a derelict restaurant. The room was cold and smelt of damp. Men arrived with weapons obtained from policeman sympathetic to the cause, or stolen from the Wehrmacht. They spoke with charged emotion of the imminent uprising.

Egon studied the accumulated weapons. 'It's not much,' he said, 'but it will have to do.'

Jana tried not to think of the well-equipped Wehrmacht but she had the feeling that she and Nela would be nursing many injured in the coming days. The course was set now; there was no turning back.

Mattresses had been laid out for the men, Nela and herself, and at night, Jana lay awake listening to the sounds around her: a grunt, a snore, a sigh. Her chattering mind allowed her no peace. Where were Papa and Babi? Had they been hurt, interrogated? *Please God, let them still be alive.*

During the days that followed, Egon sent Jana and Nela to collect scant food rations from contacts around the city. After a night below ground, Jana welcomed the fresh air. Her hair smelt of the mouldy cellar and she wondered idly when she'd last washed it.

'I don't know how the men will be able to fight with hollow stomachs,' said Jana as they walked down an avenue of pink magnolia trees, their petals a carpet on the ground.

'Oh, determination is their fuel,' said Nela.

Jana had become fond of Nela, the fierce, pretty girl who openly declared she would die if necessary to rid Prague of the Germans. She admired the resilience and fire in a girl younger than herself.

'Do you have family?' said Jana, asking Nela for the first time a personal question.

'I had four brothers working for another resistance group. Only one is still alive.' She jutted out her chin. 'They will not have died in vain.'

Jana's mouth went dry at her words.

They left the warm sunshine and entered the restaurant through a back door. Egon stood guard with one of the few semi-automatic machine guns he'd managed to acquire.

He smiled. 'Ah, angels bearing gifts.'

'Don't get too excited,' laughed Jana. 'It's hardly a feast. Do you want to eat here?' She rummaged in the shopping bag but Egon waved his hand.

'I'll wait till my watch is finished. Send up one of the boys to relieve me when they've eaten.'

The men fell on the pieces of bread and bits of cured sausage. Some devoured it in seconds and others savoured every morsel, taking their time as if it was their last meal.

The tension amongst the group in the cellar was palpable. The men paced, argued and smoked the last of the cigarettes, while Jana jittered with nervous energy, the strain of waiting unbearable. She stayed close to Nela, helping roll bandages and checking what little medical equipment they had. Egon cursed in frustration that he was unable to get a signal on the radio he'd built from parts brought by resistance members.

'We need to know the position of the allies,' he growled, thumping the equipment.

Then finally, on the evening of 4 May, Egon gathered everyone together. He gave a triumphant smile. 'Berlin has fallen to the allies. The Soviet forces have taken the Reichstag.'

Jana screamed in delight at the incredible news. They all cheered.

Once everyone quietened down, he continued solemnly. 'Tomorrow is the day we've all been waiting for. An announcer on Czech radio will give the signal at six o'clock in the morning.'

Jana held her breath as Egon continued.

'The word will go out for Czechs to rise up and take whatever weapons they have, be it a stick, brick or iron bar. Simultaneously, we will meet up with other fighters and storm the radio station. Once we have control over the broadcasts, we'll be able to instruct and inform our citizens. The Germans may have occupied our land for over six years trying to Germanise us, but spiritually, we have remained and will always remain Czechs.'

Egon pumped his fist in the air and cheers rose up. Then in a spontaneous moment of comradeship, everyone sang the national anthem. Jana released the tightness in her chest and in glorious elation, sang with more power than she'd ever sung before.

Whilst everyone prepared to settle down for the night, Jana approached Egon, who had managed to tune in to the local radio station.

'Egon, you haven't said what part I should play tomorrow. I may not be able to shoot a gun, but I can certainly wield a stick.'

He gave her a tender smile. 'I don't want you going down in

the first ten seconds. You and Nela stay here and listen to the broadcasts. Once we've secured the radio building, we'll give the order for civilians to build barricades.'

Egon's gaze flitted from Jana to Nela, who had sidled up to listen to the conversation. 'The two of you are non-combatants and should go out on the streets to help build the barricades. They will hinder fresh German troops and tanks from entering the city. Then return here to tend any wounded.'

He fell silent whilst they both considered his words.

'Try and get some sleep now,' he said and flicked off the radio.

Jana went to the restaurant's cloakroom, gave herself a quick cat wash and lay down on her mattress. She knew there would be no sleep for her tonight and the wakeful hours stretched ahead, waiting to torment her restless mind. Her thoughts sprung from Papa to Babi, from the children to Lenka, but eventually fell on Andrej. How she wished he was with her to share these moments of rising up against the Nazis. How proud and united they could've been. Together. As a pair. No longer having to hide their love. She'd prayed so long for the end of this terrible war, and now with the news that the allies were close, the possibility was within sight. Did she regret her decision to distance herself from him? With hindsight, yes. Perhaps, after the war had ended, his broken body would be found in the cellar of the Gestapo house.

Horrified at her own morbid thoughts, she pressed her fingers to her temples. She must focus, stay resolute and strong for tomorrow. She had a job to do.

49

There was little conversation at dawn the next morning as the men checked their guns and ammunition. Jana and Nela worked together silently in the restaurant kitchen. They boiled water to make acorn coffee for everyone, using the remaining powder, and cut the last of the bread into small pieces. Although she should have been hungry, Jana's stomach was clenched so tight with nerves, she could barely swallow a crumb.

When it was time for the men to go, Jana was lost for words. Was it appropriate to wish them luck? Perhaps these men were religious and she should say, *God be with you*. But that sounded like they might not return. In the end, no one said anything; the men gave each other a determined nod and Egon met Jana's eyes. After a tense smile. he turned away, waving the men forward.

Jana stood with Nela alone in the cellar, the absence of the men leaving an ominous space.

* * *

It was twenty to six: twenty minutes before the announcer would broadcast his appeal to the Czech people. The two girls sat in front of the radio. Jana switched it on and was met by a blast of static. She twirled the dial left and right, attempting to find the station, but the static just increased or decreased in volume. Nela shot her a nervous glance. Jana's fingertips trembled as she continued to search. Moments passed. She jumped as the announcer's voice burst into the room, welcoming them to Prague radio.

Jana and Nela stared at Nela's wristwatch, watching the second hand tick past. The six o'clock chimes echoed from the radio. She held her breath. The Czech announcer had, as instructed by the Nazis, been broadcasting in German but switched to Czech and gave the call to arms. He appealed to Czech police units and members of the former Czech army. The girls bolted out their chairs and up the cellar steps.

Jana's heart raced as a grey, rainy morning greeted them. Their plan was to head for the streets nearest to the radio station and help with the blockades. She looked eagerly around her for a sign of action, but there were few people to be seen. They came to a junction a couple of blocks from the radio station. Ahead, a man was pulling a cart laden with a jumble of bricks, furniture and scraps of metal. Another pushed a wheelbarrow of what looked like sacks of sand. More people appeared, men and women, their arms full of all manner of household items which they threw in a heap on the street.

Then people poured out of every doorway, pushing and shoving anything that could cause an obstruction. Jana and Nela helped heap the things into a huge pile across the street. A builder's van arrived and the crowd rushed to unload the materials.

And then came the screech of police cars. It was inevitable.

Jana stiffened, preparing herself for what was to follow. Car doors flew open and the police jumped out. The man beside her reached for one of the blockade items, an iron bar, and she grabbed a brick. Police ran towards them, their hands on their holsters. She raised the brick above her head, knowing how useless it was against a bullet, but she told herself they wouldn't shoot every single person. Or would they?

Jana and the other resistors formed a line before their unfinished barricade and braced themselves. A long-limbed policeman with a narrow face swung himself in front of them. The man with the iron bar beside her bristled.

'Looks like you need a hand here if that heap of junk is to halt the Germans.' The policeman grinned, blew his whistle and shouted, 'We stand united against the Nazis.'

She uttered a gasp of relief as she watched the police mingle amongst the resistors. With their help, the barricade was swiftly completed and she and Nela ran with the crowd to an adjacent street to start again. Gunshots echoed from the direction of the radio building followed by the rattle of machine gunfire. Had Egon and his accomplices managed to storm the building? Were they under siege?

The ominous sound of wheels rattling over cobblestones made her turn.

Wehrmacht trucks.

'Run,' a man's voice shouted.

Everyone scattered, ducking into buildings and alleyways. Jana cowered in the entrance of a laundry shop. Where was Nela? She had been right beside her. The clang of the bell above the door from behind startled her. She looked around at a stout, red-faced woman with damp hair poking from a white cap.

'Quick,' beckoned the woman.

Jana sprinted inside the shop and the woman closed the door behind them, the bell above the door clanging again.

'This way,' the woman said and led Jana past ironing boards, rails of men's shirts, soldiers' uniforms and black SS jackets. A pungent chemical smell hung in the steam-filled air.

They reached the back door.

'They may give me work, but I still hate them,' the woman hissed. 'The door in the backyard will lead you out.'

'Thank you,' Jana said before rushing across the yard and out into a back street. She paused to gain her breath and consider what to do next. Excitement and fear coursed through her and her head spun with euphoria; at last, they were rising up. The comradeship she'd experienced with others as they built the barrier was a powerful emotion. Being active, making a difference, being seen, made her spirits soar. She would find the next barricade, and the one after that. This was just the beginning.

Hurrying along, she scanned the streets for Nela but saw no sign of her. Some ordinary citizens in everyday clothes paraded with rifles and pistols, their faces resolute. It was an extraordinary sight. Jana found another barricade being built and joined the crowd hauling an array of objects to make the wall; anything to hinder trucks and hopefully tanks from moving around the city. The air was charged with excitement, purpose and determination. Rumours flew.

'The US army are south of Prague!'

'The Russians are advancing!'

'Hitler is dead!' This last one was a popular, recurrent one. If only it were true, thought Jana.

It was crowded where she stood so she moved further down and halted in surprise. Two young women, their cheeks pink from exertion, were shovelling sand from a cart. Dasha and

Karolina. Jana leaped over to them, calling their names, overcome with joy at seeing her two friends. A startled look from Dasha was followed by a huge grin and, putting her shovel aside, she threw her arms around Jana.

A thought flashed in Jana's mind; she had wondered if Dasha had suspected her of hiding children and betrayed her to the police. After all, she'd commented on the children's clothes and books. And there was the German soldier she was friendly with. But now, seeing her friend's warm smile, she doubted this to be true. Surely?

'Are you all right?' said Dasha looking her up and down. 'You look a bit—'

'Crumpled?' finished Jana, suddenly aware that she'd been wearing the same clothes for goodness knows how long.

'Well, yes. I've seen you look fresher. I came by your apartment a couple of times but no one was home.'

Jana didn't comment but turned to greet Karolina. She hugged the girl, feeling her sharp bones and caving chest.

Pulling back, she looked into her spectral face. 'How are you?' said Jana, concern in her voice.

'I've had terrible news,' Karolina said. 'Petr is seriously ill. I'm afraid he'll die in that awful prison.' Her voice was hoarse with exhaustion. 'I don't know what to do.'

'This is what you do,' said Jana. 'What we are doing now: rising up to free ourselves. If Paris can do it, then so can we. Don't lose heart, Karolina. We'll drive the Germans out and Petr will be free.'

Karolina looked unconvinced and turned her face to hide her tears.

Jana gently took the shovel from Karolina's limp hand. 'Let me take over for a while. Take a rest.'

Karolina plumped herself down on a broken chair that was

destined for the barricade whilst Jana and Dasha continued to shovel sand.

'Can we win?' said Dasha.

'We must,' said Jana, shovelling with a vigour she didn't know she possessed.

The barricade was nearly complete when the ominous trample of heavy boots sounded behind them. Panic rose in Jana's throat; they were trapped between the Germans and the barricade.

A group of anti-Nazi police amongst them stepped forward, shielding the civilians, and drew their pistols. The three girls huddled together. For a moment, time slowed down as the German rifles pointed at the police pistols. Jana looked around her frantically. There was no way out. They would all die in a hail of bullets.

A breath. A heartbeat. And then it started. Explosions of gunfire that ricocheted around the high buildings. People screaming and falling. Blood on the cobbles.

To her left, an archway. She yanked Dasha's arm. 'That way,' she yelled.

The three girls dived through the stone archway and emerged in an adjacent square with a dried-up fountain.

'My home is nearest. Come to me,' panted Dasha.

'I have somewhere else I must go,' said Jana.

There was no time to explain that she was on the run and had joined up with a resistance group.

'Go,' she urged. 'I'll find you later.'

The girls split up, Karolina fleeing with Dasha. Jana continued to wander the streets, looking for where she could help. She pulled down German signs, ripping her nails and bruising her fingers, carried metal bars to the barricades and hammered nails into planks of wood which she lay in the paths of oncoming German vehicles.

The sky darkened and it began to rain. Thousands of citizens filled the streets. The Wehrmacht were unprepared for events and struggled to control the mass of resistance without the aid of the police force, who mostly refused to shoot their fellow Czechs.

* * *

Hours later, Jana, barely able to stand, trudged through the torrential rain back to the restaurant and slipped through the back door and down into the cellar. Hearing the sound of running water, she tiptoed to the cloakroom and peered cautiously around the door. Nela stood naked by the sink splashing her grime- and blood-covered skin with cold water. Her dirty clothes lay in a heap on the floor.

'You're bleeding,' Jana said. Exhaustion made her feel outside of herself, as if someone else had spoken.

'Just scratches. You too.'

Jana looked down at her bloody hands and ripped nails and only now noticed how her skin smarted. Dazed, she left Nela to finish washing and fetched a drink of water from the kitchen, before flopping onto her mattress.

Later, she too stripped off in the cloakroom to wash and slipped on the one extra dress she had borrowed from Ramona. When she returned from the cloakroom, Nela had tuned into the radio station. The announcer was appealing to the people to continue with the barricades to halt a new influx of German troops.

'It's as if the Reich is sending every last soldier into Prague,' Jana said, sitting beside Nela.

The girl nodded, a faraway look in her eye.

Jana reached for her hand. 'After we were separated this morning, I was worried about you. It was a relief to find you back here.'

Nela withdrew her hand and avoided Jana's gaze. 'It's best not to get attached to people right now. It can distort one's judgement in a moment of crisis.'

She sounded so old for her young years.

'Let's get a couple of hours rest before we go out again,' Jana said.

There was nothing to eat so they went straight to lie down. Depleted of all energy, Jana rolled into a ball on her mattress, briefly aware of the burn of hunger before she plunged into sleep.

50

The next day, the two girls were back on the streets with thousands of people surging through the town, ripping down German flags and signs, storming German-held buildings. Jana witnessed some brutal fighting and several times stopped to aid the wounded citizens. With the lack of police support and the barricades erected the previous day, the Wehrmacht were struggling to keep control. Parts of the city were taken by the Czechs. Euphoria combined with the pent-up emotion of six years of occupation was a powerful force. Jana felt no fear. She felt driven.

Until the planes came.

Motors thrumming. A sinister sight over the beautiful city.

Jana craned her neck in horror. Surely they wouldn't bomb Prague? The city had been spared bomb attacks under the occupation. Till now.

'Take cover!' a voice yelled.

'The Luftwaffe are coming,' another shouted.

The mass of people moved, taking on a life of its own. Jana was carried along, the panicked faces becoming a blur around her. Above, the engines roared. She glanced up at the underbelly of a plane directly overhead. In that moment, she knew. Instinctively, she ducked her head, her pulse thundering in her ears.

The bomb pounded the ground with a deep boom. The explosion threw her from her feet, her bones shuddering from the vibrations. As she was propelled through the air, images swirled in front of her face: an elbow, a hat, a small hand. Something thudded into her back with a force that took her breath. Her eyes closed and the world spun. It was as if she was underwater; the only sound her heartbeat, loud and fast, resounding through her. Opening her eyes, she saw it was snowing. That's strange in May. But the snow pricked her face and her mind jolted; the snow was a torrent of shattered glass falling from the sky. She tried to fling both her arms across her face but they were pinned to her side. She turned her head to see she was jammed between people. Then sound rushed in and she heard the groans as bodies shuffled to free themselves. Moments later, another explosion rocked the city. It came from the direction of the radio station.

* * *

Again, Jana stood in the cloakroom of the restaurant, washing away blood and grime, this time from her face. Most of the cuts were slight except one deep gash across her cheek. She examined herself in the mirror, satisfied there were no glass fragments in the wound. It had taken an age to extricate herself from the crowd, most of whom lay heaped along the pavement. Luckily, most people's injuries were superficial, and after helping where she could, she'd found Nela and returned to the restaurant cellar. Their main worry was the second bomb. It seemed likely that the Luftwaffe had targeted the broadcasting building that Egon and his men had taken siege of.

There was chaos on the streets and the girls had decided it was best to wait at the restaurant in the hope Egon would return there. Jana drank several glasses of water and it occurred to her that they were lucky that the water pipes had not been damaged. She began pulling out every pot she could find and filled each one with water; best to be prepared.

Nela's urgent cry brought her running from the kitchen.

Struggling down the cellar steps with a man leaning on his shoulder was Egon, followed by others, limping or clutching themselves, their clothes stained with blood.

'The radio station is out of action,' said Egon, panting as he lowered the man to the floor. 'The bomb wasn't a direct hit, but the tower is damaged.'

Nela, switching to a nursing role, asked who was injured and where. Jana fetched water and began tending to a man she didn't know who had a leg injury. He explained he was from a different resistance group and had met Egon at the radio station.

'There's more of us following,' he said, flinching as she ripped the leg of his trousers apart.

Minutes later, more men appeared, helping those who were wounded. One man being supported was buckled over, grasping his stomach. He straightened and lifted his head. His hair was covered in debris, his angular face smeared with blood and ash. He groaned, pressing his hands against his wound. Blood oozed from between his fingers, turning his shirt crimson. The heavy-set man supporting him lowered him to floor before leaving to help another injured fighter.

Jana's head swam. She swayed, her legs weak. It couldn't be possible; her exhausted mind was playing tricks on her. She stumbled a few steps forward before her knees gave way and she collapsed beside the injured man. His dark eyes widened.

Her mouth dry and her throat tight, her voice was a rasp.

'Andrej,' she said.

He gave a weak smile. 'My darling, Jana.'

'You are alive.' Her heart lurched and tears sprung from her eyes. 'Where have you been?'

'It's a long story...' Moaning, he hunched over.

Jana's head cleared and as she wiped her tears, adrenaline kicked in. 'Have you been shot?' she asked. Her fingers shook as she undid the buttons of his blood-soaked shirt.

'No. I was hit by debris when the bomb exploded. Our group were defending the radio station. That's where I met Egon.' He spoke between breaths, flinching as Jana peeled back his shirt. She held back a gasp as she saw the gaping wound in his side; she needed to staunch the flow. Nela was already ripping a sheet into strips and handed her a length before turning to her own patient. Jana bunched up the fabric and pressed firmly against the wound.

'Are you trying to kill me?' he groaned.

'I already thought you were dead. After I saw you in the hands of the Gestapo, and then you vanished. What else should I think?' She couldn't keep the accusatory tone from her voice.

'The Gestapo were only making initial enquiries; they had nothing concrete, so they let me go. But I knew they had the scent that I was up to something and would keep digging. I moved my mother out of her apartment and she went to live with her sister in the countryside. It was the right time for me to flee Prague and join the resistance gathering in the mountains.' He touched her hand that was pressed against his side. 'I'm sorry if you were concerned.'

'I was a bit more than concerned,' she snapped. Then, gentler, she said, 'You could have told me.'

'Oh, Jana, how? I thought about you constantly but didn't want to put you at risk by making contact. With the Gestapo watching, I couldn't waltz into your bookshop and implicate you.'

'They came anyway.' She heaved a sigh. 'They have Papa. And probably my grandmother too.'

'Tell me what happened.' He squeezed her hand, his expression so full of sorrow that she fought back a new onslaught of tears.

'First, I'm going to tend to your injury. Keep pressing. I'm going to speak to Nela, a first-aid helper.'

Nela was tending to two wounded men, moving between them. Jana knelt down to her.

'My patient will need stitches,' she said.

Nela nodded to the first-aid box beside her. 'Needles and thread are there.'

'But you need to do it,' she said, alarmed. 'I have no nursing experience.'

'I have my hands full here. Can you sew?'

She thought of the puppet clothes she had carefully stitched. 'Yes, but not skin.'

'Then today is the day,' said Nela, deftly wrapping a bandage around her patient's arm. Jana swallowed and reached into the first-aid box.

She took a bowl of water, disinfectant and the sewing materials to where Andrej sat propped against the wall.

He smiled at her wryly. 'Can you stitch a wound?'

'We shall see,' she said, a tease in her voice.

Tenderness flushed through her as she dabbed away the blood, her fingertips grazing his lean, muscled torso. He clenched his jaw as she applied the disinfectant and cleaned the wound, then watched her thread the needle. Aware that his eyes were on her, her fingers jittered and it took several attempts before she succeeded.

Their eyes met as she poised, ready with the needle.

'It will be fine,' he said softly. His face was full of love and her heart quivered.

Holding the wound firmly closed, she began to sew. The first stitch was the worst but then she focused on the task, ignoring Andrej's moans. She knotted and cut the thread and applied a dressing. Then sitting back on her haunches, she admired her handiwork before going to the kitchen to wash her hands.

It took a while before she had time to return to Andrej – the other injured needed care – but finally, the patients had been made as comfortable as possible and she settled down next to him. His face was white against his black hair, and several days' hair growth covered his chin.

'How are you feeling?' she asked.

'It's just a flesh wound; I'm fine. Now tell me what happened to your father and grandmother.'

She told him how she'd arrived at Babi's to find the children packed and ready to leave.

'I've been wondering how the authorities found out.' She didn't add her suspicions about Pavel: that maybe he'd betrayed her out of revenge or financial gain, or even possibly Dasha, but continued to tell her story. When she finished, Andrej stroked her face and traced his fingers down her neck to the top of her blouse.

'Where is your locket?' His fingers lay on the base of her throat.

'A German stole it from me. A soldier named Brandt.'

Anger flashed across Andrej's face. 'I'm sorry that happened.'

They were quiet for a few moments and Jana, sitting on the floor beside him, took his hand.

'They have Papa and Babi; I'm terrified that...' Her voice trailed off.

'Don't give up hope. This will be over soon, and they will be freed.'

'How can you be sure?' She so wanted to believe his words even after the bombing that day. 'But we can no longer broadcast now that the radio station is out of action.'

'There is an alternative site planned. The resistance will have retreated there. I must join them.' He struggled to rise, but groaning, slumped back down.

'No, you're not well enough,' she said, alarmed at the idea of losing him again so soon.

'Listen, Jana. We haven't long before all German troops congregate on Prague and burst through the barricades. We're one of the last cities to be liberated and it looks like the Nazis want to use our city like a fortress: a place for a one last stand against the allies.'

'We can't let that happen,' she said.

Jana could not bear to think what the Nazis would do to the civilians in such a scenario; what revenge they would wreak before the final battle.

'Rest just a short while,' she said, desperate to keep him close a few moments more.

He sighed and leaned his head on her shoulder. She put her hands into his thick hair, pulling out pieces of debris, and stroked his head with soothing fingers. The moment was so precious, one of the few they had spent together. An urgency gripped her, as if time was running out; she wanted to know about the man she had forced herself to reject, but that her heart never had. A question burned to be answered.

'You said once that long ago there had been someone special in your life. What happened?'

He was silent for a few moments as she continued to stroke his head.

'It was seven years ago. I married young. We were in love,' he said.

Her heart jolted. 'You were married?'

'Briefly. We were expecting a child.'

Her breath caught; she had thought of Andrej as a loner.

There was a long pause before he spoke again. 'She fell from a horse. She died from her injuries a few days later.'

Jana was lost for words for a few moments.

'I'm so sorry, Andrej. And the baby?'

She felt him shake his head on her shoulder.

Her heart squeezed and she heaved a shuddering breath. Then her whole body went soft as she released all resistance and whispered, 'I love you. I've tried not to, I don't deserve to, but I can't deny it any longer. I love you, my darling.'

He lifted his head from her shoulder, his eyes wet and shining. 'My heart was in shreds while we were apart.' A tear ran down his cheek as he brought his face to hers.

Their lips met, soft and tender. The kiss was brief but it reached into the core of her soul. If only she could hold this moment, stop the clock, stop him going into battle, maybe leaving her for the last time. If only...

'Sorry if I'm interrupting but I have two important announcements.' Egon stood over them, smiling and holding a tin of something in his hand. 'I've come into possession of a treasure: several cans of beans. And the other announcement is that Hitler is dead. Unconfirmed, unfortunately.'

Jana's breath caught in her throat. Finally. Could it be true?

'Then surely the war must be over,' said Jana, hope rising in her chest. 'We don't have to fight any more.'

Andrej could stay with her, safe, and they—

'The soldiers will keep fighting till the Germans officially give the order to lay down their arms,' said Egon. 'Meanwhile, the battle continues in the streets. I'm going to join our fighters at Masaryk train station.'

'I'm coming with you,' said Andrej, fumbling to do up the buttons on his bloodstained shirt.

With a sinking heart, Jana helped Andrej to his feet, insisting he eat a couple of mouthfuls of beans before he set off.

When it was time to say goodbye, he held her face in his hands. 'I want you to know that I too have been consumed with guilt over the loss of lives in the German reprisals. But despite that, in my heart, I still believe we must never stop fighting for freedom. Whatever the price.'

'Come back to me, Andrej. Please.'

'I love you,' he said with a sad smile and limped up the cellar stairs behind Egon.

51

In the restaurant's kitchen, Jana rifled through the drawers, considering the array of implements, and chose a small knife with a fine, sharp blade. She slipped it into her pocket.

'What are you doing?' asked Nela from the doorway.

'I'm going to Masaryk station. There is fighting there and they will need help with the wounded.'

'Count me in,' said Nela, wiping the sweat from her forehead with the back of her hand. Her blouse was covered with the blood of the men she had tended.

'What about the injured? Can we leave them alone here?'

'They're settled now and none of them are seriously hurt. I've left them water to drink.'

'Then let's go.'

The two of them hurried up the cellar steps and out into the mayhem of the Prague streets. The air hung heavy with smoke; the bombs had left buildings burning and pieces of ash spun in the breeze, mingling with pink blossom. The sound of gunfire echoed around them as Jana and Nela approached a barricade defending the station. A group of resistance fighters were crouched down, and one lay wounded on the ground. One of the men, in a cloth cap and an oversized tweed jacket, turned, his eyes widening at the sight of the two girls.

'Pavel,' gasped Jana.

His expression, at first startled, turned to irritation. 'You shouldn't be here; it's far too dangerous.'

'We're here to tend the wounded,' said Jana. She glanced at Nela, who had knelt down at the injured man's side.

Pavel cracked open his rifle and slid in a round of bullets. 'I'm surprised to see you.'

Anger flared up in her.

'You informed on me, didn't you? That's why you're surprised to see me. How could you do that not just to me, but my grandmother?'

Pavel looked up from his rifle, narrowing his eyes. 'I have no idea what you're talking about.'

'Really?' she shot back. She didn't believe him for a moment. 'You're the only one I told where Michal was.'

'I don't have time for this,' he said and snapped shut his rifle.

'Neither do I,' she said, and then turned to Nela where she was attending the injured man. 'I'm heading into the station.'

Crouching down, she edged along the barricade, heading towards a side entrance to the station. Gunshots cracked above her. The ground shuddered from falling grenades. An explosion from behind hurled her from her feet and she fell onto the cobbled stones. Scrambling up, her ears whistling, she looked back the way she'd come. A plume of black smoke swirled from the spot she'd stood just moments before with Pavel and Nela. The barricade had collapsed into a burning crater.

And her friends...? She choked back a scream and stumbled

two steps towards the carnage, praying for survivors. But another grenade exploded and she was forced to dive through the station entrance.

Resistance fighters were holding off a German attempt to take the station. She saw Andrej and Egon, their rifles aimed, popping bullets through an open window. A young man lay on the stone floor, doused in blood. She moved to him and pressed her hands over the wound in an attempt to staunch the flow. The grenade explosion had left pain throbbing in her ears and the noise of the fighting was muffled as if she was underwater. She threw a glance at Andrej and caught his eye as he reloaded his gun, registering his surprise at seeing her. Bullets pinged off the stone walls and Andrej returned fire.

Above the noise, a shout went up.

'They're in the building! The Germans are here.'

'Run!' Andrej screamed at her. She looked down at the lifeless young man beneath her hands; there was nothing more she could do.

The fighters retreated towards the platform and she jolted after them. From nowhere, an arm grabbed her, encircling her neck, squeezing, squeezing. She grappled for breath and her nostrils filled with a familiar, sickly-sweet smell.

Liquorice.

Brandt rasped in her ear. 'Come with me, bookshop girl.' He dragged her backwards, increasing the pressure on her throat.

As her lungs grappled for air, she saw Andrej striding towards them, his rifle aimed at Brandt. Through her deadened ears, she heard the dim sound of a commotion outside the station, vibrations under her feet. The sound of tanks.

A flash of Wehrmacht uniforms flashed in her peripheral vision. Brandt held her in front of him, a human shield. Cold metal pressed against her temple. He laughed. 'Ah, it's our long-lost police captain. One move and I'll shoot her.' He pressed the pistol hard against the side of her head.

Andrej did not lower his rifle, but frowned, his expression uncertain. A German soldier ran between them, heading to attack the resistance fighters trapped on the platform. Andrej swung to shoot him but Brandt screamed, 'No! She's dead.'

Andrej lowered his rifle an inch, his face desperate. More Germans crossed to the platform, unhindered. Each moment that Brandt held her hostage, another resistance fighter's life was endangered. She had to do something, get free of his grasp. Brandt squeezed on her windpipe and her sight blurred and darkened. She had the sensation of falling. Edging her hand into her pocket and gathering her last ounce of strength, she withdrew the kitchen knife and swung it into Brandt's arm holding the pistol. His arm jerked and the pistol shot exploded past her face. She struck again and as he roared in pain, releasing his hold on her, she sprung away from him. In the same moment, Andrej aimed at Brandt and fired. She flew towards Andrej, her hand reaching for him.

Soldiers were pouring through the station entrance, but their uniforms were different.

Gunshots ricocheted around her. As she reached Andrej, he spun and staggered. She screamed as she watched him fall. No! A heartbeat later, her body convulsed from the force of a blow. Then another. Her limbs jerked.

Searing pain. Plummeting. Darkness rolling in.

Then nothing.

* * *

The voices came first: distant, muffled. Shadows played across Jana's eyelids. She forced them to lift. A half-open window. Curtains framing a blue and white sky.

'Miss Hajek. Can you hear me?' It was a woman's voice.

An older, round face topped with a white cap came into view.

Jana tried to speak, but her dry tongue was stuck to the roof of her mouth.

A cup appeared at her lips and cool water trickled onto her tongue. She gulped and coughed, then murmured, 'What happened?'

'You sustained bullet wounds and underwent an operation to remove three bullets. All went well,' the nurse said, giving Jana another drink.

It came back to her: the hail of bullets, the pain, Andrej falling...

'There was a man with me, Andrej Kovar. Please, how is he?'

'There were many wounded men in the shoot-out with the Germans. Fatalities too, I'm afraid. There would have been many more if the Soviet tanks hadn't arrived at the train station. Thank goodness it's over.'

'Over?' said Jana, her mind grasping to make sense of it all.

'The war. It's over and Prague is liberated.' The nurse's voice was jubilant.

It took a moment to sink in. The news she had been so desperate to hear was surreal, unbelievable, wonderful. A glow of happiness brought a smile to her lips. She needed to speak to Andrej, to see him.

'Please, find out about Andrej Kovar.'

The nurse gave a curt nod. 'I'll do my best. Your sweetheart, is he?'

'Yes,' said Jana without hesitation. 'He is.'

* * *

The ward was full of casualties, men and women lined up in tightly packed beds that ran the length of the room. Nurses rushed in and out with bed pans, medication and dressings. The less seriously injured patients called out to each other, exchanging the latest news: Germany had surrendered and the war in Europe was officially over. Hitler's body had been found in his bunker; he had committed suicide.

Jana kept watch for the nurse she'd asked to find out about Andrej. The woman was rushed off her feet and whirled past on several occasions, but Jana was unable to attract her attention.

The next day, she still hadn't heard anything and cruel doubt slipped around her heart.

She lay on her back, trying to limit her movement, the wounds in her shoulder and her arm more painful now the painkillers had worn off. A young nurse changed her dressings and explained there was not enough medication for everyone. Jana took the opportunity to ask about Andrej, but the young woman was unable to help.

Afraid to fall asleep and miss the older nurse, Jana kept watch on the door of the ward. Eventually, towards evening, the nurse appeared, but she told Jana she had no news; the hospital administration was in chaos.

The thought that Andrej should die in the last moments before the war ended was too terrible to bear. It couldn't be true; she wouldn't let it.

Night came, the hours in the humid room dragging by until, shortly before dawn, Jana succumbed to sleep. She dreamt of Andrej looking at her through the bookshop window while she knelt arranging a fan of bookmarks. Then he extended his hand and pulled her up onto the steamboat, pushing her hair away from her shoulder, whispering her name. But she said nothing and his voice grew louder.

'Jana. Jana.'

Her heart quickened and she opened her eyes.

He stood by her bed, his arm in a sling, smiling.

'I've found you,' he said.

52

Jana was too weak to get out of bed that day, so Andrej went off on his own to make further enquiries on casualties. She waited, staring at the ceiling, praying for good news about survivors from the battle. After a while, she dozed, and awoke as Andrej returned, pulling up a chair to her bedside. Her body tensed in anticipation.

He took her hand and smiled. 'I've found Nela in another ward. She's got some nasty injuries, but she's going to make it.'

Jana gasped. 'She survived! I thought she was lost. Thank God.'

'She was lucky. Two resistance fighters close to where she was found were not so lucky.'

Jana swallowed hard. 'Was one of them Pavel: Pavel Krejci?'

Andrej nodded. 'That was the name on the list. He was dead on arrival. Did you know him?'

Her chest tightened in pain as memories flashed through her mind: them eating onion soup in their little favourite restaurant, his bright eyes after she'd kissed him outside the bookshop, his bitterness when he'd spied her together with Andrej. Had she really known him? Had he betrayed her to the Nazis? He'd denied it, but now she would never know for sure.

Andrej wiped away a tear from her cheek. 'I'm sorry if he was a friend.'

He paused, giving her time. Moments passed before she asked, 'And Egon?'

Tears filled Andrej's eyes and he shook his head. 'He got caught in the crossfire between the Soviets and the Germans.'

She thought of how Egon and Ramona had embraced the night before he'd left for Prague, and gave a shuddering sigh, sadness pressing down on her.

They sat a few moments in silence, Jana taking shallow breaths as pain from her wounds shot through her.

'I have to find Papa and Babi.' It was an effort to talk as exhaustion swamped over her.

'I'll contact the police station and find out what I can.' His voice was tired, his face drawn.

'Thank you, Andrej. One more thing. Brandt. Is he dead?'

'Probably, but I don't know for sure.'

'Go back to your ward and get some rest,' said Jana, worried how ill he looked.

After he left, a nurse came and gave her newly arrived medication. Within moments Jana gave in to a merciful sleep.

* * *

Pandemonium filled the streets. Jana looked around her in awe as after four days in hospital, she gingerly made her way with Andrej on her arm. People danced, Czech music blared and Czech flags hung from every façade. It was strange to see Soviet tanks parade down the streets, and the ever-present Wehrmacht uniforms replaced by Soviet ones. Children and women threw garlands over the necks of beaming Soviet soldiers, and young men clambered onto the tanks, pumping their fists, shouting words of freedom.

But not everyone's face shared the same euphoria. There were those queuing up outside the town hall and Red Cross stations, desperate for news of missing loved ones. Scenes of the uprising were everywhere: the barricades being dismantled by the soviets, blood-stained pavements and walls, and buildings riddled with bullet holes.

'How many Czechs have been wounded or died in liberating our city?' asked Jana.

'Reports are unconfirmed, but numbers run into thousands.'

'They were all so brave.' Jana's voice broke and Andrej gave her arm a gentle squeeze.

When they arrived at the police station, Jana sighed to see the queue snake out of the front door and around the block, one anxious face after another. Andrej had tried telephoning but no one had picked up the receiver.

Andrej indicated a low, stone wall. 'Sit down and rest while I try to talk myself into the station as an ex-police captain.' She watched him walk away, slow and stiff from his injuries, thanking God that he was alive, still hardly able to believe he was back in her life. A moment of joy warmed her heart but fear for Papa and Babi snatched it away.

The clock above the police Station told her she'd been waiting for nearly two hours, watching a woman in a pink sunhat shuffle a few steps at a time as the queue moved forward. The woman still wasn't half way to the front. Jana felt hot and dizzy as the midday sun shone down and she had nothing to drink. She fixed her eyes on the entrance, willing Andrej to appear with good news.

Finally, he came. Her heart lifted; he was smiling. 'We've

found them! Both your father and grandmother are alive. They are being checked over in a Red Cross first aid centre. I have the address.'

* * *

The school had been taken over by the Red Cross, the classrooms being used to administer first aid to those whose injuries did not require hospital treatment or were being given a general check-up before being sent home. Andrej and Jana approached the front desk where three nurses flipped through registers giving out information to a queue of people. When a place became free, Jana stepped up to nurse and gave her father and Babi's names. The nurse ran her finger down the pages until she said, 'Aha. Here we are. Classroom five.' She looked up at Jana, peering over her reading glasses. 'Just to prepare you. They were freed from Gestapo headquarters.'

Jana swayed a moment and held onto Andrej, ascending the stairs with trepidation.

As she stood in the doorway of the classroom set up with camp beds, she saw Papa and Babi straight away. They were sitting next to one another on a bed by the window; small, fragile figures, mother and son together, now safe, alive. She rushed to them, calling their names, and they looked at her, startled then joyous. They stood shakily and held each other in a clumsy embrace, Jana hindered by her wounds and her father by bandaged hands.

Once their sobs and tears had subsided, they sat in a row on the bed with Jana in the middle. Andrej came to join them, standing by the window, and Jana introduced him. Then she looked down at her father's heavily bandaged hands. 'What happened, Papa?' She lay a hand on his arm and looked into his face. He now had a beard, the hairs coarse and grey, lines had deepened around his eyes, but what struck her most was the gauntness of his face, the sunken cheeks.

'For weeks we were held in the police station. It was chaos there; most of the time, they were screaming at each other about raids and round-ups. They were panicking. Things turned for the worse when they handed us over to the Gestapo.'

He paused and she waited for him to continue.

'You don't need to know the details, my darling. But my days as a puppeteer are over.'

Panic rising, she turned to Babi.

'They smashed his fingers, one by one. All of them.' Babi's head sunk.

Jana cried out, 'No Papa, no! Why?'

'They'd heard rumours that you were aiding Jewish children and wanted to know where you were.'

'But you didn't know where I was!'

'Do you think I would have told them if I had?'

She stared down at her father's bound hands in disbelief: his strong, skilful, beautiful hands that created life and character from a piece of wood. His gentle, loving hands that reached across the kitchen table to hold hers, or stroked her head when she was in search of comfort. Hot tears coursed down her cheeks and she lay her head on his shoulder. 'Papa, oh Papa...' No other words came to her.

'There, there,' he said, his lifeless hands motionless in his lap. 'I'm one of the lucky ones; I survived.'

It was true, and so was Babi. Chest heaving, she turned to Babi.

'What happened to you?' But although she'd asked the question, she was terrified of the answer.

'They had no proof of anything. I played senile and thoroughly annoyed them with my nonsense. They played their mental games with me: bright lights and music blasting. Then made me stand naked in a barrel of iced water. I can't lie, I was ready for them to shoot me. But then they just left me; it was just before the uprising and I suspect they knew things were happening and had more important jobs to handle. I didn't see the Gestapo again, just a warden that gave me water and the occasional crust of bread. Then one day, the door opened and there stood a Soviet soldier.'

53

For the second time in her life, Jana sat in a Red Cross vehicle passing through the gates of Terezin. Apart from the warm sun in a blue sky, things could not have been more different. The Germans were gone, and the streets were filled with nurses, social workers and food trucks. The former prisoners, skeletal figures in loose, tattered clothing who were too weak to stand, were tended to by aid workers, while others, clutching bowls, tottered towards the food truck. Heart thudding, Jana searched the faces looking for Lenka. Andrej, sitting beside her, squeezed her hand.

They had left Papa and Babi, who would be staying one more night at the school, and had hitched a lift from a Soviet military truck to Ivan and Lenka's apartment, hoping that Ivan would have news of Lenka. No one was home.

'He must've gone to Terezin to find Lenka,' said Jana. 'Let's go to a Red Cross point and find a truck that's going out there.'

They had been lucky and found a ride with a truck of nurses heading for the camp. Both Jana and Andrej had been flagging, pain and exhaustion taking its toll. But the Red Cross had given them food and painkillers, and after a nap on the journey, they both felt better. After they clambered out the truck, they were directed to an information point in one of the buildings which she recognised at once. It was the place where the Jewish Elders lived, where she had delivered the books to at her last visit, and where she had sneaked out the back to find Lenka.

Another queue, another wait. Finally, they reached a long table where three men sat. Jana looked twice at one of the men: now bald, with a long, silver beard, thin and stoop-shouldered. It was Samuel, who had helped her out the back window and covered for her absence when the German guard had come looking for her. She called his name. He looked across at her with vacant eyes, his face etched with fatigue.

'I came here with books about three years ago and you helped me out the building, directing me to the women's barracks.'

He peered at her closely before recognition crossed his face and he smiled, two teeth missing since she had last seen him. 'The book girl.'

Eagerly, she asked him for news on Lenka, Lillian, and Michal's parents. He showed her the few lists that he had, explaining the Germans had destroyed much of the documentation once they knew Prague would fall to the allies.

'Tens of thousands of us were transported out of here to God knows where. I suspect, over the next few weeks, we will find out what happened to them all. I'm still here because the Nazis forced the Elders Committee to organise it all, draw up the lists...' His voice broke and his head fell to his chest.

Jana reached across the desk and clasped his hands. She had suspected this was happening from the moment she'd heard Heydrich talk of his solution and read his letter to Himmler. And yet she had been unable to stop it despite her messages of warning hidden in her bookmarks. And when Heydrich had died, it was too late; the ball had already been set in motion.

'I did what I could,' Samuel sobbed. 'Held back the young, the children when possible, but they began sending anybody, the Elders too. I was due soon...'

When Samuel had composed himself, he searched through the lists he had available. He found Lillian. She was alive and still at Terezin. Jana's heart swelled. Maddie and Yveta's mother had survived.

'Where can I find her?' asked Jana.

'You can try the women's barracks. The Red Cross have erected tents there to give the women medical treatment before sending them on.'

Jana and Andrej thanked him and before they left, Samuel said, 'You might find out more information about your other friends at the former Gestapo office.'

* * *

They eventually found Lillian on a stretcher in a makeshift hospital tent, attached to a drip. She was dehydrated and malnourished but would soon recover, a nurse assured Jana. Beside her sat a man in a hat and coat, despite the warm weather. He held Lillian's hand, gazing at her in anguish. As Jana approached, her eyes fluttered open and her first words were, 'My girls! Yveta, Maddie, my girls.' Seeing Lillian's expression when she told her the children were safe was a moment so moving, Jana would never forget it.

Lillian explained that she and the man by her side had fallen in love and because he was an Elder, he had fought to keep her off the transport lists. So there was some hope and happy endings, thought Jana; it was a miracle Lillian had survived.

'I can't wait till the girls are reunited with their mother,' Jana said to Andrej as they walked away, bubbles of joy lifting her spirits.

'Let's see if we can find some more good news about Lenka and Michal's parents.'

* * *

An hour later, Jana and Andrej were sitting with Ivan on the grass outside the entrance to the Terezin Fortress. They had found him in the Gestapo building begging for information on his wife and child. But there was no mention of Lenka or Alena in the few documents that remained and they were not listed as survivors in Terezin. The official told Ivan enquiries would be made in other Nazi concentration camps, but this would take time. Ivan left his name and address.

'And that's it?' he said, now looking from Jana to Andrej. 'I should just go home and wait?'

Jana had no words. It was Andrej who spoke, his voice gentle. 'Yes. That's all you can do. Go home and wait.'

54

In the days that followed, everyone struggled with their broken bodies and shattered minds to ease themselves into a semblance of normality. Their first task was to tidy the mess in the apartment left by the Gestapo. Babi stayed with them in the apartment and slept with Jana in Papa's double bed and Papa moved into Jana's room. Andrej stayed with them too and slept uncomfortably on the settee in the living room.

One of the resistance fighters, a friend of Egon's, managed to borrow a horse and cart and rode out to break the sad news to Ramona of her husband's death and bring the children back to Prague. Jana and Lillian waited at the appointed time near the station and as the horse and cart approached with three small heads bobbing next to the driver, Lillian rushed forward to greet them. Maddie and Yveta sprung into their mother's arms with shrieks of delight and tears of happiness flowed.

The driver swung Michal down, and Jana hugged him even though her injuries were still painful.

'How did Ramona take the news?' Jana asked Egon's friend.

Then added, 'That was a stupid question. Ramona has lost her husband and now lives alone in the middle of nowhere.'

He sighed. 'Me and the wife will keep an eye on her.'

Michal looked over to Lillian and the girls and back to Jana, his face questioning.

'There's no news yet, Michal. Your parents weren't in Terezin so must have been sent somewhere else. The end of the war is rather chaotic at the moment, so we'll have to be patient, but we will find them. Till then, would you like to stay with me? Babi is there too.'

He nodded and turned again to the girls, who waved him goodbye and skipped alongside their mother as they walked towards the Jewish Quarter to discover what had become of their home.

The apartment was crowded but they were happy to be all together. Michal took over the settee and Andrej bought a second-hand mattress which he rolled out on the living-room floor. He was back at work at the police station helping to fire the fascists and appoint new staff. Jana had begun to clear up the carnage in the bookshop.

Weeks passed and Jana's wounds healed but still there had been no news of Michal's parents or Lenka. The first reports of what the prisoners had experienced in the concentration camps were so horrific that Jana found it difficult to bear. Then one morning, the letter arrived that she had been dreading: Michal's parents had died in Auschwitz.

With a heart of lead, she trudged up the stairs to the attic and pushed open the door. Michal was at Papa's workbench, carving a puppet, Papa by his side giving instructions, his crippled hands, lifeless in his lap. Yet despite his injuries, Papa was smiling. 'This boy has a natural talent. I'm going to make him my protégée and together... Goodness, Jana, whatever is wrong?'

She called Michal to her and he slipped down from the stool. They sat together on the floor and she told him. He didn't cry; he hardly reacted at all. After some moments, he said in a very quiet voice, 'I knew they wouldn't come back.'

Jana put an arm across his shoulders. 'You have us. We'll always be here for you.'

They sat there for a while in silence. Then Michal pulled away from Jana's arm and climbed back up on the stool next to Papa. 'I'd like to carry on now,' Michal said. 'How should I carve the eyes?'

* * *

Jana was determined to get the bookshop in order again and reopen. One afternoon, as she stood in the middle of the shop, planning some changes, there was a rap on the shop door. She saw it was Ivan and opened up. He stumbled inside, his face ashen, contorted.

Bile rose in Jana's throat. *No, please, no.*

Ivan crumpled to his knees, beating his fists on the floor. He howled, a terrible, feral sound that sent tremors to Jana's core. The room spun and Jana fell beside him.

'Tell me,' she said. And when he didn't reply, hot emotion erupted within her, terror and anger making her lose control.

She screamed at him, 'Tell me!'

He raged back at her, 'She's dead. Lenka is dead.'

Jana's body jerked as if bullets were ripping through her once again and she lay on the shop floor and turned on her back, waiting for the darkness to come. But it didn't. Only the deepest ache of loss and the most unspeakable sadness.

* * *

Later, upstairs, over a bottle of Vodka, Ivan filled in the details for everyone. Lenka had been sent to Ravensbrück, a concentration camp for women in Germany about a year previously. She had died six months ago, allegedly from typhus. Jana held her breath, not daring to ask the question. But Ivan looked around the anxious faces and answered it.

'My daughter was there too. But she's alive. Alena is coming home.' The tiniest light shone in his eyes.

55

The three friends sat in the yard behind the bookshop, the sun warm through the hazy sky. Jana put an arm around Karolina's shoulders and glanced at Dasha, whose expression reflected how she felt: helpless. What could they say to console their friend? After three years of anguish about her husband, Karolina had received the news that he'd died shortly before Prague was liberated. Jana could think of no platitude that would ease her friend's pain.

'You're not alone,' she said. 'Anytime you need company, we are here for you. Come to the bookshop, read or just sit and watch the customers come and go.'

Karolina raised her head, her eyes hollow in a face grown haggard from grief.

'Stop it!' she shouted, turning on Jana.

Startled, Jana dropped her arm from the woman's shoulder. 'Stop what?'

'This kindness. I can't stand it!'

Jana and Dasha exchanged shocked looks.

'I don't deserve it. It was me who put the Gestapo on to you and the children. I went to them pleading for Petr's release; he had become so ill. They said if I became an informer, they would help. I didn't know anything of use, but I was so desperate that I rambled on about everyone I knew, hoping that something I said would satisfy them.'

Jana stared at her, disbelief giving way to anger. 'What did you say?' she demanded.

'I'd seen Dasha one Sunday after she'd talked to you at the bus stop. She laughed and said you were off to your grandmother with a whole load of children's books. I remembered how you talked about the poor children in the Jewish quarter. I told the Gestapo and when that caught their attention, I told them all about our book club and how we talked about banned books; the more I said, the more they wanted to know, the whole time dangling Petr's release in front of me.' Her words came out in a torrent. Then she sprung to her feet, tipping the chair over. 'But the Gestapo lied to me. They never released him and let him die, and here I am a traitor.'

She screamed the last words and rushed from the courtyard back into the bookshop. A few seconds later, the bell above the door jangled and she was gone.

Jana stared at Dasha, both of them speechless. There had been moments when she had doubted Dasha but in the end, she'd been convinced that Pavel had betrayed her. And now Pavel was dead and she would never have the chance to tell him she was sorry for doubting him. It had never for a moment crossed her mind that Karolina had been the culprit. She recalled how she had pleaded with Andrej to intervene in Petr's arrest and how he'd managed to prevent him from being interrogated by the Gestapo before he was sent to Terezin.

'She betrayed you. You were her friend and she betrayed you,' said Dasha, shaking her head.

'And led the Germans to Babi and Papa; the children could have been murdered.'

* * *

Later that evening, once the sun had set, Jana sat in the armchair in the bookshop, reliving Karolina's words; their friendship was destroyed forever. But as Jana considered the desperate woman's motives, she knew one day, she must forgive her, but not yet. For now, the treachery sat deep in the pit of her stomach.

56

Seven weeks after the liberation, Jana was putting the finishing touches to her window display. Her heart swelling, she laid out Mama's books that had been kept hidden all these years. They were not for sale of course, but a sign of freedom, of hope.

She eased herself out of the window, able to move more freely now, her wounds nearly healed. She stood back and looked around her. How much easier she could breathe since she had removed everything German from the shop: the flag, the banner, every book pumped with propaganda and hate. After six years, she could finally sell the books she chose to sell. It would take some time until copies of the banned books would come back into circulation, but her list of customer orders grew each day.

As she tidied the children's section, memories of Michal stirred: how he'd sat in the armchair engrossed in a book that February night when his mother had been taken. Jana was looking after him till the authorities decided where he should go. She couldn't bear the thought of him in a children's home and was fighting for adoption rights but the bureaucracy was incredibly frustrating.

The bell jangled above the door and Andrej entered, his black hair glossy, his face cleanshaven. Her heart lifted and she greeted him with a kiss.

'Are you ready? We have to drink the wine before it gets warm,' he said, lifting a basket.

She locked the shop and they strolled into the balmy, summer evening.

'Where shall we go for our picnic?'

He smiled. 'Follow me.'

As they wandered along the shore away from the crowds, Jana recalled the times she'd walked this route before, both times driven with longing for Andrej. Now she laughed, light with happiness.

'Our special place.'

They sat on the small beach next to the old steamboat that still nestled under the willow tree. Andrej had brought a bottle of white wine and two glasses which they drank with bread and cheese. The swans had returned and swam back and forth, making ripples on the green water.

'I have something for you,' he said, reaching into the basket. 'Close your eyes and put out your hand.'

She thrilled with childish delight as she did so.

His finger stroked the palm of her hand, tracing a circle.

'Come on,' she giggled. 'I can't bear the anticipation.'

His touch was warm. Then something cool and smooth lay in her palm. She frowned and opened her eyes.

The gold book locket from Mama. She looked at him in wonder.

His eyes glinted.

'How?'

'I tracked down our friend, Brandt: wounded, but alive. I found him chained up and cowering in a sports hall with hundreds of other Wehrmacht soldiers awaiting transport to prisons in Siberia.' He gave a wry smile. 'Nice place. He'll soon wish he had died in battle. He didn't look very happy; his face was a mess. I think the guards are having fun with him. Anyway, he was surprisingly helpful when I asked about your locket, deluded I would put in a good word for him, save him from the hell of a Siberian prison. He told me the name of a pawn shop he'd sold it to on the other side of Prague. When I arrived at the shop, my heart sank. The place was stacked from floor to ceiling with valuables people had sold, desperate for money. But the old pawnbroker remembered the locket, saying he'd never seen one in the shape of a book before. After rummaging around for some time, he found it and I bought it back.'

'Oh, Andrej, thank you.' She opened it and smiled to see the photograph of her parents still inside. Her hands shook as she lifted the locket to her neck.

'Let me help,' he said.

She turned, lifting her hair as he closed the clasp. He brushed his lips on the back of her neck before whispering, 'Let's go inside the boat.'

They stood up and paused on the shore to kiss.

'There's one more thing.' He stroked her cheek and looked at her, his navy eyes intense.

'Yes?' She smiled, curious at his serious expression.

'A married couple would have a better chance of adopting Michal.'

She tipped her head to one side. What was he saying here?

'Have you got a couple in mind?' Her heart raced, bubbles of hope rising in her chest.

'Mr and Mrs Kovar would be very suitable.'

'Are you asking me to marry you, Mr Kovar?'

'I definitely am. I love you, Jana.'

She took his hand and led him towards the steamboat. 'Come and persuade me.'

Her head spun with joy as they climbed aboard and before her dress slipped to the floor, she whispered her answer.

EPILOGUE
SIX MONTHS LATER

The scent of cinnamon from Babi's home-baked biscuits mingled with the sharp scent of spruce that decorated the bookshop. Chatter and laughter surrounded Jana, sitting in the middle of her family and friends. As it was Christmas, Jana had decided to extend the regular book club meeting into a celebration for everyone.

Beside her was Nela, one side of her face scarred from the grenade attack, but she was smiling more that evening than Jana had ever seen her smile before; she had achieved her goal of liberating her country.

Dasha walked over with two glasses of red wine and, handing one to Jana, sat on the other side of her. They clinked glasses and wished each other Merry Christmas. How thankful she was to have Dasha as a friend; it was hard to believe she had, in those terrifying times, doubted her loyalty.

Babi appeared with her plate of Christmas biscuits and handed them around. When she came to Jana, she said, 'What a wonderful atmosphere you have created here. Your mother would have been so proud of you.'

Warmth spread in Jana's chest and she clutched the locket hanging from her neck, rubbing it between her fingers. Babi smiled at her and moved on with her biscuits.

Opposite Jana sat Ramona, chatting to Lillian. Ramona called across to Jana. 'I'm just hearing all about your wonderful book club from Lillian. Have you a space for another member?'

Lillian had joined the book club and was an enthusiastic book lover. It had been wonderful to accept her openly into the bookshop without fear of repercussions because of her religion. Delighted that Lillian was encouraging Ramona, Jana said, 'Of course we have a space for you. We'd love you to join us.' It would do Ramona good to come into Prague once a month and make new friends. Nothing could replace Egon, but perhaps friendships and the sharing of books might ease her loneliness.

Michal bounced into the circle swinging a puppet he had carved and painted himself. Everyone exclaimed their admiration, and Jana saw Papa beaming with pride from the side of the room. Michal had journeyed though various stages of grief, from his restrained distance at first, to nights of sobbing, to tantrums of anger. But in the last weeks, he'd been more settled. Jana had asked him many times if he wished her and Andrej to be his adoptive parents, and his answer had always been yes. Jana still awaited the official adoption papers, but after an initial struggle, the signs looked promising.

Michal then ran off to join Maddie and Yveta at the back of the shop, who were entertaining the younger children. Jana decided to see what the children were up to, and stood up, taking her glass with her and munching on her biscuit. As she walked through the gathering of people, she was aware that one person was missing: Karolina. The distraught girl who had betrayed Jana in a futile attempt to save her husband had left Prague to live with an aunt. When she had packed and was ready to leave, she came to the bookshop to ask Jana for forgiveness. Karolina's face shrouded in shame and grief made Jana weep. She wrapped the fragile girl in her arms. 'I understand why you did what you did. We were all going through such horrific times. I wish you well Karolina, and yes, I forgive you.' When Karolina left, Jana knew that she would never see her again.

Jana took in the scene at the back of the shop. Yveta was reading aloud to a small group of children, struggling to raise her voice above the shrieks of those running around playing tag. Andrej and Ivan stood in the other corner keeping an eye on the toddlers.

A fair-haired, three-year-old girl with a determined expression heaved a pile of picture books onto the low table. She looked at two small boys and said, 'These books.' The boys sidled up to take a look. Her authoritative voice reminded Jana of the girl's mother, Lenka. It seemed Alena had inherited Lenka's love of books. Jana hadn't been able to be there for Lenka in the end, but she was determined as godmother to be there for her daughter every step of the way.

As Ivan moved to join his daughter, Jana sauntered up to Andrej and gave him a tender kiss on the lips.

'You look beautiful this evening,' he said, studying her face.

'I feel wonderful. This is our first Christmas as a married couple.'

'I love you.' He slipped an arm around her waist.

'I love you too, and I have a very special Christmas gift for you.'

'Do I have to wait till Christmas Eve?'

'Most definitely.' She would tell him then: Michal would be having a brother or sister, and by next summer, when Prague was in full bloom along the river, and the majestic buildings shimmered in the sun, they would be a family of four.

AUTHOR NOTES

I'm often asked where my story ideas come from. As a writer of Historical Fiction, they mostly come from research, memoirs and novels. This book, however, was inspired by a film: *Anthropoid*, starring one of my favourite actors, Cillian Murphy. Set in Prague, it tells the story of the two men tasked to eliminate the tyrant, Heydrich, Governor of the country. Intrigued, I began my research of wartime Prague and came across one fascinating story after another; the 'model' town of Terezin that was presented to the world but in reality became a transportation hub of mainly Jews to extermination camps such as Auschwitz; the so called 'solution' masterminded by Heydrich who played a key role in the implementation of the Holocaust; and the terrible Lidice massacre, an event I felt compelled to include. Today, on the site of the old village, stands a sculpture of 82 bronze statues of the children murdered, and a beautiful rose garden covers the memorial area.

I visited Prague a few years ago and loved rummaging around in some of the city's wonderful bookshops and this memory combined with my research inspired *The Last Bookshop in Prague*. I hope you enjoyed the story. Thank you so much for reading.

ACKNOWLEDGEMENTS

I am extremely lucky to be published by Boldwood Books, an amazing team of talented and warm-hearted people who support and inspire their authors. As I live in Germany, initial contact was over Zoom and by email. This year, the perfect opportunity arose for me to meet everyone in person; I was nominated as a finalist by the Romantic Novelist Association for Debut of the Year 2024, for *A Mother's War*. So I booked my flight and attended the glittering ceremony in London, meeting up with my wonderful editor, Emily Yau, and the rest of the team who greeted me like family. I was also thrilled to meet many of my lovely fellow authors. A huge thank you to you all!

Thanks also goes to my agent, Clare, at the Liverpool Literary Agency who started me off on my publishing journey and has also secured foreign rights in Germany.

And finally, a huge hug of gratitude for my family and friends whose continued support keeps me going. Love you all!

ABOUT THE AUTHOR

Helen Parusel is a historical novelist, having been a teacher and a clothes buyer for M&S. She currently lives in Hamburg.

Sign up to Helen Parusel's mailing list for news, competitions and updates on future books.

Follow Helen on social media:

instagram.com/helenparusel
x.com/HelenParusel

ALSO BY HELEN PARUSEL

A Mother's War

The Austrian Bride

The Last Bookshop in Prague

Letters from *the past*

Discover page-turning historical novels from your favourite authors and be transported back in time

Join our book club Facebook group

https://bit.ly/SixpenceGroup

Sign up to our newsletter

https://bit.ly/LettersFromPastNews

Boldwood

Boldwood Books is an award-winning fiction publishing company seeking out the best stories from around the world.

Find out more at www.boldwoodbooks.com

Join our reader community for brilliant books, competitions and offers!

Follow us
@BoldwoodBooks
@TheBoldBookClub

Sign up to our weekly deals newsletter

https://bit.ly/BoldwoodBNewsletter